A CENTURY OF
SHORT STORIES

A
CENTURY
OF
SHORT
STORIES

Collected and Introduced by
AIDAN HIGGINS

BOOK CLUB ASSOCIATES LONDON

Published 1977 by
Book Club Associates

Printed in Great Britain by
Richard Clay (The Chaucer Press) Ltd,
Bungay, Suffolk

CONTENTS

Contents

6

Contents

ACKNOWLEDGMENTS

Thanks are due to the following for permission to use stories:
M. B. Yeats, Miss Anne Yeats and the Macmillan Co. of London and Basingstoke for the stories *Village Ghosts*, *Belief and Unbelief*, *A Coward*, *The Three O'Byrnes* and *The Thick Skull of the Fortunate* from *The Celtic Twilight* by Karen Blixen; Putnam & Co. Ltd. for the stories *The Giraffes go to Hamburg*, *In the Menagerie*, *Fellow Travellers*, *The Naturalist and the Monkeys*, *The Earthquake*, *George*, *A Strange Happening*, *The Parrot* from *Out of Africa* by Karen Blixen; the Executors of the James Joyce Estate for *Araby* and *Two Gallants*; Faber and Faber Ltd. for *Cassation* and *Aller et Retour* from *Spillway* by Djuna Barnes; the Estate of the late H. G. Wells and A. P. Watt & Son for *Aepyornis Island*; Baskervilles Investments Ltd. and John Murray (Publishers) Ltd. for *Borrowed Scenes* by Sir Arthur Conan Doyle from *Conan Doyle Stories*; Eudora Welty for *First Love* © 1942, renewed 1970 in the collection *The Wide Net*; the Literary Estate of William Faulkner and Chatto and Windus for *The Liar* from *New Orleans Sketches* and *Delta Autumn* from *Go Down Moses*; William Heinemann Ltd. for *First Love* and *Spring in Fialta* from *Nabakov's Dozen* by Vladimir Nabokov; the Trustees for the Copyrights of the late Dylan Thomas and J. M. Dent & Sons Ltd. for *Holiday Memory* and *A Story* from *Quite Early One Morning*; Chatto and Windus for *The Skeleton* by V. S. Pritchett from *Blind Love And Other Stories*; for *Access to the Children* © William Trevor 1972; Saul Bellow for *Mosby's Memoirs* © 1968, from the collection of the same name (Weidenfeld & Nicolson); Chatto and Windus for *The Traveller* from *Lunar Landscapes* by John Hawkes; Isaac Bashevis Singer for *The Mentor* and *The Cafeteria* from *A Friend of Kafka and Other Stories* (Cape); Richard Brautigan for *My Name* from *In Watermelon Sugar* (Cape), *The Cleveland Wrecking Yard*, *Footnote Chapter to 'Red Lip'*, *A Note*

9

Acknowledgments

of the Camping Craze that is Currently Sweeping America, Room 208, Hotel Trout Fishing in America, A Walden Pond for Winos, The Last Year the Trout came up Hayman Creek from *Trout Fishing in America* (Cape); for *Partners, Perfect California Day, Cameron* (44:40) from *Revenge of the Lawn* (Cape); John Calder (Publishers) Ltd. for *The End* by Samuel Beckett.

TELLERS OF TALES

A phrase, wrote Isaac Babel, is born into the world both good and bad at the same time. And, a stiff corollary, 'no iron can stab the heart with such force as a full stop put just at the right place'.

The combination of letters is not something to fool around with (*pace* Isaac Bashevis Singer). An error in one word or one vowel accent can 'destroy the earth'. In the beginning was the Logos. The imagination, avoiding the hegemony of the banal word, goes in search of a fabulous world.

Stories have their oldest roots in folklore, the common dreams of all language: an oral tradition. The West of Ireland stories that open this collection may belong more properly to Paddy Flynn, not to Lady Gregory or even to Yeats who later transcribed and re-transcribed them, searching for a purer diction. The poet saw the storyteller asleep under a bush, smiling.

The prescription 'I dreamed...' tilted the Tower of Babel. Some stories have no beginning, others no middle (*Mosby's Memoirs?*), and there is a Gogol story that has no end. Transcribed, because of Gogol's defective memory, the pages were baked into a pie.

Nursery rhymes, laying-on of curses, trance-speech, the Little Language of lovers (*Journal to Stella*) where the loved one is likened to monkey or snake, are all perhaps akin; as are rhyming slang, prison argot—all secret languages. The sedulous dreamers always refused to be psychoanalysed. Hence Nabokov's obligatory sneers at the Viennese witchdoctor and Freudian 'mystics', Joyce's dismissal of Dr Jung and Freud as Tweedledum and Tweedledee. The *Brüder* Grimm were always anthropologists.

Here then is an idiosyncratic collection of middle and early 20th-century short stories and aparçus published in English during the period 1890–1970. Eighty years, a lifespan. A look askance at people and things perishing, talents and vanished cities, the slow decay of manners, time's afflictions. From the groves of US Academe Nabokov sees a lost white St Petersburg, a misty Fialta, written at a time when his talent was perhaps purer. Djuna Barnes invokes a Berlin that no longer exists. Singer, another Warsaw. James Joyce, starting out on a career of notoriously straitened circumstances, looks back from Trieste towards Dublin at the turn of the century.

Some of the American stories might be regarded as *post hoc* European writing; a branch that sank underground for a generation, transmuted into a newly entangled language. Bellow might have written in Russian; Singer's English is coloured by its Polish–Yiddish origins; Beckett's work in French has to some degree modified and pared his austere English.

Behind the London clubmen, the swells and hearties, rowing men and athletes with single-sticks and boxing-gloves, dukes and baronets, names to conjure with, racehorse owners and scoundrels, lawyers and surgeons, sinister non-English persons, criminals and low fellows, wronged women, 'Penang lawyers' (a stick that could fell an ox), growlers, nice bits of blood between the shafts, that infest the pages of Conan Doyle, in a London of cabs and Bow Street runners or an unspoilt countryside sometimes luridly lit, lay another England: a land of dead bare-fist champions, ostlers and seconds, *more* Penang lawyers, and the hangman; and behind them stood the Empire, Bloemfontein, India, Gurkhas and the Raj—Sir Arthur Conan Doyle's land, boys' land. An exhumed Egyptian mummy sprints down an Oxfordshire lane, after Abercrombie Smith of all men. Elsewhere, a gigantic hellhound roams the moors.

Unmasker of the outré and the bizarre, Doyle's work is tinged with a certain Edwardian bluntness and brutality. A text teeming with the minutiae of keen observation is notable for the energy of its verbs and the marksmanship of its

adjectival clauses ('A spray of half-clad deep-breathing runners shot past him, and craning over their shoulders, he saw
Hastie pulling a steady thirty-six...'), combined with an
overall inventiveness that is hard to resist. His output was
huge, Balzacian; the sheer energy prodigious. H. G. Wells
had it also. (He once played a game of fives against Nabokov's
father.) Human dynamos.

V. S. Pritchett's writing has the mark of the just, decorous,
law-abiding English mind. Passion induces responsibility.
How English couples interact, the men shady, the women a
cross between boa-constrictor and angel. ('They spend half
their lives in the bathroom.') A self-effacing talent that does not
draw attention to itself.

William Trevor, like Pritchett, and Dickens before them,
is a sly recorder of London, its inner life and outer fringes.
Very good on middle-aged despair (The English Disease),
progressive inebriation of cocktail parties, the fog of cigarette
smoke and the warm smell of brandy, the fearful Mrs Fitch
('that man up to his tricks with women while the beauty
drains from my face'), the edgy diction of distress is well
caught. Dukelow, Belhatchet, Angusthorpe, Dutts, Miss
Efoss, Matera, Marshalsea, Abbott, Da Tanka, the Lowhrs,
Digby-Hunter, Wraggett, Buller Achen ('reputed to take
sensual interest in the sheep that roamed the mountainsides'),
no telephone directory can hold them. Echoes of early Eliot.
Curious congeries. 'I looked in a window,' admits the halfwit
dwarf Quigley, 'I saw a man and woman without their clothes
on.' Voices garrulous as Mr Jingle, sinister as Quilp. His
characters talk because they are unhappy. Stories of Ireland
too, refreshingly free of the turgidity and rank complacency
that characterizes the older Cork School; free too of the
insidious self-pity that mars much of the work of his juniors,
Born Cox, of Cork.

John Hawkes is a crafty manipulator of chilly details, not
in the contemporary American grain, but more 'European' in
approach. The Sicilian Vittorini, ('Erica') the German Robert
Musil ('Tonka'), or the Austrian Robert Walser ('Kleist in
Thun') spring to mind; mordant ambience of Bierce or Poe,
among the illustrious dead; or the surrealist Harry Mathews
among the living. Admired by Bellow.

Saul Bellow's own dramas of ideas (*Herzog, Mr Sammler's Planet*) show the anecdotal and discursive held in a vice-like grip. Exegeses proliferate. Imbued with fluctuating hope, the short declarative sentence has rarely been worked to better effect. Recapitulative epistolary forms, letters to the dead. Updated versions of *Les Liasons Dangereuses*. Chronicler of sexual intrigues and vexations, generally Jewish. A touch of Chateaubriand; Leclos.

Few writing today can match his descriptions, both acid and tender, of the tarnished Modern Megapolis and the dire condition of its citizenry. The trembling energy of the modern city (tumescent Chicago, rotting New York): 'a strip of beautifying and dramatic filth'. A keen ear for argot and slang has gone into the making of an abrasively idiomatic high style. Hemingway by comparison is ill-mannered, when not insane (*Islands in the Stream*).

William Faulkner, after a false start as poet, came to his main theme early on: the back country and woods of Mississippi, it's garrulous *habitués* and clientele of 'freed niggers'. Exhumed from the New Orleans *Times-Picayune* files, 'The Liar' (July 1925) is one of sixteen signed stories and sketches marking Faulkner's debut in fiction, written at the age of 27 during a six month sojourn in the Vieux Carré French sector of New Orleans. The story, the only one not set in the Vieux Carré, but in the back country, may have been written aboard the freighter *West Ivis*, bound for Italy and mailed back to the *Times-Picayune* office from Savannah. Like all his best work, it reads as though written on shipboard, adrift on a tempestuous sea.

Faulkner made early supererogatory claims to being 'sole owner and proprietor' of Yoknapatawpha County, Mississippi. Here already, escaped from chronology, is one loose horse troubling Mis' Harmon as its brother would trouble Mrs Littlejohn in *The Hamlet*, dispute right of way with Ratliff himself, and a whole herd of wild spotted horses go rampaging on through Frenchman's Bend. Gibson's store, give or take a prop, would become Will Varner's, all ready for the usurping Snopes dynasty.

14

Faulkner was already at work on his first novel, *Soldier's Pay*, to be published by Boni & Liveright through the agency of Sherwood Anderson; the same publishers would bring out Hemingway's *In Our Time* and early work by Djuna Barnes. Faulkner was travelling in Europe that summer.

The second story given here, 'Delta Autumn', is from *Go Down Moses* (1942). 'The Liar' is notable for much preliminary spittin' and whittlin', the 'prodigious' yellow of an outbuilding, the description of a pistol shot, with other intimations of latent powers ('the others sat in reft and silent amaze, watching the stranger leaping down the path'.) Only in the back country would his imagination take off. Those Mississippi farmers and traders spoke Elizabethan English with a tinge of Baptist fatalism. Faulkner's English would always be odd and curious, a vocabulary replete with archaicisms ('yon', 'ere' 'dasnt') and Bible tones. 'Myriad', 'doomed', 'avatar', 'apotheosis', 'redeem' and 'chastisement' recur and recur, particularly 'doomed'. 'God knows I hate for my own blooden children to reproach me,' says the father in *As I Lay Dying*. Jefferson is 'a fair piece'. In rural Ireland it would be a fair stretch, or step. Where a metal sign designates Jefferson, Corporate Limit, the pavement ends.

It is curious to compare Faulkner's early work with Joyce's, both into their first novels while engaged on short stories. Office girls took home 7s a week, a deck hand a pound a month, porter cost a penny a pint, and it was possible to dine on peas and a bottle of ginger beer (2½p, old currency), in Dublin at the turn of the century, when James Joyce came of age. Little evidence here of the later all-in-oneness of *Ulysses* (1922) or the wholesale discarding of the wideawake language of cut and dry grammar and goahead plot as discovered in *Finnegans Wake* (1939). Language topples as Europe itself topples. A sequel to *Dubliners* (1914)—*Provincials*—was never to be written.

Sponge cakes, raised umbrellas, old gentility, dusty cretonne, waltzes, unheated rooms, poorly paid servants, foul weather, crestfallen daughters, tedious aunts, craw-thumpers, *Mignon*, *The Bohemian Girl*, descant singing, the human voice, music, tenors, the dead—these stories, written at the suggestion of the middle class mystic George Russell for *The Irish Homestead*, and later included as the third and ninth in order of composition of the fifteen that made up *Dubliners*, were rejected by thirty publishers; the 'blackguard production' must since have been reprinted in as many different languages.

Written mostly in Trieste when Joyce was working on his first novel, *Stephen Hero*, it reads today more like *Little Dorret* than Checkhov. The ground already seems exhausted. Jack Mooney climbs upstairs for ever and ever, with two bottles of Bass under one arm. Prototypes of Gerty McDowell proliferate. Dublin *circa* 1906: a circumscribed area in which to settle old grievances.

'I remarked their English accents and listened vaguely to their conversation.

"O, I never said such a thing!"

"O, but you did!"

"O, but I didn't!" (*Dubliners*: 'Araby'.)'

A gap of some twenty years divides *La Fin* as written by Beckett, in French, and its appearance in English; 33 years yawns between some minor re-titling and rephrasing in the two Barnes' stories subjoined here.

Whatever happened, it happened in extraordinary times, in a season of dreams. These stories, begun at Rosses Point and ending in a rowing boat on Dublin Bay, have gone almost full circle, in three quarters of a century's patiently accumulated recording.

Aidan Higgins
1977

W. B. YEATS

'There is a war between the living and the dead and
the old Irish stories keep harping on it.'

The West of Ireland, 1890s

Village Ghosts

The ancient map-makers wrote across unexplored regions,
'Here are lions.' Across the villages of fishermen and turners
of the earth, so different are these from us, we can write but
one line that is certain, 'Here are ghosts.'

My ghosts inhabit the village of H——, in Leinster.
History has in no manner been burdened by this ancient
village, with its crooked lanes, its old abbey churchyard full
of long grass, its green background of small fir trees, and its
quay, where lie a few tarry fishing-luggers. In the annals of
entomology it is well known. For a small bay lies westward a
little, where he who watches night after night may see a
certain rare moth fluttering along the edge of the tide, just at
the end of evening or the beginning of dawn. A hundred
years ago it was carried here from Italy by smugglers in a
cargo of silks and laces. If the moth-hunter would throw
down his net, and go hunting for ghost tales or tales of those
children of Lilith we call faeries, he would have need for far
less patience.

To approach the village at night a timid man requires
great strategy. A man was once heard complaining, 'By the
Cross of Jesus! how shall I go? If I pass by the hill of Dunboy
old Captain Burney may look out on me. If I go round by the
water, and up by the steps, there is the headless one and
another on the quays, and a new one under the old churchyard wall. If I go right round the other way, Mrs Stewart is
appearing at Hillside Gate, and the Devil himself is in the
Hospital Lane.' I never heard which spirit he braved, but feel
sure it was not the one in the Hospital Lane. In cholera times
a shed had been there set up to receive patients. When the

17

need had gone by, it was pulled down, but ever since the ground where it stood has broken out in ghosts and demons and faeries. There is a farmer at H——, Paddy B—— by name, a man of great strength and a teetotaller. His wife and sister-in-law, musing on his great strength, often wonder what he would do if he drank. One night, when passing through the Hospital Lane, he saw what he supposed at first to be a tame rabbit; after a little he found that it was a white cat. When he came near, the creature slowly began to swell larger and larger, and as it grew he felt his own strength ebbing away, as though it were sucked out of him. He turned and ran.

By the Hospital Lane goes the 'Faeries' Path'. Every evening they travel from the hill to the sea, from the sea to the hill. At the sea end of their path stands a cottage. One night Mrs Arbunathy, who lived there, left her door open, as she was expecting her son. Her husband was asleep by the fire; a tall man came in and sat beside him. After he had been sitting there for a while, the woman said, 'In the name of God, who are you?' He got up and went out, saying, 'Never leave the door open at this hour, or evil may come to you.' She woke her husband and told him. 'One of the Good People has been with us,' said he.

Probably the man braved Mrs Stewart at Hillside Gate. When she lived she was the wife of the Protestant clergyman. 'Her ghost was never known to harm anyone,' say the village people; 'it is only doing penance upon the earth.' Not far from Hillside Gate, where she haunted, appeared for a short time a much more remarkable spirit. Its haunt was the boreen, a green lane leading from the western end of the village. In a cottage at the village end of the boreen lived a house-painter, Jim Montgomery, and his wife. They had several children. He was a little dandy, and came of a higher class than his neighbours. His wife was a very big woman; but he, who had been expelled from the village choir for drink, gave her a beating one day. Her sister heard of it, and came and took down one of the window shutters—Montgomery was neat about everything, and had shutters on the outside of every window—and beat him with it, being big and strong like her sister. He threatened to prosecute her; she answered that she would break every bone in his body if he did. She never spoke to her sister again, because she had allowed herself to be beaten by so small a man. Jim Montgomery grew worse and worse: his wife before long had not enough to eat, but she would tell no one, for she was very proud. Often, too, she would have no fire on a cold night. If any neighbours came in she would say she had let the fire out because she was just going to bed. The people often heard her husband beating her, but she never told anyone. She got very thin. At last one Saturday there was no food in the house for herself and the children. She could bear it no longer, and went to the priest and asked him for some money. He gave her thirty shillings. Her husband met her, and took the money, and beat her. On the following Monday she got very ill, and sent for a Mrs Kelly. Mrs Kelly, as soon as she saw her, said, 'My woman, you are dying,' and sent for the priest and the doctor. She died in an hour. After her death, as Montgomery neglected the children, the landlord had them taken to the workhouse. A few nights after they had gone, Mrs Kelly was going home through the boreen when the ghost of Mrs Montgomery appeared and followed her. It did not leave her until she reached her own house. She told the priest, Father S——, a noted antiquarian, and could not get him to believe her. A few nights afterwards Mrs Kelly again met the spirit in the same place. She was in too great terror to go the whole way, but stopped at a neighbour's cottage midway, and asked them to let her in. They answered they were going to bed. She cried out, 'In the name of God let me in, or I will break open the door.' They opened, and so she escaped from the ghost. Next day she told the priest again. This time he believed, and said it would follow her until she spoke to it.

She met the spirit a third time in the boreen. She asked what kept it from its rest. The spirit said that its children must be taken from the workhouse, for none of its relations were ever there before, and that three masses were to be said for the repose of its soul. 'If my husband does not believe you,' she said, 'show him that,' and touched Mrs Kelly's wrist with three fingers. The places where they touched swelled up and blackened. She then vanished. For a time Montgomery would not believe that his wife had appeared. 'She would not show herself to Mrs Kelly,' he said—'she with respectable people to appear to.' He was convinced by the three marks, and the children were taken from the workhouse. The priest said the masses, and the shade must have been at rest, for it has not since appeared. Some times afterwards Jim Montgomery died in the workhouse, having come to great poverty through drink.

I know some who believe they have seen the headless ghost upon the quay, and one who, when he passes the old cemetery wall at night, sees a woman with white borders to her cap* creep out and follow him. The apparition only leaves him at his own door. The villagers imagine that she follows him to avenge some wrong. 'I will haunt you when I die' is a favourite threat. His wife was once half scared to death by what she considers a demon in the shape of a dog.

These are a few of the open-air spirits; the more domestic of their tribe gather within-doors, plentiful as swallows under southern eaves.

One night a Mrs Nolan was watching by her dying child in Fluddy's Lane. Suddenly there was a sound of knocking heard at the door. She did not open, fearing it was some unhuman thing that knocked. The knocking ceased. After a little the front door and then the back door were burst open, and closed again. Her husband went to see what was wrong. He found both doors bolted. The child died. The doors were again opened and closed as before. Then Mrs Nolan remembered that she had forgotten to leave window or door open, as the custom is, for the departure of the soul. These strange openings and closings and knockings were warnings and reminders from the spirits who attend the dying.

The house ghost is usually a harmless and well-meaning creature. It is put up with as long as possible. It brings good luck to those who live with it. I remember two children who slept with their mother and sisters and brothers in one small room. In the room was also a ghost. They sold herrings in the

---

* I wonder why she had white borders to her cap. The old Mayo woman, who has told me so many tales, has told me that her brother-in-law saw 'a woman with white borders to her cap going round the stacks in a field, and soon after he got a hurt, and he died in six months.'

Dublin streets, and did not mind the ghost much, because they knew they would always sell their fish easily while they slept in the 'ha'nted' room.

I have some acquaintance among the ghost-seers of western villages. The Connacht tales are very different from those of Leinster. These H—— spirits have a gloomy, matter-of-fact way with them. They come to announce a death, to fulfil some obligation, to revenge a wrong, to pay their bills even—as did a fisherman's daughter the other day—and then hasten to their rest. All things they do decently and in order. It is demons, and not ghosts, that transform themselves into white cats or black dogs. The people who tell the tales are poor, serious-minded fishing-people, who find in the doings of the ghosts the fascination of fear. In the western tales is a whimsical grace, a curious extravagance. The people who recount them live in the most wild and beautiful scenery, under a sky ever loaded and fantastic with flying clouds. They are farmers and labourers, who do a little fishing now and then. They do not fear the spirits too much to feel an artistic and humorous pleasure in their doings. The ghosts themselves share their hilarity. In one western town, on whose deserted wharf the grass grows, these spirits have so much vigour, I have been told, that, when a misbeliever ventured to sleep in a haunted house, they flung him through the window, and his bed after him. In the surrounding villages they adopt strange disguises. A dead old gentleman steals the cabbages of his own garden in the shape of a large rabbit. A wicked sea-captain stayed for years inside the plaster of a cottage wall, in the shape of a snipe, making the most horrible noises. He was only dislodged when the wall was broken down; then out of the solid plaster the snipe rushed away whistling.

Belief and Unbelief

There are some doubters even in the western villages. One woman told me last Christmas that she did not believe either in Hell or in ghosts. Hell was an invention got up by the priest to keep people good; and ghosts would not be permitted, she held, to go 'trapsin' about the earth' at their own free will; 'but there are faeries and little leprechauns, and water-horses, and fallen angels'. I have met also a man with a Mohawk Indian tattooed upon his arm, who held exactly similar beliefs and unbeliefs. No matter what one doubts, one never doubts the faeries, for, as the man with the Mohawk Indian on his arm said, 'they stand to reason.'

A little girl who was at service in the village of Grange, close under the seaward slopes of Ben Bulben, suddenly disappeared one night about three years ago. There was at once great excitement in the neighbourhood, because it was rumoured that the faeries had taken her. A villager was said to have long struggled to hold her from them, but at last they prevailed, and he found nothing in his hands but a broomstick. The local constable was applied to, and he at once instituted a house-to-house search, and at the same time advised the people to burn all the *bucalauns* (ragweed) on the field she vanished from, because *bucalauns* are sacred to the faeries. They spent the whole night burning them, the constable repeating spells the while. In the morning the little girl was found wandering in the field. She said the faeries had taken her away a great distance, riding on a faery horse. At last she saw a big river, and the man who had tried to keep her from being carried off was drifting down it—such are the topsyturvydoms of faery glamour—in a cockle-shell. On the way her companions had mentioned the names of several people who were to die shortly in the village.

A Coward

One day I was at the house of my friend the strong farmer, who lives beyond Ben Bulben and Cope's mountain, and met there a young lad who seemed to be disliked by the two daughters. I asked why they disliked him, and was told he was a coward. This interested me, for some whom robust children of Nature take to be cowards are but men and women with a nervous system too finely made for their life and work. I looked at the lad; but no, that pink-and-white face and strong body had nothing of undue sensibility. After a little he told me his story. He had lived a wild and reckless life, until one day, two years before, he was coming home late at night, and suddenly felt himself sinking in, as it were, upon the ghostly world. For a moment he saw the face of a dead brother rise up before him, and then he turned and ran. He did not stop till he came to a cottage nearly a mile down the road. He flung himself against the door with so much of violence that he broke the thick wooden bolt and fell upon the floor. From that day he gave up his wild life, but was a hopeless coward. Nothing could ever bring him to look, either by day or night, upon the spot where he had seen the face, and he often went two miles round to avoid it; nor could, he said, 'the prettiest girl in the country' persuade him to see her home after a party if he were alone.

The Three O'Byrnes

In the dim kingdom there is a great abundance of all excellent things. There is more love there than upon the earth; there is more dancing there than upon the earth; and there is more treasure there than upon the earth. In the beginning the earth was perhaps made to fulfil the desire of man, but now it has got old and fallen into decay. What wonder if we try and pilfer the treasures of that other kingdom!

A friend was once at a village near Slieve League. One day he was straying about a rath called 'Cashel Nore.' A man with a haggard face and unkempt hair, and clothes falling in pieces, came into the rath and began digging. My friend turned to a peasant who was working near and asked who the man was. 'That is the third O'Byrne,' was the answer. A few days after he learned this story: A great quantity of treasure had been buried in the rath in pagan times, and a number of evil faeries set to guard it; but some day it was to be found and belong to the family of the O'Byrnes. Before that day three O'Byrnes must find it and die. Two had already done so. The first had dug and dug until at last he got a glimpse of the stone coffin that contained it, but immediately a thing like a huge hairy dog came down the mountain and tore him to pieces. The next morning the treasure had again vanished deep into the earth. The second O'Byrne came and dug and dug until he found the coffin, and lifted the lid and saw the gold shining within. He saw some horrible sight the next moment, and went raving mad and soon died. The treasure again sank out of sight. The third O'Byrne is now digging. He believes that he will die in some terrible way the moment he finds the treasure, but that the spell will be broken, and the O'Byrne family made rich for ever, as they were of old.

A peasant of the neighbourhood once saw the treasure. He found the shin-bone of a hare lying on the grass. He took it up; there was a hole in it; he looked through the hole, and saw the gold heaped up under the ground. He hurried home to bring a spade, but when he got to the rath again he could not find the spot where he had seen it.

The Thick Skull of the Fortunate

1

Once a number of Icelandic peasantry found a very thick skull in the cemetery where the poet Egil was buried. Its great thickness made them feel certain it was the skull of a great man, doubtless of Egil himself. To be doubly sure they put it on a wall and hit it hard blows with a hammer. It got white where the blows fell, but did not break, and they were convinced that it was in truth the skull of the poet, and worthy of every honour. In Ireland we have much kinship with the Icelanders, or 'Danes' as we call them, and all other dwellers in the Scandinavian countries. In some of our mountainous and barren places, and in our seaboard villages, we still test each other in much the same way the Icelanders tested the head of Egil. We may have acquired the custom from those ancient Danish pirates, whose descendants, the people of Rosses tell me, still remember every field and hillock in Ireland which once belonged to their forebears, and are able to describe Rosses itself as well as any native. There is one seaboard district known as Roughley, where the men are never known to shave or trim their wild red beards, and where there is a fight ever on foot. I have seen them at a boat-race fall foul of each other, and after much loud Gaelic, strike each other with oars. The first boat had gone aground, and by dint of hitting out with the long oars kept the second boat from passing, only to give the victory to the third. One day, the Sligo people say, a man from Roughley was tried in Sligo for breaking a skull in a row, and made the defence, not unknown in Ireland, that some heads are so thin you cannot be responsible for them. Having turned with a look of passionate contempt towards the solicitor who was prosecuting, and cried, 'That little fellow's skull if ye were to hit it would go like an egg-shell,' he beamed upon the judge, and said in a wheedling voice, 'but a man might wallop away at your lordship's for a fortnight.'

26

2

I wrote all this years ago, out of what were even then old memories. I was in Roughley the other day, and found it much like other desolate places. I may have been thinking of Moughorow, a much wilder place, for the memories of one's childhood are brittle things to lean upon.

1902

KAREN BLIXEN

'I began in the evenings to write stories, fairy-tales and romances, that would take my mind a long way off, to other places and times.'

Kenya, 1920s

The Giraffes go to Hamburg

I was staying in Mombasa in the house of Sheik Ali bin Salim, the Lewali of the coast, a hospitable, chivalrous old Arab gentleman.

Mombasa has all the look of a picture of Paradise, painted by a small child. The deep Sea-arm round the island forms an ideal harbour; the land is made out of whitish coral-cliff grown with broad green mango trees and fantastic bald grey Baobab trees. The Sea at Mombasa is as blue as a cornflower, and, outside the inlet to the harbour, the long breakers of the Indian Ocean draw a thin crooked white line, and give out a low thunder even in the calmest weather. The narrow-streeted town of Mombasa is all built from coral-rock, in pretty shades of buff, rose and ochre, and above the town rises the massive old Fortress, with walls and embrasure, where three hundred years ago the Portuguese and the Arabs held out against one another; it displays stronger colours than the town, as if it had, in the course of the ages, from its high site drunk in more than one stormy sunset.

The flamboyant red Acacia flowers in the gardens of Mombasa, unbelievably intense of colour and delicate of leaf. The sun burns and scorches Mombasa; the air is salt here, the breeze brings in every day fresh supplies of brine from the East, and the soil itself is salted so that very little grass grows, and the ground is bare like a dancing-floor. But the ancient mango trees have a dense dark-green foliage and give be-nignant shade; they create a circular pool of black coolness underneath them. More than any other tree that I know of, they suggest a place to meet in, a centre for human inter-

29

course; they are as sociable as the village-wells. Big markets are held under the mango trees, and the ground round their trunks is covered with hen-coops, and piled up water-melons.

Ali bin Salim had a pleasant white house on the mainland, at the curve of the Sea-arm, with a long row of stone steps down to the Sea. There were guests' houses alongside it, and in the big room of the principal building, behind the Verandah, there were collected many fine Arab and English things: old ivory and brass, china from Lamu, velvet arm-chairs, photographs, and a large gramophone. Among these, inside a satin-lined casket, were the remnants of a full tea-set in dainty English china of the forties, which had been the wedding-present of the young Queen of England and her Consort, when the Sultan of Zanzibar's son married the Shah of Persia's daughter. The Queen and the Prince had wished the married couple such happiness as they were themselves enjoying.

'And were they as happy?' I asked Sheik Ali when he took out the little cups, one by one, and placed them on the table to show them to me.

'Alas no,' said he, 'the bride would not give up riding. She had brought her horses with her, on the dhow that carried her trousseau. But the people of Zanzibar did not approve of ladies riding. There was much trouble about it, and, as the Princess would sooner give up her husband than her horses, in the end the marriage was dissolved and the Shah's daughter went back to Persia.'

In the harbour of Mombasa lay a rusty German cargo-steamer, homeward bound. I passed her in Ali bin Salim's rowing boat with his Swaheli rowers, on my way to the island and back. Upon the deck there stood a tall wooden case, and above the edge of the case rose the heads of two Giraffes. They were, Farah, who had been on board the boat, told me, coming from Portuguese East Africa, and were going to Hamburg, to a travelling Menagerie.

The Giraffes turned their delicate heads from the one side to the other, as if they were surprised, which they might well be. They had not seen the Sea before. They could only just have room to stand in the narrow case. The world had suddenly shrunk, changed and closed round them.

The Giraffes go to Hamburg

They could not know or imagine the degradation to which they were sailing. For they were proud and innocent creatures, gentle amblers of the great plains; they had not the least knowledge of captivity, cold, stench, smoke and mange, nor of the terrible boredom in a world in which nothing is ever happening.

Crowds, in dark smelly clothes, will be coming in from the wind and sleet of the streets to gaze on the Giraffes, and to realize man's superiority over the dumb world. They will point and laugh at the long slim necks when the graceful, patient, smoky-eyed heads are raised over the railings of the menagerie; they look much too long in there. The children will be frightened at the sight and cry, or they will fall in love with the Giraffes, and hand them bread. Then the fathers and mothers will think the Giraffes nice beasts, and believe that they are giving them a good time.

In the long years before them, will the Giraffes sometimes dream of their lost country? Where are they now, where have they gone to, the grass and the thorn-trees, the rivers and water-holes and the blue mountains? The high sweet air over the plains has lifted and withdrawn. Where have the other Giraffes gone to, that were side by side with them when they set going, and cantered over the undulating land? They have left them, they have all gone, and it seems that they are never coming back.

In the night where is the full moon?

The Giraffes stir, and wake up in the caravan of the Menagerie, in their narrow box that smells of rotten straw and beer.

Good-bye, good-bye, I wish for you that you may die on the journey, both of you, so that not one of the little noble heads, that are now raised, surprised, over the edge of the case, against the blue sky of Mombasa, shall be left to turn from one side to the other, all alone, in Hamburg, where no one knows of Africa.

As to us, we shall have to find someone badly transgressing against us, before we can in decency ask the Giraffes to forgive us our transgressions against them.

In The Menagerie

About a hundred years ago, a Danish traveller to Hamburg, Count Schimmelmann, happened to come upon a small itinerant Menagerie, and to take a fancy to it. While he was in Hamburg, he every day set his way round the place, although he would have found it difficult to explain what was to him the real attraction of the dirty and dilapidated caravans. The truth was that the Menagerie responded to something within his own mind. It was winter and bitterly cold outside. In the sheds the keeper had been heating the old stove until it was a clear pink in the brown darkness of the corridor, alongside the animals' cages, but still the draught and the raw air pierced people to the bone.

Count Schimmelmann was sunk in contemplation of the Hyena, when the proprietor of the Menagerie came and addressed him. The proprietor was a small pale man with a fallen-in nose, who had in his days been a student of theology, but who had had to leave the faculty after a scandal, and had since step by step come down in the world.

'Your Excellency does well to look at the Hyena,' said he. 'It is a great thing to have got a Hyena to Hamburg, where there has never been one till now. All Hyenas, you will know, are hermaphrodites, and in Africa, where they come from, on a full-moon night they will meet and join in a ring of copulation wherein each individual takes the double part of male and female. Did you know that?'

'No,' said Count Schimmelmann with a slight movement of disgust.

'Do you consider now, Your Excellency,' said the showman, 'that it should be, on account of this fact, harder to a Hyena than to other animals to be shut up by itself in a cage? Would he feel a double want, or is he, because he unites in himself the complementary qualities of creation, satisfied in himself, and in harmony? In other words, since we are all prisoners in

32

life, are we happier, or more miserable, the more talents we possess?'

'It is a curious thing,' said Count Schimmelmann, who had been following his own thoughts and had not paid attention to the showman, 'to realize that so many hundred, indeed thousands of Hyenas should have lived and died, in order that we should, in the end, get this one specimen here, so that people in Hamburg shall be able to know what a Hyena is like, and the naturalists to study from them.'

They moved on to look at the Giraffes in the neighbouring cage.

'The wild animals,' continued the Count, 'which run in a wild landscape, do not really exist. This one, now, exists, we have got a name for it, we know what it is like. The others might as well not have been, still they are the large majority. Nature is extravagant.'

The showman pushed back his worn fur-cap, underneath it he himself had not got a hair on his head. 'They see one another,' he said.

'Even that may be disputed,' said Count Schimmelmann after a short pause. 'These Giraffes, for instance, have got square markings on the skin. The Giraffes, looking at one another, will not know a square and will consequently not see a square. Can they be said to have seen one another at all?'

The showman looked at the Giraffe for some time and then said: 'God sees them.'

Count Schimmelmann smiled. 'The Giraffes?' he asked.

'Oh yes, Your Excellency,' said the showman, 'God sees the Giraffes. While they have been running about and have played in Africa, God has been watching them and has taken a pleasure in their demeanour. He has made them to please him. It is in the Bible, Your Excellency,' said the showman. 'God so loved the Giraffe that He created them. God has Himself invented the square as well as the circle, surely Your Excellency cannot deny that, He has seen the squares on their skin and everything else about them. The wild animals, Your Excellency, are perhaps a proof of the existence of God. But when they go to Hamburg,' he concluded, putting on his cap, 'the argument becomes problematic.'

Count Schimmelmann who had arranged his life according

to the ideas of other people, walked on in silence to look at the snakes, close to the stove. The showman, to amuse him, opened the case in which he kept them, and tried to make the snake within it wake up; in the end, the reptile slowly and sleepily wound itself round his arm. Count Schimmelmann looked at the group.

'Indeed, my good Kannegieter,' he said with a little surly laugh, 'if you were in my service, or if I were king and you my minister, you would now have your dismissal.'

The showman looked up at him nervously. 'Indeed, sir, should I?' he said, and slipped down the snake into the case. 'And why, sir? If I may ask so,' he added after a moment.

'Ah, Kannegieter, you are not so simple as you make out,' said the Count. 'Why? Because, my friend, the aversion to snakes is a sound human instinct, the people who have got it have kept alive. The snake is the deadliest of all the enemies of men, but what, except our own instinct of good and evil, is there to tell us so? The claws of the lions, the size, and the tusks, of the Elephant, the horns of the Buffaloes, all jump to the eye. But the snakes are beautiful animals. The snakes are round and smooth, like the things we cherish in life, of exquisite soft colouring, gentle in all their movements. Only to the godly man this beauty and gracefulness are in themselves loathsome, they smell from perdition, and remind him of the fall of man. Something within him makes him run away from the snake as from the devil, and that is what is called the voice of conscience. The man who can caress a snake can do anything.' Count Schimmelmann laughed a little at his own course of thoughts, buttoned his rich fur-coat and turned to leave the shed.

The showman had stood for a little while in deep thoughts. 'Your Excellency,' he said at last, 'you must needs love snakes. There is no way round it. Out of my own experience in life, I can tell you so, and indeed it is the best advice that I can give you: You should love the snakes. Keep in your mind, your Excellency, how often—keep in mind, your Excellency, that nearly every time that we ask the Lord for a fish, he will give us a serpent.'

Fellow Travellers

At the table on the boat to Africa I sat between a Belgian going to the Congo, and an Englishman who had been eleven times to Mexico to shoot a particular kind of wild mountain-sheep, and who was now going out to shoot bongo. In making conversation on both sides, I got mixed up in the languages, and when I meant to ask the Belgian if he had travelled much in his life, I asked him: *Avez-vous beaucoup travaillé dans votre vie?* He took no offence but, drawing out his toothpick, he answered gravely: *Enormément, Madame.* From this time he made it his object to tell me of all the labours of his life: In everything that he discussed, a certain expression came back: *Notre mission. Notre grande mission dans le Congo.*

One evening, as we were going to play cards, the English traveller told us about Mexico and of how a very old Spanish lady, who lived on a lonely farm in the mountains, when she heard of the arrival of a stranger, had sent for him and ordered him to give her the news of the world. 'Well, men fly now, Madame,' he said to her.

'Yes, I have heard of that,' said she, 'and I have had many arguments with my priest about it. Now you can enlighten us, sir. Do men fly with their legs drawn up under them, like the sparrows, or stretched out behind them, like the storks?'

He also, in the course of our talk, made a remark about the ignorance of the Natives of Mexico, and of the schools there. The Belgian, who was dealing, paused with the last card in his hand, looked piercingly at the Englishman, and said: *Il faut enseigner aux nègres à êtres honnêtes et à travailler. Rien de plus.* Laying down the card with a bang on the table, he repeated with great determination: *Rien de plus. Rien. Rien. Rien.*

The Naturalist and the Monkeys

A Swedish Professor of Natural History came out to the farm to ask me to intervene for him with the Game Department. He had come to Africa, he told me, to find out at what phase of the embryo state the foot of the monkeys, that has got a thumb to it, begins to diverge from the human foot. For this purpose he meant to go and shoot Colobus monkeys on Mount Elgon.

'You will never find out from the Colobus monkeys,' I said to him, 'they live in the tops of the cedar trees, and are shy and difficult to shoot. It would be the greatest luck should you get the embryo you want.'

The Professor was hopeful, he was going to stay out till he had got his foot, he said, even if it was to be for years. He had applied to the Game Department for permission to shoot the monkeys he wanted. The permisson he was, in view of the high scientific object of his expedition, certain to get, but so far he had had no reply.

'How many monkeys have you asked to be allowed to shoot?' I asked him.

He told me that he had, to begin with, asked for permission to shoot fifteen hundred monkeys.

Now I knew the people at the Game Department, and I assisted him to send in a second letter, asking for a reply by return of post, since the Professor was keen to get off on his research. The answer from the Game Department did, for once, come by return of post. The Game Department, they wrote, were pleased to inform Professor Landgreen that, in view of the scientific object of his expedition, they had seen their way to make an exception from their rules, and to raise the number of monkeys on his licence from four to six.

I had to read the letter over twice to the Professor. When the contents at last were clear to him, he became so downcast, so deadly shocked and hurt, that he did not say a single word. To my expressions of condolence he made no reply, but walked out of the house, got into his car and drove away sadly.

When things did not go so much against him, the Professor was an entertaining talker, and a humourist. In the course of our debates about the monkeys he enlightened me upon various facts and developed many of his ideas to me. One day he said: 'I will tell you of a highly interesting experience of mine. Up at Mount Elgon, I found it possible to believe for a moment in the existence of God, what do you think of that?'

I said that it was interesting, but I thought: There is another interesting question which is—Has it been possible to God, at Mount Elgon, to believe for a moment in the existence of Professor Landgreen?

The Earthquake

One year, about Christmas, we had an earthquake; it was strong enough to turn over a number of native huts, it was probably of the power of an angry elephant. It came in three shocks, each of them lasted a few seconds, and there was a pause of a few seconds in between them. These intervals gave people time to form their ideas of the happening.

Denys Finch-Hatton, who was at the time camped in the Masai Reserve, and was sleeping in his lorry, told me when he came back, that as he was woken up by the shock he thought, 'A rhino has got underneath the lorry.' I myself was in my bedroom going to bed when the earthquake came. At the first tug I thought, 'A leopard has got up on the roof.' When the second shock came, I thought, 'I am going to die, this is how it feels to die.' But in the short stillness between the second and the third shock, I realized what it was, it was an earthquake, and I had never thought that I should live to see that. For a moment now I believed that the earthquake was over. But when the third and last shock of it came, it brought with it such an overwhelming feeling of joy that I do not remember ever in my life to have been more suddenly and thoroughly transported.

The heavenly bodies, in their courses, have in their power to move human minds to unknown heights of delight. We are not generally conscious of them; when their idea is suddenly brought back, and actualized to us, it opens up a tremendous perspective. Keppler writes of what he felt when, after many years' work, he at last found the laws of the movements of the planets:

'I give myself over to my rapture. The die is cast. Nothing I have ever felt before is like this. I tremble, my blood leaps. God has waited six thousands years for a looker-on to his work. His wisdom is infinite, that of which we are ignorant is contained in him, as well as the little that we know.'

Indeed it was exactly the same transport which took hold

of me and shook me all through, at the time of the earthquake.

The feeling of colossal pleasure lies chiefly in the consciousness that something which you have reckoned to be
immovable, has got it in it to move on its own. That is probably one of the strongest sensations of joy and hope in the
world. The dull globe, the dead mass, the Earth itself, rose
and stretched under me. It sent me out a message, the slightest touch, but of unbounded significance. It laughed so that
the Native huts fell down and cried: *E pur si muove.*

Early next morning, Juma brought me my tea and said:
'The King of England is dead.'

I asked him how he knew.

'Did you not, Memsahib,' he said, 'feel the earth toss and
shake last night? That means that the King of England is
dead.'

But luckily the King of England lived for many years after
the earthquake.

George

The same year the grasshoppers came on the land. It was said that they came from Abyssinia; after two years of drought up there, they travelled South and ate up all vegetation on their way. Before we ever saw them, there were strange tales circulating in the country of the devastation that they had left behind them—up North, maize and wheat and fruit-farms were all one vast desert where they had passed. The settlers sent runners to their neighbours to the South to announce the coming of the grasshoppers. Still you could not do much against them even if you were warned. On all the farms people had tall piles of firewood and maize-stalks ready and set fire to them when the grasshoppers came, and they sent out all the farm-labourers with empty tins and cans, and told them to shout and yell and beat the tins to frighten them from landing. But it was a short respite only, for however much the farmers would frighten them the grasshoppers could not keep up in the air for ever, the only thing that each farmer could hope for was to drive them off to the next farm to the South, and the more farms they were scared away from, the hungrier and more desperate were they, when in the end they settled. I myself had the great plains of the Masai Reserve to the South, so that I might hope to keep the grasshoppers on the wing and send them over the river to the Masai.

I had had three or four runners announcing the arrival of the grasshoppers, from neighbourly settlers of the district, already, but nothing more had happened, and I began to believe that it was all a false alarm. One afternoon I rode over to our dhuka, a farm-shop of all goods, kept for the farm-labourers and the squatters by Farah's small brother Abdullai. It was on the highroad, and an Indian in a mule-trap outside the duca rose in his trap and beckoned to me as I passed, since he could not drive up to me on the plain.

'The grasshoppers are coming, Madam, please, on to your land,' said he when I rode up to him.

'I have been told that many times,' I said, 'but I have seen nothing of them. Perhaps it is not so bad as people tell.'

'Turn round kindly, Madam,' said the Indian.

I turned round and saw, along the Northern horizon, a shadow on the sky, like a long stretch of smoke, a town burning, 'a million-peopled city vomiting smoke in the bright air,' I thought, or like a thin cloud rising.

'What is that?' I asked.

'Grasshoppers,' said the Indian.

I saw a few grasshoppers, perhaps twenty in all, on the path across the plain as I rode back. I passed my manager's house and instructed him to have everything ready for receiving the grasshoppers. As together we looked North the black smoke on the sky had grown up a little higher. From time to time while we were watching it, a grasshopper swished past us in the air, or dropped on the ground and crawled on.

The next morning as I opened my door and looked out, the whole landscape outside was the colour of pale dull terra cotta. The trees, the lawn, the drive, all that I could see, was covered with the dye, as if in the night a thick layer of terra-cotta-coloured snow had fallen on the land. The grasshoppers were sitting there. While I stood and looked at it, all the scenery began to quiver and break, the grasshoppers moved and lifted, after a few minutes the atmosphere fluttered with wings, they were going off.

That time they did not do much damage to the farm, they had been staying with us over the night only. We had seen what they were like, about an inch and a half long, brownish grey and pink, sticky to touch. They had broken a couple of big trees in my drive simply by sitting on them, and when you looked at the trees and remembered that each of the grasshoppers could only weigh a tenth of an ounce, you began to conceive the number of them.

The grasshoppers came again; for two or three months we had continued attacks of them on the farm. We soon gave up trying to frighten them off, it was a hopeless and tragi-comical undertaking. At times a small swarm would come along, a free-corps which had detached itself from the main force, and would just pass in a rush. But at other times the grasshoppers came in big flights, which took days to pass over the farm, twelve hours incessant hurling advance in the air. When the flight was at its highest it was like a blizzard at home, whistling and shrieking like a strong wind, little hard furious wings to all sides of you and over your head, shining like thin blades of steel in the sun, but themselves darkening the sun. The grasshoppers keep in a belt, from the ground up to the top of the trees, beyond that the air is clear. They whir against your face, they get into your collar and your sleeves and shoes. The rush round you makes you giddy and fills you with a particular sickening rage and despair, the horror of the mass. The individual among it does not count, kill them and it makes no difference to anybody. After the grasshoppers have passed and have gone towards the horizon like a long streak of thinning smoke, the feeling of disgust at your own face and hands, which have been crawled upon by grasshoppers, stays with you for a long time.

A great flight of birds followed the advance of the grasshoppers, circled above them and came down and walked in the fields when they settled, living high on the horde: storks and cranes—pompous profiteers.

At times the grasshoppers settled on the farm. They did not do much harm to the coffee-plantation, the leaves of the coffee-trees, similar to laurel-leaves, are too hard for them to chew. They could only break a tree here and there in the field.

But the maize-fields were a sad sight when they had been on them and had left, there was nothing there now but a few laps of dry leaves hanging from the broken stalks. My garden by the river, that had been irrigated and kept green, was now like a dust-heap—flowers, vegetables and herbs had all gone. The shambas of the Squatters were like stretches of cleared and burnt land, rolled even by the crawling insects, with a dead grasshopper in the dust here and there as the sole fruit of the soil. The squatters stood and looked at them. The old women who had dug and planted the shambas, standing on their heads, shook their fists at the last faint black disappearing shadow in the sky.

A lot of dead grasshoppers were left behind the army

everywhere. On the high-road, where they had sat, and where the wagons and carts had passed, and had driven over them, now, after the swarm had gone, the wheel-tracks were marked, like rails of a railway, as long as you could see them, with little bodies of dead grasshoppers.

The grasshoppers had laid their eggs in the soil. Next year, after the long rains, the little black-brown hoppers appeared —grasshoppers in the first stage of life, that cannot fly, but which crawl along and eat up everything upon their march.

A Strange Happening

When I was down in the Masai Reserve, doing transport for the Government, I one day saw a strange thing, such as no one I know has ever seen. It took place in the middle of the day, while we were trekking over grass-country.

The air in Africa is more significant in the landscape than in Europe, it is filled with loomings and mirages, and is in a way the real stage of activities. In the heat of the midday the air oscillates and vibrates like the string of a violin, lifts up long layers of grass-land with thorn-trees and hills on it, and creates vast silvery expanses of water in the dry grass.

We were walking along in this burning live air, and I was, against my habit, a long way in front of the wagons, with Farah, my dog Dusk and the Toto who looked after Dusk. We were silent, for it was too hot to talk. All at once the plain at the horizon began to move and gallop with more than the atmosphere, a big herd of game was bearing down upon us from the right, diagonally across the stage.

I said to Farah: 'Look at all these Wildebeests.' But a little after, I was not sure that they were Wildebeests; I took up my field-glasses and looked at them, but that too is difficult in the middle of the day. 'Are they Wildebeests, Farah, do you think?' I asked him.

I now saw that Dusk had all his attention upon the animals, his ears up in the air, his far-seeing eyes following their advance. I often used to let him have a run after the gazelles and antelopes on the plains, but today I thought that it would be too hot, and told the Toto to fasten his lead to his collar. At that same moment, Dusk gave a short wild yell and jumped forward so that the Toto was thrown over, and I snatched the lead myself and had to hold him with all my might. I looked at the game. 'What are they?' I asked Farah.

It is very difficult to judge distances on the plains. The quivering air and the monotony of the scenery make it so, also the character of the scattered thorn-trees, which have the

44

exact shape of mighty old forest trees, but are in reality only twelve feet high, so that the Giraffes raise their heads and necks above them. You are continually deceived as to the size of the game that you see at a distance and may, in the middle of the day, mistake a jackal for an Eland, and an ostrich for a Buffalo. A minute later Farah said: 'Memsahib, these are wild dogs.'

The wild dogs are generally seen three or four at a time, but it happens that you meet a dozen of them together. The Natives are afraid of them, and will tell you that they are very murderous. Once as I was riding in the Reserve close to the farm I came upon four wild dogs which followed me at a distance of fifteen yards. The two small terriers that I had with me then kept as close to me as possible, actually under the belly of the pony, until we came across the river and on to the farm. The wild dogs are not as big as a Hyena. They are about the size of a big Alsatian dog. They are black, with a white tuft at the tip of the tail and of the pointed ears. The skin is no good, it has rough uneven hair and smells badly.

Here there must have been five hundred wild dogs. They came along in a slow canter, in the strangest way, looking neither right nor left, as if they had been frightened by something, or as if they were travelling fast with a fixed purpose on a track. They just swerved a bit as they came nearer to us; all the same they hardly seemed to see us, and went on at the same pace. When they were closest to us, they were fifty yards away. They were running in a long file, two or three or four side by side, it took time before the whole procession had passed us. In the middle of it, Farah said: 'These dogs are very tired, they have run a long way.'

When they had all gone by, and were disappearing again, we looked round for the Safari. It was still some way behind us, and exhausted by our agitation of mind we sat down where we stood in the grass, until it came up to us. Dusk was terribly upset, jerking his lead to run after the wild dogs. I took him round the neck, if I had not tied him up in time, I thought, he would by now have been eaten up.

The drivers of the wagons detached themselves from the Safari and came running up to us, to ask us what it had all been. I could not explain to them, or to myself, what had made the wild dogs come along in so great a number in such a way. The natives all took it as a very bad omen—an omen of the war, for the wild dogs are carrion-eaters. They did not afterwards discuss the happening much among themselves, as they used to discuss all the other events of the Safari.

I have told this tale to many people and not one of them has believed it. All the same it is true, and my boys can bear me witness.

The Parrot

An old Danish shipowner sat and thought of his young days and of how he had, when he was sixteen years old, spent a night in a brothel in Singapore. He had come in there with the sailors of his father's ship, and had sat and talked with an old Chinese woman. When she heard that he was a native of a distant country she brought out an old parrot, that belonged to her. Long, long ago, she told him, the parrot had been given her by a high-born English lover of her youth. The boy thought that the bird must then be a hundred years old. It could say various sentences in the languages of all the world, picked up in the cosmopolitan atmosphere of the house. But one phrase the old China-woman's lover had taught it before he sent it to her, and that she did not understand, neither had any visitor ever been able to tell her what it meant. So now for many years she had given up asking. But if the boy came from far away perhaps it was his language, and he could interpret the phrase to her.

The boy had been deeply, strangely moved at the suggestion. When he looked at the parrot, and thought that he might hear Danish from that terrible beak, he very nearly ran out of the house. He stayed on only to do the old Chinese woman a service. But when she made the parrot speak its sentence, it turned out to be classic Greek. The bird spoke its words very slowly, and the boy knew enough Greek to recognize it; it was a verse from Sappho:

> 'The moon has sunk and the Pleiads,
> And midnight is gone,
> And the hours are passing, passing,
> And I lie alone.'

The old woman, when he translated the lines to her, smacked her lips and rolled her small slanting eyes. She asked him to say it again, and nodded her head.

47

JAMES JOYCE

'Children might just as well play as not. The ogre will come in any case.'

Dublin, 1905–6

Araby

North Richmond Street, being blind, was a quiet street except at the hour when the Christian Brothers' School set the boys free. An uninhabited house of two storeys stood at the blind end, detached from its neighbours in a square ground. The other houses of the street, conscious of decent lives within them, gazed at one another with brown imperturbable faces.

The former tenant of our house, a priest, had died in the back drawing-room. Air, musty from having been long enclosed, hung in all the rooms, and the waste room behind the kitchen was littered with old useless papers. Among these I found a few paper-covered books, the pages of which were curled and damp: *The Abbot*, by Walter Scott, *The Devout Communicant* and *The Memoirs of Vidocq*. I liked the last best because its leaves were yellow. The wild garden behind the house contained a central apple-tree and a few straggling bushes, under one of which I found the late tenant's rusty bicycle-pump. He had been a very charitable priest: in his will he had left all his money to institutions and the furniture of his house to his sister.

When the short days of winter came, dusk fell before we had well eaten our dinners. When we met in the street the houses had grown sombre. The space of sky above us was the colour of ever-changing violet and towards it the lamps of the street lifted their feeble lanterns. The cold air stung us and we played till our bodies glowed. Our shouts echoed in the silent street. The career of our play brought us through the dark muddy lanes behind the houses, where we ran the gauntlet of the rough tribes from the cottages, to the back doors of the dark dripping gardens where odours arose from the ashpits, to the dark odorous stables where a coachman smoothed and combed the horse or shook music from the buckled harness. When we returned to the street, light from the kitchen windows had filled the areas. If my uncle was seen turning the corner, we hid in the shadow until we had seen him safely housed. Or if Mangan's sister came out on the doorstep to call her brother in to his tea, we watched her from our shadow peer up and down the street. We waited to see whether she would remain or go in and, if she remained, we left our shadow and walked up to Mangan's steps resignedly. She was waiting for us, her figure defined by the light from the half-opened door. Her brother always teased her before he obeyed, and I stood by the railings looking at her. Her dress swung as she moved her body, and the soft rope of her hair tossed from side to side.

Every morning I lay on the floor in the front parlour watching her door. The blind was pulled down to within an inch of the sash so that I could not be seen. When she came out on the doorstep my heart leaped. I ran to the hall, seized my books and followed her. I kept her brown figure always in my eye and, when we came near the point at which our ways diverged, I quickened my pace and passed her. This happened morning after morning. I had never spoken to her, except for a few casual words, and yet her name was like a summons to all my foolish blood.

Her image accompanied me even in places the most hostile to romance. On Saturday evenings when my aunt went marketing I had to go to carry some of the parcels. We walked through the flaring streets, jostled by drunken men and bargaining women, amid the curses of labourers, the shrill litanies of shop-boys who stood on guard by the barrels of pigs' cheeks, the nasal chanting of street-singers, who sang a *come-all-you* about O'Donovan Rossa, or a ballad about the troubles in our native land. These noises converged in a single sensation of life for me: I imagined that I bore my chalice safely through a throng of foes. Her name sprang to my lips at moments in strange prayers and praises which I myself did not understand. My eyes were often full of tears (I could not tell why) and at times a flood from my heart seemed to pour itself out into my bosom. I thought little of the future. I did not know whether I would ever speak to her or not or, if I spoke to her, how I could tell her of my confused adoration. But my body was like a harp and her words and gestures were like fingers running upon the wires.

One evening I went into the back drawing-room in which the priest had died. It was a dark rainy evening and there was no sound in the house. Through one of the broken panes I heard the rain impinge upon the earth, the fine incessant needles of water playing in the sodden beds. Some distant lamp or lighted window gleamed below me. I was thankful that I could see so little. All my senses seemed to desire to veil themselves and, feeling that I was about to slip from them, I pressed the palms of my hands together until they trembled, murmuring: '*O love! O love!*' many times.

At last she spoke to me. When she addressed the first words to me I was so confused that I did not know what to answer. She asked me was I going to *Araby*. I forgot whether I answered yes or no. It would be a splendid bazaar; she said she would love to go.

'And why can't you?' I asked.

While she spoke she turned a silver bracelet round and round her wrist. She could not go, she said, because there would be a retreat that week in her convent. Her brother and two other boys were fighting for their caps, and I was alone at the railings. She held one of the spikes, bowing her head towards me. The light from the lamp opposite our door caught the white curve of her neck, lit up her hair that rested there and, falling, lit up the hand upon the railing. It fell over one side of her dress and caught the white border of a petticoat, just visible as she stood at ease.

'It's well for you,' she said.

'If I go,' I said, 'I will bring you something.'

What innumerable follies laid waste my waking and sleeping thoughts after the evening! I wished to annihilate the tedious intervening days. I chafed against the work of school. At night in my bedroom and by day in the classroom her image came between me and the page I strove to read. The syllables of the word *Araby* were called to me through the silence in which my soul luxuriated and cast an Eastern enchantment over me. I asked for leave to go to the bazaar on Saturday night. My aunt was surprised, and hoped it was not some Freemason affair. I answered few questions in class. I watched my master's face pass from amiability to sternness; he hoped I was not beginning to idle. I could not call my wandering thoughts together. I had hardly any patience with the serious work of life which, now that it stood between me and my desire, seemed to me child's play, ugly monotonous child's play.

On Saturday morning I reminded my uncle that I wished to go to the bazaar in the evening. He was fussing at the hall-stand, looking for the hat-brush, and answered me curtly:

'Yes, boy, I know.'

As he was in the hall I could not go into the front parlour and lie at the window. I felt the house in bad humour and walked slowly towards the school. The air was pitilessly raw and already my heart misgave me.

When I came home to dinner my uncle had not yet been home. Still it was early. I sat staring at the clock for some time and, when its ticking began to irritate me, I left the room. I mounted the staircase and gained the upper part of the house. The high, cold, empty, gloomy rooms liberated me and I went from room to room singing. From the front window I saw my companions playing below in the street. Their cries reached me weakened and indistinct and, leaning my forehead against the cool glass, I looked over at the dark house where she lived. I may have stood there for an hour, seeing nothing but the brown-clad figure cast by my imagination, touched discreetly by the lamplight at the curved neck, at the hand upon the railings and at the border below the dress.

When I came downstairs again I found Mrs Mercer sitting at the fire. She was an old, garrulous woman, a pawnbrokers widow, who collected used stamps for some pious purpose. I had to endure the gossip of the tea-table. The meal was prolonged beyond an hour and still my uncle did not come. Mrs Mercer stood up to go: she was sorry she couldn't wait any longer, but it was after eight o'clock and she did not like to be out late, as the night air was bad for her. When she had gone I began to walk up and down the room, clenching my fists. My aunt said:

'I'm afraid you may put off your bazaar for this night of Our Lord.'

At nine o'clock I heard my uncle's latchkey in the hall door. I heard him talking to himself and heard the hallstand rocking when it had received the weight of his overcoat. I could interpret these signs. When he was midway through his dinner I asked him to give me the money to go to the bazaar. He had forgotten.

'The people are in bed and after their first sleep now,' he said.

I did not smile. My aunt said to him energetically:

'Can't you give him the money and let him go? You've kept him late enough as it is.'

My uncle said he was very sorry he had forgotten. He said he believed in the old saying: 'All work and no play makes Jack a dull boy.' He asked me where I was going and, when I told him a second time, he asked me did I know *The Arab's Farewell to his Steed*. When I left the kitchen he was about to recite the opening lines of the piece to my aunt.

I held a florin tightly in my hand as I strode down Buckingham Street towards the station. The sight of the streets thronged with buyers and glaring with gas recalled to me the purpose of my journey. I took my seat in a third-class carriage of a deserted train. After an intolerable delay the train moved out of the station slowly. It crept onward among ruinous houses and over the twinkling river. At Westland Row Station a crowd of people pressed to the carriage doors; but the porters moved them back, saying that it was a special train for the bazaar. I remained alone in the bare carriage. In a few minutes the train drew up beside an improvised wooden platform. I passed out on to the road and saw by the lighted dial of a clock that it was ten minutes to ten. In front of me was a large building which displayed the magical name.

I could not find any sixpenny entrance and, fearing that the bazaar would be closed, I passed in quickly through a turnstile, handing a shilling to a weary-looking man. I found myself in a big hall girded at half its height by a gallery. Nearly all the stalls were closed and the greater part of the hall was in darkness. I recognized a silence like that which pervades a church after a service. I walked into the centre of the bazaar timidly. A few people were gathered about the stalls which were still open. Before a curtain, over which the words *Café Chantant* were written in coloured lamps, two men were counting money on a salver. I listened to the fall of the coins.

Remembering with difficulty why I had come, I went over to one of the stalls and examined porcelain vases and flowered tea-sets. At the door of the stall a young lady was talking and laughing with two young gentlemen. I remarked their English accents and listened vaguely to their conversation.

'O, I never said such a thing!'

'O, but you did!'

'O, but I didn't!'

'Didn't she say that?'

'Yes. I heard her.'

'Oh, there's a ... fib!'

Observing me, the young lady came over and asked me did I wish to buy anything. The tone of her voice was not encouraging; she seemed to have spoken to me out of a sense of duty. I looked humbly at the great jars that stood like eastern guards at either side of the dark entrance to the stall and murmured:

'No, thank you.'

The young lady changed the position of one of the vases and went back to the two young men. They began to talk of the same subject. Once or twice the young lady glanced at me over her shoulder.

I lingered before her stall, though I knew my stay was useless, to make my interest in her wares seem the more real. Then I turned away slowly and walked down the middle of the bazaar. I allowed the two pennies to fall against the sixpence in my pocket. I heard a voice call from one end of the gallery that the light was out. The upper part of the hall was now completely dark.

Gazing up into the darkness I saw myself as a creature driven and derided by vanity; and my eyes burned with anguish and anger.

Two Gallants

The grey warm evening of August had descended upon the city, and a mild warm air, a memory of summer, circulated in the streets. The streets, shuttered for the repose of Sunday, swarmed with a gaily coloured crowd. Like illumined pearls the lamps shone from the summits of their tall poles upon the living texture below, which, changing shape and hue unceasingly, sent up into the warm grey evening air an unchanging, unceasing murmur.

Two young men came down the hill of Rutland Square. One of them was just bringing a long monologue to a close. The other, who walked on the verge of the path and was at times obliged to step on to the road, owing to his companion's rudeness, wore an amused, listening face. He was squat and ruddy. A yachting cap was shoved far back from his forehead, and the narrative to which he listened made constant waves of expression break forth over his face from the corners of his nose and eyes and mouth. Little jets of wheezing laughter followed one another out of his convulsed body, His eyes, twinkling with cunning enjoyment, glanced at every moment towards his companion's face. Once or twice he rearranged the light waterproof which he had slung over one shoulder in toreador fashion. His breeches, his white rubber shoes, and his jauntily slung waterproof expressed youth. But his figure fell into rotundity at the waist, his hair was scant and grey, and his face, when the waves of expression had passed over it, had a ravaged look.

When he was quite sure that the narrative had ended he laughed noiselessly for fully half a minute. Then he said:

'Well! ... That takes the biscuit!'

His voice seemed winnowed of vigour; and to enforce his words he added with humour:

'That takes the solitary, unique, and, if I may so call it, *recherché* biscuit!'

He became serious and silent when he had said this. His

tongue was tired, for he had been talking all the afternoon in a public-house in Dorset Street. Most people considered Lenehan a leech, but in spite of this reputation, his adroitness and eloquence had always prevented his friends from forming any general policy against him. He had a brave manner of coming up to a party of them in a bar and of holding himself nimbly at the borders of the company until he was included in a round. He was a sporting vagrant armed with a vast stock of stories, limericks and riddles. He was insensitive to all kinds of discourtesy. No one knew how he achieved the stern task of living, but his name was vaguely associated with racing tissues.

'And where did you pick her up, Corley?' he asked.

Corley ran his tongue swiftly along his upper lip.

'One night, man,' he said. 'I was going along Dame Street and I spotted a fine tart under Waterhouse's clock, and said good night, you know. So we went for a walk round by the canal, and she told me she was a slavey in a house in Baggot Street. I put my arm round her and squeezed her a bit that night. Then next Sunday, man, I met her by appointment. We went out to Donnybrook and I brought her into a field there. She told me she used to go with a dairyman ... It was fine, man. Cigarettes every night she'd bring me, and paying the tram out and back. And one night she brought me two bloody fine cigars—O, the real cheese, you know, that the old fellow used to smoke ... I was afraid, man, she'd get in the family way. But she's up to the dodge.'

'Maybe she thinks you'll marry her,' said Lenehan.

'I told her I was out of a job,' said Corley. 'I told her I was in Pim's. She doesn't know my name. I was too hairy to tell her that. But she thinks I'm a bit of class, you know.'

Lenehan laughed again, noiselessly.

'Of all the good ones ever I heard,' he said, 'that emphatically takes the biscuit.'

Corley's stride acknowledged the compliment. The swing of his burly body made his friend execute a few light skips from the path to the roadway and back again. Corley was the son of an inspector of police, and he had inherited his father's frame and gait. He walked with his hands by his sides, holding himself erect and swaying his head from side to side. His head was large, globular and oily; it sweated in all weathers; and his large round hat, set upon it sideways, looked like a bulb which had grown out of another. He always stared straight before him as if he were on parade, and when he wished to gaze after someone in the street, it was necessary for him to move his body from the hips. At present he was about town. Whenever any job was vacant a friend was always ready to give him the hard word. He was often to be seen walking with policemen in plain clothes, talking earnestly. He knew the inner side of all affairs and was fond of delivering final judgements. He spoke without listening to the speech of his companions. His conversation was mainly about himself: what he had said to such a person and what such a person had said to him, and what he had said to settle the matter. When he reported these dialogues he aspirated the first letter of his name after the manner of Florentines.

Lenehan offered his friend a cigarette. As the two young men walked on through the crowd Corley occasionally turned to smile at some of the passing girls, but Lenehan's gaze was fixed on the large faint moon circled with a double halo. He watched earnestly the passing of the grey web of twilight across its face. At length he said:

'Well ... tell me, Corley, I suppose you'll be able to pull it off all right, eh?'

Corley closed one eye expressively as an answer.

'Is she game for that?' asked Lenehan dubiously. 'You can never know women.'

'She's all right,' said Corley. 'I know the way to get around her, man. She's a bit gone on me.'

'You're what I call a gay Lothario,' said Lenehan. 'And the proper kind of a Lothario, too!'

A shade of mockery relieved the servility of his manner. To save himself he had the habit of leaving his flattery open to the interpretation of raillery. But Corley had not a subtle mind.

'There's nothing to touch a good slavey,' he affirmed. 'Take my tip for it.'

'By one who has tried them all,' said Lenehan.

'First I used to go with girls, you know,' said Corley, unbosoming; 'girls off the South Circular. I used to take them out, man, on the tram somewhere and pay the tram, or take them to a band or a play at the theatre, or buy them chocolate and sweets or something that way. I used to spend money on them right enough,' he added, in a convincing tone, as if he was conscious of being disbelieved.

But Lenehan could well believe it; he nodded gravely.

'I know that game,' he said, 'and it's a mug's game.'

'And damn the thing I ever got out of it,' said Corley.

'Ditto here,' said Lenehan.

'Only off of one of them,' said Corley.

He moistened his upper lip by running his tongue along it. The recollection brightened his eyes. He, too, gazed at the pale disc of the moon, now nearly veiled, and seemed to meditate.

'She was ... a bit of all right,' he said regretfully.

He was silent again. Then he added:

'She's on the turf now. I saw her driving down Earl Street one night with two fellows with her on a car.'

'I suppose that's your doing,' said Lenehan.

'There was others at her before me,' said Corley philosophically.

This time Lenehan was inclined to disbelieve. He shook his head to and fro and smiled.

'You know you can't kid me, Corley,' he said.

'Honest to God!' said Corley. 'Didn't she tell me herself?'

Lenehan made a tragic gesture.

'Base betrayer!' he said.

As they passed along the railings of Trinity College, Lenehan skipped out into the road and peered up at the clock.

'Twenty after,' he said.

'Time enough,' said Corley. 'She'll be there all right. I always let her wait a bit.'

Lenehan laughed quietly.

'Ecod! Corley, you know how to take them,' he said.

'I'm up to all their little tricks,' Corley confessed.

'But tell me,' said Lenehan again, 'are you sure you can bring it off all right? You know it's a ticklish job. They're damn close on that point. Eh? ... What?'

His bright small eyes searched his companion's face for

reassurance. Corley swung his head to and fro as if to toss aside an insistent insect, and his brows gathered.

'I'll pull it off,' he said. 'Leave it to me, can't you?'

Lenehan said no more. He did not wish to ruffle his friend's temper, to be sent to the devil and told that his advice was not wanted. A little tact was necessary. But Corley's brow was soon smooth again. His thoughts were running another way.

'She's a fine decent tart,' he said, with appreciation; 'that's what she is.'

They walked along Nassau Street and then turned into Kildare Steeet. Not far from the porch of the club a harpist stood in the roadway, playing to a little ring of listeners. He plucked at the wires heedlessly, glancing quickly from time to time at the face of each newcomer and from time to time, wearily also, at the sky. His harp, too, heedless that her coverings had fallen about her knees, seemed weary alike of the eyes of strangers and of her master's hands. One hand played in the bass the melody of *Silent, O Moyle,* while the other hand careered in the treble after each group of notes. The notes of the air sounded deep and full.

The two young men walked up the street without speaking, the mournful music following them. When they reached Stephen's Green they crossed the road. Here the noise of trams, the lights and the crowd, released them from their silence.

'There she is!' said Corley.

At the corner of Hume Street a young woman was standing. She wore a blue dress and a white sailor hat. She stood on the kerbstone, swinging a sunshade in one hand. Lenehan grew lively.

'Let's have a look at her, Corley,' he said.

Corley glanced sideways at his friend, and an unpleasant grin appeared on his face.

'Are you trying to get inside me?' he asked.

'Damn it!' said Lenehan boldly, 'I don't want an introduction. All I want is to have a look at her. I'm not going to eat her.'

'O ... A look at her?' said Corley, more amiably. 'Well ...

I'll tell you what. I'll go over and talk to her and you can pass by.'

'Right!' said Lenehan.

Corley had already thrown one leg over the chains when Lenehan called out:

'And after? Where will we meet?'

'Half ten,' answered Corley, bringing over his other leg.

'Where?'

'Corner of Merrion Street. We'll be coming back.'

'Work it all right now,' said Lenehan in farewell.

Corley did not answer. He sauntered across the road swaying his head from side to side. His bulk, his easy pace, and the solid sound of his boots had something of the conqueror in them. He approached the young woman and, without saluting, began at once to converse with her. She swung her umbrella more quickly and executed half turns on her heels. Once or twice when he spoke to her at close quarters she laughed and bent her head.

Lenehan observed them for a few minutes. Then he walked rapidly along beside the chains at some distance and crossed the road obliquely. As he approached Hume Street corner he found the air heavily scented, and his eyes made a swift anxious scrutiny of the young woman's appearance. She had her Sunday finery on. Her blue serge skirt was held at the waist by a belt of black leather. The great silver buckle of her belt seemed to depress the centre of her body, catching the light stuff of her white blouse like a clip. She wore a short black jacket with mother-of-pearl buttons, and a ragged black boa. The ends of her tulle collarette had been carefully disordered and a big bunch of red flowers was pinned in her bosom stems upwards. Lenehan's eyes noted approvingly her stout short muscular body. Frank rude health glowed in her face, on her fat red cheeks and in her unabashed blue eyes. Her features were blunt. She had broad nostrils, a straggling mouth which lay open in a contented leer, and two projecting front teeth. As he passed Lenehan took off his cap, and, after about ten seconds, Corley returned a salute to the air. This he did by raising his hand vaguely and pensively changing the angle of position of his hat.

Lenehan walked as far as the Shelbourne Hotel, where he

halted and waited. After waiting for a little time he saw them coming towards him and, when they turned to the right, he followed them, stepping lightly in his white shoes, down one side of Merrion Square. As he walked on slowly, timing his pace to theirs, he watched Corley's head which turned at every moment towards the young woman's face like a big ball revolving on a pivot. He kept the pair in view until he had seen them climbing the stairs of the Donnybrook tram; then he turned about and went back the way he had come.

Now that he was alone his face looked older. His gaiety seemed to forsake him, and as he came by the railings of the Duke's Lawn he allowed his hand to run along them. The air which the harpist had played began to control his movements. His softly padded feet played the melody while his fingers swept a scale of variations idly along the railings after each group of notes.

He walked listlessly round Stephen's Green and then down Grafton Street. Though his eyes took note of many elements of the crowd through which he passed, they did so morosely. He found trivial all that was meant to charm him, and did not answer the glances which invited him to be bold. He knew that he would have to speak a great deal, to invent and to amuse, and his brain and throat were too dry for such a task. The problem of how he could pass the hours till he met Corley again troubled him a little. He could think of no way of passing them but to keep on walking. He turned to the left when he came to the corner of Rutland Square, and felt more at ease in the dark quiet street, the sombre look of which suited his mood. He paused at last before the window of a poor-looking shop over which the words *Refreshment Bar* were printed in white letters. On the glass of the window were two flying inscriptions: *Ginger Beer* and *Ginger Ale*. A cut ham was exposed on a great blue dish, while near it on a plate lay a segment of very light plum-pudding. He eyed this food earnestly for some time, and then, after glancing warily up and down the street, went into the shop quickly.

He was hungry, for, except some biscuits which he had asked two grudging curates to bring him, he had eaten nothing since breakfast-time. He sat down at an uncovered wooden table opposite two work-girls and a mechanic. A slatternly girl waited on him.

'How much is a plate of peas?' he asked.

'Three halfpence, sir,' said the girl.

'Bring me a plate of peas,' he said, 'and a bottle of ginger beer.'

He spoke roughly in order to belie his air of gentility, for his entry had been followed by a pause of talk. His face was heated. To appear natural he pushed his cap back on his head and planted his elbows on the table. The mechanic and the two work-girls examined him point by point before resuming their conversation in a subdued voice. The girl brought him a plate of grocer's hot peas, seasoned with pepper and vinegar, a fork and his ginger beer. He ate his food greedily and found it so good that he made a note of the shop mentally. When he had eaten all the peas he sipped his ginger beer and sat for some time thinking of Corley's adventure. In his imagination he beheld the pair of lovers walking along some dark road; he heard Corley's voice in deep energetic gallantries, and saw again the leer of the young woman's mouth. This vision made him feel keenly his own poverty of purse and spirit. He was tired of knocking about, of pulling the devil by the tail, of shifts and intrigues. He would be thirty-one in November. Would he never get a good job? Would he never have a home of his own? He thought how pleasant it would be to have a warm fire to sit by and a good dinner to sit down to. He had walked the streets long enough with friends and with girls. He knew what those friends were worth: he knew the girls too. Experience had embittered his heart against the world. But all hope had not left him. He felt better after having eaten that he had felt before, less weary of his life, less vanquished in spirit. He might yet be able to settle down in some snug corner and live happily if he could only come across some good simple-minded girl with a little of the ready.

He paid twopence halfpenny to the slatternly girl, and went out of the shop to begin his wandering again. He went into Capel Street and walked along towards the City Hall. Then he turned into Dame Street. At the corner of George's Street he met two friends of his, and stopped to converse with them. He was glad that he could rest from all his walking.

His friends asked him had he seen Corley, and what was the latest. He replied that he had spent the day with Corley. His friends talked very little. They looked vacantly after some figures in the crowd, and sometimes made a critical remark. One said that he had seen Mac an hour before in Westmoreland Street. At this Lenehan said that he had been with Mac the night before in Egan's. The young man who had seen Mac in Westmoreland Street asked was it true that Mac had won a bit over a billiards match. Lenehan did not know: he said that Holohan had stood them drinks in Egan's.

He left his friends at a quarter to ten and went up George's Street. He turned to the left at the City Markets and walked on into Grafton Street. The crowd of girls and young men had thinned, and on his way up the street he heard many groups and couples bidding one another good night. He went as far as the clock of the College of Surgeons: it was on the stroke of ten. He set off briskly along the northern side of the Green, hurrying for fear Corley should return too soon. When he reached the corner of Merrion Street he took his stand in the shadow of a lamp, and brought out one of the cigarettes which he had reserved and lit it. He leaned against the lamp-post and kept his gaze fixed on the part from which he expected to see Corley and the young woman return.

His mind became active again. He wondered had Corley managed it successfully. He wondered if he had asked her yet or if he would leave it to the last. He suffered all the pangs and thrills of his friend's situation as well as those of his own. But the memory of Corley's slowly revolving head calmed him somewhat: he was sure Corley would pull it off all right. All at once the idea struck him that perhaps Corley had seen her home by another way, and given him the slip. His eyes searched the street: there was no sign of them. Yet it was surely half an hour since he had seen the clock of the College of Surgeons. Would Corley do a thing like that? He lit his last cigarette and began to smoke it nervously. He strained his eyes as each tram stopped at the far corner of the square. They must have gone home by another way. The paper of his cigarette broke and he flung it into the road with a curse.

Suddenly he saw them coming towards him. He started with delight, and keeping close to his lamp-post tried to read the result in their walk. They were walking quickly, the young woman taking quick short steps, while Corley kept beside her with his long stride. They did not seem to be speaking. An intimation of the result pricked him like the point of a sharp instrument. He knew Corley would fail; he knew it was no go.

They turned down Baggot Street, and he followed them at once, taking the other footpath. When they stopped he stopped too. They talked for a few moments, and then the young woman went down the steps into the area of a house. Corley remained standing at the edge of the path, a little distance from the front steps. Some minutes passed. Then the hall-door was opened slowly and cautiously. A woman came running down the front steps and coughed. Corley turned and went towards her. His broad figure hid hers from view for a few seconds and then she reappeared, running up the steps. The door closed on her, and Corley began to walk swiftly towards Stephen's Green.

Lenehan hurried on in the same direction. Some drops of light rain fell. He took them as a warning, and glancing back towards the house which the young woman had entered to see that he was not observed, he ran eagerly across the road. Anxiety and his swift run made him pant. He called out:

'Hallo, Corley!'

Corley turned his head to see who had called him, and then continued walking as before. Lenehan ran after him, settling the waterproof on his shoulders with one hand.

'Hallo, Corley!' he cried again.

He came level with his friend and looked keenly in his face. He could see nothing there.

'Well?' he said. 'Did it come off?'

They had reached the corner of Ely Place. Still without answering, Corley swerved to the left and went up the side street. His features were composed in stern calm. Lenehan kept up with his friend, breathing uneasily. He was baffled, and a note of menace pierced through his voice.

'Can't you tell us?' he said. 'Did you try her?'

Corley halted at the first lamp and stared grimly before him. Then with a grave gesture he extended a hand towards the light and, smiling, opened it slowly to the gaze of his disciple. A small gold coin shone in the palm.

DJUNA BARNES

'Each race to its wrestling!'
Nice and Berlin, 1923

Aller et Retour

The train travelling from Marseilles to Nice had on board a
woman of great strength.

She was well past forty and a little top-heavy. Her bosom
was tightly cross-laced, the busk bending with every breath,
and as she breathed and moved she sounded with many
chains in coarse gold links, the ring of large heavily set jewels
marking off her lighter gestures. From time to time she raised
a long-handled *lorgnette* to her often winking brown eyes,
surveying the countryside blurred in smoke from the train.

At Toulon, she pushed down the window, leaning out,
calling for beer, the buff of her hip-fitting skirt rising in a
peak above tan boots laced high on shapely legs, and above
that the pink of woollen stockings. She settled back, drinking
her beer with pleasure, controlling the jarring of her body
with the firm pressure of her small plump feet against the
rubber matting.

She was a Russian, a widow. Her name was Erling von
Bartmann. She lived in Paris.

In leaving Marseilles she had purchased a copy of *Madame
Bovary*, and now she held it in her hands, elbows slightly
raised and out.

She read a few sentences with difficulty, then laid the book
on her lap, looking at the passing hills.

Once in Marseilles, she traversed the dirty streets slowly,
holding the buff skirt well above her boots, in a manner at
once careful and absent. The thin skin of her nose quivered
as she drew in the foul odours of the smaller passages, but she
looked neither pleased nor displeased.

She went up the steep narrow littered streets abutting on
the port, staring right and left, noting every object.

65

A gross woman, with wide set legs, sprawled in the doorway to a single room, gorged with a high-posted rusting iron bed. The woman was holding a robin loosely in one huge plucking hand. The air was full of floating feathers, falling and rising about girls with bare shoulders, blinking under coarse dark bangs. Madame von Bartmann picked her way carefully.

At a ship-chandler's she stopped, smelling the tang of tarred rope. She took down several coloured postcards showing women in the act of bathing; of happy mariners leaning above full-busted sirens with sly cogged eyes. Madame von Bartmann touched the satins of vulgar, highly coloured bedspread laid out for sale in a side alley. A window, fly-specked, dusty and cracked, displayed, terrace upon terrace, white and magenta funeral wreaths, wired in beads, flanked by images of the Bleeding Heart, embossed in tin, with edgings of beaten flame, the whole beached on a surf of metal lace.

She returned to her hotel room and stood, unpinning her hat and veil before the mirror in the tall closet door. She sat, to unlace her boots, in one of eight chairs, arranged in perfect precision along the two walls. The thick boxed velvet curtains blocked out the court where pigeons were sold. Madame von Bartmann washed her hands with a large oval of coarse red soap, drying them, trying to think.

In the morning, seated on the stout linen sheets of the bed, she planned the rest of her journey. She was two or three hours too early for her train. She dressed and went out. Finding a church, she entered and drew her gloves off slowly. It was dark and cold and she was alone. Two small oil lamps burned on either side of the figures of St Anthony and St Francis. She put her leather bag on a form and went into a corner, kneeling down. She turned the stones of her rings out and put her hands together, the light shining between the little fingers; raising them she prayed, with all her vigorous understanding, to God, for a common redemption.

She got up, peering about her, angry that there were no candles burning to the *Magnifique*—feeling the stuff of the altar-cloth.

At Nice she took an omnibus, riding second class, reaching the outskirts about four. She opened the high rusty gates to a private park, with a large iron key, and closed it behind her.

The lane of flowering trees with their perfumed cups, the moss that leaded the broken paving stones, the hot musky air, the incessant rustling wings of unseen birds—all ran together in a tangle of singing textures, light and dark.

The avenue was long and without turning until it curved between two massive jars, spiked with spirals of cacti, and just behind these, the house of plaster and stone.

There were no shutters open on the avenue because of insects, and Madame von Bartmann went slowly, still holding her skirts, around to the side of the house, where a long-haired cat lay softly in the sun. Madame von Bartmann looked up at the windows, half shuttered, paused, thought better of it and struck off into the wood beyond.

The deep pervading drone of ground insects ceased about her chosen steps and she turned her head, looking up into the occasional touches of sky.

She still held the key to the gate in her gloved hand, and the seventeen-year-old girl who came up from a bush took hold of it, walking beside her.

The child was still in short dresses, and the pink of her knees was dulled by the dust of the underbrush. Her squirrel-coloured hair rose in two ridges of light along her head, descending to the lobes of her long ears, where it was caught into a faded green ribbon.

'Richter!' Madame von Bartmann said (her husband had wanted a boy).

The child put her hands behind her back before answering.

'I've been out there, in the field.'

Madame von Bartmann, walking on, made no answer.

'Did you stop in Marseilles, Mother?'

She nodded.

'Long?'

'Two days and a half.'

'Why a half?'

'The trains.'

'Is it a big city?'

'Not very, but dirty.'

'Is there anything nice there?'

67

Madame von Bartmann smiled: 'The Bleeding Heart— sailors——'

Presently they came out into the open field, and Madame von Bartmann, turning her skirt back, sat down on a knoll, warm with tempered grass.

The child, with slight springiness of limb, due to youth, sat beside her.

'Shall you stay home now?'

'For quite a while.'

'Was Paris nice?'

'Paris was Paris.'

The child was checked. She began pulling at the grass. Madame von Bartmann drew off one of her tan gloves, split at the turn of the thumb, and stopped for a moment before she said: 'Well, now that your father is dead——'

The child's eyes filled with tears; she lowered her head.

'I come flying back,' Madame von Bartmann continued good-naturedly, 'to look at my own. Let me see you,' she continued, turning the child's chin up in the palm of her hand. 'Ten, when I last saw you, and now you are a woman.' With this she dropped the child's chin and put on her glove.

'Come,' she said, rising, 'I haven't seen the house in years.' As they went down the dark avenue, she talked.

'Is the black marble Venus still in the hall?'

'Yes.'

'Are the chairs with the carved legs still in existence?'

'Only two. Last year Erna broke one, and the year be- fore——'

'Well?'

'I broke one.'

'Growing up,' Madame von Bartmann commented. 'Well, well. Is the great picture still there, over the bed?'

The child, beneath her breath, said: 'That's my room.'

Madame von Bartmann, unfastening her *lorgnette* from its hook on her bosom, put it to her eyes and regarded the child.

'You are very thin.'

'I'm growing.'

'I grew, but like a pigeon. Well, one generation can't be exactly like another. You have your father's red hair. That,' she said abruptly, 'was a queer, mad fellow, that Herr von Bartmann. I never could see what we were doing with each other. As for you,' she added, shutting her glasses, 'I'll have to see what he has made of you.'

In the evening, in the heavy house with its heavy furniture, Richter watched her mother, still in hat and spotted veil, playing on the sprawling lanky grand, high up behind the terrace window. It was a waltz. Madame von Barthmann played fast, with effervescence, the sparkles of her jewelled fingers bubbled over the keys.

In the dark of the garden, Richter listened to Schubert streaming down the light from the open casement. The child was cold now, and she shivered in the fur coat that touched the chill of her knees.

Still swiftly, with a *finale* somewhat in the Grand Opera manner, Madame von Bartmann closed the piano, stood a moment on the balcony inhaling the air, fingering the coarse links of her chain, the insects darting vertically across her vision.

Presently she came out and sat down on a stone bench, quietly, waiting.

Richter stood a few steps away and did not approach or speak. Madame von Bartmann began, though she could not see the child without turning:

'You have been here always, Richter?'

'Yes,' the child answered.

'In this park, in this house, with Herr von Bartmann, the tutors and the dogs?'

'Yes.'

'Do you speak German?'

'A little.'

'Let me hear.'

'Müde bin Ich, geh' zu Ruh.'

'French?'

'O nuit désastreuse! O nuit effroyable!'

'Russian?'

The child did not answer.

'Ach!' said Madame von Bartmann. Then: 'Have you been to Nice?'

'Oh, yes, often.'

'What did you see there?'

'Everything.'

Madame von Bartmann laughed. She leaned forward, her elbow on her knee, her face in her palm. The ear-rings in her ears stood still, the drone of the insects was clear and soft; pain lay fallow.

'Once,' she said, 'I was a child like you. Fatter, better health—nevertheless like you. I loved nice things. But,' she added, 'a different kind, I imagine. Things that were positive. I liked to go out in the evening, not because it was sweet and voluptuous—but to frighten myself, because I'd known it such a little while, and after me it would exist so long. But that——' she interrupted herself, 'is beside the point. Tell me how you feel.'

The child moved in the shadow. 'I can't.'

Madame von Bartmann laughed again, but stopped abruptly.

'Life,' she said, 'is filthy; it is also frightful. There is everything in it: murder, pain, beauty, disease—death. Do you know this?'

The child answered, 'Yes.'

'How do you know?'

The child answered again, 'I don't know.'

'You see!' Madame von Bartmann went on, 'you know nothing. You must know *everything*, and *then* begin. You must have a great understanding, or accomplish a fall. Horses hurry you away from danger; trains bring you back. Paintings give the heart a mortal pang—they hung over a man you loved and perhaps murdered in his bed. Flowers hearse up the heart because a child was buried in them. Music incites to the terror of repetition. The crossroads are where lovers vow, and taverns are for thieves. Contemplation leads to prejudice; and beds are fields where babies fight a losing battle. Do you know all this?'

There was no answer from the dark.

'Man is rotten from the start,' Madame von Bartmann continued. 'Rotten with virtue and with vice. He is strangled by the two and made nothing; and God is the light the mortal insect kindled, to turn to, and to die by. That is very wise, but it must not be misunderstood. I do not want you to turn your nose up at any whore in any street; pray and wallow and cease, but without prejudice. A murderer may have less prejudice than a saint; sometimes it is better to be a saint. Do not be vain about your indifference, should you be possessed of indifference; and don't,' she said, 'misconceive the value of your passions; it is only seasoning to the whole horror. I wish...' She did not finish, but quietly took her pocket handkerchief and silently dried her eyes.

'What?' the child asked from the darkness.

Madame von Bartmann shivered. 'Are you thinking?' she said.

'No,' the child answered.

'Then *think*,' Madame von Bartmann said loudly, turning to the child. 'Think everything, good, bad, indifferent; everything, and *do* everything, *everything*! Try to know what you are before you die. And,' she said, putting her head back and swallowing with shut eyes, 'come back to me a good woman.'

She got up then and went away, down the long aisle of trees.

That night, at bedtime, Madame von Bartmann, rolled up in a bed with a canopy of linen roses, frilled and smelling of lavender, called through the curtains:

'Richter, do you play?'

'Yes,' answered Richter.

'Play me something.'

Richter heard her mother turn heavily, breathing comfort.

Touchingly, with frail legs pointed to the pedals, Richter, with a thin technique and a light touch, played something from Beethoven.

'*Brava!*' her mother called, and she played again, and this time there was silence from the canopied bed. The child closed the piano, pulling the velvet over the mahogany, put the light out and went, still shivering in her short coat, out on to the balcony.

A few days later, having avoided her mother, looking shy, frightened and offended, Richter came into her mother's room. She spoke directly and sparingly:

'Mother, with your consent, I should like to announce my engagement to Gerald Teal.' Her manner was stilted. 'Father approved of him. He knew him for years: if you permit——'

'Good heavens!' exclaimed Madame von Bartmann, and swung clear around on her chair. 'Who is he? What is he like?'

'He is a clerk in government employ; he is young——'

'Has he money?'

'I don't know: father saw to that.'

There was a look of pain and relief on Madame von Bartmann's face.

'Very well,' she said, 'I shall have dinner for you two at eight-thirty sharp.'

At eight-thirty sharp they were dining. Madame von Bartmann, seated at the head of the table, listened to Mr Teal speaking.

'I shall do my best to make your daughter happy. I am a man of staid habits, no longer too young,' he smiled. 'I have a house on the outskirts of Nice. My income is assured—a little left me by my mother. My sister is my housekeeper, she is a maiden lady, but very cheerful and very good.' He paused, holding a glass of wine to the light. 'We hope to have children—Richter will be occupied. As she is delicate we shall travel, to Vichy, once a year. I have two very fine horses and a carriage with sound springs. She will drive in the afternoons, when she is indisposed—though I hope she will find her greatest happiness at home.'

Richter, sitting at her mother's right hand, did not look up.

Within two months Madame von Bartmann was once again in her travelling clothes, hatted and veiled, strapping her umbrella as she stood on the platform, waiting for the train to Paris. She shook hands with her son-in-law, kissed the cheek of her daughter and climbed into a second class smoker.

Once the train was in motion, Madame Erling von Bartmann slowly drew her gloves through her hand, from fingers to cuff, stretching them firmly across her knee.

'Ah, how unnecessary.'

Cassation

'Do you know Germany, Madame, Germany in the spring? It is charming then, do you not think so? Wide and clean, the Spree winding thin and dark—and the roses! the yellow roses in the windows; and the bright talkative Americans passing through groups of German men staring over their *steins*, at the light and laughing women.

'It was such a spring, three years ago, that I came into Berlin from Russia. I was just sixteen, and my heart was a dancer's heart. It is that way sometimes; one's heart is all one thing for months, then—although another thing, *nicht wahr*? I used to sit in the café at the end of the Zelten, eating eggs and drinking coffee, watching the sudden rain of sparrows. Their feet struck the table all together, and all together they cleared the crumbs, and all together they flew into the sky, so that the café was as suddenly without birds as it had been suddenly full of birds.

'Sometimes a woman came here, at about the same hour as myself, around four in the afternoon; once she came with a little man, quite dreamy and uncertain. But I must explain how she looked: *temperamentvoll* and tall, *kraftvoll* and thin. She must have been forty then, dressed richly and carelessly. It seemed as though she could hardly keep her clothes on; her shoulders were always coming out, her skirt would be hanging on a hook, her pocket book would be mislaid, but all the time she was savage with jewels, and something purposeful and dramatic came in with her, as if she were the centre of a whirlpool, and her clothes a temporary debris.

'Sometimes she clucked the sparrows, and sometimes she talked to the *weinschenk*, clasping her fingers together until the rings stood out and you would see through them, she was so vital and so wasted. As for her dainty little man, she would talk to him in English, so that I did not know where they came from.

'Then one week I stayed away from the café because I was

trying out for the *Schauspielhaus*, I heard they wanted a ballet dancer, and I was very anxious to get the part, so of course I thought of nothing else. I would wander, all by myself, through the *Tiergarten*, or I would stroll down the *Sieges-Allee* where all the great German emperors' statues are, looking like widows. Then suddenly I thought of the *Zelten*, and of the birds, and of that tall odd woman and so I went back there, and there she was, sitting in the garden sipping beer and chuck-chucking the sparrows.

'When I came in, she got up at once and came over to me and said: "Why, how do you do, I have missed you. Why did you not tell me that you were going away? I should have seen what I could do about it."'

'She talked like that; a voice that touched the heart because it was so unbroken and clear. "I have a house," she said, "just on the Spree. You could have stayed with me. It is a big, large house, and you could have the room just off my room. It is difficult to live in, but it is lovely—Italian you know, like the interiors you see in Venetian paintings, where young girls lie dreaming of the Virgin. You could find that you could sleep there, because you have dedication."

'Somehow it did not seem at all out of the way that she should come to me and speak to me. I said I would meet her again some day in the garden, and we could go "home" together, and she seemed pleased, but did not show surprise.

'Then one evening we came into the garden at the same moment. It was late and the fiddles were already playing. We sat together without speaking, just listening to the music, and admiring the playing of the only woman member of the orchestra. She was very intent on the movement of her fingers, and seemed to be leaning over her chin to watch. Then suddenly the lady got up, leaving a small rain of coin, and I followed her until we came to a big house and she let herself in with a brass key. She turned to the left and went into a dark room and switched on the lights and sat down and said: "This is where we sleep; this is how it is."

'Everything was disorderly, and expensive and melancholy. Everything was massive and tall, or broad and wide. A chest of drawers rose above my head. The china stove was enormous and white, enamelled in blue flowers. The bed was so high that you could only think of it as something that might be overcome. The walls were all bookshelves, and all the books were bound in red morocco, on the back of each, in gold, was stamped a coat of arms, intricate and oppressive. She rang for tea and began taking off her hat.

'A great painting hung over the bed; the painting and the bed ran together in encounter, the huge rumps of the stallions reined into the pillows. The generals, with foreign helmets and dripping swords, raging through rolling smoke and the bleeding ranks of the dying, seemed to be charging the bed, so large, so rumpled, so devastated. The sheets were trailing, the counterpane hung torn, and the feathers shivered along the floor, trembling in the slight wind from the open window. The lady was smiling in a sad grave way, but she said nothing, and it was not until some moments later that I saw a child, not more than three years old, a small child, lying in the centre of the pillows, making a thin noise, like the buzzing of a fly, and I thought it was a fly.

'She did not talk to the child, indeed she paid no attention to it, as if it were in her bed and she did not know it. When the tea was brought in she poured it, but she took none, instead she drank small glasses of Rhine wine.

'"You have seen Ludwig," she said in her faint and grieving voice, "we were married a long time ago, he was just a boy then. I? Me? I am an Italian, but I studied English and German because I was with a travelling company. You," she said abruptly, "you must give up the ballet—the theatre—acting." Somehow I did not think it odd that she should know of my ambition, though I had not mentioned it. "And," she went on, "you are not for the stage; you are for something quieter, more withdrawn. See here, I like Germany very much, I have lived here a good many years. You will stay and you will see. You have seen Ludwig, you have noticed that he is not strong; he is always declining, you must have noticed it yourself; he must not be distressed, he can't bear anything. He has his room to himself." She seemed suddenly tired, and she got up and threw herself across the bed, at the foot, and fell asleep, almost instantly, her hair all about her. I went away then, but I came back that night and tapped at the window. She came to the window and signed to me, and presently appeared at another window to the right of the bedroom, and beckoned with her hand, and I came up and climbed in, and did not mind that she had not opened the door for me. The room was dark except for the moon, and two thin candles burning, before the Virgin.

'It was a beautiful room, Madame, *"traurig"* as she said. Everything was important and old and gloomy. The curtains about the bed were red velvet, Italian you know, and fringed in gold bullion. The bed cover was a deep red velvet with the same gold fringe: on the floor, beside the bed, a stand on which was a tasselled red cushion, on the cushion a Bible in Italian, lying open.

'She gave me a long nightgown, it came below my feet and came back up again almost to my knees. She loosened my hair, it was long then, and yellow. She plaited it in two plaits; she put me down at her side and said a prayer in German, then in Italian, and ended, "God bless you," and I got into bed. I loved her very much because there was nothing between us but this strange preparation for sleep. She went away then. In the night I heard the child crying, but I was tired.

'I stayed a year. The thought of the stage had gone out of my heart. I had become a *religieuse*; a gentle religion that began with the prayer I had said after her the first night, and the way I had gone to sleep, though we never repeated the ceremony. It grew with the furniture and the air of the whole room, and with the Bible lying open at a page that I could not read; a religion, Madame, that was empty of need, therefore it was not holy perhaps, and not as it should have been in its manner. It was that I was happy, and I lived there for one year. I almost never saw Ludwig, and almost never Valentine, for that was her child's name, a little girl.

'But at the end of that year I knew there was trouble in other parts of the house. I heard her walking in the night, sometimes Ludwig would be with her, I could hear him crying and talking, but I could not hear what was said. It sounded like a sort of lesson, a lesson for a child to repeat, but if so, there would have been no answer, for the child never uttered a sound, except that buzzing cry.

'Sometimes it is wonderful in Germany, Madame, *nicht*

wahr? There is nothing like a German winter. She and I used to walk about the Imperial Palace, and she stroked the cannon, and said they were splendid. We talked about philosophy, for she was troubled with too much thinking, but she always came to the same conclusion, that one must be, or try to be, like everyone else. She explained that to be like everyone, all at once, in your own person, was to be holy. She said that people did not understand what was meant by "Love thy neighbour as thyself." It meant, she said, that one should be like all people *and* oneself, then, she said, one was both ruined and powerful.

'Sometimes it seemed that she was managing it, that she was all Germany, at least in her Italian heart. She seemed so irreparably collected and yet distressed, that I was afraid of her, and not afraid.

'That is the way it was, Madame, she seemed to wish it to be that way, though at night she was most scattered and distraught, I could hear her pacing in her room.

'Then she came in one night and woke me and said that I must come into her room. It was in a most terrible disorder. There was a small cot bed that had not been there before. She pointed to it and said that it was for me.

'The child was lying in the great bed against a large lace pillow. Now it was four years old and yet it did not walk, and I never heard it say a thing, or make a sound, except that buzzing cry. It was beautiful in the corrupt way of idiot children; a sacred beast without a taker, tainted with innocence and waste time; honey-haired and failing, like those dwarf angels on holy prints and valentines, if you understand me, Madame, something saved for a special day that would not arrive, not for life at all: and my lady was talking quietly, but I did not recognize any of her former state.

' "You must sleep here now," she said, "I brought you here for this if I should need you, and I need you. You must stay, you must stay for ever." Then she said, "Will you?" And I said no, I could not do that.

'She took up the candle and put it on the floor beside me, and knelt beside it, and put her arms about my knees. "Are you a traitor?" she said, "have you come into my house, Ludwig's house, the house of my child, to betray us?" And I

77

said, no, I had not come to betray. "Then," she said, "you will do as I tell you. I will teach you slowly, slowly; it will not be too much for you, but you must begin to forget, you must forget *everything*. You must forget all the things people have told you. You must forget arguments and philosophy. I was wrong in talking of such things; I thought it would teach you how to lag with her mind, to undo time for her as it passes, to climb into her bereavement and her dispossession. I brought you up badly; I was vain. You will do better. Forgive me." She put the palms of her hands on the floor, her face to my face. "You must never see any other room than this room. It was a great vanity that I took you out walking. Now you will stay here safely, and you will see. You will like it, you will learn to like it the very best of all. I will bring you breakfast, and luncheon and supper. I will bring it to you both, myself. I will hold you on my lap, I will feed you like the birds. I will rock you to sleep. You must not argue with me—above all we must have no arguments, no talk about man and his destiny—man has no destiny—that is my secret—I have been keeping it from you until today, this very hour. Why not before? Perhaps I was jealous of the knowledge, yes, that must be it, but now I give it to you, I share it with you. I am an old woman," she said, still holding me by the knees. "When Valentine was born, Ludwig was only a boy." She got up and stood behind me. "He is not strong, he does not understand that the weak are the strongest things in the world, because he is one of them. He cannot help her, they are adamant together. I need you, it must be you." Suddenly she began talking to me as she talked with the child, and I did not know which of us she was talking to. "Do not repeat anything after me. Why should children repeat what people say? The whole world is nothing but a noise, as hot as the inside of a tiger's mouth. They call it civilization—that is a lie! But some day you may have to go out, someone will try to take you out, and you will not understand them or what they are saying, unless you understand nothing, absolutely nothing, then you will manage." She moved around so that she faced us, her back against the wall. "Look," she said, "it is all over, it has gone away, you do not need to be afraid; there is only you. The stars are out, and the snow is falling down

and covering the world, the hedges, the houses and the lamps.
No, no!" she said to herself, "wait. I will put you on your
feet, and tie you up in ribbons, and we will go out together,
out into the garden where the swans are, and the flowers and
the bees and small beasts. And the students will come,
because it will be summer, and they will read in their
books..." She broke off, then took her wild speech up again,
this time as though she were really speaking to the child,
"Katya will go with you. She will instruct you, she will tell
you there are no swans, no flowers, no beasts, no boys—
nothing, nothing at all, just as you like it. No mind, no
thought, nothing whatsoever else. No bells will ring, no
people will talk, no birds will fly, no boys will move, there'll
be no birth and no death; no sorrow, no laughing, no kissing,
no crying, no terror, no joy; no eating, no drinking, no
games, no dancing; no father, no mother, no sisters, no
brothers—only you, only you!"

'I stopped her and I said, "Gaya, why is it that you suffer so,
and what am I to do?" I tried to put my arms around her, but
she struck them down crying, "Silence!" Then she said,
bringing her face close to my face, "She has no claws to hang
by; she has no hunting foot; she has no mouth for the meat—
vacancy!"

'Then, Madame, I got up. It was very cold in the room. I
went to the window and pulled the curtain, it was a bright
and starry night, and I stood leaning my head against the
frame, saying nothing. When I turned around, she was
regarding me, her hands held apart, and I knew that I had to
go away and leave her. So I came up to her and said, "Good-
bye, my Lady." And I went and put on my street clothes, and
when I came back she was leaning against the battle picture,
her hands hanging. I said to her, without approaching her,
"God-bye, my love," and went away.

'Sometimes it is beautiful in Berlin. Madame, *nicht wahr?*
There was something new in my heart, a passion to see Paris,
so it was natural that I said *lebe wohl* to Berlin.

'I went for the last time to the café in the Zelten, ate my
eggs, drank my coffee and watched the birds coming and
going just as they used to come and go—altogether here then
altogether gone. I was happy in my spirit, for that is the way

it is with my spirit, Madame, when I am going away.

'But I went back to her house just once. I went in quite easily by the door, for all the doors and windows were open—perhaps they were sweeping that day. I came to the bedroom door and knocked, but there was no answer. I pushed, and there she was, sitting up in the bed with the child, and she and the child were making that buzzing cry, and no human sound between them, and as usual, everything was in disorder. I came up to her, but she did not seem to know me. I said, "I am going away; I am going to Paris. There is a longing in me to be in Paris. So I have come to say farewell."

'She got down off the bed and came to the door with me. She said, "Forgive me—I trusted you—I was mistaken. I did not know that I could do it myself, but you see, I can do it myself." Then she got back on to the bed and said, "Go away," and I went.

'Things are like that, when one travels, *nicht wahr*, Madame?'

JOSEPH CONRAD

'I verily believe mine was the only case of a boy of my
nationality and antecedents taking a, so to speak, standing jump out of his racial surroundings and association.'

Incident off Cambodia, 1910

The Secret Sharer

1

On my right hand there were lines of fishing-stakes resembling a mysterious system of half-submerged bamboo fences,
incomprehensible in its division of the domain of tropical
fishes, and crazy of aspect as if abandoned for ever by some
nomad tribe of fishermen now gone to the other end of the
ocean; for there was no sign of human habitation as far as the
eye could reach. To the left a group of barren islets, sug-
gesting ruins of stone walls, towers and blockhouses, had its
foundations set in a blue sea that itself looked solid, so still
and stable did it lie below my feet; even the track of light
from the westering sun shone smoothly, without that anim-
ated glitter which tells of an imperceptible ripple. And when
I turned my head to take a parting glance at the tug which
had just left us anchored outside the bar, I saw the straight
line of the flat shore joined to the stable sea, edge to edge,
with a perfect and unmarked closeness, in one levelled floor
half brown, half blue under the enormous dome of the sky.
Corresponding in their insignificance to the islets of the sea,
two small clumps of trees, one on each side of the only fault
in the impeccable joint, marked the mouth of the river
Meinam we had just left on the first preparatory stage of our
homeward journey; and, far back on the inland level, a larger
and loftier mass, the grove surrounding the great Paknam
pagoda, was the only thing on which the eye could rest from
the vain task of exploring the monotonous sweep of the
horizon. Here and there gleams as of a few scattered pieces of
silver marked the windings of the great river; and on the
nearest of them, just within the bar, the tug steaming right

into the land became lost to my sight, hull and funnel and masts, as though the impassive earth had swallowed her up without an effort, without a tremor. My eye followed the light cloud of her smoke, now here, now there, above the plain, according to the devious curves of the stream, but always fainter and farther away, till I lost it at last behind the mitre-shaped hill of the great pagoda. And then I was left alone with my ship, anchored at the head of the Gulf of Siam.

She floated at the starting-point of a long journey, very still in an immense stillness, the shadows of her spars flung far to the eastward by the setting sun. At that moment I was alone on her decks. There was not a sound in her—and around us nothing moved, nothing lived, not a canoe on the water, not a bird in the air, not a cloud in the sky. In this breathless pause at the threshold of a long passage we seemed to be measuring our fitness for a long and arduous enterprise, the appointed task of both our existences to be carried out, far from all human eyes, with only sky and sea for spectators and for judges.

There must have been some glare in the air to interfere with one's sight, because it was only just before the sun left us that my roaming eyes made out beyond the highest ridge of the principal islet of the group something which did away with the solemnity of perfect solitude. The tide of darkness flowed on swiftly; and with tropical suddenness a swarm of stars came out above the shadowy earth, while I lingered yet, my hand resting lightly on my ship's rail as if on the shoulder of a trusted friend. But, with all that multitude of celestial bodies staring down at one, the comfort of quiet communion with her was gone for good. And there were also disturbing sounds by this time—voices, footsteps forward; the steward flitted along the main-deck, a busily ministering spirit; a hand-bell tinkled urgently under the poop-deck...

I found my two officers waiting for me near the supper table, in the lighted cuddy. We sat down at once, and as I helped the chief mate, I said:

'Are you aware that there is a ship anchored inside the islands? I saw her mastheads above the ridge as the sun went down.'

He raised sharply his simple face, overcharged by a terrible growth of whisker, and emitted his usual ejaculations: 'Bless my soul, sir! You don't say so!'

My second mate was a round-cheeked, silent young man, grave beyond his eyes, I thought; but as our eyes happened to meet I detected a slight quiver on his lips. I looked down at once. It was not my part to encourage sneering on board my ship. It must be said, too, that I knew very little of my officers. In consequence of certain events of no particular significance, except to myself, I had been appointed to the command only a fortnight before. Neither did I know much of the hands forward. All these people had been together for eighteen months or so, and my position was that of the only stranger on board. I mention this because it has some bearing on what is to follow. But what I felt most was my being a stranger to the ship; and if all the truth must be told, I was somewhat of a stranger to myself. The youngest man on board (barring the second mate), and untried as yet by a position of the fullest responsibility, I was willing to take the adequacy of the others for granted. They had simply to be equal to their tasks; but I wondered how far I should turn out faithful to that ideal conception of one's own personality every man sets up for himself secretly.

Meantime the chief mate, with an almost visible effect of collaboration on the part of his round eyes and frightful whiskers, was trying to evolve a theory of the anchored ship. His dominant trait was to take all things into earnest consideration. He was of a painstaking turn of mind. As he used to say, he 'liked to account to himself' for practically everything that came in his way, down to a miserable scorpion he had found in his cabin a week before. The why and the wherefore of that scorpion—how it got on board and came to select his room rather than the pantry (which was a dark place and more what a scorpion would be partial to), and how on earth it managed to drown itself in the inkwell of his writing-desk—had exercised him infinitely. The ship within the islands was much more easily accounted for; and just as we were about to rise from table he made his pronouncement. She was, he doubted not, a ship from home lately arrived. Probably she drew too much water to cross the bar except at the top of spring tides. Therefore she went into that natural harbour to wait for a few days in preference to remaining in an open roadstead.

'That's so,' confirmed the second mate, suddenly, in his slightly hoarse voice. 'She draws over twenty feet. She's the Liverpool ship *Sephora* with a cargo of coal. Hundred and twenty-three days from Cardiff.'

We looked at him in surprise.

'The tugboat skipper told me when he came on board for your letters, sir,' explained the young man. 'He expects to take her up the river the day after tomorrow.'

After thus overwhelming us with the extent of his information he slipped out of the cabin. The mate observed regretfully that he 'could not account for that young fellow's whims.' What prevented him telling us all about it at once, he wanted to know.

I detained him as he was making a move. For the last two days the crew had had plenty of hard work, and the night before they had very little sleep. I felt painfully that I—a stranger—was doing something unusual when I directed him to let all hands turn in without setting an anchor-watch. I proposed to keep on deck myself till one o'clock or thereabouts. I would get the second mate to relieve me at that hour.

'He will turn out the cook and the steward at four,' I concluded, 'and then give you a call. Of course at the slightest sign of any sort of wind we'll have the hands up and make a start at once.'

He concealed his astonishment. 'Very well, sir.' Outside the cuddy he put his head in the second mate's door to inform him of my unheard-of caprice to take a five hours' anchor-watch on myself. I heard the other raise his voice incredulously—'What? The Captain himself?' Then a few more murmurs, a door closed, then another. A few moments later I went on deck.

My strangeness, which had made me sleepless, had prompted that unconventional arrangement, as if I had expected in those solitary hours of the night to get on terms with the ship of which I knew nothing, manned by men of whom I knew very little more. Fast alongside a wharf, littered like any ship

in port with a tangle of unrelated things, invaded by unrelated shore people, I had hardly seen her yet properly.
Now, as she lay cleared for sea, the stretch of her main-deck
seemed to me very fine under the stars. Very fine, very roomy
for her size, and very inviting. I descended the poop and
paced the waist, my mind picturing to myself the coming passage through the Malay Archipelago, down the Indian Ocean
and up the Atlantic. All its phases were familiar enough to
me, every characteristic, all the alternatives which were likely
to face me on the high seas—everything! ... except the novel
responsibility of command. But I took heart from the reasonable thought that the ship was like other ships, the men like
other men, and that the sea was not likely to keep any special
surprises expressly for my discomfiture.

Arrived at that comforting conclusion, I bethought myself
of a cigar and went below to get it. All was still down there.
Everybody at the after end of the ship was sleeping pro-
foundly. I came out again on the quarter-deck, agreeably at
ease in my sleeping-suit on that warm breathless night, barefooted, a glowing cigar in my teeth, and, going forward, I was
met by the profound silence of the fore end of the ship. Only
as I passed the door of the forecastle I heard a deep, quiet,
trustful sigh of some sleeper inside. And suddenly I rejoiced
in the great security of the sea as compared with the unrest of
the land, in my choice of that untempted life presenting no
disquieting problems, invested with an elementary moral
beauty by the absolute straightforwardness of its appeal and
by the singleness of its purpose.

The riding-light in the fore-rigging burned with a clear,
untroubled, as if symbolic, flame, confident and bright in the
mysterious shades of the night. Passing on my way aft along
the other side of the ship, I observed that the rope side-
ladder, put over, no doubt, for the master of the tug when he
came to fetch away our letters, had not been hauled in as it
should have been. I became annoyed at this, for exactitude in
small matters is the very soul of discipline. Then I reflected
that I had myself peremptorily dismissed my officers from
duty, and by my own act had prevented the anchor-watch
being formally set and things properly attended to. I asked
myself whether it was wise ever to interfere with the estab-

lished routine of duties even from the kindest of motives. My action might have made me appear eccentric. Goodness only knew how that absurdly whiskered mate would 'account' for my conduct, and what the whole ship thought of that informality of their new captain. I was vexed with myself.

Not from compunction certainly, but, as it were mechanically, I proceeded to get the ladder in myself. Now a side-ladder of that sort is a light affair and comes in easily, yet my vigorous tug, which should have brought it flying on board, merely recoiled upon my body in a totally unexpected jerk. What the devil! ... I was so astounded by the immovableness of that ladder that I remained stock-still, trying to account for it to myself like that imbecile mate of mine. In the end, of course, I put my head over the rail.

The side of the ship made an opaque belt of shadow on the darkling glassy shimmer of the sea. But I saw at once something elongated and pale floating very close to the ladder. Before I could form a guess a faint flash of phosphorescent light, which seemed to issue suddenly from the naked body of a man, flickered in the sleeping water with the elusive, silent play of summer lightning in a night sky. With a gasp I saw revealed to my stare a pair of feet, the long legs, a broad livid back immersed right up to the neck in a greenish cadaverous glow. One hand, awash, clutched the bottom rung of the ladder. He was complete but for the head. A headless corpse! The cigar dropped out of my gaping mouth with a tiny plop and a short hiss quite audible in the absolute stillness of all things under heaven. At that I suppose he raised up his face, a dimly pale oval in the shadow of the ship's side. But even then I could only barely make out down there the shape of his black-haired head. However, it was enough for the horrid, frost-bound sensation which had gripped me about the chest to pass off. The moment of vain exclamations was past, too. I only climbed on the spare spar and leaned over the rail as far as I could, to bring my eyes nearer to that mystery floating alongside.

As he hung by the ladder, like a resting swimmer, the sea-lightning played about his limbs at every stir; and he appeared in it ghastly, silvery, fish-like. He remained as mute as a fish, too. He made no motion to get out of the water, either. It was inconceivable that he should not attempt to come on board, and strangely troubling to suspect that perhaps he did not want to. And my first words were prompted by just that troubled incertitude.

'What's the matter?' I asked in my ordinary tone, speaking down to the face upturned exactly under mine.

'Cramp,' it answered, no louder. Then slightly anxious, 'I say, no need to call anyone.'

'I was not going to,' I said.

'Are you alone on deck?'

'Yes.'

I had somehow the impression that he was on the point of letting go the ladder to swim away beyond my ken—mysterious as he came. But, for the moment, this being appearing as if he had risen from the bottom of the sea (it was certainly the nearest land to the ship) wanted only to know the time. I told him. And he, down there, tentatively:

'I suppose your captain's turned in?'

'I am sure he isn't,' I said.

He seemed to struggle with himself, for I heard something like the low, bitter murmur of doubt. 'What's the good?' His next words came out with a hesitating effort.

'Look here, my man. Could you call him out quietly?'

I thought the time had come to declare myself.

'*I* am the captain.'

I heard a 'By Jove!' whispered at the level of the water. The phosphorescence flashed in the swirl of the water all about his limbs, his other hand seized the ladder.

'My name's Leggatt.'

The voice was calm and resolute. A good voice. The self-possession of that man had somehow induced a corresponding state in myself. It was very quietly that I remarked:

'You must be a good swimmer.'

'Yes. I've been in the water practically since nine o'clock. The question for me now is whether I am to let go this ladder and go on swimming till I sink from exhaustion, or—to come on board here.'

I felt this was no mere formula of desperate speech, but a real alternative in the view of a strong soul. I should have gathered from this that he was young; indeed, it is only the young who are ever confronted by such clear issues. But at the time it was pure intuition on my part. A mysterious communication was established already between us two—in the face of that silent, darkened tropical sea. I was young, too; young enough to make no comment. The man in the water began suddenly to climb up the ladder, and I hastened away from the rail to fetch some clothes.

Before entering the cabin I stood still, listening in the lobby at the foot of the stairs. A faint snore came through the closed door of the chief mate's room. The second mate's door was on the hook, but the darkness in there was absolutely soundless. He, too, was young and could sleep like a stone. Remained the steward, but he was not likely to wake up before he was called. I got a sleeping-suit out of my room and, coming back on desk, saw the naked man from the sea sitting on the main-hatch, glimmering white in the darkness, his elbows on his knees and his head in his hands. In a moment he had concealed his damp body in a sleeping-suit of the same grey-stripe pattern as the one I was wearing and followed me like my double on the poop. Together we moved right aft, barefooted, silent.

'What is it?' I asked in a deadened voice, taking the lighted lamp out of the binnacle, and raising it to his face.

'An ugly business.'

He had rather regular features; a good mouth; light eyes under somewhat heavy, dark eyebrows; a smooth, square forehead; no growth on his cheeks; a small, brown moustache, and a well-shaped, round chin. His expression was concentrated, meditative, under the inspecting light of the lamp I held up to his face; such as a man thinking hard in solitude might wear. My sleeping-suit was just right for his size. A well-knit young fellow of twenty-five at most. He caught his lower lip with the edge of white, even teeth.

'Yes,' I said, replacing the lamp in the binnacle. The warm, heavy tropical night closed upon his head again.

'There's a ship over there,' he murmured.

'Yes, I know. The *Sephora*. Did you know of us?'

'Hadn't the slightest idea. I am the mate of her——' He paused and corrected himself. 'I should say I *was*.'

'Aha! Something wrong?'

'Yes, very wrong indeed. I've killed a man.'

'What do you mean? Just now?'

'No, on the passage. Weeks ago. Thirty-nine south. When I say a man——'

'Fit of temper,' I suggested, confidently.

The shadowy, dark head, like mine, seemed to nod imperceptibly above the ghostly grey of my sleeping-suit. It was, in the night, as though I had been faced by my own reflection in the depths of a sombre and immense mirror.

'A pretty thing to have to own up to for a Conway boy,' murmured my double, distinctly.

'You're a Conway boy?'

'I am,' he said, as if startled. Then, slowly ... 'Perhaps you too——'

It was so; but being a couple of years older I had left before he joined. After a quick interchange of dates a silence fell; and I thought suddenly of my absurd mate with his terrific whiskers and the 'Bless my soul—you don't say so' type of intellect. My double gave me an inkling of his thoughts by saying: 'My father's a parson in Norfolk. Do you see me before a judge and jury on that charge? For myself I can't see the necessity. There are fellows that an angel from heaven—— And I am not that. He was one of those creatures that are just simmering all the time with a silly sort of wickedness. Miserable devils that have no business to live at all. He wouldn't do his duty and wouldn't let anybody else do theirs. But what's the good of talking! You know well enough the sort of ill-conditioned snarling cur——'

He appealed to me as if our experiences had been as identical as our clothes. And I knew well enough the pestiferous danger of such a character where there are no means of legal repression. And I knew well enough also that my double there was no homicidal ruffian. I did not think of asking him for details, and he told me the story roughly in brusque, disconnected sentences. I needed no more. I saw it all going on as though I were myself inside that other sleeping-suit.

'It happened while we were setting a reefed foresail, at dusk. Reefed foresail! You understand the sort of weather. The only sail we had left to keep the ship running; so you may guess what it had been like for days. Anxious sort of job, that. He gave me some of his cursed insolence at the sheet. I tell you I was overdone with this terrific weather that seemed to have no end to it. Terrific, I tell you—and a deep ship. I believe the fellow himself was half crazed with funk. It was no time for gentlemanly reproof, so I turned round and felled him like an ox. He up and at me. We closed just as an awful sea made for the ship. All hands saw it coming and took to the rigging, but I had him by the throat, and went on shaking him like a rat, the men above us yelling, "Look out! look out!" Then a crash as if the sky had fallen on my head. They say that for over ten minutes hardly anything was to be seen of the ship—just the three masts and a bit of the forecastle head and of the poop all awash driving along in a smother of foam. It was a miracle that they found us, jammed together behind the forebits. It's clear that I meant business, because I was holding him by the throat still when they picked us up. He was black in the face. It was too much for them. It seems they rushed us aft together, gripped as we were, screaming "Murder!" like a lot of lunatics, and broke into the cuddy. And the ship running for her life, touch and go all the time, any minute her last in a sea fit to turn your hair grey only a-looking at it. I understand that the skipper, too, started raving like the rest of them. The man had been deprived of sleep for more than a week, and to have this sprung on him at the height of a furious gale nearly drove him out of his mind. I wonder they didn't fling me overboard after getting the carcass of their precious shipmate out of my fingers. They had rather a job to separate us, I've been told. A sufficiently fierce story to make an old judge and a respectable jury sit up a bit. The first thing I heard when I came to myself was the maddening howling of that endless gale, and on that the voice of the old man. He was hanging on to my bunk, staring into my face out of his sou'wester.

'"Mr Legatt, you have killed a man. You can act no longer as chief mate of this ship."'

His care to subdue his voice made it sound monotonous. He rested a hand on the end of the skylight to steady himself with, and all that time did not stir a limb, so far as I could see. 'Nice little tale for a quiet tea-party,' he concluded in the same tone.

One of my hands, too, rested on the end of the skylight; neither did I stir a limb, so far as I knew. We stood less than a foot from each other. It occurred to me that if old 'Bless my soul—you don't say so' were to put his head up the companion and catch sight of us, he would think he was seeing double, or imagine himself come upon a scene of weird witchcraft; the strange captain having a quiet confabulation by the wheel with his own grey ghost. I became very much concerned to prevent anything of the sort. I heard the other's soothing undertone.

'My father's a parson in Norfolk,' it said. Evidently he had forgotten he had told me this important fact before. Truly a nice little tale.

'You had better slip down into my stateroom now,' I said, moving off stealthily. My double followed my movements; our bare feet made no sound; I let him in, closed the door with care and, after giving a call to the second mate, returned on deck for my relief.

'Not much sign of any wind yet,' I remarked when he approached.

'No, sir. Not much,' he assented, sleepily, in his hoarse voice, with just enough deference, no more, and barely suppressing a yawn.

'Well, that's all you have to look out for. You have got your orders.'

'Yes, sir.'

I paced a turn or two on the poop and saw him take up his position face forward with his elbow in the ratlines of the mizzen-rigging before I went below. The mate's faint snoring was still going on peacefully. The cuddy lamp was burning over the table on which stood a vase with flowers, a polite attention from the ship's provision merchant—the last flowers we should see for the next three months at the very least. Two bunches of bananas hung from the beam symmetrically, one on each side of the rudder-casing. Everything was as before in the ship—except that two of her captain's sleeping-suits were simultaneously in use, one motionless in the cuddy, the other keeping very still in the captain's stateroom.

It must be explained here that my cabin had the form of

the capital letter L the door being within the angle and opening into the short part of the letter. A couch was to the left, the bed-place to the right; my writing-desk and the chronometers' table faced the door. But any one opening it, unless he stepped right inside, had no view of what I call the long (or vertical) part of the letter. It contained some lockers surmounted by a bookcase; and a few clothes, a thick jacket or two, caps, oilskin coat and such like, hung on hooks. There was at the bottom of that part a door opening into my bath-room, which could be entered also directly from the saloon. But that way was never used.

The mysterious arrival had discovered the advantage of this particular shape. Entering my room, lighted strongly by a big bulkhead lamp swung on gimbals above my writing-desk, I did not see him anywhere till he stepped out quietly from behind the coats hung in the recessed part.

'I heard somebody moving about, and went in there at once,' he whispered.

I, too, spoke under my breath.

'Nobody is likely to come in here without knocking and getting permission.'

He nodded. His face was thin and the sunburn faded, as though he had been ill. And no wonder. He had been, I heard presently, kept under arrest in his cabin for nearly seven weeks. But there was nothing sickly in his eyes or in his expression. He was not a bit like me, really; yet, as we stood leaning over my bed-place, whispering side by side, with our dark heads together and our backs to the door, anybody bold enough to open it stealthily would have been treated to the uncanny sight of a double captain busy talking in whispers with his other self.

'But all this doesn't tell me how you came to hang on to our side-ladder,' I inquired, in the hardly audible murmurs we used, after he had told me something more of the proceedings on board the *Sephora* once the bad weather was over.

'When we sighted Java Head I had had time to think all those matters out several times over. I had six weeks of doing nothing else, and with only an hour or so every evening for a tramp on the quarter-deck.'

He whispered, his arms folded on the side of my bedplace,

staring through the open port. And I could imagine perfectly the manner of this thinking out—a stubborn if not a steadfast operation; something of which I should have been perfectly incapable.

'I reckoned it would be dark before we closed with the land,' he continued, so low that I had to strain my hearing, near as we were to each other, shoulder touching shoulder almost. 'So I asked to speak to the old man. He always seemed very sick when he came to see me—as if he could not look me in the face. You know, that foresail saved the ship. She was too deep to have run long under bare poles. And it was I that managed to set it for him. Anyway, he came. When I had him in my cabin—he stood by the door looking at me as if I had the halter round my neck already—I asked him right away to leave my cabin door unlocked at night while the ship was going through Sunda Straits. There would be the Java coast within two or three miles, off Angier Point. I wanted nothing more. I've had a prize for swimming my second year in the Conway.'

'I can believe it,' I breathed out.

'God only knows why they locked me in every night. To see some of their faces you'd have thought they were afraid I'd go about at night strangling people. Am I a murdering brute? Do I look it? By Jove! if I had been he wouldn't have trusted himself like that into my room. You'll say I might have chucked him aside and bolted out, there and then—it was dark already. Well, no. And for the same reason I wouldn't think of trying to smash the door. There would have been a rush to stop me at the noise, and I did not mean to get into a confounded scrimmage. Somebody else might have got killed—for I would not have broken out only to get chucked back, and I did not want any more of that work. He refused, looking more sick than ever. He was afraid of the men, and also of that old second mate of his who had been sailing with him for years—a grey-headed old humbug; and his steward, too, had been with him devil knows how long— seventeen years or more—a dogmatic sort of loafer who hated me like poison, just because I was the chief mate. No chief mate ever made more than one voyage in the *Sephora*, you know. Those two old chaps ran the ship. Devil only knows what the skipper wasn't afraid of (all his nerve went to pieces altogether in that hellish spell of bad weather we had)—of what the law would do to him—of his wife, perhaps. Oh, yes! she's on board. Though I don't think she would have meddled. She would have been only too glad to have me out of the ship in any way. The 'brand of Cain' business, don't you see. That's all right. I was ready enough to go off wandering on the face of the earth—and that was price enough to pay for an Abel of that sort. Anyhow, he wouldn't listen to me. 'This thing must take its course. I represent the law here.' He was shaking like a leaf. 'So you won't?' 'No!' 'Then I hope you will be able to sleep on that,' I said, and turned my back on him. 'I wonder that *you* can,' cries he, and locks the door.

'Well, after that, I couldn't. Not very well. That was three weeks ago. We have had a slow passage through the Java Sea; drifted about Carimata for ten days. When we anchored here they thought, I suppose, it was all right. The nearest land (and that's five miles) is the ship's destination; the consul would soon set about catching me; and there would have been no object in bolting to these islets there. I don't suppose there's a drop of water on them. I don't know how it was, but tonight that steward, after bringing me my supper, went out to let me eat it, and left the door unlocked. And I ate it—all there was, too. After I had finished I strolled out on the quarter-deck. I don't know that I meant to do anything. A breath of fresh air was all I wanted, I believe. Then a sudden temptation came over me. I kicked off my slippers and was in the water before I had made up my mind fairly. Somebody heard the splash and they raised an awful hullabaloo. 'He's gone! Lower the boats! He's committed suicide! No, he's swimming.' Certainly I was swimming. It's not so easy for a swimmer like me to commit suicide by drowning. I landed on the nearest islet before the boat left the ship's side. I heard them pulling about in the dark, hailing, and so on, but after a bit they gave up. Everything quieted down and the anchorage became as still as death. I sat down on a stone and began to think. I felt certain they would start searching for me at daylight. There was no place to hide on those stony things— and if there had been, what would have been the good? But now I was clear of that ship, I was not going back. So after a

while I took off all my clothes, tied them up in a bundle with
a stone inside, and dropped them in the deep water on the
outer side of that islet. That was suicide enough for me. Let
them think what they liked, but I didn't mean to drown
myself. I meant to swim till I sank—but that's not the same
thing. I struck out for another of these little islands, and it
was from that one that I first saw your riding-light. Something to swim for. I went on easily, and on the way I came
upon a flat rock a foot or two above water. In the daytime, I
dare say, you might make it out with a glass from your poop. I
scrambled up on it and rested myself for a bit. Then I made
another start. That last spell must have been over a mile.'

His whisper was getting fainter and fainter, and all the
time he stared straight out through the port-hole, in which
there was not even a star to be seen. I had not interrupted
him. There was something that made comment impossible in
his narrative, or perhaps in himself; a sort of feeling, a
quality, which I can't find a name for. And when he ceased,
all I found was a futile whisper: 'So you swam for our light?'

'Yes—straight for it. It was something to swim for. I
couldn't see any stars low down because the coast was in the
way, and I couldn't see the land, either. The water was like
glass. One might have been swimming in a confounded
thousand-feet deep cistern with no place for scrambling out
anywhere; but what I didn't like was the notion of swimming
round and round like a crazed bullock before I gave out; and
as I didn't mean to go back ... No. Do you see me being
hauled back, stark naked, off one of these little islands by the
scruff of the neck and fighting like a wild beast? Somebody
would have got killed for certain, and I did not want any of
that. So I went on. Then your ladder——'

'Why didn't you hail the ship?' I asked, a little louder.

He touched my shoulder lightly. Lazy footsteps came right
over our heads and stopped. The second mate had crossed
from the other side of the poop and might have been hanging
over the rail, for all we knew.

'He couldn't hear us talking—could he?' My double
breathed into my very ear, anxiously.

His anxiety was an answer, a sufficient answer, to the
question I had put to him. An answer containing all the

difficulty of that situation. I closed the porthole quietly, to make sure. A louder word might have been overheard.

'Who's that?' he whispered then.

'My second mate. But I don't know much more of the fellow than you do.'

And I told him a little about myself. I had been appointed to take charge while I least expected anything of the sort, not quite a fortnight ago. I didn't know either the ship or the people. Hadn't had the time in port to look about me or size anybody up. And as to the crew, all they knew was that I was appointed to take the ship home. For the rest, I was almost as much of a stranger on board as himself, I said. And at the moment I felt it most acutely. I felt that it would take very little to make me a suspect person in the eyes of the ship's company.

He had turned about meantime; and we, the two strangers in the ship, faced each other in identical attitudes.

'Your ladder——' he murmured, after a silence.

'Who'd have thought of finding a ladder hanging over at night in a ship anchored out here! I felt just then a very unpleasant faintness. After the life I've been leading for nine weeks, anybody would have got out of condition. I wasn't capable of swimming round as far as your rudder-chains. And, lo and behold! there was a ladder to get hold of. After I gripped it I said to myself, "What's the good?" When I saw a man's head looking over I thought I would swim away presently and leave him shouting—in whatever language it was. I didn't mind being looked at. I—I liked it. And then you speaking to me so quietly—as if you had expected me—made me hold on a little longer. It had been a confounded lonely time—I don't mean while swimming. I was glad to talk a little to somebody that didn't belong to the *Sephora*. As to asking for the captain, that was a mere impulse. It could have been no use, with all the ship knowing about me and the other people pretty certain to be round here in the morning. I don't know—I wanted to be seen, to talk with somebody, before I went on. I don't know what I would have said ... "Fine night, isn't it?" or something of the sort.'

'Do you think they will be round here presently?' I asked with some incredulity.

'Quite likely,' he said, faintly.

He looked extremely haggard all of a sudden. His head rolled on his shoulders.

'H'm. We shall see then. Meantime get into that bed.' I whispered. 'Want help? There.'

It was a rather high bed-place with a set of drawers underneath. This amazing swimmer really needed the lift I gave him by seizing his leg. He tumbled in, rolled over on his back, and flung one arm across his eyes. And then, with his face nearly hidden, he must have looked exactly as I used to look in that bed. I gazed upon my other self for a while before drawing across carefully the two green serge curtains which ran on a brass rod. I thought for a moment of pinning them together for greater safety, but I sat down on the couch, and once there I felt unwilling to rise and hunt for a pin. I would do it in a moment. I was extremely tired, in a peculiarly intimate way, by the strain of stealthiness, by the effort of whispering and the general secrecy of this excitement. It was three o'clock by now and I had been on my feet since nine, but I was not sleepy; I could not have gone to sleep. I sat there, fagged out, looking at the curtains, trying to clear my mind of the confused sensation of being in two places at once, and greatly bothered by an exasperating knocking in my head. It was a relief to discover suddenly that it was not in my head at all, but on the outside of the door. Before I could collect myself the words 'Come in' were out of my mouth, and the steward entered with a tray, bringing in my morning coffee. I had slept, after all, and I was so frightened that I shouted, 'This way! I am here, steward,' as though he had been miles away. He put down the tray on the table next the couch and only then said, very quietly, 'I can see you are here, sir.' I felt him give me a keen look, but I dared not meet his eyes just then. He must have wondered why I had drawn the curtains of my bed before going to sleep on the couch. He went out, hooking the door open as usual.

I heard the crew washing decks above me. I knew I would have been told at once if there had been any wind. Calm, I thought, and I was doubly vexed. Indeed, I felt dual more than ever. The steward reappeared suddenly in the doorway. I jumped up from the couch so quickly that he gave a start.

'What do you want here?'

'Close your port, sir—they are washing decks.'

'It is closed,' I said, reddening.

'Very well, sir.' But he did not move from the doorway and returned my stare in an extraordinary, equivocal manner for a time. Then his eyes wavered, all his expression changed, and in a voice unusually gentle, almost coaxingly:

'May I come in to take the empty cup away, sir?'

'Of course!' I turned my back on him while he popped in and out. Then I unhooked and closed the door and even pushed the bolt. This sort of thing could not go on very long. The cabin was as hot as an oven, too. I took a peep at my double, and discovered that he had not moved, his arm was still over his eyes; but his chest heaved; his hair was wet; his chin glistened with perspiration. I reached over him and opened the port.

'I must show myself on deck,' I reflected.

Of course, theoretically, I could do what I liked, with no one to say nay to me within the whole circle of the horizon; but to lock my cabin door and take the key away I did not dare. Directly I put my head out of the companion I saw the group of my two officers, the second mate bare-footed, the chief mate in long india-rubber boots, near the break of the poop and the steward half-way down the poop-ladder talking to them eagerly. He happened to catch sight of me and dived, the second ran down on the main-deck shouting some order or other and the chief mate came to meet me, touching his cap.

There was a sort of curiosity in his eye that I did not like. I don't know whether the steward had told them that I was 'queer' only, or downright drunk, but I know the man meant to have a good look at me. I watched him coming with a smile which, as he got into point-blank range, took effect and froze his very whiskers. I did not give him time to open his lips.

'Square the yards by lifts and braces before the hands go to breakfast.'

It was the first particular order I had given on board that ship; and I stayed on deck to see it executed, too. I had felt the need of asserting myself without loss of time. That sneering young cub got taken down a peg or two on that occasion, and I also seized the opportunity of having a good look at the face of every foremast man as they filed past me to go to the after braces. At breakfast time, eating nothing myself, I presided with such frigid dignity that the two mates were only too glad to escape from the cabin as soon as decency permitted; and all the time the dual working of my mind distracted me almost to the point of insanity. I was constantly watching myself, my secret self, as dependent on my actions as my own personality, sleeping in that bed, behind that door which faced me as I sat at the head of the table. It was very much like being mad, only it was worse because one was aware of it.

I had to shake him for a solid minute, but when at last he opened his eyes it was in the full possession of his senses, with an inquiring look.

'All's well so far,' I whispered. 'Now you must vanish into the bathroom.'

He did so, as noiseless as a ghost, and then I rang for the steward, and facing him boldly, directed him to tidy up my stateroom while I was having my bath—'and be quick about it.' As my tone admitted of no excuses, he said, 'Yes, sir,' and ran off to fetch his dust-pan and brushes. I took a bath and did most of my dressing, splashing, and whistling softly for the steward's edification, while the secret sharer of my life stood drawn up bolt upright in that little space, his face looking very sunken in daylight, his eyelids lowered under the stern, dark line of his eyebrows drawn together by a slight frown.

When I left him there to go back to my room the steward was finishing dusting. I sent for the mate and engaged him in some insignificant conversation. It was, as it were, trifling with the terrific character of his whiskers; but my object was to give him an opportunity for a good look at my cabin. And then I could at last shut, with a clear conscience, the door of my stateroom and get my double back into the recessed part. There was nothing else for it. He had to sit still on a small folding stool, half smothered by the heavy coats hanging there. We listened to the steward going into the bathroom out of the saloon, filling the water-bottles there, scrubbing the bath, setting things to rights, whisk, bang, clatter—out again into the saloon—turn the key—click. Such was my scheme for keeping my second self invisible. Nothing better could be contrived under the circumstances. And there we sat; I at my writing-desk ready to appear busy with some papers, he behind me out of sight of the door. It would not have been prudent to talk in daytime; and I could not have stood the excitement of that queer sense of whispering to myself. Now and then, glancing over my shoulder, I saw him far back there, sitting rigidly on the low stool, his bare feet close together, his arms folded, his head hanging on his breast—and perfectly still. Anybody would have taken him for me.

I was fascinated by it myself. Every moment I had to glance over my shoulder. I was looking at him when a voice outside the door said:

'Beg pardon, sir.'

'Well!' ... I kept my eyes on him, and so when the voice outside the door announced, 'There's a ship's boat coming our way, sir,' I saw him give a start—the first movement he had made for hours. But he did not raise his bowed head.

'All right. Get the ladder over.''

I hesitated. Should I whisper something to him? But what? His immobility seemed to have been never disturbed. What could I tell him he did not know already? ... Finally I went on deck.

2

The skipper of the *Sephora* had a thin red whisker all round his face, and the sort of complexion that goes with hair of that colour; also the particular, rather smeary shade of blue in the eyes. He was not exactly a showy figure; his shoulders were high, his stature but middling—one leg, slightly more bandy than the other. He shook hands, looking vaguely around. A spiritless tenacity was his main characteristic, I judged. I behaved with a politeness which seemed to disconcert him. Perhaps he was shy. He mumbled to me as if he were ashamed of what he was saying; gave his name (it was something like Archbold—but at this distance of years I hardly am sure), his ship's name, and a few other particulars of that sort, in the manner of a criminal making a reluctant and doleful confession. He had had terrible weather on the passage out—terrible—terrible—wife aboard, too.

But this time we were seated in the cabin and the steward brought in a tray with a bottle and glasses. 'Thanks! No.' Never took liquor. Would have some water, though. He drank two tumblerfuls. Terrible thirsty work. Ever since daylight had been exploring the islands round his ship.

'What was that for—fun?' I asked, with an appearance of polite interest.

'No!' He sighed. 'Painful duty.'

As he persisted in his mumbling and I wanted my double to hear every word, I hit upon the notion of informing him that I regretted to say I was hard of hearing.

'Such a young man, too!' he nodded, keeping his smeary blue, unintelligent eyes fastened upon me. What was the cause of it—some disease? he inquired, without the least sympathy and as if he thought that, if so, I'd got no more than I deserved.

'Yes; disease,' I admitted in a cheerful tone which seemed to shock him. But my point was gained, because he had to raise his voice to give me his tale. It is not worth while to record that version. It was just over two months since all this had happened, and he had thought so much about it that he seemed completely muddled as to its bearings, but still immensely impressed.

'What would you think of such a thing happening on board your own ship? I've had the *Sephora* for these fifteen years. I am a well-known shipmaster.'

He was densely distressed—and perhaps I should have sympathized with him if I had been able to detach my mental vision from the unsuspected sharer of my cabin as though he were my second self. There he was on the other side of the bulkhead, four or five feet from us, no more, as we sat in the saloon. I looked politely at Captain Archbold (if that was his name), but it was the other I saw, in a grey sleeping-suit, seated on a low stool, his bare feet close together, his arms folded, and every word said between us falling into the ears of his dark head bowed on his chest.

'I have been at sea now, man and boy, for seven-and-thirty years, and I've never heard of such a thing happening in an

English ship. And that it should be my ship. Wife on board, too.'

I was hardly listening to him.

'Don't you think,' I said, 'that the heavy sea which, you told me, came aboard just then might have killed the man? I have seen the sheer weight of a sea kill a man very neatly, by simply breaking his neck.'

'Good God!' he uttered, impressively, fixing his smeary blue eyes on me. 'The sea! No man killed by the sea ever looked like that.' He seemed positively scandalized at my suggestion. And as I gazed at him, certainly not prepared for anything original on his part, he advanced his head close to mine and thrust his tongue out at me so suddenly that I couldn't help starting back.

After scoring over my calmness in this graphic way he nodded wisely. If I had seen the sight, he assured me, I would never forget it as long as I lived. The weather was too bad to give the corpse a proper sea burial. So next day at dawn they took it up on the poop, covering its face with a bit of bunting; he read a short prayer, and then, just as it was, in its oilskins and long boots, they launched it among those mountainous seas that seemed ready every moment to swallow up the ship herself and the terrified lives on board of her.

'That reefed foresail saved you,' I threw in.

'Under God—it did,' he exclaimed fervently. 'It was by a special mercy, I firmly believe, that it stood some of those hurricane squalls.'

'It was the setting of that sail which——' I began.

'God's own hand in it,' he interrupted me. 'Nothing less could have done it. I don't mind telling you that I hardly dared give the order. It seemed impossible that we could touch anything without losing it, and then our last hope would have been gone.'

The terror of that gale was on him yet. I let him go on for a bit, then said, casually—as if returning to a minor subject:

'You were very anxious to give up your mate to the shore people, I believe?'

He was. To the law. His obscure tenacity on that point had in it something incomprehensible and a little awful; something, as it were, mystical, quite apart from his anxiety that he should not be suspected of 'countenancing any doings of that sort'. Seven-and-thirty virtuous years at sea, of which over twenty of immaculate command, and the last fifteen in the *Sephora,* seemed to have laid him under some pitiless obligation.

'And you know,' he went on, groping shamefacedly among his feelings, 'I did not engage that young fellow. His people had some interest with my owners. I was in a way forced to take him on. He looked very smart, very gentlemanly, and all that. But do you know—I never liked him, somehow. I am a plain man. You see, he wasn't exactly the sort for the chief mate of a ship like the *Sephora.'*

I had become so connected in thoughts and impressions with the secret sharer of my cabin that I felt as if I, personally, were being given to understand that I, too, was not the sort that would have done for the chief mate of a ship like the *Sephora.* I had no doubt of it in my mind.

'Not at all the style of man. You understand,' he insisted, superfluously, looking hard at me.

I smiled urbanely. He seemed at a loss for a while.

'I suppose I must report a suicide.'

'Beg pardon?'

'Sui-cide! That's what I'll have to write to my owners directly I get in.'

'Unless you manage to recover him before tomorrow,' I assented, dispassionately ... 'I mean, alive.'

He mumbled something which I really did not catch, and I turned my ear to him in a puzzled manner. He fairly bawled:

'The land—I say, the mainland is at least seven miles off my anchorage.'

'About that.'

My lack of excitement, of curiosity, of surprise, of any sort of pronounced interest, began to arouse his distrust. But except for the felicitous pretence of deafness I had not tried to pretend anything. I had felt utterly incapable of playing the part of ignorance properly, and therefore was afraid to try. It is also certain that he had brought some ready-made suspicions with him, and that he viewed my politeness as a strange and unnatural phenomenon. And yet how else could

I have received him? Not heartily! That was impossible for psychological reasons, which I need not state here. My only object was to keep off his inquiries. Surlily? Yes, but surliness might have provoked a point-blank question. From its novelty to him and from its nature, punctilious courtesy was the manner best calculated to restrain the man. But there was the danger of his breaking through my defence bluntly. I could not, I think, have met him by a direct lie, also for psychological (not moral) reasons. If he had only known how afraid I was of his putting my feeling of identity with the other to the test! But, strangely enough—(I thought of it only afterwards)—I believe that he was not a little disconcerted by the reverse side of that weird situation, by something in me that reminded him of the man he was seeking—suggested a mysterious similitude to the young fellow he had distrusted and disliked from the first.

However that might have been, the silence was not very prolonged. He took another oblique step.

'I reckon I had no more than a two-mile pull to your ship. Not a bit more.'

'And quite enough, too, in this awful heat,' I said.

Another pause full of mistrust followed. Necessity, they say, is mother of invention, but fear, too, is not barren of ingenious suggestions. And I was afraid he would ask me point-blank for news of my other self.

'Nice little saloon, isn't it?' I remarked, as if noticing for the first time the way his eyes roamed from one closed door to the other. 'And very well fitted out, too. Here, for instance,' I continued, reaching over the back of my seat negligently and flinging the door open, 'is my bathroom.'

He made an eager movement, but hardly gave it a glance. I got up, shut the door of the bathroom, and invited him to have a look round, as if I were very proud of my accommodation. He had to rise and be shown round, but he went through the business without any raptures whatever.

'And now we'll have a look at my stateroom,' I declared, in a voice as loud as I dared to make it, crossing the cabin to the starboard side with purposely heavy steps.

He followed me in and gazed around. My intelligent double had vanished. I played my part.

'Very convenient—isn't it?'

'Very nice. Very comf...' He didn't finish and went out brusquely as if to escape from some unrighteous wiles of mine. But it was not to be. I had been too frightened not to feel vengeful; I felt I had him on the run, and I meant to keep him on the run. My polite insistence must have had something menacing in it, because he gave in suddenly. And I did not let him off a single item; mate's room, pantry, storerooms, the very sail-locker which was also under the poop—he had to look into them all. When at last I showed him out on the quarter-deck he drew a long, spiritless sigh, and mumbled dismally that he must really be going back to his ship now. I desired my mate, who had joined us, to see to the captain's boat.

The man of whiskers gave a blast on the whistle which he used to wear hanging round his neck, and yelled, '*Sephora's* away!' My double down there in my cabin must have heard, and certainly could not feel more relieved than I. Four fellows came running out from somewhere forward and went over the side, while my own men, appearing on deck too, lined the rail. I escorted my visitor to the gangway ceremoniously, and nearly overdid it. He was a tenacious beast. On the very ladder he lingered, and in that unique, guiltily conscientious manner of sticking to the point:

'I say ... you ... you don't think that——'

I covered his voice loudly:

'Certainly not ... I am delighted. Good-bye.'

I had an idea of what he meant to say, and just saved myself by the privilege of defective hearing. He was too shaken generally to insist, but my mate, close witness of that parting, looked mystified and his face took on a thoughtful cast. As I did not want to appear as if I wished to avoid all communication with my officers, he had the opportunity to address me.

'Seems a very nice man. His boat's crew told our chaps a very extraordinary story, if what I am told by the steward is true. I suppose you had it from the captain, sir?'

'Yes. I had a story from the captain.'

'A very horrible affair—isn't it, sir?'

'It is.

'Beats all these tales we hear about murders in Yankee ships.'

'I don't think it beats them. I don't think it resembles them in the least.'

'Bless my soul—you don't say so! But of course I've no acquaintance whatever with American ships, not I, so I couldn't go against your knowledge. It's horrible enough for me ... But the queerest part is that those fellows seemed to have some idea the man was hidden aboard here. They had really. Did you ever hear of such a thing?'

'Preposterous—isn't it?'

We were walking to and fro athwart the quarter-deck. No one of the crew forward could be seen (the day was Sunday), and the mate pursued:

'There was some little dispute about it. Our chaps took offence. "As if we would harbour a thing like that," they said. "Wouldn't you like to look for him in our coal-hole?" Quite a tiff. But they made it up in the end. I suppose he did drown himself. Don't you, sir?'

'I don't suppose anything.'

'You have no doubt in the matter, sir?'

'None whatever.'

I left him suddenly. I felt I was producing a bad impression, but with my double down there it was most trying to be on deck. And it was almost as trying to be below. Altogether a nerve-trying situation. But on the whole I felt less torn in two when I was with him. There was no one in the whole ship whom I dared take into my confidence. Since the hands had got to know his story, it would have been impossible to pass him off for anyone else, and an accidental discovery was to be dreaded now more than ever ...

The steward being engaged in laying the table for dinner, we could talk only with our eyes when I first went down. Later in the afternoon we had a cautious try at whispering. The Sunday quietness of the ship was against us; the stillness of air and water around her was against us; the elements, the men were against us—everything was against us in our secret partnership; time itself—for this could not go on for ever. The very trust in Providence was, I suppose, denied to his guilt. Shall I confess that this thought cast me down very much? And as to the chapter of accidents which counts for so much in the book of success, I could only hope that it was closed. For what favourable accident could be expected?

'Did you hear everything?' were my first words as soon as we took up our position side by side, leaning over my bed-place.

He had. And the proof of it was his earnest whisper, 'The man told you he hardly dared to give the order.'

I understood the reference to be to that saving foresail.

'Yes. He was afraid of it being lost in the setting.'

'I assure you he never gave the order. He may think he did, but he never gave it. He stood there with me on the break of the poop after the maintopsail blew away, and whimpered about our last hope—positively whimpered about it and nothing else—and the night coming on! To hear one's skipper go on like that in such weather was enough to drive any fellow out of his mind. It worked me up into a sort of desperation. I just took it into my own hands and went away from him, boiling, and—— But what's the use telling you? *You* know! ... Do you think that if I had not been pretty fierce with them I should have got the men to do anything? Not it! The bo's'n perhaps? Perhaps! It wasn't a heavy sea—it was a sea gone mad! I suppose the end of the world will be something like that; and a man may have the heart to see it coming once and be done with it—but to have to face it day after day—— I don't blame anybody. I was precious little better than the rest. Only—I was an officer of that old coal-wagon, anyhow——'

'I quite understand,' I conveyed that sincere assurance into his ear. He was out of breath with whispering; I could hear him pant slightly. It was all very simple. The same strung-up force which had given twenty-four men a chance, at least, for their lives, had, in a sort of recoil, crushed an unworthy mutinous existence.

But I had no leisure to weigh the merits of the matter—footsteps in the saloon, a heavy knock. 'There's enough wind to get under way with, sir.' Here was the call of a new claim upon my thoughts and even upon my feelings.

'Turn the hands up,' I cried through the door. 'I'll be on deck directly.'

I was going out to make the acquaintance of my ship. Before I left the cabin our eyes met—the eyes of the only two strangers on board. I pointed to the recessed part where the little camp-stool awaited him and laid my finger on my lips. He made a gesture—somewhat vague—a little mysterious, accompanied by a faint smile, as if of regret.

This is not the place to enlarge upon the sensations of a man who feels for the first time a ship move under his feet to his own independent word. In my case they were not unalloyed. I was not wholly alone with my command; for there was that stranger in my cabin. Or rather, I was not completely and wholly with her. Part of me was absent. That mental feeling of being in two places at once affected me physically as if the mood of secrecy had penetrated my very soul. Before an hour had elapsed since the ship had begun to move, having occasion to ask the mate (he stood by my side) to take a compass bearing of the Pagoda, I caught myself reaching up to his ear in whispers. I say I caught myself, but enough had escaped to startle the man. I can't describe it otherwise than by saying that he shied. A grave, preoccupied manner, as though he were in possession of some perplexing intelligence, did not leave him henceforth. A little later I moved away from the rail to look at the compass with such a stealthy gait that the helmsman noticed it—and I could not help noticing the unusual roundness of his eyes. These are trifling instances, though it's to no commander's advantage to be suspected of ludicrous eccentricities. But I was also more seriously affected. There are to a seaman certain words, gestures, that should in given conditions come as naturally, as instinctively as the winking of a menaced eye. A certain order should spring on to his lips without thinking; a certain sign should get itself made, so to speak, without reflection. But all unconscious alertness had abandoned me. I had to make an effort of will to recall myself back (from the cabin) to the conditions of the moment. I felt that I was appearing an irresolute commander to those people who were watching me more or less critically.

And, besides, there were the scares. On the second day out, for instance, coming off the deck in the afternoon (I had straw slippers on my bare feet) I stopped at the open pantry door and spoke to the steward. He was doing something there with his back to me. At the sound of my voice he nearly jumped out of his skin, as the saying is, and incidentally broke a cup.

'What on earth's the matter with you?' I asked, astonished.

He was extremely confused. 'Beg your pardon, sir. I made sure you were in your cabin.'

'You see I wasn't.'

'No, sir. I could have sworn I had heard you moving in there not a moment ago. It's most extraordinary ... very sorry, sir.'

I passed on with an inward shudder. I was so identified with my secret double that I did not even mention the fact in those scanty, fearful whispers we exchanged. I suppose he had made some slight noise of some kind or other. It would have been miraculous if he hadn't at one time or another. And yet, haggard as he appeared, he looked always perfectly self-controlled, more than calm—almost invulnerable. On my suggestion he remained almost entirely in the bathroom, which, upon the whole, was the safest place. There could be really no shadow of an excuse for anyone ever wanting to go in there, once the steward had done with it. It was a very tiny place. Sometimes he reclined on the floor, his legs bent, his head sustained on one elbow. At others I would find him on the camp-stool, sitting in his grey sleeping-suit and with his cropped dark hair like a patient, unmoved convict. At night I would smuggle him into my bed-place, and we would whisper together, with the regular footfalls of the officer of the watch passing and repassing over our heads. It was an infinitely miserable time. It was lucky that some tins of fine preserves were stowed in a locker in my stateroom; hard bread I could always get hold of; and so he lived on stewed chicken, paté de foie gras, asparagus, cooked oysters, sardines—on all sorts of abominable sham delicacies out of tins. My early morning coffee he always drank; and it was all I dared do for him in that respect.

Every day there was the horrible manoeuvring to go through so that my room and then the bathroom should be done in the usual way. I came to hate the sight of the steward, to abhor the voice of that harmless man. I felt that it was he who would bring on the disaster of discovery. It hung like a sword over our heads.

The fourth day out, I think (we were then working down the east side of the Gulf of Siam, tack for tack, in light winds and smooth water)—the fourth day, I say, of this miserable juggling with the unavoidable, as we sat at our evening meal, that man, whose slightest movement I dreaded, after putting down the dishes ran up on deck busily. This could not be dangerous. Presently he came down again; and then it appeared that he had remembered a coat of mine which I had thrown over a rail to dry after having been wetted in a shower which had passed over the ship in the afternoon. Sitting stolidly at the head of the table I became terrified at the sight of the garment on his arm. Of course he made for my door. There was no time to lose.

'Steward,' I thundered. My nerves were so shaken that I could not govern my voice and conceal my agitation. This was the sort of thing that made my terrifically whiskered mate tap his forehead with his forefinger. I had detected him using that gesture while talking on deck with a confidential air to the carpenter. It was too far to hear a word, but I had no doubt that this pantomime could only refer to the strange new captain.

'Yes, sir,' the pale-faced steward turned resignedly to me. It was this maddening course of being shouted at, checked without rhyme or reason, arbitrarily chased out of my cabin, suddenly called into it, sent flying out of his pantry on incomprehensible errands, that accounted for the growing wretchedness of his expression.

'Where are you going with that coat?'

'To your room, sir.'

'Is there another shower coming?'

'I'm sure I don't know, sir. Shall I go up again and see, sir?'

'No! never mind.'

My object was attained, as of course my other self in there would have heard everything that passed. During this interlude my two officers never raised their eyes off their respective plates; but the lip of that confounded cub, the second mate, quivered visibly.

I expected the steward to hook my coat on and come out at once. He was very slow about it; but I dominated my nervousness sufficiently not to shout after him. Suddenly I became aware (it could be heard plainly enough) that the fellow for some reason or other was opening the door of the bathroom. It was the end. The place was literally not big enough to swing a cat in. My voice died in my throat and I went stony all over. I expected to hear a yell of surprise and terror, and made a movement, but had not the strength to get on my legs. Everything remained still. Had my second self taken the poor wretch by the throat? I don't know what I could have done next moment if I had not seen the steward come out of my room, close the door and then stand quietly by the sideboard.

'Saved,' I thought. 'But, no! Lost! Gone! He was gone!'

I laid my knife and fork down and leaned back in my chair. My head swam. After a while, when sufficiently recovered to speak in a steady voice, I instructed my mate to put the ship round at eight o'clock himself.

'I won't come on deck,' I went on. 'I think I'll turn in, and unless the wind shifts I don't want to be disturbed before midnight. I feel a bit seedy.'

'You did look middling bad a little while ago,' the chief mate remarked without showing any great concern.

They both went out, and I stared at the steward clearing the table. There was nothing to be read on that wretched man's face. But why did he avoid my eyes I asked myself. Then I thought I should like to hear the sound of his voice.

'Steward!'

'Sir!' Startled as usual.

'Where did you hang up that coat?'

'In the bathroom, sir.' The usual anxious tone. 'It's not quite dry yet, sir.'

For some time longer I sat in the cuddy. Had my double vanished as he had come? But of his coming there was an explanation, whereas his disappearance would be inexplicable ... I went slowly into my dark room, shut the door, lighted the lamp and for a time dared not turn round. When at last I did I saw him standing bolt-upright in the narrow recessed part. It would not be true to say I had a shock, but an irresistible doubt of his bodily existence flitted through my mind. Can it be, I asked myself, that he is not visible to other eyes than mine? It was like being haunted. Motionless, with a grave face, he raised his hands slightly at me in a gesture which meant clearly, 'Heavens! what a narrow escape!' Narrow indeed. I think I had come creeping quietly as near insanity as any man who has not actually gone over the border. That gesture restrained me, so to speak.

The mate with the terrific whiskers was now putting the ship on the other tack. In the moment of profound silence which follows upon the hands going to their stations I heard on the poop his raised voice: 'Hard alee!' and the distant shout of the order repeated on the maindeck. The sails, in that light breeze, made but a faint fluttering noise. It ceased. The ship was coming round slowly; I held my breath in the renewed stillness of expectation; one wouldn't have thought that there was a single living soul on her decks. A sudden brisk shout. 'Mainsail haul!' broke the spell. and in the noisy cries and rush overhead of the men running away with the main-brace we two, down in my cabin, came together in our usual position by the bed-place.

He did not wait for my question. 'I heard him fumbling here and just managed to squat myself down in the bath,' he whispered to me. 'The fellow only opened the door and put his arm in to hang the coat up. All the same——'

'I never thought of that,' I whispered back, even more appalled than before at the closeness of the shave, and marvelling at that something unyielding in his character which was carrying him through so finely. There was no agitation in his whisper. Whoever was being driven distracted, it was not he. He was sane. And the proof of his sanity was continued when he took up the whispering again.

'It would never do for me to come to life again.'

It was something that a ghost might have said. But what he was alluding to was his old captain's reluctant admission of the theory of suicide. It would obviously serve his turn—if I had understood at all the view which seemed to govern the unalterable purpose of his action.

'You must maroon me as soon as ever you can get among these islands off the Cambodje shore,' he went on.

'Maroon you! We are not living in a boy's adventure tale,' I protested. His scornful whispering took me up.

'We aren't indeed! There's nothing of a boy's tale in this. But there's nothing else for it. I want no more. You don't suppose I am afraid of what can be done to me? Prison or gallows or whatever they may please. But you don't see me coming back to explain such things to an old fellow in a wig and twelve respectable tradesmen, do you? What can they know whether I am guilty or not—or of *what* I am guilty, either? That's my affair. What does the Bible say? "Driven off the face of the earth." Very well. I am off the face of the earth now. As I came at night so I shall go.'

'Impossible!' I murmured. 'You can't.'

'Can't? ... Not naked like a soul on the Day of Judgement. I shall freeze on to this sleep-suit. The Last Day is not yet—and ... you have understood thoroughly. Didn't you?'

I felt suddenly ashamed of myself. I may say truly that I understood—and my hesitation in letting that man swim away from my ship's side had been a mere sham sentiment, a sort of cowardice.

'It can't be done now till next night,' I breathed out. 'The ship is on the off-shore tack and the wind may fail us.'

'As long as I know that you understand,' he whispered. 'But of course you do. It's a great satisfaction to have got somebody to understand. You seem to have been there on purpose.' And in the same whisper, as if we two whenever we talked had to say things to each other which were not fit for the world to hear, he added, 'It's very wonderful.'

We remained side by side talking in our secret way—but sometimes silent or just exchanging a whispered word or two at long intervals. And as usual he stared through the port. A breath of wind came now and again into our faces. The ship might have been moored in dock, so gently and on an even keel she slipped through the water, that did not murmur even at our passage, shadowy and silent like a phantom sea.

At midnight I went on deck, and to my mate's great surprise put the ship round on the other tack. His terrible whiskers flitted round me in silent criticism. I certainly should not have done it if it had been only a question of getting out of that sleepy gulf as quickly as possible. I believe he told the second mate, who relieved him, that it was a great want of judgement. The other only yawned. That intolerable cub shuffled about so sleepily and lolled against the rails in such a slack, improper fashion that I came down on him sharply.

'Aren't you properly awake yet?'

'Yes, sir! I am awake.'

'Well, then, be good enough to hold yourself as if you were. And keep a look-out. If there's any current we'll be closing with some islands before daylight.'

The east side of the gulf is fringed with islands, some solitary, others in groups. On the blue background of the high coast they seem to float on silvery patches of calm water, arid and grey, or dark green and rounded like clumps of evergreen bushes, with the larger ones, a mile or two long, showing the outlines of ridges, ribs of grey rock under the dank mantle of matted leafage. Unknown to trade, to travel, almost to geography, the manner of life they harbour is an unsolved secret. There must be villages—settlements of fishermen at least—on the largest of them, and some communication with the world is probably kept up by native craft. But all that forenoon, as we headed for them, fanned along by the faintest of breezes, I saw no sign of man or canoe in the field of the telescope I kept on pointing at the scattered group.

At noon I gave no orders for a change of course, and the mate's whiskers became much concerned and seemed to be offering themselves unduly to my notice. At last I said:

'I am going to stand right in. Quite in—as far as I can take her.'

The stare of extreme surprise imparted an air of ferocity also to his eyes, and he looked truly terrific for a moment.

'We're not doing well in the middle of the gulf,' I continued, casually. 'I am going to look for the land breezes tonight.'

'Bless my soul! Do you mean, sir, in the dark among the lot of all them islands and reefs and shoals?'

'Well—if there are any regular land breezes at all on this coast one must get close inshore to find them, mustn't one?'

'Bless my soul!' he exclaimed again under his breath. All that afternoon he wore a dreamy, contemplative appearance which in him was a mark of perplexity. After dinner I went into my stateroom as if I meant to take some rest. There we two bent our dark heads over a half-unrolled chart lying on my bed.

'There,' I said. 'It's got to be Koh-ring. I've been looking at it ever since sunrise. It has got two hills and a low point. It must be inhabited. And on the coast opposite there is what look like the mouth of a biggish river—with some town, no doubt, not far up. It's the best chance for you that I can see.'

'Anything. Koh-ring let it be.'

He looked thoughtfully at the chart as if surveying chances and distances from a lofty height—and following with his eyes his own figure wandering on the blank land of Cochin-China, and then passing off that piece of paper clean out of sight into uncharted regions. And it was as if the ship had two captains to plan her course for her. I had been so worried and restless running up and down that I had not had the patience to dress that day. I had remained in my sleeping-suit, with straw slippers and a soft floppy hat. The closeness of the heat in the gulf had been most oppressive, and the crew were used to see me wandering in that airy attire.

'She will clear the south point as she heads now,' I whispered into his ear. 'Goodness only knows when, though, but certainly after dark. I'll edge her in to half a mile, as far as I may be able to judge in the dark——'

'Be careful,' he murmured, warningly—and I realized suddenly that all my future, the only future for which I was fit, would perhaps go irretrievably to pieces in any mishap to my first command.

I could not stop a moment longer in the room. I motioned him to get out of sight and made my way on the poop. That unplayful cub had the watch. I walked up and down for a while thinking things out, then beckoned him over.

'Send a couple of hands to open the two quarter-deck ports,' I said, mildly.

He actually had the impudence, or else so forgot himself in his wonder at such an incomprehensible order, as to repeat:

'Open the quarter-deck ports! What for, sir?'

'The only reason you need concern yourself about is

because I tell you to do so. Have them open wide and fastened properly.'

He reddened and went off, but I believe made some jeering remark to the carpenter as to the sensible practice of ventilating a ship's quarter-deck. I know he popped into the mate's cabin to impart the fact to him because the whiskers came on deck, as it were by chance, and stole glances at me from below—for signs of lunacy or drunkenness, I suppose.

A little before supper, feeling more restless than ever, I rejoined, for a moment, my second self. And to find him sitting so quietly was surprising, like something against nature, inhuman.

I developed my plan in a hurried whisper.

'I shall stand in as close as I dare and then put her round. I will presently find means to smuggle you out of here into the sail-locker, which communicates with the lobby. But there is an opening, a sort of square for hauling the sails out, which gives straight on the quarter-deck and which is never closed in fine weather, so as to give air to the sails. When the ship's way is deadened in stays and all the hands are aft at the mainbraces you will have a clear road to slip out and get overboard through the open quarter-deck port. I've had them both fastened up. Use a rope's end to lower yourself into the water so as to avoid a splash—you know. It could be heard and cause some beastly complication.'

He kept silent for a while, then whispered, 'I understand.'

'I won't be there to see you go,' I began with an effort. 'The rest ... I only hope I have understood, too.'

'You have. From first to last'—and for the first time there seemed to be a faltering, something strained in his whisper. He caught hold of my arm, but the ringing of the supper bell made me start. He didn't, though; he only released his grip.

After supper I didn't come below again till well past eight o'clock. The faint, steady breeze was loaded with dew; and the wet, darkened sails held all there was of propelling power in it. The night, clear and starry, sparkled darkly, and the opaque, lightless patches shifting slowly against the low stars were the drifting islets. On the port bow there was a big one more distant and shadowily imposing by the great space of sky it eclipsed.

On opening the door I had a back view of my very own self looking at a chart. He had come out of the recess and was standing near the table.

'Quite dark enough,' I whispered.

He stepped back and leaned against my bed with a level, quiet glance. I sat on the couch. We had nothing to say to each other. Over our heads the officer of the watch moved here and there. Then I heard him move quickly. I knew what that meant. He was making for the companion; and presently his voice was outside my door.

'We are drawing in pretty fast, sir. Land looks rather close.'

'Very well,' I answered. 'I am coming on deck directly.'

I waited till he was gone out of the cuddy, then rose. My double moved too. The time had come to exchange our last whispers, for neither of us was ever to hear each other's natural voice.

'Look here!' I opened a drawer and took out three sovereigns. 'Take this anyhow. I've got six and I'd give you the lot, only I must keep a little money to buy some fruit and vegetables for the crew from native boats as we go through Sunda Straits.'

He shook his head.

'Take it,' I urged him, whispering desperately. 'No one can tell what——'

He smiled and slapped meaningly the only pocket of the sleeping-jacket. It was not safe, certainly. But I produced a large old silk handkerchief of mine, and tying the three pieces of gold in a corner, pressed it on him. He was touched, I suppose, because he took it at last and tied it quickly round his waist under the jacket, on his bare skin.

Our eyes met; several seconds elapsed, till, our glances still mingled, I extended my hand and turned the lamp out. Then I passed through the cuddy, leaving the door of my room wide open ... 'Steward!'

He was still lingering in the pantry in the greatness of his zeal, giving a rub-up to a plated cruet stand the last thing before going to bed. Being careful not to wake up the mate, whose room was opposite, I spoke in an undertone.

He looked round anxiously. 'Sir!'

'Can you get me a little hot water from the galley?'

'I am afraid, sir, the galley fire's been out for some time now.'

'Go and see.'

He flew up the stairs.

'Now,' I whispered, loudly, into the saloon—too loudly, perhaps, but I was afraid I couldn't make a sound. He was by my side in an instant—the double captain slipped past the stairs—through a tiny dark passage ... a sliding door. We were in the sail-locker, scrambling on our knees over the sails. A sudden thought struck me. I saw myself wandering barefooted, bareheaded, the sun beating on my dark poll. I snatched off my floppy hat and tried hurriedly in the dark to ram it on my other self. He dodged and fended off silently. I wonder what he thought had come to me before he understood and suddenly desisted. Our hands met gropingly, lingered united in a steady, motionless clasp for a second ... No word was breathed by either of us when they separated.

I was standing quietly by the pantry door when the steward returned.

'Sorry, sir. Kettle barely warm. Shall I light the spirit-lamp?'

'Never mind.'

I came out on deck slowly. It was now a matter of conscience to shave the land as close as possible—for now he must go overboard whenever the ship was put in stays. Must! There could be no going back for him. After a moment I walked over to leeward and my heart flew into my mouth at the nearness of the land on the bow. Under any other circumstances I would not have held on a minute longer. The second mate had followed me anxiously.

I looked on till I felt I could command my voice.

'She may weather,' I said then in a quiet tone.

'Are you going to try that, sir?' he stammered out incredulously.

I took no notice of him and raised my tone just enough to be heard by the helmsman.

'Keep her good full.'

'Good full, sir.'

The wind fanned my cheek, the sails slept, the world was silent. The strain of watching the dark loom of the land grow bigger and denser was too much for me. I had shut my eyes—because the ship must go closer. She must! The stillness was intolerable. Were we standing still?

When I opened my eyes the second view started my heart with a thump. The black southern hill of Koh-ring seemed to hang right over the ship like a towering fragment of the everlasting night. On that enormous mass of blackness there was not a gleam to be seen, not a sound to be heard. It was gliding irresistibly towards us and yet seemed already within reach of the hand. I saw the vague figures of the watch grouped in the waist, gazing in awed silence.

'Are you going on, sir?' inquired an unsteady voice at my elbow.

I ignored it. I had to go on.

'Keep her full. Don't check her way. That won't do now,' I said, warningly.

'I can't see the sails very well,' the helmsman answered me, in strange, quavering tones.

Was she close enough? Already she was, I won't say in the shadow of the land, but in the very blackness of it, already swallowed up as it were, gone too close to be recalled, gone from me altogether.

'Give the mate a call,' I said to the young man who stood at my elbow as still as death. 'And turn all hands up.'

My tone had a borrowed loudness reverberated from the height of the land. Several voices cried out together: 'We are all on deck, sir.'

Then stillness again, with the great shadow gliding closer, towering higher, without light, without a sound. Such a hush had fallen on the ship that she might have been a bark of the dead floating in slowly under the very gate of Erebus.

'My God! Where are we?'

It was the mate moaning at my elbow. He was thunderstruck, and as it were deprived of the moral support of his whiskers. He clapped his hands and absolutely cried out, 'Lost!'

'Be quiet,' I said, sternly.

He lowered his tone, but I saw the shadowy gesture of his despair. 'What are we doing here?'

'Looking for the land wind.'

He made as if to tear his hair, and addressed me recklessly.

'She will never get out. You have done it, sir. I knew it'd end in something like this. She will never weather, and you are too close now to stay. She'll drift ashore before she's round. O my God!'

I caught his arm as he was raising it to batter his poor devoted head, and shook it violently.

'She's ashore already,' he wailed, trying to tear himself away.

'Is she? ... Keep good full there!'

'Good full, sir,' cried the helmsman in a frightened, thin, child-like voice.

I hadn't let go the mate's arm and went on shaking it. 'Ready about, do you hear? You go forward'—shake—'and stop there'—shake—'and hold your noise'—shake—'and see these head-sheets properly overhauled'—shake, shake—shake.

And all the time I dared not look towards the land lest my heart should fail me. I released my grip at last and he ran forward as if fleeing for dear life.

I wondered what my double there in the sail-locker thought of this commotion. He was able to hear every-thing—and perhaps he was able to understand why, on my conscience, it had to be thus close—no less. My first order 'Hard alee!' re-echoed ominously under the towering shadow of Koh-ring as if I had shouted in a mountain gorge. And then I watched the land intently. In that smooth water and light wind it was impossible to feel the ship coming-to. No! I could not feel her, And my second self was making now ready to slip out and lower himself overboard. Perhaps he was gone already...?

The great black mass brooding over our very mastheads began to pivot away from the ship's side silently. And now I forgot the secret stranger ready to depart, and remembered only that I was a total stranger to the ship. I did not know her. Would she do it? How was she to be handled?

I swung the mainyard and waited helplessly. She was per-haps stopped, and her very fate hung in the balance, with the black mass of Koh-ring like the gate of the everlasting night towering over her taffrail. What would she do now? Had she way on her yet? I stepped to the side swiftly, and on the shadowy water I could see nothing except a faint phosphorescent flash revealing the glassy smoothness of the sleeping surface. It was impossible to tell—and I had not learned yet the feel of my ship. Was she moving? What I needed was something easily seen, a piece of paper, which I could throw overboard and watch. I had nothing on me. To run down for it I didn't dare. There was no time. All at once my strained, yearning stare distinguished a white object floating within a yard of the ship's side. White on the black water. A phosphorescent flash passed under it. What was that thing? ... I recognized my own floppy hat. It must have fallen off his head ... and he didn't bother. Now I had what I wanted—the saving mark for my eyes. But I hardly thought of my other self, now gone from the ship, to be hidden for ever from all friendly faces, to be a fugitive and a vagabond on the earth, with no brand of the curse on his sane forehead to stay a slaying hand ... too proud to explain.

And I watched the hat—the expression of my sudden pity for his mere flesh. It had been meant to save his homeless head from the dangers of the sun. And now—behold—it was saving the ship, by serving me for a mark to help out the ignorance of my strangeness. Ha! It was drifting forward, warning me just in time that the ship had gathered sternway.

'Shift the helm,' I said in a low voice to the seaman standing still like a statue.

The man's eyes glistened wildly in the binnacle light as he jumped round to the other side and spun round the wheel.

I walked to the break of the poop. On the overshadowed deck all hands stood by the forebraces waiting for my order. The stars ahead seemed to be gliding from right to left. And all was so still in the world that I heard the quiet remark 'She's round,' passed in a tone of intense relief between two seamen.

'Let's go and haul.'

The foreyards ran round with a great noise, admist cheery cries. And now the frightful whiskers made themselves heard giving various orders. Already the ship was drawing ahead. And I was alone with her. Nothing! no one in the world should stand now between us, throwing a shadow on the way of silent knowledge and mute affection, the perfect communion of a seaman with his first command.

Walking to the taffrail, I was in time to make out, on the very edge of a darkness thrown by a towering black mass like the very gateway of Erebus—yes, I was in time to catch an evanescent glimpse of my white hat left behind to mark the spot where the secret sharer of my cabin and of my thoughts, as though he were my second self, had lowered himself into the water to take his punishment: a free man, a proud swimmer striking out for a new destiny.

H. G. WELLS

'... Mr Egbert Caine, an artist, bathing near Newyln, threw up his arms, shrieked, and was drawn under.'

Christmas, 1894

Aepyornis Island

The man with the scarred face leant over the table and looked at my bundle.

'Orchids?' he asked.

'A few,' I said.

'Cypripediums,' he said.

'Chiefly,' said I.

'Anything new? I thought not. *I* did these islands twenty-five—twenty-seven years ago. If you find anything new here—well, it's brand new. I didn't leave much.'

'I'm not a collector,' said I.

'I was young then,' he went on. 'Lord! how I used to fly round.' He seemed to take my measure. 'I was in the East Indies two years and in Brazil seven. Then I went to Madagascar.'

'I know a few explorers by name,' I said, anticipating a yarn. 'Whom did you collect for?'

'Dawsons'. I wonder if you've heard the name of Butcher ever?'

'Butcher—Butcher?' The name seemed vaguely present in my memory; then I recalled *Butcher* v. *Dawson*. 'Why!' said I, 'you are the man who sued them for four years' salary—got cast away on a desert island...'

'Your servant,' said the man with the scar, bowing. 'Funny case, wasn't it? Here was me, making a little fortune on that island, doing nothing for it neither, and them quite unable to give me notice. It often used to amuse me thinking over it while I was there. I did calculations of it—big—all over the blessed atoll in ornamental figuring.'

123

'How did it happen?' said I. 'I don't rightly remember the case.'

'Well ... You've heard of the Aepyornis?'

'Rather. Andrews was telling me of a new species he was working on only a month or so ago. Just before I sailed. They've got a thigh-bone, it seems, nearly a yard long. Monster the thing must have been!'

'I believe you,' said the man with the scar. 'It *was* a monster. Sindbad's roc was just a legend of 'em. But when did they find these bones?'

'Three or four years ago—'91, I fancy. Why?'

'Why? Because *I* found them—Lord!—it's nearly twenty years ago. If Dawsons' hadn't been silly about that salary they might have made a perfect ring in 'em ... *I* couldn't help the infernal boat going adrift.'

He paused. 'I suppose it's the same place. A kind of swamp about ninety miles north of Antananarivo. Do you happen to know? You have to go to it along the coast by boats. You don't happen to remember, perhaps?'

'I don't. I fancy Andrews said something about a swamp.'

'It must be the same. It's on the east coast. And somehow there's something in the water that keeps things from decaying. Like creosote it smells. It reminded me of Trinidad. Did they get any more eggs? Some of the eggs I found were a foot and a half long. The swamp goes circling round, you know, and cuts off this bit. It's mostly salt, too. Well ... What a time I had of it! I found the things quite by accident. We went for eggs, me and two native chaps, in one of those rum canoes all tied together, and found the bones at the same time. We had a tent and provisions for four days, and we pitched on one of the firmer places. To think of it brings that odd tarry smell back even now. It's funny work. You go probing into the mud with iron rods, you know. Usually the egg gets smashed. I wonder how long it is since these Aepyornises really lived. The missionaries say the natives have legends about when they were alive, but I never heard any such stories myself.* But certainly those eggs we got were as fresh as if they had been new laid. Fresh! Carrying them down to the boat one

* No European is known to have seen a live Aepyornis, with the doubtful exception of Maver, who visited Madagascar in 1745—H.G.W.

of my nigger chaps dropped one on a rock and it smashed. How I lammed into the beggar! But sweet it was, as if it was new laid, not even smelly, and its mother dead these four hundred years, perhaps. Said a centipede had bit him. However, I'm getting off the straight with the story. It had taken us all day to dig into the slush and get these eggs out unbroken, and we were all covered with beastly black mud, and naturally I was cross. So far as I knew they were the only eggs that have ever been got out not even cracked. I went afterwards to see the ones they have at the Natural History Museum in London; all of them were cracked and just stuck together like a mosaic, and bits missing. Mine were perfect, and I meant to blow them when I got back. Naturally I was annoyed at the silly duffer dropping three hours' work just on account of a centipede. I hit him about rather.'

The man with the scar took out a clay pipe. I placed my pouch before him. He filled up absent-mindedly.

'How about the others? Did you get those home? I don't remember——'

'That's the queer part of the story. I had three others. Perfectly fresh eggs. Well, we put 'em in the boat, and then I went up to the tent to make some coffee, leaving my two heathens down by the beach—the one fooling about with his sting and the other helping him. It never occurred to me that the beggar would take advantage of the peculiar position I was in to pick a quarrel. But I suppose the centipede poison and the kicking I had given him had upset the one—he was always a cantankerous sort—and he persuaded the other.

'I remember I was sitting and smoking and boiling up the water over a spirit-lamp business I used to take on these expeditions. Incidentally I was admiring the swamp under the sunset. All black and blood-red it was, in streaks—a beautiful sight. And up beyond the land rose grey and hazy to the hills, and the sky behind them red, like a furnace mouth. And fifty yards behind the back of me was these blessed heathen—quite regardless of the tranquil air of things—plotting to cut off with the boat and leave me all alone with three days' provisions and a canvas tent, and nothing to drink whatsoever beyond a little keg of water. I heard a kind of yelp behind me, and there they were in this canoe affair—it wasn't properly a boat—and, perhaps, twenty yards from land. I realized what was up in a moment. My gun was in the tent, and, besides, I had no bullets—only duck shot. They knew that. But I had a little revolver in my pocket, and I pulled that out as I ran down to the beach.

' "Come back!" says I, flourishing it.

'They jabbered something at me, and the man that broke the egg jeered. I aimed at the other—because he was un-wounded and had the paddle, and I missed. They laughed. However, I wasn't beat. I knew I had to keep cool, and I tried him again and made him jump with the whang of it. He didn't laugh that time. The third time I got his head, and over he went, and the paddle with him. It was a precious lucky shot for a revolver. I reckon it was fifty yards. He went right under. I don't know if he was shot, or simply stunned and drowned. Then I began to shout to the other chap to come back, but he huddled up in the canoe and refused to answer. So I fired out my revolver at him and never got near him.

'I felt a precious fool, I can tell you. There I was on this rotten black beach, flat swamp all behind me, and the flat sea, cold after the sun set, and just this black canoe drifting steadily out to sea. I tell you I damned Dawsons' and Jam-rach's and Museums and all the rest of it just to rights. I bawled to this nigger to come back, until my voice went up into a scream.

'There was nothing for it but to swim after him and take my luck with the sharks. So I opened my clasp-knife and put it in my mouth, and took off my clothes and waded in. As soon as I was in the water I lost sight of the canoe, but I aimed, as I judged, to head it off. I hoped the man in it was too bad to navigate it, and that it would keep on drifting in the same direction. Presently it came up over the horizon again to the south-westward about. The afterglow of sunset was well over now and the dim of night creeping up. The stars were coming through the blue. I swam like a champion, though my legs and arms were soon aching.

'However, I came up to him by the time the stars were fairly out. As it got darker I began to see all manner of glowing things in the water—phosphorescence, you know. At times it made me giddy. I hardly knew which was stars and which was phosphorescence, and whether I was swimming on my head or my heels. The canoe was as black as sin, and the ripple under the bows like liquid fire. I was naturally chary of clambering up into it. I was anxious to see what he was up to first. He seemed to be lying cuddled up in a lump in the bows, and the stern was all out of the water. The thing kept turning round slowly as it drifted—kind of waltzing, don't you know. I went to the stern and pulled it down, expecting him to wake up. Then I began to clamber in with my knife in my hand, and ready for a rush. But he never stirred. So there I sat in the stern of the little canoe, drifting away over the calm phosphorescent sea and with all the host of stars above me, waiting for something to happen.

'After a long time I called him by name, but he never answered. I was too tired to take any risks by going along to him. So we sat there. I fancy I dozed once or twice. When the dawn came I saw he was as dead as a door-nail and all puffed up and purple. My three eggs and the bones were lying in the middle of the canoe, and the keg of water and some coffee and biscuits wrapped in a Cape *Argus* by his feet, and a tin of methylated spirit underneath him. There was no paddle, nor, in fact, anything except the spirit tin that I could use as one, so I settled to drift until I was picked up. I held an inquest on him, brought in a verdict against some snake, scorpion or centipede unknown, and sent him overboard.

'After that I had a drink of water and a few biscuits, and took a look round. I suppose a man low down as I was don't see very far; leastways, Madagascar was clean out of sight, and any trace of land at all. I saw a sail going south-westward—looked like a schooner but her hull never came up. Presently the sun got high in the sky and began to beat down upon me. Lord! it pretty near made my brains boil. I tried dipping my head in the sea, but after a while my eye fell on the Cape *Argus*, and I lay down flat in the canoe and spread this over me. Wonderful things these newspapers! I never read one through thoroughly before, but it's odd what you get up to when you're alone, as I was. I suppose I read that blessed old Cape *Argus* twenty times. The pitch in the canoe simply reeked with the heat and rose up into big blisters.

'I drifted ten days,' said the man with the scar. 'It's a little thing in the telling, isn't it? Every day was like the last. Except in the morning and the evening I never kept a look-out even—the blaze was so infernal. I didn't see a sail after the first three days, and those I saw took no notice of me. About the sixth night a ship went by scarcely half a mile away from me, with all its lights ablaze and its ports open, looking like a big firefly. There was music aboard. I stood up and shouted and screamed at it. The second day I broached one of the Aepyornis eggs, scraped the shell away at the end bit by bit, and tried it, and I was glad to find it was good enough to eat. A bit flavoury—not bad, I mean—but with something of the taste of a duck's egg. There was a kind of circular path, about six inches across, on one side of the yolk, and with streaks of blood and a white mark like a ladder in it that I thought queer, but I did not understand what this meant at the time, and I wasn't inclined to be particular. The egg lasted me three days, with biscuits and a drink of water. I chewed coffee-berries too—invigorating stuff. The second egg I opened about the eighth day, and it scared me.'

The man with the scar paused. 'Yes,' he said, 'developing.'

'I dare say you find it hard to believe. I did, with the thing before me. There the egg had been, sunk in that cold black mud, perhaps three hundred years. But there was no mistaking it. There was the—what is it?—embryo, with its big head and curved back, and its heart beating under its throat, and the yolk shrivelled up and great membranes spreading inside of the shell and all over the yolk. Here was I hatching out the eggs of the biggest of all extinct birds, in a little canoe in the midst of the Indian Ocean. If only Dawson had known that! It was worth four years' salary. What do *you* think?

'However, I had to eat that precious thing up, every bit of it, before I sighted the reef, and some of the mouthfuls were beastly unpleasant. I left the third one alone. I held it up to the light, but the shell was too thick for me to get any notion of what might be happening inside; and though I fancied I heard blood pulsing, it might have been the rustle in my own ears, like what you listen to in a seashell.

'Then came the atoll. Came out of the sunrise, as it were, suddenly, close to me. I drifted straight towards it until I was about half a mile from shore, not more, and then the current took a turn, and I had to paddle as hard as I could with my hands and bits of the Aepyornis shell to make the place. However, I got there. It was just a common atoll about four miles round, with a few trees growing and a spring in one place, and the lagoon full of parrot-fish. I took the egg ashore and put it in a good place, well above the tide lines and in the sun, to give it all the chance I could, and pulled the canoe up safe, and loafed about prospecting. It's rum how dull an atoll is. As soon as I had found a spring all the interest seemed to vanish. When I was a kid I thought nothing could be finer or more adventurous than the Robinson Crusoe business, but that place was as monotonous as a book of sermons. I went round finding eatable things and generally thinking; but I tell you I was bored to death before the first day was out. It shows my luck—the very day I landed the weather changed. A thunderstorm went by to the north and flicked its wing over the island, and in the night there came a drencher and a howling wind slap over us. It wouldn't have taken much, you know, to upset that canoe.

'I was sleeping under the canoe, and the egg was luckily among the sand higher up the beach, and the first thing I remember was a sound like a hundred pebbles hitting the boat at once, and a rush of water over my body. I'd been dreaming of Antananarivo, and I sat up and halloed to Intoshi to ask her what the devil was up, and clawed out at the chair where the matches used to be. Then I remembered where I was. There were phosphorescent waves rolling up as if they meant to eat me, and all the rest of the night as black as pitch. The air was simply yelling. The cloud seemed down on your head almost, and the rain fell as if heaven was sinking and they were bailing out the waters above the firmament. One great roller came writhing at me, like a fiery serpent, and I bolted. Then I thought of the canoe, and ran down to it as the water went hissing back again; but the thing had gone. I wondered about the egg, then, and felt my way to it. It was all right and well out of reach of the maddest waves, so I sat down beside it and cuddled it for company. Lord! what a night that was!

'The storm was over before the morning. There wasn't a

rag of cloud left in the sky when the dawn came, and all along the beach there were bits of plank scattered—which was the disarticulated skeleton, so to speak, of my canoe. However, that gave me something to do, for taking advantage of two of the trees being together, I rigged up a kind of storm-shelter with these vestiges. And that day the egg hatched.

'Hatched, sir, when my head was pillowed on it and I was asleep. I heard a whack and felt a jar and sat up, and there was the end of the egg pecked out and a rum little brown head looking out at me, "Lord!" I said, "You're welcome," and with a little difficulty he came out.

'He was a nice friendly little chap at first, about the size of a small hen—very much like most other young birds, only bigger. His plumage was a dirty brown to begin with, with a sort of grey scab that fell off it very soon, and scarcely feathers—a kind of downy hair. I can hardly express how pleased I was to see him. I tell you, Robinson Crusoe don't make near enough of his loneliness. But here was interesting company. He looked at me and winked his eye from the front backwards, like a hen, and gave a chirp and began to peck about at once, as though being hatched three hundred years too late was just nothing. "Glad to see you, Man Friday," says I, for I had naturally settled he was to be called Man Friday if ever he was hatched, as soon as ever I found the egg in the canoe had developed. I was a bit anxious about his feed, so I gave him a lump of raw parrot-fish at once. He took it, and opened his beak for more. I was glad of that, for, under the circumstances, if he'd been at all fanciful, I should have had to eat him after all.

'You'd be surprised what an interesting bird that Aep-yornis chick was. He followed me about from the very beginning. He used to stand by me and watch while I fished in the lagoon, and go shares in anything I caught. And he was sensible, too. There were nasty green warty things, like pickled gherkins, used to lie about on the beach, and he tried one of these and it upset him. He never even looked at any of them again.

'And he grew. You could almost see him grow. And as I was never much of a society man, his quiet friendly ways suited me to a T. For nearly two years we were as happy as we could be on that island. I had no business worries, for I knew my salary was mounting up at Dawsons'. We would see a sail now and then, but nothing ever came near us. I amused myself, too, by decorating the island with designs worked in sea-urchins and fancy shells of various kinds. I put AEPYORNIS ISLAND all around the place very neatly in big letters, like what you see done with coloured stones at railway stations in the old country, and mathematical calculations and drawings of various sorts. And I used to lie watching the blessed bird stalking round and growing, growing; and think how I could make a living out of him by showing him about if I ever got taken off. After his first moult he began to get handsome, with a crest and a blue wattle, and a lot of green feathers at the behind of him. And then I used to puzzle whether Dawsons' had any right to claim him or not. Stormy weather and in the rainy season we lay snug under the shelter I had made out of the old canoe, and I used to tell him lies about my friends at home. And after a storm we would go round the island together to see if there was any drift. It was a kind of idyll, you might say. If only I had had some tobacco it would have been simply just like heaven.

'It was about the end of the second year our little paradise went wrong. Friday was then about fourteen feet high to the bill of him, with a big, broad head like the end of a pickaxe, and two huge brown eyes with yellow rims, set together like a man's—not out of sight of each other like a hen's. His plumage was fine—none of the half-mourning style of your ostrich—more like a cassowary as far as colour and texture go. And then it was he began to cock his comb at me and give himself airs, and show signs of a nasty temper...

'At last came a time when my fishing had been rather unlucky, and he began to hang about me in a queer, medita-tive way. I thought he might have been eating sea-cucumbers or something, but it was really just discontent on his part. I was hungry, too, and when at last I landed a fish I wanted it for myself. Tempers were short that morning on both sides. He pecked at it and grabbed it, and I gave him a whack on the head to make him leave go. And at that he went for me. Lord! ...

'He gave me this in the face.' The man indicated his scar.

'Then he kicked me. It was like a cart-horse. I got up, and, seeing he hadn't finished, I started off full tilt with my arms doubled up over my face. But he ran on those gawky legs of his faster than a racehorse, and kept landing out at me with sledge-hammer kicks and bringing his pick-axe down on the back of my head. I made for the lagoon, and went in up to my neck. He stopped at the water, for he hated getting his feet wet, and began to make a shindy, something like a peacock's, only hoarser. He started strutting up and down the beach. I'll admit I felt small to see this blessed fossil lording it there. And my head and face were all bleeding, and—well, my body just one jelly of bruises.

'I decided to swim across the lagoon and leave him alone for a bit, until the affair blew over. I shinned up the tallest palm-tree, and sat there thinking of it all. I don't suppose I ever felt so hurt by anything before or since. It was the brutal ingratitude of the creature. I'd been more than a brother to him. I'd hatched him, educated him. A great gawky, out-of-date bird! And me a human being—heir of the ages and all that.

'I thought after a time he'd begin to see things in that light himself, and feel a little sorry for his behaviour. I thought if I was to catch some nice little bits of fish, perhaps, and go to him presently in a casual kind of way, and offer them to him, he might do the sensible thing. It took me some time to learn how unforgiving and cantankerous an extinct bird can be. Malice!

'I won't tell you all the little devices I tried to get that bird round again. I simply can't. It makes my cheek burn with shame even now to think of the snubs and buffets I had from this infernal curiosity. I tried violence. I chucked lumps of coral at him from a safe distance, but he only swallowed them. I shied my open knife at him and almost lost it, though it was too big for him to swallow. I tried starving him out and struck fishing, but he took to picking along the beach at low water after worms, and rubbed along on that. Half my time I spent up to my neck in the lagoon, and the rest up the palm-trees. One of them was scarcely high enough, and when he caught me up it he had a regular Bank Holiday with the calves of my legs. It got unbearable. I don't know if you have ever tried sleeping up a palm-tree. It gave me the most horrible nightmares. Think of the shame of it, too! Here was this extinct animal mooning about my island like a sulky duke, and me not allowed to rest the sole of my foot on the place. I used to cry with weariness and vexation. I told him straight that I didn't mean to be chased about a desert island by any damned anachronisms. I told him to go and peck a navigator of his own age. But he only snapped his beak at me. Great ugly bird, all legs and neck!

'I shouldn't like to say how long that went on altogether. I'd have killed him sooner if I'd known how. However, I hit on a way of settling him at last. It is a South American dodge. I joined all my fishing-lines together with stems of seaweed and things, and made a stoutish string, perhaps twelve yards in length or more, and I fastened two lumps of coral rock to the ends of this. It took me some time to do, because every now and then I had to go into the lagoon or up a tree as the fancy took me. This I whirled rapidly round my head, and then let it go at him. The first time I missed, but the next time the string caught his legs beautifully, and wrapped round them again and again. Over he went. I threw it standing waist-deep in the lagoon, and as soon as he went down I was out of the water and sawing at his neck with my knife...

'I don't like to think of that even now. I felt like a murderer while I did it, though my anger was hot against him. When I stood over him and saw him bleeding on the white sand, and his beautiful great legs and neck writhing in his last agony ... Pah!

'With that tragedy loneliness came upon me like a curse. Good Lord! you can't imagine how I missed that bird. I sat by his corpse and sorrowed over him, and shivered as I looked round the desolate, silent reef. I thought of what a jolly little bird he had been when he was hatched, and of a thousand pleasant tricks he had played before he went wrong. I thought if I'd only wounded him I might have nursed him round into a better understanding. If I'd had any means of digging into the coral rock I'd have buried him. I felt exactly as if he was human. As it was, I couldn't think of eating him, so I put him in the lagoon, and the little fishes picked him clean. I didn't even save the feathers. Then one day a chap cruising about in a yacht had a fancy to see if my atoll still existed.

'He didn't come a moment too soon, for I was about sick enough of the desolation of it, and only hesitating whether I should walk out into the sea and finish up the business that way, or fall back on the green things...

'I sold the bones to a man named Winslow—a dealer near the British Museum, and he says he sold them to old Havers. It seems Havers didn't understand they were extra large, and it was only after his death they attracted attention. They called 'em Aepyornis—what was it?'

'*Aepyornis vastus*,' said I, 'It's funny, the very thing was mentioned to me by a friend of mine. When they found an Aepyornis with a thigh a yard long, they thought they had reached the top of the scale, and called him *Aepyornis maximus*. Then someone turned up another thigh-bone four feet six or more, and that they called *Aepyornis titan*. Then your *vastus* was found after old Havers died, in his collection, and then the *vastissimus* turned up.'

'Winslow was telling me as much,' said the man with the scar. 'If they get any more Aepyornises, he reckons some scientific swell will go and burst a blood-vessel. But it was a queer thing to happen to a man, wasn't it—altogether?'

'Get up, you chaps!' he cried. 'I believe Merryweather has been shot by the dervishes.'

Sussex, 1906

Borrowed Scenes

Yes, I tried and my experience may interest other people. You must imagine, then, that I am soaked in George Borrow, especially in his *Lavengro* and his *Romany Rye*, that I have modelled both my thoughts, my speech and my style very carefully upon those of the master, and that finally I set forth one summer day actually to lead the life of which I had read. Behold me, then, upon the country road which leads from the railway-station to the Sussex village of Swinehurst.

As I walked, I entertained myself by recollections of the founders of Sussex, of Cerdic that mighty sea-rover, and of Ella his son, said by the bard to be taller by the length of a spear-head than the tallest of his fellows. I mentioned the matter twice to peasants whom I met upon the road. One, a tallish man with a freckled face, sidled past me and ran swiftly towards the station. The other, a smaller and older man, stood entranced while I recited to him that passage of the Saxon Chronicle which begins, 'Then came Leija with longships forty-four, and the fyrd went out against him.' I was pointing out to him that the Chronicle had been written partly by the monks of Saint Albans and afterwards by those of Peterborough, but the fellow sprang suddenly over a gate and disappeared.

The village of Swinehurst is a straggling line of half-timbered houses of the early English pattern. One of these houses stood, as I observed, somewhat taller than the rest, and seeing by its appearance and by the sign which hung before it that it was the village inn, I approached it, for indeed I had not broken my fast since I had left London. A stoutish man, five foot eight perhaps in height, with black coat and trousers

135

of a greyish shade, stood outside, and to him I talked in the fashion of the master.

'Why a rose and why a crown?' I asked as I pointed upwards.

He looked at me in a strange manner. The man's whole appearance was strange. 'Why not?' he answered, and shrank a little backwards.

'The sign of a king,' said I.

'Surely,' said he. 'What else should we understand from a crown?'

'And which king?' I asked.

'You will excuse me,' said he, and tried to pass.

'Which king?' I repeated.

'How should I know?' he asked.

'You should know by the rose,' said I, 'which is the symbol of that Tudor-ap-Tudor, who, coming from the mountains of Wales, yet seated his posterity upon the English throne. Tudor,' I continued, getting between the stranger and the door of the inn, through which he appeared to be desirous of passing, 'was of the same blood as Owen Glendower, the famous chieftain, who is by no means to be confused with Owen Gwynedd, the father of Madoc of the Sea, of whom the bard made the famous cnylyn, which runs in the Welsh as follows——'

I was about to repeat the famous stanza of Dafydd-ap-Gwilyn when the man, who had looked very fixedly and strangely at me as I spoke, pushed past me and entered the inn. 'Truly,' said I aloud, 'it is surely Swinehurst to which I have come, since the same means the grove of the hogs.' So saying I followed the fellow into the bar parlour, where I perceived him seated in a corner with a large chair in front of him. Four persons of various degrees were drinking beer at a central table, while a small man of active build, in a black, shiny suit, which seemed to have seen much service, stood before the empty fireplace. Him I took to be the landlord, and I asked him what I should have for my dinner.

He smiled, and said that he could not tell.

'But surely, my friend,' said I, 'you can tell me what is ready?'

'Even that I cannot do,' he answered; 'but I doubt not that

the landlord can inform us.' On this he rang the bell, and a fellow answered, to whom I put the same question.

'What would you have?' he asked.

I thought of the master, and I ordered a cold leg of pork to be washed down with tea and beer.

'Did you say tea *and* beer?' asked the landlord.

'I did.'

'For twenty-five years have I been in business,' said the landlord, 'and never before have I been asked for tea and beer.'

'The gentleman is joking,' said the man with the shining coat.

'Or else——' said the elderly man in the corner.

'Or what, sir?' I asked.

'Nothing,' said he—'nothing.' There was something very strange in this man in the corner—him to whom I had spoken of Dafydd-ap-Gwilyn.

'Then you are joking,' said the landlord.

I asked him if he had read the works of my master, George Borrow. He said that he had not. I told him that in those five volumes he would not, from cover to cover, find one trace of any sort of a joke. He would also find that my master drank tea and beer together. Now it happens that about tea I have read nothing either in the sagas or in the bardic cnylynions, but, while the landlord had departed to prepare my meal, I recited to the company those Icelandic stanzas which praise the beer of Gunnar, the long-haired son of Harold the Bear. Then, lest the language should be unknown to some of them, I recited my own translation, ending with the line——

'If the beer be small, then let the mug be large.'

I then asked the company whether they went to church or to chapel. The question surprised them, and especially the strange man in the corner, upon whom I now fixed my eye. I had read his secret, and as I looked at him he tried to shrink behind the clock-case.

'The church or the chapel?' I asked him.

'The church,' he gasped.

'*Which* church?' I asked.

He shrank farther behind the clock. 'I have never been so questioned,' he cried.

I showed him that I knew his secret. 'Rome was not built in a day,' said I.

'He! He!' he cried. Then, as I turned away, he put his head from behind the clock-case and tapped his forehead with his forefinger. So also did the man with the shiny coat, who stood before the empty fireplace.

Having eaten the cold leg of pork—where is there a better dish, save only boiled mutton with capers?—and having drunk both the tea and the beer, I told the company that such a meal had been called 'to box Harry' by the master, who had observed it to be in great favour with commercial gentlemen out of Liverpool. With this information and a stanza or two from Lopez de Vega I left the Inn of the Rose and Crown behind me, having first paid my reckoning. At the door the landlord asked me for my name and address.

'And why?' I asked.

'Lest there should be inquiry for you,' said the landlord.

'But why should they inquire for me?'

'Ah, who knows?' said the landlord, musing. And so I left him at the door of the Inn of the Rose and Crown whence came, I observed, a great tumult of laughter. 'Assuredly,' thought I, 'Rome was not built in a day.'

Having walked down the main street of Swinehurst, which, as I have observed, consists of half-timbered buildings in the ancient style, I came out upon the country road, and proceeded to look for those wayside adventures, which are, according to the master, as thick as blackberries for those who seek them upon an English highway. I had already received some boxing lessons before leaving London, so it seemed to me that if I should chance to meet some traveller whose size and age seemed such as to encourage the venture, I would ask him to strip off his coat and settle any differences which he could find in the Old English fashion. I waited, therefore, by a stile for anyone who should chance to pass, and it was while I stood there that the screaming horror came upon me, even as it came upon the master in the dingle. I gripped the bar of the stile, which was of good British oak. Oh, who can tell the terrors of the screaming horror! That was what I thought as I grasped the oaken bar of the stile. Was it the beer—or was it the tea? Or was it that the landlord was right and that other, the man with the black, shiny coat, he who had answered the sign of the strange man in the corner? But the master drank tea with beer. Yes, but the master also had the screaming horror. All this I thought as I grasped the bar of British oak, which was the top of the stile. For half an hour the horror was upon me. Then it passed, and I was left feeling very weak and still grasping the oaken bar.

I had not moved from the stile, where I had been seized by the screaming horror, when I heard the sound of steps behind me, and turning round I perceived that a pathway led across the field upon the farther side of the stile. A woman was coming towards me along this pathway, and it was evident to me that she was one of those gipsy Rias, of whom the master has said so much. Looking beyond her, I could see the smoke of a fire from a small dingle, which showed where her tribe were camping. The woman herself was of a moderate height, neither tall nor short, with a face which was much sunburned and freckled. I must confess that she was not beautiful, but I do not think that anyone, save the master, has found very beautiful women walking about upon the high-roads of England. Such as she was I must make the best of her, and well I knew how to address her, for many times had I admired the mixture of politeness and audacity which should be used in such a case. Therefore, when the woman had come to the stile, I held out my hand and helped her over.

'What says the Spanish poet Calderon?' said I. 'I doubt not that you have read the couplet which has been thus Englished:

> *"Oh, maiden, may I humbly pray*
> *That I may help you on your way." '*

The woman blushed, but said nothing.

'Where,' I asked, 'are the Romany chals and the Romany chis?'

She turned her head away and was silent.

'Though I am a gorgio,' said I, 'I know something of the Romany lil,' and to prove it I sang the stanza——

'Coliko, coliko saulo wer
Apopli to the farming ker
Will wel and mang him mullo,
Will wel and mang his truppo.'

The girl laughed, but said nothing. It appeared to me from her appearance that she might be one of those who make a living at telling fortunes or 'dukkering', as the master calls it, at racecourses and other gatherings of the sort.

'Do you dukker?' I asked.

She slapped me on the arm. 'Well, you *are* a pot of ginger!' said she.

I was pleased at the slap, for it put me in mind of the peerless Belle. 'You can use Long Melford,' said I, an expression which, with the master, meant fighting.

'Get along with your sauce!' said she, and struck me again.

'You are a very fine young woman,' said I, 'and remind me of Grunelda, the daughter of Hjalmar, who stole the golden bowl from the King of the Islands.'

She seemed annoyed at this. 'You keep a civil tongue, young man,' said she.

'I meant no harm, Belle. I was but comparing you to one of whom the saga says her eyes were like the shine of sun upon icebergs.'

This seemed to please her, for she smiled. 'My name ain't Belle,' she said at last.

'What is your name?'

'Henrietta.'

'The name of a queen,' I said aloud.

'Go on,' said the girl.

'Of Charles's queen,' said I, 'of whom Waller the poet (for the English also have their poets, though in this respect far inferior to the Basques)—of whom, I say, Waller the poet said:

"That she was Queen was the Creator's act,
Belated man could but endorse the fact."'

'I say!' cried the girl. 'How you do go on!'

'So now,' said I, 'since I have shown you that you are a

queen you will surely give me a choomer'—this being a kiss in Romany talk.

'I'll give you one on the ear-hole,' she cried.

'Then I will wrestle with you,' said I. 'If you should chance to put me down, I will do penance by teaching you the Armenian alphabet—the very word alphabet, as you will perceive, shows us that our letters came from Greece. If, on the other hand, I should chance to put you down, you will give me a choomer.'

I had got so far, and she was climbing the stile with some pretence of getting away from me, when there came a van along the road, belonging, as I discovered, to a baker in Swinehurst. The horse, which was of a brown colour, was such as is bred in the New Forest, being somewhat under fifteen hands and of a hairy, ill-kempt variety. As I know less than the master about horses, I will say no more of this horse, save to repeat that its colour was brown—nor indeed had the horse or the horse's colour anything to do with my narrative. I might add, however, that it could either be taken as a small horse or as a large pony, being somewhat tall for the one, but undersized for the other. I have now said enough about this horse, which has nothing to do with my story, and I will turn my attention to the driver.

This was a man with a broad, florid face and brown side-whiskers. He was of a stout build and had rounded shoulders, with a small mole of a reddish colour over his left eyebrow. His jacket was of velveteen, and he had large, iron-shod boots, which were perched upon the splashboard in front of him. He pulled up the van as he came up to the stile near which I was standing with the maiden who had come from the dingle, and in a civil fashion he asked me if I could oblige him with a light for his pipe. Then, as I drew a matchbox from my pocket, he threw his reins over the splashboard, and removing his large, iron-shod boots he descended on to the road. He was a burly man, but inclined to fat and scant of breath. It seemed to me that it was a chance for one of those wayside boxing adventures which were so common in the olden times. It was my intention that I should fight the man, and that the maiden from the dingle standing by me should tell me when to use my right or my left, as the case might be, picking me up also in case I should be so unfortunate as to be knocked down by the man with the iron-shod boots and the small mole of a reddish colour over his left eyebrow.

'Do you use Long Melford?' I asked.

He looked at me in some surprise, and said that any mixture was good enough for him.

'By Long Melford,' said I, 'I do not mean, as you seem to think, some form of tobacco, but I mean that art and science of boxing which was held in such high esteem by our ancestors, that some famous professors of it, such as the great Gully, have been elected to the highest offices of the State. There were men of the highest character among the bruisers of England, of whom I would particularly mention Tom of Hereford, better known as Tom Spring, though his father's name, as I have been given to understand, was Winter. This, however, has nothing to do with the matter in hand, which is that you must fight me.'

The man with the florid face seemed very much surprised at my words, so that I cannot think that adventures of this sort were as common as I had been led by the master to expect.

'Fight!' said he. 'What about?'

'It is a good old English custom,' said I, 'by which we may determine which is the better man.'

'I've nothing against you,' said he.

'Nor I against you,' I answered. 'So that we will fight for love, which was an expression much used in olden days. It is narrated by Harold Sygvynson that among the Danes it was usual to do so even with battle-axes, as is told in his second set of runes. Therefore you will take off your coat and fight.' As I spoke, I stripped off my own.

The man's face was less florid than before. 'I'm not going to fight,' said he.

'Indeed you are,' I answered, 'and this young woman will doubtless do you the service to hold your coat.'

'You're clean balmy,' said Henrietta.

'Besides,' said I, 'if you will not fight me for love, perhaps you will fight me for this,' and I held out a sovereign. 'Will you hold his coat?' I said to Henrietta.

'I'll hold the thick 'un,' said she.

'No, you don't,' said the man, and put the sovereign into the pocket of his trousers, which were of a corduroy material. 'Now,' said he, 'what am I to do to earn this?'

'Fight,' said I.

'How do you do it?' he asked.

'Put up your hands,' I answered.

He put them up as I had said, and stood there in a sheepish manner with no idea of anything further. It seemed to me that if I could make him angry he would do better, so I knocked off his hat, which was black and hard, of the kind which is called billy-cock.

'Heh, guv'nor!' he cried. 'what are you up to?'

'That was to make you angry,' said I.

'Well, I am angry,' said he.

'Then here is your hat,' said I, 'and afterwards we shall fight.'

I turned as I spoke to pick up his hat, which had rolled behind where I was standing. As I stooped to reach it, I received such a blow that I could neither rise erect nor yet sit down. This blow which I received as I stooped for his billy-cock hat was not from his fist, but from his iron-shod boot, the same which I had observed upon the splashboard. Being unable either to rise erect or yet to sit down, I leaned upon the oaken bar of the stile and groaned loudly on account of the pain of the blow which I had received. Even the screaming horror had given me less pain than this blow from the iron-shod boot. When at last I was able to stand erect, I found that the florid-faced man had driven away with his cart, which could no longer be seen. The maiden from the dingle was standing at the other side of the stile, and a ragged man was running across the field from the direction of the fire.

'Why did you not warn me, Henrietta?' I asked.

'I hadn't time,' said she. 'Why were you such a chump as to turn your back on him like that?'

The ragged man had reached us, where I stood talking to Henrietta by the stile. I will not try to write his conversation as he said it, because I have observed that the master never condescends to dialect, but prefers by a word introduced here and there to show the fashion of a man's speech. I will only say that the man from the dingle spoke as did the Anglo-Saxons who were wont, as is clearly shown by the venerable Bede, to call their leaders 'Enjist and 'Orsa, two words which in their proper meaning signify a horse and a mare.

'What did he hit you for?' asked the man from the dingle. He was exceedingly ragged, with a powerful frame, a lean brown face, and an oaken cudgel in his hand. His voice was very hoarse and rough, as is the case with those who live in the open air. 'The bloke hit you,' said he. 'What did the bloke hit you for?'

'He asked him to,' said Henrietta.

'Asked him to—asked him what?'

'Why, he asked him to hit him. Gave him a thick 'un to do it.'

The ragged man seemed surprised. 'See here, gov'nor,' said he. 'If you're collectin', I could let you have one half-price.'

'He took me unawares,' said I.

'What else would the bloke do when you bashed his hat?' said the maiden from the dingle.

By this time I was able to straighten myself up by the aid of the oaken bar which formed the top of the stile. Having quoted a few lines of the Chinese poet Lo-tun-an to the effect that, however hard a knock might be, it might always conceivably be harder, I looked about for my coat, but could by no means find it.

'Henrietta,' I said, 'what have you done with my coat?'

'Look here, gov'nor,' said the man from the dingle, 'not so much Henrietta, if it's the same to you. This woman's my wife. Who are you to call her Henrietta?'

I assured the man from the dingle that I had meant no disrespect to his wife. 'I had thought she was a mort,' said I; 'but the ria of a Romany chal is always sacred to me.'

'Clean balmy,' said the woman.

'Some other day,' said I, 'I may visit you in your camp in the dingle and read you the master's book about the Romanys.'

'What's Romanys?' asked the man.

Myself. Romanys are gipsies.

The Man. We ain't gipsies.

Myself. What are you then?

144

The Man. We are hoppers.

Myself (to Henrietta). Then how did you understand all I have said to you about gipsies?

Henrietta. I didn't.

I again asked for my coat, but it was clear now that before offering to fight the florid-faced man with the mole over his left eyebrow I must have hung my coat upon the splashboard of his van. I therefore recited a verse from Ferideddin-Atar, the Persian poet, which signifies that it is more important to preserve your skin than your clothes, and bidding farewell to the man from the dingle and his wife I returned into the old English village of Swinehurst, where I was able to buy a second-hand coat, which enabled me to make my way to the station, where I should start for London. I could not but remark with some surprise that I was followed to the station by many of the villagers, together with the man with the shiny coat, and that other, the strange man, he who had slunk behind the clock-case. From time to time I turned and approached them, hoping to fall into conversation with them; but as I did so they would break and hasten down the road. Only the village constable came on, and he walked by my side and listened while I told him the history of Hunyadi Janos and the events which occurred during the wars between that hero, known also as Corvinus or the crow-like, and Mahommed the second, he who captured Constantinople, better known as Byzantium, before the Christian epoch. Together with the constable I entered the station, and seating myself in a carriage I took paper from my pocket and I began to write upon the paper all that had occurred to me, in order that I might show that it was not easy in these days to follow the example of the master. As I wrote, I heard the constable talk to the station-master, a stout, middle-sized man with a red neck-tie, and tell him of my own adventures in the old English village of Swinehurst.

'He is a gentleman too,' said the constable, 'and I doubt not that he lives in a big house in London town.'

'A very big house if every man had his rights,' said the station-master, and waving his hand he signalled that the train should proceed.

EUDORA WELTY

'Whatever happened, it happened in extraordinary times.'

Natchez Trace, January 1807

First Love

Whatever happened, it happened in extraordinary times, in a season of dreams, and in Natchez it was the bitterest winter of them all. The north wind struck one January night in 1807 with an insistent penetration, as if it followed the settlers down by their own course, screaming down the river bends to drive them further still. Afterwards there was the strange drugged fall of snow. When the sun rose the air broke into a thousand prisms as close as the flash-and-turn of gulls' wings. For a long time afterwards it was so clear that in the evening the little companion-star to Sirius could be seen plainly in the heavens by travellers who took their way by night, and Venus shone in the daytime in all its course through the new transparency of the sky.

The Mississippi shuddered and lifted from its bed, reaching like a somnambulist driven to go in new places; the ice stretched far out over the waves. Flatboats and rafts continued to float downstream, but with unsignalling passengers submissive and huddled, mere bundles of sticks; bets were laid on shore as to whether they were alive or dead, but it was impossible to prove it either way.

The coated moss hung in blue and shining garlands over the trees along the changed streets in the morning. The town of little galleries was all laden roofs and silence. In the fastness of Natchez it began to seem then that the whole world, like itself, must be in a transfiguration. The only clamour came from the animals that suffered in their stalls, or from the wildcats that howled in closer rings each night from the frozen cane. The Indians could be heard from greater distances and in greater numbers than had been guessed, sending up placating but proud messages to the sun in continual ceremonies of dancing. The red percussion of their fires could be seen night and day by those waiting in the dark trance of the frozen town. Men were caught by the cold, they dropped in its snare-like silence. Bands of travellers moved closer together, with intenser caution, through the glassy tunnels of the Trace, for all proportion went away, and they followed one another like insects going at dawn through the heavy grass. Natchez people turned silently to look when a solitary man that no one had ever seen before was found and carried in through the streets, frozen the way he had crouched in a hollow tree, grey and huddled like a squirrel, with a little bundle of goods clasped to him.

Joel Mayes, a deaf boy twelve years old, saw the man brought in and knew it was a dead man, but his eyes were for something else, something wonderful. He saw the breaths coming out of people's mouths, and his dark face, losing just now a little of its softness, showed its secret desire. It was marvellous to him when the infinite designs of speech became visible in formations on the air, and he watched with awe that changed to tenderness whenever people met and passed in the road with an exchange of words. He walked alone, slowly through the silence, with the sturdy and yet dreamlike walk of the orphan, and let his own breath out through his lips, pushed it into the air, and whatever word it was it took the shape of a tower. He was as pleased as if he had had a little conversation with someone. At the end of the street, where he turned into the Inn, he always bent his head and walked faster, as if all frivolity were done, for he was boot-boy there.

He had come to Natchez some time in the summer. That was through great worlds of leaves, and the whole journey from Virginia had been to him a kind of childhood wandering in oblivion. He had remained to himself: always to himself at first, and afterwards too—with the company of Old Man McCaleb who took him along when his parents vanished in the forest, were cut off from him, and in spite of his last backward look, dropped behind. Arms bent on destination dragged him forward through the sharp bushes, and leaves came towards his face which he finally put his hands out to stop. Now that he was a boot-boy, he had thought little, frugally, almost stonily, of that long time … until lately Old Man McCaleb had reappeared at the Inn, bound for no telling where, his tangled beard like the beards of old men in dreams; and in the act of cleaning his boots, which were uncommonly heavy and burdensome with mud, Joel came upon a little part of the old adventure, for there it was, dark and crusted … came back to it, and went over it again …

He rubbed, and remembered the day after his parents had left him, the day when it was necessary to hide from the Indians. Old Man McCaleb, his stern face lighting in the most unexpected way, had herded them, the whole party alike, into the dense cane brake, deep down off the Trace— the densest part, where it grew as thick and locked as some kind of wild teeth. There they crouched, and each one of them, man, woman and child, had looked at all the others from a hiding place that seemed the least safe of all, watching in an eager wild instinct for any movement or betrayal. Crouched by his bush, Joel had cried; all his understanding would desert him suddenly and because he could not hear he could not see or touch or find a familiar thing in the world. He wept, and Old Man McCaleb first felled the excited dog with the blunt end of his axe, and then he turned a fierce face towards him and lifted the blade in the air, in a kind of ecstasy of protecting the silence they were keeping. Joel had made a sound … He gasped and put his mouth quicker than thought against the earth. He took the leaves in his mouth … In that long time of lying motionless with the men and women in the cane brake he had learned what silence meant to other people. Through the danger he had felt acutely, even with horror, the nearness of his companions, a speechless embrace of which he had had no warning, a powerful, crushing unity. The Indians had then gone by, followed by an old woman—in solemn, single file, careless of the inflaming arrows they carried in their quivers, dangling in their hands a few strings of catfish. They passed in the length of the old woman's yawn. Then one by one McCaleb's charges had to rise up and come out of the hiding place. There was little talking together, but a kind of shame and shuffling. As soon as the party reached Natchez, their little cluster dissolved completely. The old man had given each of them one long, rather forlorn look for a farewell, and had gone away, no less preoccupied than he had ever been. To the man who had saved his life Joel lifted the gentle, almost indifferent face of the child who has asked for nothing. Now he remembered the white gulls flying across the sky behind the old man's head.

Joel had been deposited at the Inn, and there was nowhere else for him to go, for it stood there and marked the foot of the long Trace, with the river back of it. So he remained. It was a non-committal arrangement: he never paid them any-thing for his keep, and they never paid him anything for his work. Yet time passed, and he became a little part of the place where it passed over him. A small private room became his own; it was on the ground floor behind the saloon, a dark little room paved with stones with its ceiling rafters curved not higher than a man's head. There was a fireplace and one window, which opened on the courtyard filled always with the tremor of horses. He curled up every night on a high-backed bench, when the weather turned cold he was given a collection of old coats to sleep under, and the room was almost excessively his own, as it would have been a stray kitten's that came to the same spot every night. He began to keep his candlestick carefully polished, he set it in the centre of the puncheon table, and at night when it was lighted all the messages of love carved into it with a knife in Spanish words, with a deep Spanish gouging, came out in black relief, for anyone to read who came knowing the language.

Late at night, nearer morning, after the travellers had all certainly pulled off their boots to fall into bed, he waked by habit and passed with the candle shielded up the stairs and through the hall and rooms, and gathered up the boots. When he had brought them all down to his table he would sit and take his own time cleaning them, while the firelight would come gently across the paving stones. It seemed then that his whole life was safely alighted, in the sleep of everyone else, like a bird on a bough, and he was alone in the way he liked to be. He did not despise boots at all—he had learned boots; under his hand they stood up and took a good shape. This was not a slave's work, or a child's either. It had dignity: it was dangerous to walk about among sleeping men.

More than once he had been seized and the life half shaken out of him by a man waking up in a sweat of suspicion or nightmare, but he dealt nimbly as an animal with the violence and quick frenzy of dreamers. It might seem to him that the whole world was sleeping in the lightest of trances, which the least movement would surely wake; but he only walked softly, stepping around and over, and got back to his room. Once a rattlesnake had shoved its head from a boot as he stretched out his hand; but that was not likely to happen again in a thousand years.

It was in his own room, on the night of the first snowfall, that a new adventure began for him. Very late in the night, towards morning, Joel sat bolt upright in bed and opened his eyes to see the whole room shining brightly, like a brimming lake in the sun. Boots went completely out of his head, and he was left motionless. The candle was lighted in its stick, the fire was high in the grate, and from the window a wild tossing illumination came, which he did not even identify at first as the falling of snow. Joel was left in the shadow of the room, and there before him, in the centre of the strange multiplied light, were two men in black capes sitting at his table. They sat in profile to him, tall under the little arch of the rafters, facing each other across the good table he used for everything, and talking together. They were not of Natchez, and their names were not in the book. Each of them had a white glitter upon his boots—it was the snow; their capes were drawn together in front, and in the blackness of the folds, snowflakes were just beginning to melt.

Joel had never been able to hear the knocking at a door, and still he knew what that would be; and he surmised that these men had never knocked even lightly to enter his room. When he found that at some moment outside his knowledge or consent two men had seemingly fallen from the clouds on to the two stools at his table and had taken everything over for themselves, he did not keep the calm heart with which he had stood and regarded all men up to Old Man McCaleb, who snored upstairs.

He did not at once betray the violation that he felt. Instead, he simply sat, still bolt upright, and looked with the feasting the eyes do in secret—at their faces, the one eye of each that he could see, the cheeks, the half-hidden mouths—the faces each firelit, and strange with a common reminiscence or speculation ... Perhaps he was saved from giving a cry by knowing it could be heard. Then the gesture one of the men made in the air transfixed him where he waited.

One of the two men lifted his right arm—a tense, yet gentle and easy motion—and made the dark wet cloak fall back. To Joel it was like the first movement he had ever seen, as if the world had been up to that night inanimate. It was like the signal to open some heavy gate or paddock, and it did open to his complete astonishment upon a panorama in his own head, about which he knew first of all that he would never be able to speak—it was nothing but brightness, as full as the brightness on which he had opened his eyes. Inside his room was still another interior, this meeting upon which all the light was turned, and within that was one more mystery, all that was being said. The men's heads were inclined together against the blaze, their hair seemed light and floating. Their elbows rested on the boards, stirring the crumbs where Joel had eaten his biscuit. He had no idea of how long they had stayed when they got up and stretched their arms and walked out through the door, after blowing the candle out.

When Joel woke up again at daylight, his first thought was of Indians, his next of ghosts, and then the vision of what had happened came back into his head. He took a light beating for forgetting to clean the boots, but then he forgot the beating. He wondered for how long a time the men had been meeting in his room while he was asleep, and whether they had ever seen him, and what they might be going to do to him, whether they would take him each by the arm and drag him on further, through the leaves. He tried to remember everything of the night before, and he rubbed belatedly at a boot in a long and deepening dream. His memory could work like the slinging of a noose to catch a wild pony. It reached back and hung trembling over the very moment of terror in which he had become separated from his parents, and then it turned and started in the opposite direction, and it would have discerned some shape, but he would not let it, of the future. In the meanwhile, all day long, everything in the passing moment and each little deed assumed the gravest importance. He divined every change in the house, in the angle of the doors, in the height of the fires, and whether the logs had been stirred by a boot or had only fallen in an empty room. He was seized and possessed by mystery. He waited for night. In his own room the candlestick now stood on the table covered with the wonder of having been touched by unknown hands in his absence and seen in his sleep.

It was while he was cleaning boots again that the identity of the men came to him all at once. Like part of his meditations, the names came into his mind. He ran out into the street with this knowledge rocking in his head, remembering then the tremor of a great arrival which had shaken Natchez, caught fast in the grip of the cold, and shaken it through the lethargy of the snow, and it was clear now why the floors swayed with running feet and unsteady hands shoved him aside at the bar. There was no one to inform him that the men were Aaron Burr and Harman Blennerhassett, but he knew. No one had pointed out to him any way that he might know which was which, but he knew that: it was Burr who had made the gesture.

They came to his room every night, and indeed Joel had not expected that the one visit would be the end. It never occurred to him that the first meeting did not mark a beginning. It took a little time always for the snow to melt from their capes—for it continued all this time to snow. Joel sat up with his eyes wide open in the shadows and looked out like the lone watcher of a conflagration. The room grew warm, burning with the heat from the little grate, but there was something of fire in all that happened. It was from Aaron Burr that the flame was springing, and it seemed to pass across the table with certain words and through the sudden nobleness of the gesture, and touch Blennerhassett. Yet the breath of their speech was no simple thing like the candle's gleam between them. Joel saw them still only in profile, but he could see that the secret was endlessly complex, for in two nights it was apparent that it could never be all told. All that they said never finished their conversation. They would always have to meet again. The ring Burr wore caught the firelight repeatedly and started it up again in the intricate

whirlpool of a signet. Quicker and fuller still was his eye, darting its look about, but never at Joel. Their eyes had never
really seen his room ... the fine polish he had given the
candlestick, the clean boards from which he had scraped the
crumbs, the wooden bench where he was himself, from which
he put outward—just a little, carelessly—his hand ... Everything in the room was conquest, all was a dream of delights
and powers beyond its walls ... The light-filled hair fell over
Burr's sharp forehead, his cheek grew taut, his smile was
sudden, his lips drove the breath through. The other man's
face, with its quiet mouth, for he was the listener, changed
from ardour to gloom and back to ardour ... Joel sat still and
looked from one man to the other.

At first he believed that he had not been discovered. Then
he knew that they had learned somehow of his presence, and
that it had not stopped them. Somehow that appalled him ...
They were aware that if it were only before him, they could
talk for ever in his room. Then he put it that they accepted
him. One night, in his first realization of this, his defect
seemed to him a kind of hospitality. A joy came over him, he
was moved to gaiety, he felt wit stirring in his mind, and he
came out of his hiding place and took a few steps towards
them. Finally, it was too much: he broke in upon the circle of
their talk, and set food and drink from the kitchen on the
table between them. His hands were shaking, and they looked
at him as if from great distances, but they were not surprised,
and he could smell the familiar black wetness of travellers'
clothes steaming up from them in the firelight. Afterwards he
sat on the floor perfectly still, with Burr's cloak hanging just
beside his own shoulder. At such moments he felt a dizziness
as if the cape swung him about in a great arc of wonder, but
Aaron Burr turned his full face and looked down at him only
with gravity, the high margin of his brows lifted above tireless eyes.

There was a kind of dominion promised in his gentlest
glance. When he first would come and throw himself down to
talk and the fire would flame up and the reflections of the
snowy world grew bright, even the clumsy table seemed to
change its substance and to become a part of a ceremony.
He might have talked in another language, in which there

was nothing but evocation. When he was seen so plainly, all his movements and his looks seemed part of a devotion that was curiously patient and had the illusion of wisdom all about it. Lights shone in his eyes like travellers' fires seen far out on the river. Always he talked, his talking was his appearance, as if there were no eyes, nose or mouth to remember; in his face there was every subtlety and eloquence, and no features, no kindness, for there was no awareness whatever of the present. Looking up from the floor at his speaking face, Joel knew all at once some secret of temptation and an anguish that would reach out after it like a closing hand. He would allow Burr to take him with him wherever it was that he meant to go.

Sometimes in the nights Joel would feel himself surely under their eyes, and think they must have come; but that would be a dream, and when he sat up on his bench he often saw nothing more than the dormant firelight stretched on the empty floor, and he would have a strange feeling of having been deserted and lost, not quite like anything he had ever felt in his life. It was likely to be early dawn before they came.

When they were there, he sat restored, though they paid no more attention to him than they paid the presence of the firelight. He brought all the food he could manage to give them; he saved a little out of his own suppers, and one night he stole a turkey pie. He might have been their safety, for the way he sat up so still and looked at them at moments like a father at his playing children. He never for an instant wished for them to leave, though he would so long for sleep that he would stare at them finally in bewilderment and without a single flicker of the eyelid. Often they would talk all night. Blennerhassett's wide vague face would grow out of devotion into exhaustion. But Burr's hand would always reach across and take him by the shoulder as if to rouse him from a dull sleep, and the radiance of his own face would heighten always with the passing of time. Joel sat quietly, waiting for the full revelation of the meetings. All his love went out to the talkers. He would not have known how to hold it back.

In the idle mornings, in some morning need to go looking at the world, he wandered down to the Esplanade and stood under the trees which bent heavily over his head. He frowned

out across the ice-covered racetrack and out upon the river.
There was one hour when the river was the colour of smoke,
as if it were more a thing of the woods than an element and a
power in itself. It seemed to belong to the woods, to be gentle
and watched over, a tethered and grazing pet of the forest,
and then when the light spread higher and colour stained the
world, the river would leap suddenly out of the shining ice
around, into its full-grown torrent of life, and its strength and
its churning passage held Joel watching over it like the spell
unfolding by night in his room. If he could not speak to the
river, and he could not, still he would try to read in the
river's blue and violet skeins a working of the momentous
event. It was hard to understand. Was any scheme a man had,
however secret and intact, always broken upon by the very
current of its working? One day, in anguish, he saw a raft
torn apart in midstream and the men scattered from it. Then
all that he felt move in his heart at the sight of the inscrutable river went out in hope for the two men and their
genius that he sheltered.

It was when he returned to the Inn that he was given a
notice to paste on the saloon mirror saying that the trial of
Aaron Burr for treason would be held at the end of the
month at Washington, capitol of Mississippi Territory, on the
campus of Jefferson College, where the crowds might be
amply accommodated. In the meanwhile, the arrival of the
full, armed flotilla was being awaited, and the price of whisky
would not be advanced in this tavern, but there would be a
slight increase in the tariff on a bed upstairs, depending on
how many slept in it.

The month wore on, and now it was full moonlight. Late at
night the whole sky was lunar, like the surface of the moon
brought as close as a cheek. The luminous ranges of all the
clouds stretched one beyond the other in heavenly order.
They seemed to be the streets where Joel was walking
through the town. People now lighted their houses in enter-
tainments as if they copied after the sky, with Burr in the
centre of them always, dancing with the women, talking with
the men. They followed and formed cotillion figures about
the one who threatened or lured them, and their minuets

skimmed across the nights like a pebble expertly skipped across water. Joel would watch them take sides, and watch the arguments, all the frilled motions and the toasts, and he thought they were to decide whether Burr was good or evil. But all the time, Joel believed, when he saw Burr go dancing by, that did not touch him at all. Joel knew his eyes saw nothing there and went always beyond the room, although usually the most beautiful woman there was somehow in his arms when the set was over. Sometimes they drove him in their carriages down to the Esplanade and pointed out the moon to him, to end the evening. There they sat showing everything to Aaron Burr, nodding with a magnificence that approached fatigue towards the reaches of the ice that stretched over the river like an impossible bridge, some extension to the West of the Natchez Trace; and a radiance as soft and near as rain fell on their hands and faces, and on the plumes of the breaths from the horses' nostrils, and they were as gracious and as grand as Burr.

Each day that drew the trial closer, men talked more hotly on the corners and the saloon at the Inn shook with debate; every night Burr was invited to a finer and later ball; and Joel waited. He knew that Burr was being allotted, by an almost specific consent, this free and unmolested time till dawn, to meet in conspiracy, for the sake of continuing and perfecting the secret. This knowledge Joel gathered to himself by being, himself, everywhere; it decreed his own suffering and made it secret and filled with private omens.

One day he was driven to know everything. It was the morning he was given a little fur cap, and he set it on his head and started out. He walked through the dark trodden snow all the way up the Trace to the Bayou Pierre. The great trees began to break that day. The pounding of their explosions filled the subdued air; to Joel it was as if a great foot had stamped on the ground. And at first he thought he saw the fulfilment of all the rumour and promise—the flotilla coming around the bend, and he did not know whether he felt terror or pride. But then he saw that what covered the river over was a chain of great perfect trees floating down, lying on their sides in postures like slain giants and heroes of battle, black cedars and stone-white sycamores, magnolias with their leavy leaves shining as if they were in bloom, a long procession. Then it was terror that he felt.

He went on. He was not the only one who had made the pilgrimage to see what the original flotilla was like, that had been taken from Burr. There were many others: there was Old Man McCaleb, at a little distance ... In care not to show any excitement of expectation, Joel made his way through successive little groups that seemed to meditate there above the encampment of militia on the snowy bluff, and looked down at the water.

There was no galley there. There were nine small flatboats tied to the shore. They seemed so small and delicate that he was shocked and distressed, and looked around at the faces of the others, who looked coolly back at him. There was no sign of weapon about the boats or anywhere, except in the hands of the men on guard. There were barrels of molasses and whisky, rolling and knocking each other like drowned men, and stowed to one side of one of the boats, in a dark place, a strange little collection of blankets, a silver bridle with bells, a book swollen with water, and a little flute with a narrow ridge of snow along it. Where Joel stood looking down upon them, the boats floated in clusters of three, as small as water-lilies on a still bayou. A canoe filled with crazily wrapped-up Indians passed at a little distance, and with severe open mouths the Indians all laughed.

But the soldiers were sullen with cold, and very grave or angry, and Old Man McCaleb was there with his beard flying and his finger pointing prophetically in the direction of upstream. Some of the soldiers and all the women nodded their heads, as though they were the easiest believers, and one woman drew her child tightly to her. Joel shivered. Two of the young men hanging over the edge of the bluff flung their arms in sudden exhilaration about each other's shoulders, and a look of wildness came over their faces.

Back in the streets of Natchez, Joel met part of the militia marching and stood with his heart racing, back out of the way of the line coming with bright guns tilted up in the sharp air. Behind them, two of the soldiers dragged along a young dandy whose eyes glared at everything. There where they held him he was trying over and over again to make Aaron

Burr's gesture, and he never convinced anybody.

Joel went in all three times to the militia's encampment on the Bayou Pierre, the last time on the day before the trial was to begin. Then out beyond a willow point a rowboat with one soldier in it kept laconic watch upon the north.

Joel returned on the frozen path to the Inn, and stumbled into his room, and waited for Burr and Blennerhassett to come and talk together. His head ached ... All his walking about was no use. Where did people learn things? Where did they go to find them? How far?

Burr and Blennerhassett talked across the table, and it was growing late on the last night. Then there in the doorway with a fiddle in her hand stood Blennerhassett's wife, wearing breeches, come to fetch him home. The fiddle she had simply picked up in the Inn parlour as she came through, and Joel did not think she bothered now to speak at all. But she waited there before the fire, still a child and so clearly related to her husband that their sudden movements at the encounter were alike and made at the same time. They stood looking at each other there in the firelight like creatures balancing together on a raft, and then she lifted the bow and began to play.

Joel gazed at the girl, not much older than himself. She leaned her cheek against the fiddle. He had never examined a fiddle at all, and when she began to play it she frightened and dismayed him by her almost insect-like motions, the pensive antennae of her arms, her mask of a countenance. When she played she never blinked her eye. Her legs, fantastic in breeches, were separated slightly, and from her bent knees she swayed back and forth as if she were weaving the tunes with her body. The sharp odour of whisky moved with her. The slits of her eyes were milky. The songs she played seemed to him to have no beginnings and no endings, but to be about many hills and valleys, and chains of lakes. She, like the men, knew of a place ... All of them spoke of a country.

And quite clearly, and altogether to his surprise, Joel saw a sight that he had nearly forgotten. Instead of the fire on the hearth, there was a mimosa tree in flower. It was in the little back field at his home in Virginia and his mother was leading him by the hand. Fragile, delicate, cloudlike it rose on its pale trunk and spread its long level arms. His mother pointed to it. Among the trembling leaves the feathery puffs of sweet bloom filled the tree like thousands of paradisical birds all alighted at an instant. He had known then the story of the Princess Labam, for his mother had told it to him, how she was so radiant that she sat on the roof-top at night and lighted the city. It seemed to be the mimosa tree that lighted the garden, for its brightness and fragrance overlaid all the rest. Out of its graciousness this tree suffered their presence and shed its splendour upon him and his mother. His mother pointed again, and its scent swayed like the Asiatic princess moving up and down the pink steps of its branches. Then the vision was gone. Aaron Burr sat in front of the fire, Blennerhassett faced him, and Blennerhassett's wife played on the violin.

There was no compassion in what this woman was doing, he knew that—there was only a frightening thing, a stern allurement. Try as he might, he could not comprehend it, though it was so calculated. He had instead a sensation of pain, the ends of his fingers were stinging. At first he did not realize that he had heard the sounds of her song, the only thing he had ever heard. Then all at once as she held the lifted bow still for a moment he gasped for breath at the interruption, and he did not care to learn her purpose or to wonder any longer, but bent his head and listened for the note that she would fling down upon them. And it was so gentle then, it touched him with surprise; it made him think of animals sleeping on their cushioned paws.

For a moment his love went like sound into a myriad life and was divided among all the people in his room. While they listened, Burr's radiance was somehow quenched, or theirs was raised to equal it, and they were all alike. There was one thing that shone in all their faces, and that was how far they were from home, how far from everywhere that they knew. Joel put his hand to his own face, and hid his pity from them while they listened to the endless tunes.

But she ended them. Sleep all at once seemed to overcome her whole body. She put down the fiddle and took Blennerhassett by both hands. He seemed tired too, more tired than talking could ever make him. He went out when she led him. They went wrapped under one cloak, his arm about her.

Burr did not go away immediately. First he walked up and down before the fire. He turned each time with diminishing violence, and light and shadow seemed to stream more softly with his turning cloak. Then he stood still. The firelight threw its changes over his face. He had no one to talk to. His boots smelled of the fire's closeness. Of course he had forgotten Joel, he seemed quite alone. At last with a strange naturalness, almost with a limp, he went to the table and stretched himself full length upon it.

He lay on his back. Joel was astonished. That was the way they laid out the men killed in duels in the Inn yard; and that was the table they laid them on.

Burr fell asleep instantly, so quickly that Joel felt he should never be left alone. He looked at the sleeping face of Burr, and the time and the place left him, and all that Burr had said that he had tried to guess left him too—he knew nothing in the world except the sleeping face. It was quiet. The eyes were almost closed, only dark slits lay beneath the lids. There was a small scar on the cheek. The lips were parted. Joel thought, I could speak if I would, or I could hear. Once I did each thing ... Still he listened ... and it seemed that all that would speak, in this world, was listening. Burr was silent; he demanded nothing, nothing ... A boy or a man could be so alone in his heart that he could not even ask a question. In such silence as falls over a lonely man there is childlike supplication, and all arms might wish to open to him but there is no speech. This was Burr's last night: Joel knew that. This was the moment before he would ride away. Why would the heart break so at absence? Joel knew that it was because nothing had been told. The heart is secret even when the moment it dreamed of has come, a moment when there might have been a revelation ... Joel stood motionless; he lifted his gaze from Burr's face and stared at nothing ... If love does a secret thing always, it is to reach backward, to a time that could not be known—for it makes a history of the sorrow and the dream it has contemplated in some instant of recognition. What Joel saw before him he had a terrible wish to speak out loud, but he would have had to find names for the places of the heart and the times for its shadowy and tragic events, and they seemed of great magnitude, heroic and terrible and splendid, like the legends of the mind. But for lack of a way to tell how much was known, the boundaries would lie between him and the others, all the others, until he died.

Presently Burr began to toss his head and to cry out. He talked, his face drew into a dreadful set of grimaces, which it followed over and over. He could never stop talking. Joel was afraid of these words, and afraid that eavesdroppers might listen to them. Whatever words they were, they were being taken by some force out of his dream. In horror, Joel put out his hand. He could never in his life have laid it across the mouth of Aaron Burr, but he thrust it into Burr's spread-out fingers. The fingers closed and did not yield; the clasp grew so fierce that it hurt his hand, but he saw that the words had stopped.

As if a silent love had shown him whatever new thing he would ever be able to learn, Joel had some wisdom in his fingers now which only this long month could have brought. He knew with what gentleness to hold the burning hand. With the gravity of his very soul he received the furious pressure of this man's dream. At last Burr drew his arm back beside his quiet head, and his hand hung like a child's in sleep, released in oblivion.

The next morning, Joel was given a notice to paste on the saloon mirror that conveyances might be rented at the Inn daily for the excursion to Washington for the trial of Mr Burr, payment to be made in advance. Joel went out and stood on a corner, and joined with a group of young boys walking behind the militia.

It was warm—a 'false spring' day. The little procession from Natchez, decorated and smiling in all they owned or whatever they borrowed or chartered or rented, moved grandly through the streets and on up the Trace. To Joel, somewhere in the line, the blue air that seemed to lie between the high banks held it all in a mist, softly coloured, the fringe waving from a carriage top, a few flags waving, a sword shining when some gentleman made a flourish. High up on their horses a number of the men were wearing their Revolutionary War uniforms, as if to reiterate that Aaron Burr fought once at their sides as a hero.

Under the spreading live-oaks at Washington, the trial opened like a festival. There was a theatre of benches, and a promenade; stalls were set out under the trees and glasses of whisky, and coloured ribbons, were sold. Joel sat somewhere among the crowds. Breezes touched the yellow and violet of dresses and stirred them, horses pawed the ground, and the people pressed upon him and seemed more real than those in dreams, and yet their pantomime was like those choruses and companies whose movements are like the waves running together. A hammer was then pounded, there was sudden attention from all the spectators, and Joel felt the great solidifying of their silence.

He had dreaded the sight of Burr. He had thought there might be some mark or disfigurement that would come from his panic. But all his grace was back upon him, and he was smiling to greet the studious faces which regarded him. Before their bright façade others rose first, declaiming men in turn, and then Burr.

In a moment he was walking up and down with his shadow on the grass and the patches of snow. He was talking again, talking now in great courtesy to everybody. There was a flickering light of sun and shadow on his face.

Then Joel understood. Burr was explaining away, smoothing over all that he had held great enough to have dreaded once. He walked back and forth elegantly in the sun, turning his wrist ever so airily in its frill, making light of his dream that had terrified him. And it was the deed they had all come to see. All around Joel they gasped, smiled, pressed one another's arms, nodded their heads; there were tender smiles on the women's faces. They were at Aaron Burr's feet at last, learning their superiority. They loved him now, in their condescension. They leaned forward in delight at the parading spectacle he was making. And when it was over for the day, they shook each other's hands, and Old Man McCaleb could be seen spitting on the ground, in the anticipation of another day as good as this one.

Blennerhassett did not come that night.

Burr came very late. He walked in the door, looked down at Joel where he sat among his boots, and suddenly stooped and took the dirty cloth out of his hand. He put his face quickly into it and pressed and rubbed it against his skin. Joel saw that all his clothes were dirty and ragged. The last thing he did was to set a little cap of turkey feathers on his head. Then he went out.

Joel followed him along behind the dark houses and through a ravine. Burr turned towards the Halfway Hill. Joel turned too, and he saw Burr walk slowly up and open the great heavy gate.

He saw him stop beside a tall camellia bush as solid as a tower and pick up one of the frozen buds which were shed all around it on the ground. For a moment he held it in the palm of his hand, and then he went on. Joel, following behind, did the same. He held the bud, and studied the burned edges of its folds by the pale half-light of the East. The bud came apart in his hand, its layers like small velvet shells, still iridescent, the shrivelled flower inside. He held it tenderly and yet timidly, in a kind of shame, as though all disaster lay pitifully disclosed now to the eyes.

He knew the girl Burr had often danced with under the rings of tapers when she came out in a cloak across the shadowy hill. Burr stood, quiet and graceful as he had always been as her partner at the balls. Joel felt a pain like a sting while she first merged with the dark figure and then drew back. The moon, late-risen and waning, came out of the clouds. Aaron Burr made the gesture there in the distance, towards the West, where the clouds hung still and red, and when Joel looked at him in the light he saw as she must have seen the absurdity he was dressed in, the feathers on his head. With a curious feeling of revenge upon her, he watched her turn, draw smaller within her own cape, and go away.

Burr came walking down the hill, and passed close to the camellia bush where Joel was standing. He walked stiffly in his mock Indian dress with the boot polish on his face. The youngest child in Natchez would have known that this was a remarkable and wonderful figure that had humiliated itself by disguise.

Pausing in an open space, Burr lifted his hand once more and a slave led out from the shadows a majestic horse with silver trappings shining in the light of the moon. Burr mounted from the slave's hand in all the clarity of his true elegance, and sat for a moment motionless in the saddle. Then he cut his whip through the air, and rode away.

Joel followed him on foot towards the Liberty Road. As he walked through the streets of Natchez he felt a strange mourning to know that Burr would never come again by that way. If he had left in disguise, the thirst that was in his face was the same as it had ever been. He had eluded judgement, that was all he had done, and Joel was glad while he still trembled. Joel would never know now the true course, or the true outcome of any dream: this was all he felt. But he walked on, in the frozen path into the wilderness, on and on. He did not see how he could ever go back and still be the boot-boy at the Inn.

He did not know how far he had gone on the Liberty Road when the possee came riding up behind and passed him. He walked on. He saw that the bodies of the frozen birds had fallen out of the trees, and he fell down and wept for his father and mother, to whom he had not said good-bye.

WILLIAM FAULKNER

'Tell me about the South. What's it like there. What
do they do there. Why do they live there. Why do they
live at all—'

Mississippi, Summer, 1925. November 1942

The Liar

Four men sat comfortably on the porch of Gibson's store,
facing the railroad tracks and two nondescript yellow buildings. The two buildings belonged to the railroad company,
hence they were tidy in an impersonal way, and were painted
the same prodigious yellow. The store, not belonging to the
railroad company, was not painted. It squatted stolidly
against a rising hill, so that the proprietor could sit at ease,
spitting into the valley, and watch the smoke-heralded passing of casual trains. The store and the proprietor resembled
each other, slovenly and comfortable; and it was seldom that
the owner's was the only chair tilted against the wall, and his
the only shavings littering the floor.

Today he had four guests. Two of these had ridden in from
the hills for trivial necessities, the other two had descended
from the morning's local freight; and they sat in easy amity,
watching the smoke from the locomotive dwindle away down
the valley.

'Who's that feller, coming up from the deepo?' spoke one
at last. The others followed his gaze and the stranger
mounted the path from the station under their steady pro-
vincial stare. He was roughly dressed—a battered felt hat, a
coarse blue cloth jacket and corduroy trousers—a costume
identical with that of at least one of the watchers.

'Never seen him before. He don't live hereabouts, that I
know of,' murmured the proprietor. 'Any of you boys know
him?'

They shook their heads. 'Might be one of them hill fellers.
They stays back yonder all the year round, some of 'em ain't
never been out.' The speaker, a smallish man with a large

round bald head and a long saturnine face in which his two bleached eyes were innocent and keen—like a depraved priest—continued: 'Feller over to Mitchell says one of 'em brung his whole family into town one day last month to let 'em see a train. Train blowed, and his wife and six–seven children started milling round kind of nervous; but when she come in sight around the bend the whole bunch broke for the woods.

'Old man Mitchell himself had drove down fer his paper, and them hill folks run right spang over his outfit: tore his buggy all to pieces and scart his hoss so bad it took 'em till next day noon to catch him. Yes, sir, heard 'em whooping and hollering all night, trying to head that hoss into something with a fence around it. They say he run right through old Mis' Harmon's house——' The narrator broke down over his own invention. His audience laughed too, enjoying the humour, but tolerantly, as one laughs at a child. His fabling was well known. And though like all peoples who live close to the soil, they were by nature veracious, they condoned his unlimited imagination for the sake of the humour he achieved and which they understood.

The laughter ceased, for the newcomer was near. He mounted the shaky steps and stood among them, a dark-favoured man. 'Morning, gentlemen,' he greeted them without enthusiasm.

The proprietor, as host, returned his greeting. The others muttered something, anything, as was the custom. The stranger entered the store and the owner rose reluctantly and luxuriously to follow him.

'Say,' spoke the raconteur, 'ever notice how spry Will is for trade? See him jump up when a customer comes in, and nigh tromps his heels off herding him inside? Minds me of the time——'

'Shet up, Ek,' another told him equably. 'You already told one lie this morning. Give a man time to smoke a pipe betwixt 'em, leastways. Mebbe that stranger'd like to hear ye. And Will'd hate to miss it, too.' The others guffawed, and spat.

Gibson and his customer returned; the proprietor sank with a sigh into his chair and the other, bearing a piece of cheese and a paper sack of crackers, lowered himself on to the top step, his back against a post, partly facing them. He began his meal while they stared at him, gravely and without offence, as children, and all whose desires and satisfactions are simple, can.

'Say, Will,' said one after a while, 'you come near missing one of Ek's yarns. Us fellers stopped him, though. Now, Ek, you kin go ahead.'

'Lissen,' said the one called Ek, readily, 'all you boys think that ever' time I open my mouth it's to do a little blanket stretching, but lemme tell you something cur'ous that reely happened. 'Twas like this——'

He was interrupted. 'H'y, Will, git out yer hoss medicine: Ek's took sick.'

'Musta had a stroke. We kept telling him ter stay outen them sunny fields.'

'Yes, sir; shows what work'll do fer you.'

'No, boys, it's that licker them Simpson boys makes: Makes a man tell the truth all the time. Sho' better keep it outen the courts, or ever'body'll be in jail.'

Ek had vainly striven to surmount the merriment. 'You fellers don't know nothing,' he roared. 'Feller comes trying to tell you the truth——' They shouted him down again, and Will Gibson summed the matter up.

'Why, Ek, we ain't doubting your ability to tell the truth when it's necessary, like in court or meeting house; but they ain't no truth ever happened as entertaining as your natural talk, hey boys? He's better'n a piece in the theaytre, ain't he, fellers?'

The others assented loudly, but Ek refused to be mollified. He sat in offended dignity. The others chuckled at intervals, but at last the merriment was gone and there was no sound save the stranger's methodical crunching. He, seemingly, had taken no part in the laughter. Far up the valley a train whistled; echo took the sound and toyed with it, then let it fade back into silence.

But silence was unbearable to Ek. At last it overcame his outraged dignity. 'Say,' he went easily into narrative, 'lemme tell you something cur'ous that reely happened to me yest'day. I was over to Mitchell yest'day waiting for the early local, when I meets up with Ken Rogers, the sheriff. We passed the time of day and he says to me, what am I doing today, and I tells him I aim to ride No. 12 over home. Then he says he's looking for somebody like me, asking me wasn't I raised in the hills. I tells him I was, and how when I turned twenty-one, paw decided I had ought to wear shoes. I hadn't never worn no shoes, and was young and skittish as a colt in them days.

'Well, sir, you may believe it or not, but when they come to my pallet that morning with them new shoes, I up and lit out of there in my shirt tail and took to the woods. Paw sent word around to the neighbours and they organized a hunt same as a bear hunt, with axes and ropes and dogs. No guns, though; paw held that to shoot me would be a waste of man-power, as I could stand up to a day's work with any of 'em.

'Well, sir, it took 'em two days to git me, and they only got me then when them big man-eating hounds of Lem Haley's put me up a tree in Big Sandy bottom, twenty miles from home. And mebbe you won't believe it, but it took paw and three strong men to put them shoes on me.' He led the laughter himself, which the stranger joined. 'Yes, sir; them was the days. But lemme see, I kind of got off the track. Where was I? Oh, yes. Well, the sheriff he says to me can't I go back in the hills a ways with him. And I says, well, I dunno; I got some business in Sidon to tend to today——'

'Same business you're tending to now, I reckon?' interrupted one of his audience. 'Got to git back where folks believe him when he says he's telling the truth.'

'Now, look-a-here,' began the affronted narrator, when the proprietor interfered. 'Hush up, you Lafe; let him finish his tale. G'on, Ek, won't no body bother you again.'

Ek looked at him in gratitude and resumed. 'Well, listen. The sheriff, he says to me, he needs a man that knows them hill folks to go in with him. Been some trouble of some kind and he wants to clear it up. But them hill people is so leary that they's liable to shoot first, before a man kin state his point. So he wants I should go along with him and kind of mollify 'em, you might say, promising to get me back in time to catch the evening train. Well, they ain't nothing I couldn't put off a day or so, so I goes with him. He's got his car all ready and a deppity waiting, so we piles in and lit out.

'It was as putty a day as I ever see and we was having a good time, laughing and talking back and forth——'

Lafe interrupted again: 'Must of been with a set of fellers't never heard your lies before.'

'Be quiet, Lafe,' Gibson commanded peremptorily.

'—and first thing I knew, we come to a place where the road played out altogether. "Have to walk from here on," sheriff says, so we runs the car off the road a ways, and struck out afoot. Well, sir, I was born and raised in them hills, but I never seen that stretch where we was before—all ridges, and gullies where you could sling a hoss off and lose him. Finally the sheriff says to me: "Ek," he says, "place we're heading for is jest across that ridge. You go on over to the house, and tell Mrs Starnes who you are; and Tim and me'll go around yonder way. Probably catch Joe in his lower field. We'll meet you at the house. Might ask Mis' Starnes if she kin git us a little snack ready."

'"All right, sheriff," I says, "but I don't know nobody through here."

'"That's all right," sheriff says, "jest go up to the house and tell her me and Joe and Tim'll be 'long soon." And him and Tim started on around the ridge, and I took the route he give me. Well, sir, I moseyed on up to the top of the ridge, and sho' 'nough, there was a house and a barn setting in the next valley. It didn't look like much of a farm and I just decided them Starneses was average shif'less hill folks. There was a lot of rocks on the ridge where I was, and just as I was thinking what a good place for snakes it was and starting on down to'rds the house—bzzzrrr! went something right behind me. Gentlemen, I jumped twenty foot and lit grabbing rocks. When I had throwed a couple the rattler was gone into a hole; and then I seen three others laying with their heads mashed, and I knowed I must of stumbled into a regular den of 'em. They hadn't been dead long, and from the sample I'd had I knowed how mad the others must be, so I lit a shuck out of there. But I wasn't far from the feller had killed them three, but just how close I never learnt till later.

'I dropped on down through the brush, coming to the house from behind. Down the hill from the barn and between me and the house was a spring in a rocky gully. The spring was railed off from cattle. There was gullies and rocks ever'-where: I never seen such pore, rocky and—sink holes full of rocks and narrer as wells. I had to jump 'em lik a goat.

'I was about half-way down the hill when I seen a feller moving down at the spring I hadn't seen him before. He jest wasn't there when I looked once, but there he was when I looked again, rising up by the spring. He had a wooden box under his arm. I never knowed where he come from.

'Knowing how skittish them hill folks are, I was jest about to sing out when he put his finger in his mouth and whistled. I thought mebbe he was calling his dog, and I was thinking to myself it was a sorry dog that never suspicioned me when I was this close, when a woman come to the back door of the house. She stood there a minute, shading her eyes and looking all around at the ridges, but she never did look to'rds the spring. Then she stepped out, toting something in her hand, and started fer the spring on the run. Then I could see she had her Sunday hat on, and that the thing in her hand was a carpetbag. Fellers, she jest flew down that hill.

' "Uh, uh," thinks I to myself, "they's something going on here that I don't know about, and that Starnes don't know nothing about, neither." The sheriff seemed mighty certain he wouldn't be to home, and I never seen a man and wife go to all that trouble to go anywheres.

'Well, sir, they met at the spring. The feller had set his little box down careful, and they was clamped together like two sheep in a storm, and was a-kissing. "Uh, uh!" thinks I, "here's something else me and Starnes don't know nothing about, and what'd make him itch if he did." I was higher up than them two, and I taken a look around fer sheriff and Tim, and I seen a lone feller coming down the valley. They couldn't see him a tall, but jest when I seen him, he spied them. He stopped a minute like he was studying, then he come on, not hiding exactly, but walking careful.

'Meanwhile, them two at the spring was bent over the feller's little box, and I seen her jump back and kind of squeal. Well, sir, things was getting cur'ouser and cur'ouser ever' minute, and I was a-wishing and a-griping for sheriff and Tim to git there. "If sheriff's wanting something to clear up," I thinks to myself, "I got it here waiting fer him." And about then things begun to pop.

'Them two at the spring looked up all on a sudden. They had either seen or heard the other feller; so he walked in bold as you please. The woman she kind of comes behind the first feller; then she drops her bag and makes a bee-line fer the other one, the feller that jest come up, and tries to grab him round the neck. He flings her off and she fell flat, but jumped up and tried to grab him again.

'Well, sir, she kep' on trying to hold his arm and he kep' on a-flinging her off, all the time walking not fast but steady to'rds number one. Finally she sees she can't stop 'em, so she backed off with her hands kind of against her side, and I can see she is scared most to death. Them two fellers is about a yard apart, when number two hauled off and knocked the other one clean into the spring. He jumped up right away and grabbed up a rail from the fence that kep' cattle out of the spring. The woman hollered and grabbed at number two again, and while he was shaking her loose, number one ups and hits him over the head with his rail, and he dropped like a ox. Them hill folks has got hard heads, but it seemed to me I could hear that feller's skull bust. Leastways, he never moved again. The woman backed off, clamping her head betwixt her hands; and the feller watched him awhile, then throwed away his rail.

'Well, sir, you could of knocked me down with a straw. There I was, watching murder, skeered to move, and no sign of sheriff and Tim. I've got along fine without no law officers, but I sho' needed one then.' Ek stopped, with consummate art, and gazed about on his hearers. Their eyes were enraptured on his face, the hot black gaze of the stranger seemed like a blade spitting him against the wall, like a pinned moth. The train whistled again, unheard.

'Go on, go on,' breathed Gibson.

He drew his gaze from the stranger's by an effort of will, and found that the pleasant May morning was suddenly chill. For some reason he did not want to continue.

'Well, sir, I didn't know whether the feller would finish his job right then or not; seemed like he didn't know himself. And all the time the woman was like she was took by a spell.

Finally he walked over and picked the unconscious feller up, and carried him about fifteen foot down the gulley, then dumped him like a sack of meal into one of them narrow sink holes. And all the time the woman was watching him like she was turned to stone.' The train whistled again and the locomotive came in sight, but not one turned his eyes from the narrator's face.

'Seemed like he had decided what to do now. He run back to'rds where the woman was, and I thinks, my God, he's going to kill her, too. But no, he's just after his box. He grabs it up and come back to where he had throwed the other feller. Well, sir, if I could have been cur'ous over anything right then, I would have been cur'ous over what he was a-doing now. But as it was, I was past thinking: jest goggle-eyed, like a fish when you jerk him out the water.

'And all the time this feller is fiddling with his box, standing on the edge of that sink hole. All on a sudden he helt it out from him, shaking it over the hole. Finally something all knotted and shiny like a big watch chain fell out of it and dropped, shining and twisting, into the place where the other feller was.

'Then I knowed who'd killed them rattlers.'

'My God,' said someone.

'Yes, sir. They'd planned to fix that there snake where number two'd stumble on it when he come in, only he come too soon for 'em.'

'My God!' repeated the voice, then the one called Lafe screamed:

'Look out!'

A pistol said whow, the sound slammed against the front of the store and roared across the porch. Ek rolled from his chair and thumped on the floor, tried to rise, and fell again. Lafe sprang erect, but the others sat in reft and silent amaze, watching the stranger leaping down the path towards the track and the passing train; saw him recklessly grasp a car ladder and, shaving death by inches, scramble aboard.

Later, when the doctor had ridden ten miles, dressed Ek's shoulder, cursed him for a fool and gone, the four of them took him to task.

'Well, Ek, I guess you learnt your lesson. You'll know better than tell the truth again.'

'Ain't it the beatingest thing? Here's a man lied his way through life fer forty years and never got a scratch, then sets out to tell the truth fer once in his life, and gets shot.'

'But what was your point,' Will Gibson reiterated, 'in telling your fool yarn right in front of the feller that did it? Didn't you know him again?'

Ek turned his fever exasperated face to them. 'I tell you that it was all a lie, ever last word of it. I wasn't nowhere near Mitchell yest'day.'

They shook their heads at his obstinacy; then Gibson, seeing that they were increasing the patient's fever, drove them out. The last to go, he turned at the door for a parting shot.

'I don't know whether you were lying, or were telling the truth, but either way, you must get a whole lot of satisfaction out of this. If you were lying, you ought to be shot for telling one so prob'le that it reely happened somewhere; and if you were telling the truth, you ought to be shot for having no better sense than to blab it out in front of the man that done the killing. Either way, if you ain't learnt a lesson, I have. And this is, don't talk at all lessen you have to, and when you got to talk, tell the truth.'

'Aw, get out of here,' snarled Ek. And convicted of both truthfulness and stupidity, he turned his face bitterly to the wall, knowing that his veracity as a liar was gone for ever.

Delta Autumn

Soon now they would enter the Delta. The sensation was familiar to him. It had been renewed like this each last week in November for more than fifty years—the last hill, at the foot of which the rich unbroken alluvial flatness began as the sea began at the base of its cliffs, dissolving away beneath the unhurried November rain as the sea itself would dissolve away.

At first they had come in wagons: the guns, the bedding, the dogs, the food, the whisky, the keen heart-lifting anticipation of hunting; the young men who could drive all night and all the following day in the cold rain and pitch a camp in the rain and sleep in the wet blankets and rise at daylight the next morning and hunt. There had been bear then. A man shot a doe or a fawn as quickly as he did a buck, and in the afternoons they shot wild turkey with pistols to test their stalking skill and marksmanship, feeding all but the breast to the dogs. But that time was gone now. Now they went in cars, driving faster and faster each year because the roads were better and they had farther and farther to drive, the territory in which game still existed drawing yearly inward as his life was drawing inward, until now he was the last of those who had once made the journey in wagons without feeling it and now those who accompanied him were the sons and even grandsons of the men who had ridden for twenty-four hours in the rain or sleet behind the steaming mules. They called him 'Uncle Ike' now, and he no longer told anyone how near eighty he actually was because he knew as well as they did that he no longer had any business making such expeditions, even by car.

In fact, each time now, on that first night in camp, lying aching and sleepless in the harsh blankets, his blood only faintly warmed by the single thin whisky-and-water which he allowed himself, he would tell himself that this would be his last. But he would stand that trip—he still shot almost as well as he ever had, still killed almost as much of the game he saw as he ever killed; he no longer even knew how many deer had fallen before his gun—and the fierce long heat of the next summer would renew him. Then November would come again, and again in the car with two of the sons of his old companions, whom he had taught not only how to distinguish between the prints left by a buck or a doe but between the sound they made in moving, he would look ahead past the jerking arc of the windshield wiper and see the land flatten suddenly and swoop, dissolving away beneath the rain as the sea itself would dissolve, and he would say, 'Well, boys, there it is again.'

This time though, he didn't have time to speak. The driver of the car stopped it, slamming it to a skidding halt on the greasy pavement without warning, actually flinging the two passengers forward until they caught themselves with their braced hands against the dash. 'What the hell, Roth!' the man in the middle said. 'Can't you whistle first when you do that? Hurt you, Uncle Ike?'

'No,' the old man said. 'What's the matter?' The driver didn't answer. Still leaning forward, the old man looked sharply past the face of the man between them, at the face of his kinsman. It was the youngest face of them all, aquiline, saturnine, a little ruthless, the face of his ancestor too, tempered a little, altered a little, staring sombrely through the streaming windshield across which the twin wipers flicked and flicked.

'I didn't intend to come back in here this time,' he said suddenly and harshly.

'You said that back in Jefferson last week,' the old man said. 'Then you changed your mind. Have you changed it again? This ain't a very good time to——'

'Oh, Roth's coming,' the man in the middle said. His name was Legate. He seemed to be speaking to no one, as he was looking at neither of them. 'If it was just a buck he was coming all this distance for, now. But he's got a doe in here. Of course a old man like Uncle Ike can't be interested in no doe, not one that walks on two legs—when she's standing up, that is. Pretty light-coloured, too. The one he was after them nights last fall when he said he was coon-hunting, Uncle Ike.

The one I figured maybe he was still running when he was gone all that month last January. But of course a old man like Uncle Ike ain't got no interest in nothing like that.' He chortled, still looking at no one, not completely jeering.

'What?' the old man said. 'What's that?' But he had not even so much as glanced at Legate. He was still watching his kinsman's face. The eyes behind the spectacles were the blurred eyes of an old man, but they were quite sharp too; eyes which could still see a gun-barrel and what ran beyond it as well as any of them could. He was remembering himself now: how last year, during the final stage by motor-boat in to where they camped, a box of food had been lost overboard and how on the next day his kinsman had gone back to the nearest town for supplies and had been gone overnight. And when he did return, something had happened to him. He would go into the woods with his rifle each dawn when the others went, but the old man, watching him, knew that he was not hunting. 'All right,' he said. 'Take me and Will on to shelter where we can wait for the truck, and you can go on back.'

'I'm going in,' the other said harshly. 'Don't worry. Because this will be the last of it.'

'The last of deer hunting, or of doe hunting?' Legate said. This time the old man paid no attention to him even by speech. He still watched the young man's savage and brooding face.

'Why?' he said.

'After Hitler gets through with it? Or Smith or Jones or Roosevelt or Wilkie or whatever he will call himself in this country?'

'We'll stop in this country,' Legate said. 'Even if he calls himself George Washington.'

'How?' Edmonds said. 'By singing God bless America in bars at midnight and wearing dime-store flags in our lapels?'

'So that's what's worrying you,' the old man said. 'I ain't noticed this country being short of defenders yet, when it needed them. You did some of it yourself twenty-odd years ago, before you were a grown man even. This country is a little mite stronger than any one man or group of men, outside of it or even inside of it either. I reckon, when the time comes and some of you have done got tired of hollering we are whipped if we don't go to war and some more are hollering we are whipped if we do, it will cope with one Austrian paper-hanger, no matter what he will be calling himself. My pappy and some other better men than any of them you named tried once to tear it in two with a war, and they failed.'

'And what have you got left?' the other said. 'Half the people without jobs and half the factories closed by strikes. Half the people on public dole that won't work and half that couldn't work even if they would. Too much cotton and corn and hogs, and not enough for people to eat and wear. The country full of people to tell a man how he can't raise his own cotton whether he will or won't, and Sally Rand with a sergeant's stripes and not even the fan couldn't fill the army rolls. Too much not-butter and not even the guns——'

'We got a deer camp—if we ever get to it,' Legate said. 'Not to mention does.'

'It's a good time to mention does,' the old man said. 'Does and fawns both. The only fighting anywhere that ever had anything of God's blessing on it has been when men fought to protect does and fawns. If it's going to come to fighting, that's a good thing to mention and remember too.'

'Haven't you discovered in—how many years more than seventy is it?—that women and children are one thing there's never any scarcity of?' Edmonds said.

'Maybe that's why all I am worrying about right now is that ten miles of river we still have got to run before we can make camp,' the old man said. 'So let's go on.'

They went on. Soon they were going fast again, as Edmonds always drove, consulting neither of them about the speed just as he had given neither of them any warning when he slammed the car to stop. The old man relaxed again. He watched, as he did each recurrent November while more than sixty of them passed, the land which he had seen change. At first there had been only the old towns along the River and the old towns along the hills, from each of which the planters with their gangs of slaves and then of hired labourers had wrested from the impenetrable jungle of water-standing cane and cypress, gum and holly and oak and ash, cotton patches which as the years passed became fields and then plantations. The paths made by deer and bear became roads and then highways, with towns in turn springing up along them and along the rivers Tallahatchie and Sunflower which joined and became the Yazoo, the River of the Dead of the Choctaws—the thick, slow, black, unsunned streams almost without current, which once each year ceased to flow at all and then reversed, spreading, drowning the rich land and subsiding again, leaving it still richer.

Most of that was gone now. Now a man drove two hundred miles from Jefferson before he found wilderness to hunt in. Now the land lay open from the cradling hills on the East to the impenetrable jungle of water-standing cane and cypress, cotton for the world's looms—the rich black land, imponderable and vast, fecund up to the very doorsteps of the Negroes who worked it and of the white men who owned it; which exhausted the hunting life of a dog in one year, the working life of a mule in five and of a man in twenty—the land in which neon flashed past them from the little countless towns and countless shining this-year's automobiles sped past them on the board plumb-ruled highways, yet in which the only permanent mark of man's occupation seemed to be the tremendous gins, constructed in sections of sheet iron and in a week's time though they were, since no man, millionaire though he be, would build more than a roof and walls to shelter the camping equipment he lived from when he knew that once each ten years or so his house would be flooded to the second storey and all within it ruined—the land across which there came now no scream of panther but instead the long hooting of locomotives: trains of incredible length and drawn by a single engine, since there was no gradient anywhere and no elevation save those raised by forgotten aboriginal hands as refuges from the yearly water and used by their Indian successors to sepulchre their fathers' bones, and all that remained of that old time were the Indian names on the little towns and usually pertaining to water—Aluschaskuna, Tillatoba, Homochitto, Yazoo.

By early afternoon, they were on water. At the last little Indian-named town at the end of pavement they waited until the other car and the two trucks—the one carrying the bedding and tents and food, the other the horses—overtook them. They left the concrete and, after another mile or so, the gravel too. In caravan they ground on through the ceaselessly dissolving afternoon, with skid-chains on the wheels now, lurching and splashing and sliding among the ruts, until presently it seemed to him that the retrograde of his remembering had gained an inverse velocity from their own slow progress, that the land had retreated not in minutes from the last spread of gravel but in years, decades, back towards what it had been when he first knew it: the road they now followed once more the ancient pathway of bear and deer, the diminishing fields they now passed once more scooped punily and terrifically by axe and saw and mule-drawn plough from the wilderness's flank, out of the brooding and immemorial tangle, in place of ruthless mile-wide parallelograms wrought by ditching the dyking machinery.

They reached the river landing and unloaded, the horses to go overland down stream to a point opposite the camp and swim the river, themselves and the bedding and food and dogs and guns in the motor-launch. It was himself, though no horseman, no farmer, not even a countryman save by his distant birth and boyhood, who coaxed and soothed the two horses, drawing them by his own single frail hand until, backing, filling, trembling a little, they surged, halted, then sprang scrambling down from the truck, possessing no affinity for them as creatures, beasts, but being merely insulated by his years and time from the corruption of steel and oiled moving parts which tainted the others.

Then, his old hammer double gun which was only twelve years younger than he standing between his knees, he watched even the last puny marks of man—cabin, clearing, the small and irregular fields which a year ago were jungle and in which the skeleton stalks of this year's cotton stood almost as tall and rank as the old cane had stood, as if man had to marry his planting to the wilderness in order to conquer it—fall away and vanish. The twin banks marched with wilderness as he remembered it—the tangle of brier and cane impenetrable even to sight twenty feet away, the tall tremendous soaring of oak and gum and ash and hickory which had rung to no axe save the hunter's, had echoed to no

machinery save the beat of old-time steam-boats traversing it
or to the snarling of launches like their own of people going
into it to dwell for a week or two weeks because it was still
wilderness. There was some of it left, although now it was two
hundred miles from Jefferson when once it had been thirty.
He had watched it, not being conquered, destroyed, so much
as retreating since its purpose was served now and its time an
outmoded time, retreating southward through this inverted-
apex, this ∇-shaped section of earth between hills and river
until what was left of it seemed now to be gathered and for
the time arrested in one tremendous destiny of brooding and
inscrutable impenetrability at the ultimate funnelling tip.

They reached the site of their last-year's camp with still
two hours left of light. 'You go on over under that driest tree
and set down,' Legate told him. '—if you can find it. Me and
these other young boys will do this.' He did neither. He was
not tired yet. That would come later. *Maybe it won't come at
all this time*, he thought, as he had thought at this point each
November for the last five or six of them. *Maybe I will go out
on stand in the morning too*; knowing that he would not, not
even if he took the advice and sat down under the driest
shelter and did nothing until camp was made and supper
cooked. Because it would not be the fatigue. It would be
because he would not sleep tonight but would lie instead
wakeful and peaceful on the cot amid the tent-filling snoring
and the rain's whisper as he always did on the first night in
camp; peaceful, without regret or fretting, telling himself
that was all right too, who didn't have so many of them left as
to waste one sleeping.

In his slicker he directed the unloading of the boat—the
tents, the stove, the bedding, the food for themselves and the
dogs until there should be meat in camp. He sent two of
the Negroes to cut firewood; he had the cook-tent raised and
the stove up and a fire going and supper cooking while the big
tent was still being staked down. Then in the beginning of
dusk he crossed in the boat to where the horses waited, backing and snorting at the water. He took the lead-ropes and
with no more weight than that and his voice, he drew them
down into the water and held them beside the boat with only
their heads above the surface, as though they actually were

suspended from his frail and strengthless old man's hands, while the boat recrossed and each horse in turn lay prone in the shallows, panting and trembling, its eyes rolling in the dusk, until the same weightless hand and unraised voice gathered it surging upward, splashing and thrashing up the bank.

Then the meal was ready. The last of light was gone now save the thin stain of it snared somewhere between the river's surface and the rain. He had the single glass of thin whisky-and-water, then, standing in the churned mud beneath the stretched tarpaulin, he said grace over the fried slabs of pork, the hot soft shapeless bread, the canned beans and molasses and coffee in iron plates and cups—the town food, brought along with them—then covered himself again, the others following. 'Eat,' he said. 'Eat it all up. I don't want a piece of town meat in camp after breakfast tomorrow. Then you boys will hunt. You'll have to. When I first started hunting in this bottom sixty years ago with old General Compson and Major de Spain and Roth's grandfather and Will Legate's too, Major de Spain wouldn't allow but two pieces of foreign grub in his camp. That was one side of pork and one ham of beef. And not to eat for the first supper and breakfast neither. It was to save until along towards the end of camp when every-body was so sick of bear meat and coon and venison that we couldn't even look at it.'

'I thought Uncle Ike was going to say the pork and beef was for the dogs,' Legate said, chewing. 'But that's right; I remember. You just shot the dogs a mess of wild turkey every evening when they got tired of deer guts.'

'Times are different now,' another said. 'There was game here then.'

'Yes,' the old man said quietly. 'There was game here then.'

'Besides, they shot does then too,' Legate said. 'As it is now, we ain't got but one doe-hunter in——'

'And better men hunted it,' Edmonds said. He stood at the end of the rough plank table, eating rapidly and steadily as the others ate. But again the old man looked sharply across at the sullen, handsome, brooding face which appeared now darker and more sullen still in the light of the smoky lantern. 'Go on. Say it.'

'I didn't say that,' the old man said. 'There are good men everywhere, at all times. Most men are. Some are just unlucky, because most men are a little better than their circumstances give them a chance to be. And I've known some that even the circumstances couldn't stop.'

'Well, I wouldn't say——' Legate said.

'So you've lived almost eighty years,' Edmonds said. 'And that's what you finally learned about the other animals you lived among. I suppose the question to ask you is, where have you been all the time you were dead?'

There was a silence; for the instant even Legate's jaw stopped chewing while he gaped at Edmonds. 'Well, by God, Roth——' the third speaker said. But it was the old man who spoke, his voice still peaceful and untroubled and merely grave:

'Maybe so,' he said. 'But if being what you call alive would have learned me any different, I reckon I'm satisfied, wherever it was I've been.'

'Well, I wouldn't say that Roth——' Legate said.

The third speaker was still leaning forward a little over the table, looking at Edmonds, 'Meaning that it's only because folks happen to be watching him that a man behaves at all,' he said. 'Is that it?'

'Yes,' Edmonds said. 'A man in a blue coat, with a badge on it watching him. Maybe just the badge.'

'I deny that,' the old man said. 'I don't——'

The other two paid no attention to him. Even Legate was listening to them for the moment, his mouth still full of food and still open a little, his knife with another lump of something balanced on the tip of the blade arrested half-way to his mouth. 'I'm glad I don't have your opinion of folks,' the third speaker said. 'I take it you include yourself.'

'I see,' Edmonds said. 'You prefer Uncle Ike's opinion of circumstances. All right. Who makes the circumstances?'

'Luck,' the third said. 'Chance. Happen so. I see what you are getting at. But that's just what Uncle Ike said: that now and then, maybe most of the time, man is a little better than the net result of his and his neighbours' doings, when he gets the chance to be.'

This time Legate swallowed first. He was not to be stopped

this time. 'Well, I wouldn't say that Roth Edmonds can hunt one doe every day and night for two weeks and was a poor hunter or a unlucky one neither. A man that still have the same doe left to hunt on again next year——'

'Have some meat,' the man next to him said.

'—ain't no unlucky. What?' Legate said.

'Have some meat.' The other offered the dish.

'I got some,' Legate said.

'Have some more,' the third speaker said. 'You and Roth Edmonds both. Have a heap of it. Clapping your jaws together that way with nothing to break the shock.' Someone chortled. Then they all laughed, with relief, the tension broken. But the old man was speaking, even into the laughter, in that peaceful and still untroubled voice:

'I still believe. I see proof everywhere. I grant that man made a heap of his circumstances, him and his living neighbours between them. He even inherited some of them already made, already almost ruined even. A while ago Henry Wyatt there said how there used to be more game here. There was. So much that we even killed does. I seem to remember Will Legate mentioning that too——' Someone laughed, a single guffaw, stillborn. It ceased and they all listened, gravely, looking down at their plates. Edmonds was drinking his coffee, sullen, brooding, inattentive.

'Some folks still kill does,' Wyatt said. 'There won't be just one buck hanging in this bottom tomorrow night without any head to fit it.'

'I didn't say all men,' the old man said. 'I said most men. And not just because there is a man with a badge to watch us. We probably won't even see him unless maybe he will stop here about noon tomorrow and eat dinner with us and check our licences——'

'We don't kill does because if we did kill does in a few years there wouldn't even be any bucks left to kill, Uncle Ike,' Wyatt said.

'According to Roth yonder, that's one thing we won't never have to worry about,' the old man said. 'He said on the way here this morning that does and fawns—I believe he said women and children—are two things this world ain't ever lacked. But that ain't all of it,' he said. 'That just the mind's reason a man has to give himself because the heart don't always have time to bother with thinking up words that fit together. God created man and He created the world for him to live in and I reckon He created the kind of world He would have wanted to live in if He had been a man—the ground to walk on, the big woods, the trees and the water, and the game to live in it. And maybe He didn't put the desire to hunt and kill game in man but I reckon He knew it was going to be there, that man was going to teach it to himself, since he wasn't quite God himself yet——'

'When will he be?' Wyatt said.

'I think that every man and woman, at the instant when it don't even matter whether they marry or not, I think that whether they marry then or afterwards or don't never, at that instant the two of them together were God.'

'Then there are some Gods in this world I wouldn't want to touch, and with a damn long stick,' Edmonds said. He set his coffee cup down and looked at Wyatt. 'And that includes myself, if that's what you want to know. I'm going to bed.' He was gone. There was a general movement among the others. But it ceased and they stood again about the table, not looking at the old man, apparently held there yet by his quiet and peaceful voice as the heads of the swimming horses had been held above the water by his weightless hand. The three Negroes—the cook and his helper and old Isham—were sitting quietly in the entrance of the kitchen tent, listening too, the three faces dark and motionless and musing.

'He put them both here: man, and the game he would follow and kill, foreknowing it. I believe He said, "So be it." I reckon He even foreknew the end. But He said, "I will give him his chance. I will give him warning and foreknowledge too, along with the desire to follow and the power to slay. The woods and fields he ravages and the game he devastates will be the consequence and signature of his crime and guilt, and his punishment." Bed time,' he said. His voice and inflexion did not change at all. 'Breakfast at four o'clock, Isham. We want meat on the ground by sunup time.'

There was a good fire in the sheet-iron heater; the tent was warm and was beginning to dry out, except for the mud underfoot. Edmonds was already rolled into his blankets, motionless, his face to the wall. Isham had made up his bed too—the strong, battered iron cot, the stained mattress which was not quite soft enough, the worn, often-washed blankets which as the years passed were less and less warm enough. But the tent was warm; presently, when the kitchen was cleaned up and readied for breakfast, the young Negro would come in to lie down before the heater, where he could be roused to put fresh wood into it from time to time. And then, he knew now he would not sleep tonight anyway; he no longer needed to tell himself that perhaps he would. But it was all right now. The day was ended now and night faced him, but alarmless, empty of fret. *Maybe I came for this*, he thought: *Not to hunt, but for this. I would come anyway, even if only to go back home tomorrow.* Wearing only his bagging woollen underwear, his spectacles folded away in the worn case beneath the pillow where he could reach them readily and his lean body fitted easily into the old worn groove of mattress and blankets, he lay on his back, his hands crossed on his breast and his eyes closed while the others undressed and went to bed and the last of the sporadic talking died into snoring. Then he opened his eyes and lay peaceful and quiet as a child, looking up at the motionless belly of rain-murmured canvas upon which the glow of the heater was dying slowly away and would fade still further until the young Negro, lying on two planks before it, would sit up and stoke it and lie back down again.

They had a house once. That was sixty years ago, when the Big Bottom was only thirty miles from Jefferson and old Major de Spain, who had been his father's cavalry commander in '61 and '2 and '3 and '4, and his cousin (his older brother; his father too) had taken him into the woods for the first time. Old Sam Fathers was alive then, born in slavery, son of a Negro slave and a Chickasaw chief, who had taught him how to shoot, not only when to shoot but when not to; such a November dawn as tomorrow would be and the old man led him straight to the great cypress and he had known the buck would pass exactly there because there was something running in Sam Fathers's veins which ran in the veins of the buck too, and they stood there against the tremendous trunk, the old man of seventy and the boy of twelve, and there was nothing save the dawn until suddenly the buck was there, smoke-coloured out of nothing, magnificent with speed: and Sam Fathers said, 'Now. Shoot quick and shoot slow': and the gun levelled rapidly without haste and crashed and he walked to the buck lying still intact and still in the shape of that magnificent speed and bled it with Sam's knife and Sam dipped his hands into the hot blood and marked his face for ever while he stood trying not to tremble, humbly and with pride too though the boy of twelve had been unable to phrase it then: *I slew you: my bearing must not shame your quitting life. My conduct for ever onward must become your death:* marking him for that and for more than that: that day and himself and McCaslin juxtaposed not against the wilderness but against the tamed land, the old wrong and shame itself, in repudiation and denial at least of the land and the wrong and shame even if he couldn't cure the wrong and eradicate the shame, who at fourteen when he learned of it had believed he could do both when he became competent and when at twenty-one he became competent he knew that he could do neither but at least he could repudiate the wrong and shame, at least in principle, and at least the land itself in fact, for his son at least: and did, thought he had: then (married then) in a rented cubicle in a back-street stock-traders' boarding-house, the first and last time he ever saw her naked body, himself and his wife juxtaposed in their turn against that same land, that same wrong and shame from whose regret and grief he would at least save and free his son and, saving and freeing his son, lost him. They had the house then. That roof, the two weeks of each November which they spent under it, had become his home. Although since that time they had lived during the two fall weeks in tents and not always in the same place two years in succession and now his companions were the sons and even the grandsons of them with whom he had lived in the house and for almost fifty years now the house itself had not even existed, the conviction, the sense and feeling of home, had been merely transferred into the canvas. He owned a house in Jefferson, a good house though small, where he had had a wife and lived with her and lost her, ay, lost her even though he had lost her in the rented cubicle before he and his old clever dipso-

maniac partner had finished the house for them to move into
it: but lost her, because she loved him. But women hope for
so much. They never live too long to still believe that anything within the scope of their passionate wanting is likewise
within the range of their passionate hope: and it was still
kept for him by his dead wife's widowed niece and her
children and he was comfortable in it, his wants and needs
and even the small trying harmless crotchets of an old man
looked after by blood at least related to the blood which he
had elected out of all the earth to cherish. But he spent the
time within those walls waiting for November, because even
this tent with its muddy floor and the bed which was not wide
enough nor soft enough nor even warm enough, was his home
and these men, some of whom he only saw during these two
November weeks and not one of whom even bore any name
he used to know—De Spain and Compson and Ewell and
Hogganbeck—were more his kin than any. Because this was
his land——

The shadow of the youngest Negro loomed. It soared,
blotting the heater's dying glow from the ceiling, the wood
billets thumping into the iron maw until the glow, the flame,
leaped high and bright across the canvas. But the Negro's
shadow still remained, by its length and breadth, standing,
since it covered most of the ceiling, until after a moment he
raised himself on one elbow to look. It was not the Negro, it
was his kinsman; when he spoke the other turned sharp
against the red firelight the sullen and ruthless profile.

'Nothing,' Edmonds said. 'Go on back to sleep.'

'Since Will Legate mentioned it,' McCaslin said, 'I remember you had some trouble sleeping in here last fall too.
Only you called it coon-hunting then. Or was it Will Legate
called it that?' The other didn't answer. Then he turned and
went back to his bed, McCaslin, still propped on his elbow,
watched until the other's shadow sank down the wall and
vanished, became one with the mass of sleeping shadows.
'That's right,' he said. 'Try to get some sleep. We must have
meat in camp tomorrow. You can do all the setting up you
want to after that.' He lay down again, his hands crossed
again on his breast, watching the glow of the heater on the
canvas ceiling. It was steady again now, the fresh wood

accepted, being assimiliated; soon it would begin to fade again, taking with it the last echo of that sudden upflare of a young man's passion and unrest. Let him lie awake for a little while, he thought; He will lie still some day for a long time without even dissatisfaction to disturb him. And lying awake here, in these surroundings, would soothe him if anything could, if anything could soothe a man just forty years old. Yes, he thought; Forty years old or thirty, or even the trembling and sleepless ardour of a boy; already the tent, the rain-murmured canvas globe, was once more filled with it. He lay on his back, his eyes closed, his breathing quiet and peaceful as a child's, listening to it—that silence which was never silence but was myriad. He could almost see it, tremendous, primeval, looming, musing downward upon this puny evanescent clutter of human sojourn which after a single brief week would vanish and in another week would be completely healed, traceless in the unmarked solitude. Because it was his land, although he had never owned a foot of it. He had never wanted to, not even after he saw plain its ultimate doom, watching it retreat year by year before the onslaught of axe and saw the log-lines and then dynamite and tractor ploughs, because it belonged to no man. It belonged to all; they had only to use it well, humbly and with pride. Then suddenly he knew why he had never wanted to own any of it, arrest at least that much of what people called progress, measure his longevity at least against that much of its ultimate fate. It was because there was just exactly enough of it. He seemed to see the two of them—himself and the wilderness—as coevals, his own span as a hunter, a woodsman, not contemporary with his first breath but transmitted to him, assumed by him gladly, humbly, with joy and pride, from that old Major de Spain and that old Sam Fathers who had taught him to hunt, the two spans running out together, not towards oblivion, nothingness, but into a dimension free of both time and space where once more the untreed land warped and wrung to mathematical squares of rank cotton for the frantic old-world people to turn into shells to shoot at one another, would find ample room for both—the names, the faces of the old men he had known and loved and for a little while outlived, moving again among the shades of tall unaxed trees and sightless brakes where the wild strong immortal game ran for ever before the tireless belling immortal hounds, falling and rising phoenix-like to the soundless guns.

He had been asleep. The lantern was lighted now. Outside in the darkness the oldest Negro, Isham, was beating a spoon against the bottom of a tin pan and crying, 'Raise up and get yo foa clock coffy. Raise up and get yo foa clock coffy,' and the tent was full of low talk and of men dressing, and Legate's voice, repeating: 'Get out of here now and let Uncle Ike sleep. If you wake him up, he'll go out with us. And he ain't got any business in the woods this morning.'

So he didn't move. He lay with his eyes closed, his breathing gentle and peaceful, and heard them one by one leave the tent. He listened to the breakfast sounds from the table beneath the tarpaulin and heard them depart—the horses, the dogs, the last voice until it died away and there was only the sounds of the Negroes clearing breakfast away. After a while he might possibly even hear the first faint clear cry of the first hound ring through the wet woods from where the buck had bedded, then he would go back to sleep again—The tent-flap swung in and fell. Something jarred sharply against the end of the cot and a hand grasped his knee through the blanket before he could open his eyes. It was Edmonds, carrying a shotgun in place of his rifle. He spoke in a harsh, rapid voice:

'Sorry to wake you. There will be a——'

'I was awake,' McCaslin said. 'Are you going to shoot that shotgun today?'

'You just told me last night you want meat,' Edmonds said. 'There will be a——'

'Since when did you start having trouble getting meat with your rifle?'

'All right,' the other said, with that harsh, restrained, furious impatience. Then McCaslin saw in his hand a thick oblong: an envelope. 'There will be a message here some time this morning, looking for me. Maybe it won't come. If it does, give the messenger this and tell h—— say I said No.'

'A what?' McCaslin said. 'Tell who?' He half rose on to his elbow as Edmonds jerked the envelope on to the blanket, already turning towards the entrance, the envelope striking

solid and heavy and without noise and already sliding from
the bed until McCaslin caught it, divining by feel through
the paper as instantaneously and conclusively as if he had
opened the envelope and looked, the thick sheaf of banknotes. 'Wait,' he said. 'Wait:'—more than the blood kinsman, more even than the senior in years, so that the other
paused, the canvas lifted, looking back, and McCaslin saw
that outside it was already day. 'Tell her No,' he said. 'Tell
her.' They stared at one another—the old face, wan, sleep-
raddled above the tumbled bed, the dark and sullen younger
one at once furious and cold. 'Will Legate was right. This is
what you called coon-hunting. And now this.' He didn't raise
the envelope. He made no motion, no gesture to indicate it.
'What did you promise her that you haven't the courage to
face her and retract?'

'Nothing!' the other said. 'Nothing! This is all of it. Tell
her I said No.' He was gone. The tent flap lifted on an in-
waft of faint light and the constant murmur of rain, and fell
again, leaving the old man still half-raised on to one elbow,
the envelope clutched in the other shaking hand. Afterwards,
it seemed to him that he had begun to hear the approaching
boat almost immediately, before the other could have got out
of sight even. It seemed to him that there had been no
interval whatever: the tent flap falling on the same out-waft
of faint and rain-filled light like the suspiration and expira-
tion of the same breath and then in the next second lifted
again—the mounting snarl of the outboard engine, increasing,
nearer and nearer and louder and louder then cut short off,
ceasing with the absolute instantaneity of a blown-out candle,
into the lap and plop of water under the bows as the skiff slid
in to the bank, the youngest Negro, the youth, raising the
tent flap beyond which for that instant he saw the boat—a
small skiff with a Negro man sitting in the stern beside the up-
slanted motor—then the woman entering, in a man's hat and
a man's slicker and rubber boots, carrying the blanket-
swaddled bundle on one arm and holding the edge of the
unbuttoned raincoat over it with the other hand: and bringing something else, something intangible, an effluvium
which he knew he would recognize in a moment because
Isham had already told him, warned him, by sending the

young Negro to the tent to announce the vistor instead of coming himself, the flap falling at last on the young Negro and they were alone—the face indistinct and as yet only young and with dark eyes, queerly colourless but not ill and not that of a country woman despite the garments she wore, looking down at him where he sat upright on the cot now, clutching the envelope, the soiled undergarment bagging about him and the twisted blankets huddled about his hips.

'Is that his?' he cried. 'Don't lie to me!'

'Yes,' she said. 'He's gone.'

'Yes. He's gone. You won't jump him here. Not this time. I don't reckon even you expected that. He left you this. Here.' He fumbled at the envelope. It was not to pick it up, because it was still in his hand; he had never put it down. It was as if he had to fumble somehow to co-ordinate physically his heretofore obedient hand with what his brain was commanding of it, as if he had never performed such an action before, extending the envelope at last, saying again. 'Here. Take it. Take it:' until he became aware of her eyes, or not the eyes so much as the look, the regard fixed now on his face with that immersed contemplation, that bottomless and intent candour, of a child. If she had ever seen either the envelope or his movement to extend it, she did not show it.

'You're Uncle Isaac,' she said.

'Yes,' he said. 'But never mind that. Here. Take it. He said to tell you No.' She looked at the envelope, then she took it. It was sealed and bore no superscription. Nevertheless, even after she glanced at the front of it, he watched her hold it in the one free hand and tear the corner off with her teeth and manage to rip it open and tilt the neat sheaf of bound notes on to the blanket without even glancing at them and look into the empty envelope and take the edge between her teeth and tear it completely open before she crumpled and dropped it.

'That's just money,' she said.

'What did you expect? What else did you expect? You have known him long enough or at least often enough to have got that child, and you don't know him any better than that?'

'Not very often. Not very long. Just that week here last fall, and in January he sent for me and we went West, to New Mexico. We were there six weeks, where I could at least sleep in the same apartment where I cooked for him and looked after his clothes——'

'But not marriage,' he said. 'Not marriage. He didn't promise you that. Don't lie to me. He didn't have to.'

'No. He didn't have to. I didn't ask him to. I knew what I was doing. I knew that to begin with, long before honour I imagine he called it told him the time had come to tell me in so many words what his code I suppose he would call it would forbid him for ever to do. And we agreed. Then we agreed again before he left New Mexico, to make sure. That that would be all of it. I believed him. No, I don't mean that; I mean I believed myself. I wasn't even listening to him any more by then because by that time it had been a long time since he had had anything else to tell me for me to have to hear. By then I wasn't even listening enough to ask him to please stop talking. I was listening to myself. And I believed it. I must have believed it. I don't see how I could have helped but believe it, because he was gone then as we had agreed and he didn't write as we had agreed, just the money came to the bank in Vicksburg in my name but coming from nobody as we had agreed. So I must have believed it. I even wrote him last month to make sure again and the letter came back unopened and I was sure. So I left the hospital and rented myself a room to live in until the deer season opened so I could make sure myself and I was waiting beside the road yesterday when your car passed and he saw me and so I was sure.'

'Then what do you want?' he said. 'What do you want? What do you expect?'

'Yes,' she said. And while he glared at her, his white hair awry from the pillow and his eyes, lacking the spectacles to focus them, blurred and irisless and apparently pupilless, he saw again that grave, intent, speculative and detached fixity like a child watching him. 'His great great—Wait a minute— great great *great* grandfather was your grandfather. McCaslin. Only it got to be Edmonds. Only it got to be more than that. Your cousin McCaslin was there that day when your father and Uncle Buddy won Tennie from Mr Beauchamp for the one that had no name but Terrel so you called him Tomey's Terrel to marry. But after that it got to be Edmonds.' She regarded him, almost peacefully, with that unwinking and heatless fixity—the dark wide bottomless eyes in the face's dead and toneless pallor which to the old man looked anything but dead, but young and incredibly and even ineradicably alive—as though she were not only not looking at anything, she was not even speaking to anyone but herself. 'I would have made a man of him. He's not a man yet. You spoiled him. You, and Uncle Lucas and Aunt Mollie. But mostly you.'

'Me?' he said. 'Me?'

'Yes. When you gave to his grandfather that land which didn't belong to him, not even half of it by will or even law.'

'And never mind that too,' he said. 'Never mind that too. You,' he said. 'You sound like you have been to college even. You sound almost like a Northerner even, not like the draggle-tailed women of these Delta peckerwoods. Yet you meet a man on the street one afternoon just because a box of groceries happened to fall out of a boat. And a month later you go off with him and live with him until he got a child on you: and then, by your own statement, you sat there while he took his hat and said good-bye and walked out. Even a Delta peckerwood would look after even a draggle-tail better than that. Haven't you got any folks at all?'

'Yes,' she said. 'I was living with one of them. My aunt, in Vicksburg. I came to live with her two years ago when my father died; we lived in Indianapolis then. But I got a job, teaching school here in Aluschaskuna, because my aunt was a widow, with a big family, taking in washing to sup——'

'Took in what?' he said. 'Took in washing?' He sprang, still seated even, flinging himself backward on to one arm, awry-haired, glaring. Now he understood what it was she had brought into the tent with her, what old Isham had already told him by sending the youth to bring her in to him—the pale lips, the skin pallid and dead-looking yet not ill, the dark and tragic and fore-knowing eyes. *Maybe in a thousand or two thousand years in America*, he thought. *But not now! Not now!* He cried, not loud, in a voice of amazement, pity and outrage: 'You're a nigger!'

'Yes,' she said. 'James Beauchamp—you called him Tennie's Jim though he had a name—was my grandfather. I said you were Uncle Isaac.'

'And he knows?'

'No,' she said. 'What good would that have done?'

'But you did,' he cried. 'But you did. Then what do you expect here?'

'Nothing.'

'Then why did you come here? You said you were waiting in Aluschaskuna yesterday and he saw you. Why did you come this morning?'

'I'm going back North. Back home. My cousin brought me up the day before yesterday in his boat. He's going to take me on to Leland to get the train.'

'Then go,' he said. Then he cried again in that thin not loud and grieving voice: 'Get out of here! I can do nothing for you! Can't nobody do nothing for you!' She moved; she was not looking at him again, towards the entrance. 'Wait,' he said. She paused again, obediently still, turning. He took up the sheaf of banknotes and laid it on the blanket at the foot of the cot and drew his hand back beneath the blanket. 'There,' he said.

Now she looked at the money, for the first time, one brief blank glance, then away again. 'I don't need it. He gave me money last winter. Besides the money he sent to Vicksburg. Provided. Honour and code too. That was all arranged.'

'Take it,' he said. His voice began to rise again, but he stopped it. 'Take it out of my tent.' She came back to the cot and took up the money; whereupon once more he said, 'Wait:' although she had not turned, still stooping, and he put out his hand. But, sitting, he could not complete the reach until she moved her hand, the single hand which held the money, until he touched it. He didn't grasp it, he merely touched it—the gnarled, bloodless, bone-light bone-dry old man's fingers touching for a second the smooth young flesh where the strong old blood ran after its long-lost journey back to home. 'Tennie's Jim,' he said. 'Tennie's Jim.' He drew the hand back beneath the blanket again: he said harshly now: 'It's a boy, I reckon. They usually are, except that one that was its own mother too.'

'Yes,' she said. 'It's a boy.' She stood for a moment longer, looking at him. Just for an instant her free hand moved as though she were about to lift the edge of the raincoat away from the child's face. But she did not. She turned again when once more he said Wait and moved beneath the blanket.

'Turn your back,' he said. 'I am going to get up. I ain't got my pants on.' Then he could not get up. He sat in the huddled blanket, shaking, while again she turned and looked down at him in dark interrogation. 'There,' he said harshly, in the thin and shaking old man's voice. 'On the nail there. The tentpole.'

'What?' she said.

'The horn!' he said harshly. 'The horn.' She went and got it, thrust the money into the slicker's side pocket as if it were a rag, a soiled handkerchief, and lifted down the horn, the one which General Compson had left him in his will, covered with the unbroken skin from a buck's shank and bound with silver.

'What?' she said.

'It's his. Take it.'

'Oh,' she said. 'Yes. Thank you.'

'Yes,' he said, harshly, rapidly, but not so harsh now and soon not harsh at all but just rapid, urgent, until he knew that his voice was running away with him and he had neither intended it nor could stop it: 'That's right. Go back North. Marry: a man in your own race. That's the only salvation for you—for a while yet, maybe a long while yet. We will have to wait. Marry a black man. You are young, handsome, almost white; you could find a black man who would see in you what it was you saw in him, who would ask nothing of you and expect less and get even still less than that, if it's revenge you want. Then you will forget all this, forget it ever happened, that he ever existed——' until he could stop it at last and did, sitting there in his huddle of blankets during the instant when, without moving at all, she blazed silently down at him. Then that was gone too. She stood in the gleaming and still dripping slicker, looking quietly down at him from under the sodden hat.

'Old man,' she said, 'have you lived so long and forgotten so much that you don't remember anything you ever knew or felt or even heard about love?'

Then she was gone too. The waft of light and the murmur of the constant rain flowed into the tent and then out again as the flap fell. Lying back once more, trembling, panting, the blanket huddled to his chin and his hands crossed on his breast, he listened to the pop and snarl, the mounting then fading whine of the motor until it died away and once again the tent held only silence and the sound of rain. And cold too: he lay shaking faintly and steadily in it, rigid save for the shaking. This Delta, he thought: This Delta. *This land which man has deswamped and denuded and derivered in two generations so that white men can own plantations and commute every night to Memphis and black men own plantations and ride in jim crow cars to Chicago to live in millionaires' mansions on Lakeshore Drive, where white men rent farms and live like niggers and niggers crop on shares and live like animals, where cotton is planted and grows man-tall in the very cracks of the sidewalks, and usury and mortgage and bankruptcy and measureless wealth, Chinese and African and Aryan and Jew, all breed and spawn to-gether until no man has time to say which one is which nor cares* ... No wonder the ruined woods I used to know don't cry for retribution! he thought: The people who have destroyed it will accomplish its revenge.

The tent flap jerked rapidly in and fell. He did not move save to turn his head and open his eyes. It was Legate. He went quickly to Edmonds's bed and stopped, rummaging hurriedly among the still-tumbled blankets.

'What is it?' he said.

'Looking for Roth's knife,' Legate said. 'I come back to get a horse. We got a deer on the ground.' He rose, the knife in his hand, and hurried towards the entrance.

'Who killed it?' McCaslin said. 'Was it Roth?'

'Yes,' Legate said, raising the flap.

'Wait,' McCaslin said. He moved, suddenly, on to his elbow. 'What was it?' Legate paused for an instant beneath the lifted flap. He did not look back.

'Just a deer, Uncle Ike,' he said impatiently. 'Nothing extra.' He was gone; again the flap fell behind him, wafting out of the tent again the faint light and the constant and grieving rain. McCaslin lay back down, the blanket once more drawn to his chin, his crossed hands once more weight-less on his breast in the empty tent.

'It was a doe,' he said.

VLADIMIR NABOKOV

'What it would be actually to see again my former surroundings, I can hardly imagine. Sometimes I fancy myself revisiting them with a false passport, and under an
assumed name.'

Nord Express, 1909

First Love

1

In the early years of this century, a travel agency on Nevski
Avenue displayed a three-foot long model of an oak-brown
international sleeping car. In delicate verisimilitude it completely outranked the painted tin of my clockwork trains.
Unfortunately it was not for sale. One could make out the
blue upholstery inside, the embossed leather lining of the
compartment wall, their polished panels, inset mirrors, tulip-
shaped reading lamps and other maddening details. Spacious
windows alternated with narrower ones, single or geminate,
and some of these were of frosted glass. In a few of the com-
partments, the beds had been made.

The then great and glamorous Nord Express (it was never
the same after the First World War), consisting solely of such
international cars and running but twice a week, connected
St Petersburg with Paris. I would have said: directly with
Paris, had passengers not been obliged to change from one
train to a superficially similar one at the Russo-German
frontier, (Verzhbolovo–Eydtkuhnen), where the ample and
lazy Russian sixty-and-a-half-inch gauge was replaced by the
fifty-six-and-a-half-inch standard of Europe, and coal succeeded birch logs.

In the far end of my mind I can unravel, I think, at least
five such journeys to Paris, with the Riviera or Biarritz as
their ultimate destination. In 1909, the year I now single out,
my two small sisters had been left at home with nurses and
aunts. Wearing gloves and a travelling cap, my father sat
reading a book in the compartment he shared with our tutor.

My brother and I were separated from them by a washroom.
My mother and her maid occupied a compartment adjacent
to ours. The odd one of our party, my father's valet, Osip
(whom, a decade later, the pedantic Bolsheviks were to shoot,
because he appropriated our bicycles instead of turning them
over to the nation), had a stranger for companion.

In April of that year, Peary had reached the North Pole. In
May, Chaliapin had sung in Paris. In June, bothered by
rumours of new and better Zeppelins, the United States War
Department had told reporters of plans for an aerial Navy. In
July, Blériot had flown from Calais to Dover (with a little
additional loop when he lost his bearings). It was late August
now. The firs and marshes of north-western Russia sped by,
and on the following day gave way to German pine barrens
and heather.

At a collapsible table, my mother and I played a card game
called *durachki*. Although it was broad daylight, our cards, a
glass and on a different plane the locks of a suitcase were
reflected in the window. Through forest and field, and in
sudden ravines, and among scuttling cottages, those discarn-
ate gamblers kept steadily playing on for steadily sparkling
stakes.

'*Ne budet-li, ti ved' ustal* [Haven't you had enough, aren't
you tired]?' my mother would ask, and then would be lost in
thought as she slowly shuffled the cards. The door of the
compartment was open and I could see the corridor window,
where the wires—six thin black wires—were doing their best
to slant up, to ascend skywards, despite the lightning blows
dealt them by one telegraph pole after another; but just as all
six, in a triumphant swoop of pathetic elation, were about to
reach the top of the window, a particularly vicious blow
would bring them down, as low as they had ever been, and
they would have to start all over again.

When, on such journeys as these, the train changed its
pace to a dignified amble and all but grazed house fronts and
shop signs, as we passed through some big German town, I
used to feel a twofold excitement, which terminal stations
could not provide. I saw a city with its toy-like trams, linden
trees and brick walls enter the compartment, hobnob with the
mirrors and fill to the brim the windows on the corridor side.

This informal contact between train and city was part of the thrill. The other was putting myself in the place of some passer-by who, I imagined, was moved as I would be moved myself to see the long, romantic, auburn cars, with their intervestibular connecting curtains as black as bat wings and their metal lettering copper-bright in the low sun, unhurriedly negotiate an iron bridge across an everyday thoroughfare and then turn, with all windows suddenly ablaze, around a last block of houses.

There were drawbacks to those optical amalgamations. The wide-windowed dining-car, a vista of chaste bottles of mineral water, mitre-folded napkins and dummy chocolate bars (whose wrappers—Cailler, Kohler and so forth—enclosed nothing but wood) would be perceived at first as a cool haven beyond a consecution of reeling blue corridors; but as the meal progressed towards its fatal last course, one would keep catching the car in the act of being recklessly sheathed, lurching waiters and all, in the landscape, while the landscape itself went through a complex system of motion, the day-time moon stubbornly keeping abreast of one's plate, the distant meadows opening fanwise, the near trees sweeping up on invisible swings towards the track, a parallel rail line all at once committing suicide by anastomosis, a bank of nicitating grass, rising, rising, rising, until the little witness of mixed velocities was made to disgorge his portion of *omelette aux confitures de fraises*.

It was at night, however, that the Compagnie Internationale des Wagons-Lits et des Grands Express Européens lived up to the magic of its name. From my bed under my brother's bunk (Was he asleep? Was he there at all?) in the semi-darkness of our compartment, I watched things, and parts of things, and shadows, and sections of shadows cautiously moving about and getting nowhere. The woodwork gently creaked and crackled. Near the door that led to the toilet, a dim garment on a peg and, higher up, the tassel of the blue, bivalved night light swung rhythmically. It was hard to correlate those halting approaches, that hooded stealth, with the headlong rush of the outside night, which I knew *was* rushing by, spark-streaked, illegible.

I would put myself to sleep by the simple act of identifying myself with the engine driver. A sense of drowsy wellbeing invaded my veins as soon as I had everything nicely arranged—the carefree passengers in their rooms enjoying the ride I was giving them, smoking, exchanging knowing smiles, nodding, dozing; the waiters and cooks and train guards (whom I had to place somewhere) carousing in the diner; and myself, goggled and begrimed, peering out of the engine cab at the tapering track, at the ruby or emerald point in the black distance. And then, in my sleep, I would see something totally different—a glass marble rolling under a grand piano or a toy engine lying on its side with its wheels still working gamely.

A change in the speed of the train sometimes interrupted the current of my sleep. Slow lights were stalking by; each in passing, investigated the same chink, and then a luminous compass measured the shadows. Presently, the train stopped with a long-drawn Westinghousian sigh. Something (my brother's spectacles, as it proved next day) fell from above. It was marvellously exciting to move to the foot of one's bed, with part of the bedclothes following, in order to undo cautiously the catch of the window shade, which could be made to slide only halfway up, impeded as it was by the edge of the upper berth.

Like moons around Jupiter, pale moths revolved about a lone lamp. A dismembered newspaper stirred on a bench. Somewhere on the train one could hear muffled voices, somebody's comfortable cough. There was nothing particularly interesting in the portion of station platform before me, and still I could not tear myself away from it until it departed of its own accord.

Next morning, wet fields with misshapen willows along the radius of a ditch or a row of poplars afar, traversed by a horizontal band of milky-white mist, told one that the train was spinning through Belgium. It reached Paris at 4 p.m.; and even if the stay was only an overnight one, I had always time to purchase something—say, a little brass Tour Eiffel, rather roughly coated with silver paint—before we boarded at noon the following day the Sud Express, which, on its way to Madrid, dropped us around 10 p.m. at the La Négresse station of Biarritz, a few miles from the Spanish frontier.

2

Biarritz still retained its quiddity in those days. Dusty black-berry bushes and weedy *terrains à vendre* bordered the road that led to our villa. The Carlton was still being built. Some thirty-six years had to elapse before Brigadier-General Samuel McCroskey would occupy the royal suite of the Hôtel du Palais, which stands on the site of a former palace, where, in the sixties, that incredibly agile medium, Daniel Home, is said to have been caught stroking with his bare foot (in imitation of a ghost hand) the kind, trustful face of Empress Eugénie. On the promenade near the Casino, an elderly flower-girl, with carbon eyebrows and a painted smile, nimbly slipped the plump torus of a carnation into the buttonhole of an intercepted stroller whose left jowl accentu-ated its royal fold as he glanced down sideways at the coy insertion of the flower.

Along the black line of the *plage*, various seaside chairs and stools supported the parents of straw-hatted children who were playing in front on the sand. I could be seen on my knees trying to set a found comb aflame by means of a magnifying glass. Men sported white trousers that to the eye of today would look as if they had comically shrunk in the washing; ladies wore, that particular season, light coats with silk-faced lapels, hats with big crowns and wide brims, dense embroidered white veils, frill-fronted blouses, frills at their wrists, frills on their parasols. The breeze salted one's lips. At a tremendous pace a stray golden-orange butterfly came dash-ing across the palpitating *plage*.

Additional movement and sound were provided by vendors hawking *cacahauètes*, sugared violets, pistachio ice-cream of a heavenly green, cachou pellets, and huge convex pieces of dry, gritty, waferlike stuff that came from a red barrel. With a distinctness that no later superpositions have dimmed, I see that waffle-man stomp along through deep mealy sand, with the heavy cast on his bent back. When called, he would sling it off his shoulder by a twist of its strap, bang it down on the sand in a Tower of Pisa position, wipe his face with his sleeve and proceed to manipulate a kind of arrow-and-dial arrangement with numbers on the lid of the cask. The arrow rasped and whirred around. Luck was supposed to fix the size of a sou's worth of wafer. The bigger the piece, the more I was sorry for him.

The process of bathing took place on another part of the beach. Professional bathers, burly Basques in black bathing suits, were there to help ladies and children enjoy the terrors of the surf. Such a *baigneur* would place you with your back to the incoming wave and hold you by the hand as the rising, rotating mass of foamy, green water violently descended upon you from behind, knocking you off your feet with one mighty wallop. After a dozen of these tumbles, the *baigneur*, glistening like a seal, would lead his panting, shivering, moistly snuffling charge landward, to the flat foreshore, where an unforgettable old woman with grey hairs on her chin promptly chose a bathing robe from several hanging on a clothesline. In the security of a little cabin, one would be helped by yet another attendant to peel off one's soggy, sand-heavy bathing suit. It would plop on to the boards, and, still shivering, one would step out of it and trample on its bluish, diffuse stripes. The cabin smelt of pine. The attendant, a hunchback with beaming wrinkles, brought a basin of steaming-hot water, in which one immersed one's feet. From him I learned, and have preserved ever since in a glass cell of my memory, that 'butterfly' in the Basque language is *misericoletea*—or at least it sounded so (among the seven words I have found in dictionaries the closest approach is *micheletea*).

3

On the browner and wetter part of the *plage,* that part which at low tide yielded the best mud for castles, I found myself digging, one day, side by side with a little French girl called Colette.

She would be ten in November, I had been ten in April. Attention was drawn to a jagged bit of violet mussel shell upon which she had stepped with the bare sole of her narrow long-toed foot. No, I was not English. Her greenish eyes seemed flecked with the overflow of the freckles that covered her sharp-featured face. She wore what might now be termed a play-suit, consisting of a blue jersey with rolled-up sleeves and blue knitted shorts. I had taken her at first for a boy and then had been puzzled by the bracelet on her thin wrist and the corkscrew brown curls dangling from under her sailor cap.

She spoke in birdlike bursts of rapid twitter, mixing governess English and Parisian French. Two years before, on the same *plage*, I had been much attached to the lovely, suntanned little daughter of a Serbian physician; but when I met Colette, I knew at once that this was the real thing. Colette seemed to me so much stranger than all my other chance playmates at Biarritz! I somehow acquired the feeling that she was less happy than I, less loved. A bruise on her delicate, downy forearm gave rise to awful conjectures. 'He pinches as bad as my mummy,' she said, speaking of a crab. I evolved various schemes to save her from her parents, who were '*des bourgeois de Paris*' as I heard somebody tell my mother with a slight shrug. I interpreted the disdain in my own fashion, as I knew that those people had come all the way from Paris in their blue-and-yellow limousine (a fashionable adventure in those days) but had drably sent Colette with her dog and governess by an ordinary coach train. The dog was a female fox terrier with bells on her collar and a most waggly behind. From sheer exuberance, she would lap up salt water out of Colette's toy pail. I remember the sail, the sunset and the lighthouse pictured on that pail, but I cannot recall the dog's name and this bothers me.

During the two months of our stay at Biarritz, my passion for Colette all but surpassed my passion for butterflies. Since my parents were not keen to meet hers, I saw her only on the beach but I thought of her constantly. If I noticed she had been crying, I felt a surge of helpless anguish that brought tears to my eyes. I could not destroy the mosquitoes that had left their bites on her frail neck, but I could, and did, have a successful fist fight with a red-haired boy who had been rude to her. She used to give me warm handfuls of hard candy. One day, as we were bent together over a starfish, and Colette's ringlets were tickling my ear, she suddenly turned towards me and kissed me on the cheek. So great was my emotion that all I could think of saying was. 'You little monkey.'

I had a gold coin that I assumed would pay for our elopement. Where did I want to take her? Spain? America? The mountains above Pau? '*Là-bas, là-bas, dans la montagne,*' as I had heard Carmen sing at the opera. One strange night, I lay awake, listening to the recurrent thud of the ocean and planning our flight. The ocean seemed to rise and grope in the darkness and then heavily fall on its face.

Of our actual getaway, I have little to report. My memory retains a glimpse of her obediently putting on rope-soled canvas shoes, on the lee side of a flapping tent, while I stuffed a folding butterfly net into a brown paper bag. The next glimpse is of our evading pursuit by entering a pitch-dark *cinéma* near the Casino (which, of course, was absolutely out of bounds). There we sat, holding hands across the dog, which now and then gently jingled in Colette's lap, and were shown a jerky, drizzly, but highly exciting bullfight at San Sebastián. My final glimpse is of myself being led along the promenade by my tutor. His long legs move with a kind of ominous briskness and I can see the muscles of his grimly set jaw working under the tight skin. My bespectacled brother, aged nine, whom he happens to hold with his other hand, keeps trotting out forward to peer at me with awed curiosity, like a little owl.

Among the trivial souvenirs acquired at Biarritz before leaving, my favourite was not the small bull of black stone and not the sonorous sea shell but something which now seems almost symbolic—a meerschaum penholder with a tiny peephole of crystal in its ornamental part. One held it quite close to one's eye, screwing up the other, and when one had got rid of the shimmer of one's own lashes, a miraculous photographic view of the bay and of the line of cliffs ending in a lighthouse could be seen inside.

And now a delightful thing happens. The process re-creating that penholder and the microcosm in its eyelet stimulates my memory to a last effort. I try again to recall the name of Colette's dog—and, sure enough, along those remote beaches, over the glossy evening sands of the past, where each footprint slowly fills up with sunset water, here it comes, here it comes, echoing and vibrating: Floss, Floss, Floss!

Colette was back in Paris by the time we stopped there for

a day before continuing our homeward journey; and there in a fawn park under a cold blue sky, I saw her (by arrangement between our mentors, I believe) for the last time. She carried a hoop and a short stick to drive it with, and everything about her was extremely proper and stylish in an autumnal, Parisian, *tenure-deville-pour-filletts* way. She took from her governess and slipped into my brother's hand a farewell present, a box of sugar-coated almonds, meant, I know, solely for me; and instantly she was off, tap-tapping her glinting hoop through light and shade, around and around a fountain choked with dead leaves near where I stood. The leaves mingle in my memory with the leather of her shoes and gloves, and there was, I remember, some detail in her attire (perhaps a ribbon on her Scottish cap, or the pattern of her stockings) that reminded me then of the rainbow spiral in a glass marble. I still seem to be holding that wisp of iridescence, now knowing exactly where to fit it, while she runs with her hoop ever faster around me and finally dissolves among the slender shadows cast on the gravelled path by the interlaced arches of its low looped fence.

Boston, 1948

Spring in Fialta

Spring in Fialta is cloudy and dull. Everything is damp: the piebald trunks of the plane trees, the juniper shrubs, the railings, the gravel. Far away, in a watery vista between the jagged edges of pale bluish houses, which tottered up from their knees to climb the slope (a cypress indicating the way), the blurred Mount St George is more than ever remote from its likeness on the picture postcards which since 1910, say (those straw hats, those youthful cabmen), have been courting the tourist from the sorry-go-round of their prop, among amethyst-toothed lumps of rock and the mantelpiece dreams of sea-shells. The air is windless and warm, with a faint tang of burning. The sea, its salt drowned in a solution of rain, is less glaucous than grey with waves too sluggish to break into foam.

It was on such a day in the early thirties that I found myself, all my senses wide open, on one of Fialta's steep little streets, taking in everything at once, that marine rococo on the stand, and the coral crucifixes in a show window, and the dejected poster of a visiting circus, one corner of its drenched paper detached from the wall, and a yellow bit of unripe orange peel on the old, slate-blue sidewalk, which retained here and there a fading memory of ancient mosaic design. I am fond of Fialta; I am fond of it because I feel in the hollow of those violaceous syllables the sweet dark dampness of the most rumpled of small flowers, and because the alto-like name of a lovely Crimean town is echoed by its viola; and also because there is something in the very somnolence of its humid Lent that especially anoints one's soul. So I was happy to be there again, to trudge uphill in inverse direction to the rivulet of the gutter, hatless, my head wet, my skin already suffused with warmth, although I wore only a light macintosh over my shirt.

I had come on the Capparabella express, which, with that reckless gusto peculiar to trains in mountainous country, had done its thundering best to collect throughout the night as many tunnels as possible. A day or two, just as long as a breathing spell in the midst of a business trip would allow me, was all I expected to stay. I had left my wife and children at home, and that was an island of happiness always present in the clear north of my being, always floating beside me, and even through me, I dare say, but yet keeping on the outside of me most of the time.

A pantless infant of the male sex, with a taut mud-grey little belly, jerkily stepped down from a doorstep and waddled off, bow-legged, trying to carry three oranges at once, but continuously dropping the variable third, until he fell himself, and then a girl of twelve or so, with a string of heavy beads around her dusky neck and wearing a skirt as long as that of a gipsy, promptly took away the whole lot with her more nimble and more numerous hands. Nearby, on the wet terrace of a café, a waiter was wiping the slabs of tables; a melancholy brigand hawking local lollipops, elaborate-looking things with a lunar gloss, had placed a hopelessly full basket on the cracked balustrade, over which the two were conversing. Either the drizzle had stopped or Fialta had got so used to it that she herself did not know whether she was breathing moist air or warm rain. Thumb-filling his pipe from a rubber pouch as he walked, a plus-foured Englishman of the solid exportable sort came from under an arch and entered a pharmacy, where large pale sponges in a blue vase were dying a thirsty death behind their glass. What luscious elation I felt rippling through my veins, how gratefully my whole being responded to the flutters and effluvia of that grey day saturated with a vernal essence which itself it seemed slow in perceiving! My nerves were unusually receptive after a sleepless night; I assimilated everything: the whistling of a thrush in the almond trees beyond the chapel, the peace of the crumbling houses, the pulse of the distant sea, panting in the mist, all this together with the jealous green of bottle glass bristling along the top of a wall and the fast colours of a circus advertisement featuring a feathered Indian on a rearing horse in the act of lassoing a boldly endemic zebra, while some thoroughly fooled elephants sat brooding upon their star-spangled thrones.

Presently the same Englishman overtook me. As I absorbed him along with the rest, I happened to notice the sudden side-roll of his big blue eye straining at its crimson canthus, and the way he rapidly moistened his lips—because of the dryness of those sponges, I thought; but then I followed the direction of his glance, and saw Nina.

Every time I had met her during the fifteen years of our—well, I fail to find the precise term for our kind of relationship—she had not seemed to recognize me at once; and this time too she remained quite still for a moment, on the opposite sidewalk, half turning towards me in sympathetic incertitude mixed with curiosity, only her yellow scarf already on the move like those dogs that recognize you before their owners do—and then she uttered a cry, her hands up, all her ten fingers dancing, and in the middle of the street, with merely the frank impulsiveness of an old friendship (just as she would rapidly make the sign of the cross over me every time we parted), she kissed me thrice with more mouth than meaning, and then walked beside me, hanging on to me, adjusting her stride to mine, hampered by her narrow brown skirt perfunctorily slit down the side.

'Oh yes, Ferdie is here too,' she replied and immediately in her turn inquired nicely after Elena.

'Must be loafing somewhere around with Segur,' she went on in reference to her husband. 'And I have some shopping to do; we leave after lunch. Wait a moment, where are you leading me, Victor dear?'

Back into the past, back into the past, as I did every time I met her, repeating the whole accumulation of the plot from the very beginning up to the last increment—thus in Russian fairy tales the already told is bunched up again at every new turn of the story. This time we had met in warm and misty Fialta, and I could not have celebrated the occasion with greater art, could not have adorned with bright vignettes the list of fate's former services, even if I had known that this was to be the last one; the last one, I maintain, for I cannot imagine any heavenly firm of brokers that might consent to arrange me a meeting with her beyond the grave.

My introductory scene with Nina had been laid in Russia quite a long time ago, around 1917 I should say, judging by certain left-wing theatre rumblings back-stage. It was at some birthday party at my aunt's on her country estate, near Luga, in the deepest folds of winter (how well I remember the first sign of nearing the place: a red barn in a white wilderness). I had just graduated from the Imperial Lyceum; Nina was already engaged: although she was of my age and of that of the century, she looked twenty at least, and this in spite or perhaps because of her neat slender build, whereas at thirty-two that very slightness of hers made her look younger. Her fiancé was a guardsman on leave from the front, a handsome heavy fellow, incredibly well-bred and stolid, who weighed every word on the scales of the most exact common sense and spoke in a velvety baritone, which grew smoother when he addressed her; his decency and devotion probably got on her nerves; and he is now a successful if somewhat lonesome engineer in a most distant tropical country.

Windows light up and stretch their luminous lengths upon the dark billowy snow, making room for the reflection of the fan-shaped light above the front door between them. Each of the two side-pillars is fluffily fringed with white, which rather spoils the lines of what might have been a perfect *ex-libris* for the book of our two lives. I cannot recall why we had all wandered out of the sonorous hall into the still darkness, peopled only with firs, snow-swollen to twice their size; did the watchmen invite us to look at a sullen red glow in the sky, portent of nearing arson? Possibly. Did we go to admire an equestrian statue of ice sculptured near the pond by the Swiss tutor of my cousins? Quite as likely. My memory revives only on the way back to the brightly symmetrical mansion towards which we tramped in single file along a narrow furrow between snow-banks, with that crunch-crunch-crunch which is the only comment that a taciturn winter night makes upon humans. I walked last; three singing steps ahead of me walked a small bent shape; the firs gravely showed their burdened paws. I slipped and dropped the dead flashlight someone had forced upon me; it was devilishly hard to retrieve; and instantly attracted by my curses, with an eager, low laugh in anticipation of fun, Nina dimly veered towards me. I call her Nina, but I could hardly have known her name yet, hardly could we have had time, she and I, for any preliminary. 'Who's that?' she asked with interest—and I was already kissing her neck, smooth and quite fiery hot from the long fox fur of her coat-collar, which kept getting into my way until she clasped my shoulder, and with the candour so peculiar to her gently fitted her generous, dutiful lips to mine.

But suddenly parting as by its explosion of gaiety, the theme of a snowball fight started in the dark, and someone, fleeing, falling, crunching, laughing and panting, climbed a drift, tried to run, and uttered a horrible groan: deep snow had performed the amputation of an Arctic. And soon after, we all dispersed to our respective homes, without my having talked with Nina, nor made any plans about the future, about those fifteen itinerant years that had already set out towards the dim horizon, loaded with the parts of our un-assembled meetings; and as I watched her in the maze of gestures and shadows of gestures of which the rest of that evening consisted (probably parlour games—with Nina per-sistently in the other camp), I was astonished, I remember, not so much by her inattention to me after that warmth in the snow as by the innocent naturalness of that inattention, for I did not yet know that had I said a word it would have changed at once into a wonderful sunburst of kindness, a cheerful, compassionate attitude with all possible co-opera-tion, as if woman's love were spring water containing salubri-ous salts which at the least notion she ever so willingly gave anyone to drink.

'Let me see, where did we last meet,' I began (addressing the Fialta version of Nina) in order to bring to her small face with prominent cheek-bones and dark-red lips a certain ex-pression I knew; and sure enough, the shake of her head and the puckered brow seemed less to imply forgetfulness than to deplore the flatness of an old joke; or to be more exact, it was as if all those cities where fate had fixed our various rendez-vous without ever attending them personally, all those plat-forms and stairs and three-walled rooms and dark back alleys, were trite settings remaining after some other lives all brought to a close long before and were so little related to the acting out of our own aimless destiny that it was almost bad taste to mention them.

I accompanied her into a shop under the arcades; there, in the twilight beyond a beaded curtain, she fingered some red leather purses stuffed with tissue paper, peering at the price tags, as if wishing to learn their museum names. She wanted, she said, exactly that shape but in fawn, and when after ten minutes of frantic rustling the old Dalmatian found such a freak by a miracle that has puzzled me ever since, Nina, who was about to pick some money out of my hand, changed her mind and went through the streaming beads without having bought anything.

Outside it was just as milky dull as before; the same smell of burning, stirring by Tartar memories, drifted from the bare windows of the pale houses; a small swarm of gnats was busy darning the air above a mimosa, which bloomed list-lessly, her sleeves trailing to the very ground; two workmen in broad-brimmed hats were lunching on cheese and garlic; their backs against a circus billboard, which depicted a red hussar and an orange tiger of sorts; curious—in his effort to make the beast as ferocious as possible, the artist had gone so far that he had come back from the other side, for the tiger's face looked positively human.

'*Au fond*, I wanted a comb,' said Nina with belated regret.

How familiar to me were her hesitations, second thoughts, third thoughts mirroring first ones, ephemeral worries be-tween trains. She had always either just arrived or was about to leave, and of this I find it hard to think without feeling humiliated by the variety of intricate routes one feverishly follows in order to keep that final appointment which the most confirmed dawdler knows to be unavoidable. Had I to submit before judges of our earthly existence a specimen of her average pose, I would have perhaps placed her leaning upon a counter at Cook's, left calf crossing right shin, left toe tapping floor, sharp elbows and coin-spilling bag on the counter, while the employee, pencil in hand, pondered with her over the plan of an eternal sleeping car.

After the exodus from Russia, I saw her—and that was the second time—in Berlin at the house of some friends. I was about to get married; she had just broken with her fiancé. As I entered that room I caught sight of her at once and, having glanced at the other guests, I instinctively determined which of the men knew more about her than I. She was sitting in the corner of a couch, her feet pulled up, her small comfortable body folded in the form of a Z; an ash-tray stood aslant on the couch near one of her heels; and, having squinted at me and listened to my name, she removed her stalk-like cigarette holder from her lips and proceeded to utter slowly and joyfully, 'Well, of all people——' and at once it became clear to everyone, beginning with her, that we had long been on intimate terms: unquestionably, she had forgotten all about the actual kiss, but somehow because of that trivial occurrence she found herself recollecting a vague stretch of warm, pleasant friendship, which in reality had never existed between us. Thus the whole cast of our relationship was fraudulently based upon an imaginary amity—which had nothing to do with her random goodwill. Our meeting proved quite insignificant in regard to the words we said, but already no barriers divided us; and when that night I happened to be seated beside her at supper, I shamelessly tested the extent of her secret patience.

Then she vanished again; and a year later my wife and I were seeing my brother off to Posen, and when the train had gone, and we were moving towards the exit along the other side of the platform, suddenly near a car of the Paris express I saw Nina, her face buried in the bouquet she held, in the midst of a group of people whom she had befriended without my knowledge and who stood in a circle gaping at her as idlers gape at a street row, a lost child or the victim of an accident. Brightly she signalled to me with her flowers; I introduced her to Elena, and in that life-quickening atmosphere of a big railway station where everything is something trembling on the brink of something else, thus to be clutched and cherished, the exchange of a few words was enough to enable two totally dissimilar women to start calling each other by their pet names the very next time they met. That day, in the blue shade of the Paris car, Ferdinand was first mentioned: I learned with a ridiculous pang that she was about to marry him. Doors were beginning to slam; she quickly but piously kissed her friends, climbed into the vestibule, disappeared; and then I saw her through the glass settling herself in her compartment, having suddenly forgotten about us or passed

into another world, and we all, our hands in our pockets,
seemed to be spying upon an utterly unsuspecting life
moving in that aquarium dimness, until she grew aware of us
and drummed on the window-pane, then raised her eyes,
fumbling at the frame as if hanging a picture, but nothing
happened; some fellow passenger helped her, and she leaned
out, audible and real, beaming with pleasure; one of us,
keeping up with the stealthily gliding car, handed her a
magazine and a Tauchnitz (she read English only when
travelling); all was slipping away with beautiful smoothness,
and I held a platform ticket crumpled beyond recognition,
while a song of the last century (connected, it has been
rumoured, with some Parisian drama of love) kept ringing in
my head, having emerged, God knows why, from the music-
box of memory, a sobbing ballad which often used to be sung
by an old maiden aunt of mine, with a face as yellow as
Russian church wax, but whom nature had given such a
powerful, ecstatically full voice that it seemed to swallow her
up in the glory of a fiery cloud as soon as she would begin:

> *On dit que tu te maries,*
> *tu sais que j'en vais mourir,*

and that melody, the pain, the offence, the link between
hymen and death evoked by the rhythm and the voice itself
of the dead singer, which accompanied the recollection as the
sole owner of the song, gave me no rest for several hours after
Nina's departure and even later arose at increasing intervals
like the last flat little waves sent to the beach by a passing
ship, lapping ever more infrequently and dreamily, or like
the bronze agony of a vibrating belfry after the bell-ringer
has already reseated himself in the cheerful circle of his
family. And another year or two later, I was in Paris on
business; and one morning on the landing of a hotel, where I
had been looking up a film-actor fellow, there she was again,
clad in a grey tailored suit, waiting for the elevator to take
her down, a key dangling from her fingers. 'Ferdinand has
gone fencing,' she said conversationally; her eyes rested on
the lower part of my face as if she were lip-reading, and after
a moment of reflection (her amatory comprehension was

matchless), she turned and rapidly swaying on slender ankles led me along the sea-blue carpeted passage. A chair at the door of her room supported a tray with the remains of breakfast—a honey-stained knife, crumbs on the grey porcelain; but the room had already been done, and because of our sudden draught a wave of muslin embroidered with white dahlias got sucked in, with a shudder and knock, between the responsive halves of the french window, and only when the door had been locked did they let go that curtain with something like a blissful sigh; and a little later I stepped out on the diminutive cast-iron balcony beyond to inhale a combined smell of dry maple leaves and gasoline—the dregs of the hazy blue morning street; and as I did not yet realize the presence of that growing morbid pathos which was to embitter so my subsequent meetings with Nina, I was probably quite as collected and carefree as she was, when from the hotel I accompanied her to some office or other to trace a suitcase she had lost, and thence to the café where her husband was holding session with his court of the moment.

I will not mention the name (and what bits of it I happen to give here appear in decorous disguise) of that man, that Franco-Hungarian writer ... I would rather not dwell upon him at all, but I cannot help it—he is surging up from under my pen. Today one does not hear much about him; and this is good, for it proves that I was right in resisting his evil spell, right in experiencing a creepy chill down my spine whenever this or that new book of his touched my hand. The fame of his life circulates briskly but soon grows heavy and stale; and as for history it will limit his life story to the dash between two dates. Lean and arrogant, with some poisonous pun ever ready to fork out and quiver at you, and with a strange look of expectancy in his dull brown veiled eyes, this false wag had, I daresay, an irresistible effect on small rodents. Having mastered the art of verbal invention to perfection, he particularly prided himself on being a weaver of words, a title he valued higher than that of a writer; personally, I never could understand what was the good of thinking up books, of penning things that had not really happened in some way or other; and I remember once saying to him as I braved the mockery of his encouraging nods that, were I a writer, I should allow only my heart to have imagination, and for the rest rely upon memory, that long-drawn sunset shadow of one's personal truth.

I had known his books before I knew him; a faint disgust was already replacing the aesthetic pleasure which I had suffered his first novel to give me. At the beginning of his career, it had been possible perhaps to distinguish some human landscape, some old garden, some dream-familiar disposition of trees through the stained glass of his prodigious prose ... but with every new book the tints grew still more dense, the gules and purpure still more ominous; and today one can no longer see anything at all through that blazoned, ghastly rich glass, and it seems that were one to break it, nothing but a perfectly black void would face one's shivering soul. But how dangerous he was in his prime, what venom he squirted, with what whips he lashed when provoked! The tornado of his passing satire left a barren waste where felled oaks lay in a row, and the dust still twisted, and the unfortunate author of some adverse review, howling with pain, spun like a top in the dust.

At the time we met, his *Passage à niveau* was being acclaimed in Paris; he was, as they say, 'surrounded', and Nina (whose adaptability was an amazing substitute for the culture she lacked) had already assumed if not the part of a muse at least that of a soul mate and subtle adviser, following Ferdinand's creative convolutions and loyally sharing his artistic tastes; for although it is wildly improbable that she had ever waded through a single volume of his, she had a magic knack of gleaning all the best passages from the shop talk of literary friends.

An orchestra of women was playing when we entered the café, first I noted the ostrich thigh of a harp reflected in one of the mirror-faced pillars, and then I saw the composite table (small ones drawn together to form a long one) at which, with his back to the plush wall, Ferdinand was presiding; and for a moment his whole attitude, the position of his parted hands and the faces of his table companions all turned towards him reminded me in a grotesque, nightmarish way of something I did not quite grasp, but when I did so in retrospect, the suggested comparison struck me as hardly less sacrilegious than

Vladimir Nabokov

the nature of his art itself. He wore a white turtle-neck sweater under a tweed coat; his glossy hair was combed back from the temples, and above it cigarette smoke hung like a halo; his bony, Pharaoh-like face was motionless: the eyes alone roved this way and that, full of dim satisfaction. Having forsaken the two or three obvious haunts where naïve amateurs of Mont-parnassian life would have expected to find him, he had started patronizing this perfectly bourgeois establishment because of his peculiar sense of humour, which made him derive ghoulish fun from the pitiful *spécialité de la maison*—this orchestra composed of half a dozen weary-looking, self-conscious ladies interlacing mild harmonies on a crammed platform and not knowing, as he put it, what to do with their motherly bosoms, quite superfluous in the world of music. After each number he would be convulsed by a fit of epileptic applause, which the ladies had stopped acknow-ledging and which was already arousing, I thought, certain doubts in the minds of the proprietor of the café and its fundamental customers, but which seemed highly diverting to Ferdinand's friends. Among these I recall: an artist with an impeccably bald though slightly chipped head, which under various pretexts he constantly painted into his eye-and-guitar canvases; a poet, whose special gag was the ability to represent, if you asked him, Adam's Fall by means of five matches; a humble business man who financed surrealist ventures (and paid for the *apéritifs*) if permitted to print in a corner eulogistic allusions to the actress he kept; a pianist, presentable in so far as the face was concerned, but with a dreadful expression of the fingers; a jaunty but linguistically impotent Soviet writer fresh from Moscow, with an old pipe and a new wrist watch, who was completely and ridiculously unaware of the sort of company he was in; there were several other gentlemen present who have become confused in my memory, and doubtless two or three of the lot had been intimate with Nina. She was the only woman at the table; there she stooped, eagerly sucking at a straw, the level of her lemonade sinking with a kind of childish celerity, and only when the last drop had gurgled and squeaked, and she had pushed away the straw with her tongue, only then did I finally catch her eye, which I had been obstinately seeking,

218

still not being able to cope with the fact that she had had
time to forget what had occurred earlier in the morning—to
forget it so thoroughly that upon meeting my glance, she
replied with a blank questioning smile, and only after peering more closely did she remember suddenly what kind of
answering smile I was expecting. Meanwhile, Ferdinand (the
ladies having temporarily left the platform after pushing
away their instruments like so many pieces of furniture) was
juicily drawing his cronies' attention to the figure of an
elderly luncher in a far corner of the café, who had, as some
Frenchmen for some reason or other have, a little red ribbon
or something on his coat lapel and whose grey beard combined with his moustaches to form a cosy yellowish nest for
his sloppily munching mouth. Somehow the trappings of old
age always amused Ferdie.

I did not stay long in Paris, but that week proved sufficient
to engender between him and me that fake chumminess the
imposing of which he had such a talent for. Subsequently I
even turned out to be of some use to him: my firm acquired
the film rights of one of his more intelligible stories, and then
he had a good time pestering me with telegrams. As the years
passed, we found ourselves every now and then beaming at
each other in some place, but I never felt at ease in his
presence, and that day in Fialta, too, I experienced a familiar
depression upon learning that he was on the prowl nearby;
one thing, however, considerably cheered me up: the flop of
his recent play.

And there he was coming towards us, garbed in an absolutely waterproof coat with belt and pocket flaps, a camera
across his shoulder, double rubber soles to his shoes, sucking
with an imperturbability that was meant to be funny a long
stick of moonstone candy, that speciality of Fialta's. Beside
him walked the dapper, doll-like, rosy Segur, a lover of art
and a perfect fool; I never could discover for what purpose
Ferdinand needed him; and I still hear Nina exclaiming with
a moaning tenderness that did not commit her to anything:
'Oh, he is such a darling, Segur!' They approached; Ferdinand and I greeted each other lustily, trying to crowd into
handshake and backslap as much fervour as possible, knowing
by experience that actually that was all but pretending it was

only a preface; and it always happened like that: after every separation we met to the accompaniment of strings being excitedly tuned, in a bustle of geniality, in the hubbub of sentiments taking their seats; but the ushers would close the doors, and after that no one was admitted.

Segur complained to me about the weather, and at first I did not understand what he was talking about; even if the moist, grey, greenhouse essence of Fialta might be called 'weather', it was just as much outside of anything that could serve us as a topic of conversation as was, for instance, Nina's slender elbow, which I was holding between finger and thumb, or a bit of tin-foil someone had dropped, shining in the middle of the cobbled street in the distance.

We four moved on, vague purchases still looming ahead. 'God, what an Indian!' Ferdinand suddenly exclaimed with fierce relish, violently nudging me and pointing at a poster, Farther on, near a fountain, he gave his stick of candy to a native child, a swarthy girl with beads round her pretty neck; we stopped to wait for him: he crouched saying something to her, addressing her sooty-black lowered eyelashes, and then he caught up with us, grinning and making one of those remarks with which he loved to spice his speech. Then his attention was drawn by an unfortunate object exhibited in a souvenir shop; a dreadful marble imitation of Mount St George showing a black tunnel at its base, which turned out to be the mouth of an inkwell, and with a compartment for pens in the semblance of railroad tracks. Open-mouthed, quivering, all agog with sardonic triumph, he turned that dusty, cumbersome and perfectly irresponsible thing in his hands, paid without bargaining, and with his mouth still open came out carrying the monster. Like some autocrat who surrounds himself with hunchbacks and dwarfs, he would become attached to this or that hideous object; this infatu-ation might last from five minutes to several days or even longer if the thing happened to be animate.

Nina wistfully alluded to lunch, and seizing the oppor-tunity when Ferdinand and Segur stopped at a post office, I hastened to lead her away. I still wonder what exactly she meant to me, that small dark woman of the narrow shoulders and 'lyrical limbs' (to quote the expression of a mincing *émigré* poet, one of the few men who had sighed platonically after her), and still less do I understand what was the purpose of fate in bringing us constantly together. I did not see her for quite a long while after my sojourn in Paris, and then one day when I came home from my office I found her having tea with my wife and examining on her silk-hosed hand, with her wedding ring gleaming through, the texture of some stockings bought cheap in Tauentzienstrasse. Once I was shown her photograph in a fashion magazine full of autumn leaves and gloves and wind-swept golf links. On a certain Christmas she sent me a picture postcard with snow and stars. On a Riviera beach she almost escaped my notice behind her dark glasses and terracotta tan. Another day, having dropped in on an ill-timed errand at the house of some strangers where a party was in progress, I saw her scarf and fur coat among alien scarecrows on a coat rack. In a bookshop she nodded to me from a page of one of her husband's stories, a page referring to an episodic servant girl, but smuggling in Nina in spite of the author's intention: 'Her face,' he wrote, 'was rather nature's snapshot than a meticulous portrait, so that when ... tried to imagine it, all he could visualize were fleeting glimpses of disconnected features: the downy outline of her pommettes in the sun, the amber-tinted brown darkness of quick eyes, lips shaped into a friendly smile which was always ready to change into an ardent kiss.'

Again and again she hurriedly appeared in the margins of my life, without influencing in the least its basic text. One summer morning (Friday—because housemaids were thumping out carpets in the sun-dusted yard), my family was away in the country and I was lolling and smoking in bed when I heard the bell ring with tremendous violence—and there she was in the hall having burst in to leave (incidentally) a hairpin and (mainly) a trunk illuminated with hotel labels, which a fortnight later was retrieved for her by a nice Austrian boy, who (according to intangible but sure symptoms) belonged to the same very cosmopolitan association of which I was a member. Occasionally, in the middle of a conversation her name would be mentioned and she would run down the steps of a chance sentence, without turning her head. While travelling in the Pyrenees, I spent a week at the château belonging to people with whom she and Ferdinand happened to be staying, and I shall never forget my first night there: how I waited, how certain I was that without my having to tell her she would steal to my room, how she did not come, and the din thousands of crickets made in the delirious depth of the rocky garden dripping with moonlight, the mad bubbling brooks, and my struggle between blissful southern fatigue after a long day of hunting on the screes and the wild thirst for her stealthy coming, low laugh, pink ankles above the swan's-down trimming of high-heeled slippers; but the night raved on, and she did not come, and when next day, in the course of a general ramble in the mountains, I told her of my waiting, she clasped her hands in dismay—and at once with a rapid glance estimated whether the backs of the gesticulating Ferd and his friend had sufficiently receded. I remember talking to her on the telephone across half of Europe (on her husband's business) and not recognizing at first her eager barking voice; and I remember once dreaming of her: I dreamt that my eldest girl had run in to tell me the doorman was sorely in trouble—and when I had gone down to him, I saw lying on a trunk, a roll of burlap under her head, pale-lipped and wrapped in a woollen kerchief, Nina fast asleep, as miserable refugees sleep in God-forsaken railway stations. And regardless of what happened to me or to her, in between, we never discussed anything, as we never thought of each other during the intervals in our destiny, so that when we met the pace of life altered at once, all its atoms were recombined, and we lived in another, lighter time-medium, which was measured not by the lengthy separations but by those few meetings of which a short, supposedly frivolous life was thus artificially formed. And with each new meeting I grew more and more apprehensive; no—I did not experience any inner emotional lapse, the shadow of tragedy did not haunt our revels, my married life remained unimpaired, while on the other hand her electric husband ignored her casual affairs although deriving some profit from them in the way of pleasant and useful connections. I grew apprehensive because something lovely, delicate and unrepeatable was being wasted: something which I abused by snapping off poor bright bits in gross haste while neglecting the modest but true core which perhaps it kept offering me in a pitiful whisper. I was apprehensive because, in the long run, I was somehow accepting Nina's life, the lies, the futility, the gibberish of that life. Even in the absence of any sentimental discord, I felt myself bound to seek for a rational, if not moral, interpretation of my existence, and this meant choosing between the world in which I sat for my portrait, with my wife, my young daughters, the Doberman pinscher (idyllic garlands, a signet ring, a slender cane), between that happy, wise and good world ... and what? Was there any practical chance of life together with Nina, life I could barely imagine, for it would be penetrated, I knew, with a passionate, intolerable bitterness and every moment of it would be aware of a past, teeming with protean partners. No, the thing was absurd. And moreover was she not chained to her husband by something stronger than love—the staunch friendship between two convicts? Absurd! But then what should I have done with you, Nina, how should I have disposed of the store of sadness that had gradually accumulated as a result of our seemingly carefree, but really hopeless meetings?

Fialta consists of the old town and of the new one; here and there, past and present are interlaced, struggling either to disentangle themselves or to thrust each other out; each one has its own methods: the newcomer fights honestly—importing palm trees, setting up smart tourist agencies, painting with creamy lines the red smoothness of tennis courts; whereas the sneaky old-timer creeps out from behind a corner in the shape of some little street on crutches or the steps of stairs leading nowhere. On our way to the hotel, we passed a half-built white villa, full of litter within, on a wall of which again the same elephants, their monstrous baby knees wide apart, sat on huge, gaudy drums; in ethereal bundles the equestrienne (already with a pencilled moustache) was resting on a broad-backed steed; and a tomato-nosed clown was walking a tight-rope, balancing an umbrella ornamented with those recurrent stars—a vague symbolic recollection of the heavenly fatherland of circus performers. Here, in the Riviera part of Fialta, the wet gravel crunched in a more luxurious manner, and the lazy sighing of the sea was more audible. In the back yard of the hotel, a kitchen boy armed with a knife was pursuing a hen which was clucking madly as it raced for its life. A boot-black offered me his ancient throne with a toothless smile. Under the plane trees stood a motor-cycle of German make, a mud-bespattered limousine and a yellow-bodied Icarus that looked like a giant scarab: ('That's ours—Segur's, I mean,' said Nina, adding: 'Why don't you come with us, Victor?' although she knew very well that I could not come); in the lacquer of its elytra a gouache of sky and branches was engulfed; in the metal of one of the bomb-shaped lamps we ourselves were momentarily reflected, lean film-land pedestrians passing along the convex surface; and then, after a few steps, I glanced back and foresaw, in an almost optical sense, as it were, what really happened an hour or so later: the three of them wearing motoring helmets, getting in, smiling and waving to me, transparent to me like ghosts, with the colour of the world shining through them, and then they were moving, receding, diminishing (Nina's last ten-fingered farewell); but actually the automobile was still standing quite motionless, smooth and whole like an egg, and Nina under my outstretched arm was entering a laurel-flanked doorway, and as we sat down we could see through the window Ferdinand and Segur, who had come by another way, slowly approaching.

There was no one on the veranda where we lunched except the Englishman I had recently observed; in front of him, a long glass containing a bright crimson drink threw an oval reflection on the tablecloth. In his eyes, I noticed the same bloodshot desire, but now it was in no sense related to Nina; that avid look was not directed at her at all, but was fixed on the upper right-hand corner of the broad window near which he was sitting.

Having pulled the gloves off her small thin hands, Nina, for the last time in her life, was eating the shellfish of which she was so fond. Ferdinand also busied himself with food. and I took advantage of his hunger to begin a conversation which gave me the semblance of power over him: to be specific, I mentioned his recent failure. After a brief period of fashion-able religious conversation, during which grace descended upon him and he undertook some rather ambiguous pilgrim-ages, which ended in a decidedly scandalous adventure, he had turned his dull eyes towards barbarous Moscow. Now, frankly speaking, I have always been irritated by the complacent conviction that a ripple of stream consciousness, a few healthy obscenities and a dash of Communism in any old slop-pail will alchemically and automatically produce ultra-modern literature; and I will contend until I am shot that art as soon as it is brought into contact with politics inevitably sinks to the level of any ideological trash. In Ferdinand's case, it is true, all this was rather irrelevant: the muscles of his muse were exceptionally strong, to say nothing of the fact that he didn't care a damn for the plight of the underdog; but because of certain obscurely mischievous undercurrents of that sort, his art had become still more repulsive. Except for a few snobs none had understood the play; I had not seen it myself, but could well imagine that elaborate Kremlinesque night along the impossible spirals of which he spun various wheels of dismembered symbols; and now, not without pleasure, I asked him whether he had read a recent bit of criticism about himself.

'Criticism!' he exclaimed. 'Fine criticism! Every slick jackanapes sees fit to read me a lecture. Ignorance of my work is their bliss. My books are touched gingerly, as one touches something that may go bang. Criticism! They are examined from every point of view except the essential one. It is as if a naturalist in describing the equine genus, started to jaw about saddles or Mme de V.' (he named a well-known literary hostess, who indeed strongly resembled a grinning horse). 'I would like some of that pigeon's blood, too,' he continued in the same loud, ripping voice, addressing the waiter, who understood his desire only after he had looked in the direction of the long-nailed finger which unceremoniously pointed at the Englishman's glass. For some reason or other, Segur mentioned Ruby Rose, the lady who painted flowers on her breast, and the conversation took on a less insulting character. Meanwhile the big Englishman suddenly made up his mind, got up on a chair, stepped from there on to the window-sill and stretched up till he reached that coveted corner of the frame where rested a compact furry moth, which he deftly slipped into a pill-box.

'... rather like Wouwerman's white horse,' said Ferdinand,

in regard to something he was discussing with Segur.

'*Tu es très hippique ce matin*,' remarked the latter.

Soon they both left to telephone. Ferdinand was particularly fond of long-distance calls, and particularly good at endowing them, no matter what the distance, with a friendly warmth when it was necessary, as for instance now, to make sure of free lodgings.

From afar came the sounds of music—a trumpet, a zither. Nina and I set out to wander again. The circus on its way to Fialta had apparently sent out runners: an advertising pageant was tramping by; but we did not catch its head, as it had turned uphill into a side alley: the gilded back of some carriage was receding, a man in a burnous led a camel, a file of four mediocre Indians carried placards on poles, and behind them, by special permission, a tourist's small son in a sailor suit sat reverently on a tiny pony.

We wandered by a café where the tables were now almost dry but still empty; the waiter was examining (I hope he adopted it later) a horrible foundling, the absurd inkstand affair, stowed by Ferdinand on the banisters in passing. At the next corner we were attracted by an old stone stairway, and we climbed up, and I kept looking at the sharp angle of Nina's step as she ascended, raising her skirt, its narrowness requiring the same gesture as formerly length had done; she diffused a familiar warmth, and going up beside her, I recalled the last time we had come together. It had been in a Paris house, with many people around, and my dear friend Jules Darboux, wishing to do me a refined aesthetic favour, had touched my sleeve and said, 'I want you to meet——' and led me to Nina, who sat in the corner of a couch, her body folded Z-wise, with an ash-tray at her heel, and she took a long turquoise cigarette holder from her lips and joyfully, slowly exclaimed, 'Well, of all people——' and then all the evening my heart felt like breaking, as I passed from group to group with a sticky glass in my fist, now and then looking at her from a distance (she did not look . . .), and listened to scraps of conversation, and overheard one man saying to another, 'Funny, how they all smell alike, burnt leaf through whatever perfume they use, those angular dark-haired girls,' and as it often happens, a trivial remark related to some unknown topic coiled and clung to one's own intimate recollection, a parasite of its sadness.

At the top of the steps, we found ourselves on a rough kind of terrace. From here one could see the delicate outline of the dove-coloured Mount St George with a cluster of bone-white flecks (some hamlet) on one of its slopes; the smoke of an indiscernible train undulated along its rounded base—and suddenly disappeared; still lower, above the jumble of roofs, one could perceive a solitary cypress, resembling the moist-twirled black tip of a water-colour brush; to the right, one caught a glimpse of the sea, which was grey, with silver wrinkles. At our feet lay a rusty old key, and on the wall of the half-ruined house adjoining the terrace, the ends of some wire still remained hanging ... I reflected that formerly there had been life here, a family had enjoyed the coolness at night-fall, clumsy children had coloured pictures by the light of a lamp ... We lingered there as if listening to something; Nina, who stood on higher ground, put a hand on my shoulder and smiled, and carefully, so as not to crumple her smile, kissed me. With an unbearable force, I relived (or so it now seems to me) all that had ever been between us beginning with a similar kiss; and I said (substituting for our cheap, formal 'thou' that strangely full and expressive 'you' to which the circumnavigator, enriched all around, returns), 'Look here— what if I love you?' Nina glanced at me, I repeated those words, I wanted to add ... but something like a bat passed swiftly across her face, a quick, queer, almost ugly expression, and she, who would utter coarse words with perfect sim-plicity, became embarrassed; I also felt awkward ... 'Never mind, I was only joking,' I hastened to say, lightly encircling her waist. From somewhere a firm bouquet of small dark, unselfishly smelling violets appeared in her hands, and before she returned to her husband and car, we stood for a little while longer by the stone parapet, and our romance was even more hopeless than it had ever been. But the stone was as warm as flesh, and suddenly I understood something I had been seeing without understanding—why a piece of tin-foil had sparkled so on the pavement, why the gleam of a glass had trembled on a tablecloth, why the sea was a-shimmer: somehow, by imperceptible degrees, the white sky above

Fialta had got saturated with sunshine, and now it was sun-pervaded throughout, and this brimming white radiance grew broader and broader, all dissolved in it, all vanished, all passed, and I stood on the station platform of Mlech with a freshly bought newspaper, which told me that the yellow car I had seen under the plane trees had suffered a crash beyond Fialta, having run at full speed into the truck of a travelling circus entering the town, a crash from which Ferdinand and his friend, those invulnerable rogues, those salamanders of fate, those basilisks of good fortune, had escaped with local and temporary injury to their scales, while Nina, in spite of her long-standing, faithful imitation of them, had turned out after all to be mortal.

Paris, 1938

DYLAN THOMAS

'A fanfare of sunshades opening.'

1945

Holiday Memory

August Bank Holiday—a tune on an ice-cream cornet. A slap of sea and a tickle of sand. A fanfare of sunshades opening. A wince and whinny of bathers dancing into deceptive water. A tuck of dresses. A rolling of trousers. A compromise of paddlers. A sunburn of girls and a lark of boys. A silent hullabaloo of balloons.

I remember the sea telling lies in a shell held to my ear for a whole harmonious, hollow minute by a small, wet girl in an enormous bathing suit marked Corporation Property.

I remember sharing the last of my moist buns with a boy and a lion. Tawny and savage, with cruel nails and capacious mouth, the little boy tore and devoured. Wild as seedcake, ferocious as a hearthrug, the depressed and verminous lion nibbled like a mouse at his half a bun and hiccupped in the sad dusk of his cage.

I remember a man like an alderman or a bailiff, bowlered and collarless, with a bag of monkeynuts in his hand, crying 'Ride 'em cowboy!' time and again as he whirled in his chairaplane giddily above the upturned laughing faces of the town girls bold as brass and the boys with padded shoulders and shoes sharp as knives; and the monkeynuts flew through the air like salty hail.

Children all day capered or squealed by the glazed or bashing sea, and the steam-organ wheezed its waltzes in the threadbare playground and the waste lot, where the dodgems dodged, behind the pickle factory.

And mothers loudly warned their proud pink daughters or sons to put that jellyfish down; and fathers spread newspapers over their faces; and sandfleas hopped on the picnic lettuce;

and someone had forgotten the salt.

In those always radiant, rainless, lazily rowdy and skyblue summers departed, I remember August Monday from the rising of the sun over the stained and royal town to the husky hushing of the roundabout music and the dowsing of the naphtha jets in the seaside fair: from bubble-and-squeak to the last of the sandy sandwiches.

There was no need, that holiday morning, for the sluggardly boys to be shouted down to breakfast; out of their jumbled beds they tumbled, and scrambled into their rumpled clothes; quickly at the bathroom basin they catlicked their hands and faces, but never forgot to run the water loud and long as though they washed like colliers; in front of the cracked looking-glass, bordered with cigarette cards, in their treasure-trove bedrooms, they whisked a gap-tooth comb through their surly hair; and with shining cheeks and noses and tidemarked necks, they took the stairs three at a time.

But for all their scramble and scamper, clamour on the landing, catlick and toothbrush flick, hair-whisk and stair-jump, their sisters were always there before them. Up with the lady lark, they had prinked and frizzed and hot-ironed; and smug in their blossoming dresses, ribboned for the sun, in gymshoes white as the blanco'd snow, neat and silly with doilies and tomatoes they helped in the higgledy kitchen. They were calm; they were virtuous; they had washed their necks; they did not romp, or fidget; and only the smallest sister put out her tongue at the noisy boys.

And the woman who lived next door came into the kitchen and said that her mother, an ancient uncertain body who wore a hat with cherries, was having one of her days and had insisted, that very holiday morning, in carrying, all the way to the tramstop, a photograph album and the cutglass fruit-bowl from the front room.

This was the morning when father, mending one hole in the thermos-flask, made three; when the sun declared war on the butter, and the butter ran; when dogs, with all the sweet-binned backyards to wag and sniff and bicker in, chased their tails in the jostling kitchen, worried sandshoes, snapped at flies, writhed between legs, scratched among towels, sat smiling on hampers.

And if you could have listened at some of the open doors of some of the houses in the street you might have heard:

'Uncle Owen says he can't find the bottle-opener——'

 'Has he looked under the hallstand?'

'Willy's cut his finger——'

 'Got your spade?'

'If somebody doesn't kill that dog——'

'Uncle Owen says why should the bottle-opener be under the hallstand?'

'Never again, never again——'

'I know I put the pepper somewhere——'

 'Willy's bleeding——'

'Look, there's a bootlace in my bucket——'

 'Oh come *on*, come *on*——'

'Let's have a look at the bootlace in your bucket——'

 'If I lay my hands on that dog——'

'Uncle Owen's found the bottle-opener——'

 'Willy's bleeding over the cheese——'

And the trams that hissed like ganders took us all to the beautiful beach.

There was cricket on the sand, and sand in the spongecake, sandflies in the watercress, and foolish, mulish, religious donkeys on the unwilling trot. Girls undressed in slipping tents of propriety; under invisible umbrellas, stout ladies dressed for the male and immoral sea. Little naked navvies dug canals; children with spades and no ambition built fleeting castles; wispy young men, outside the bathing-huts, whistled at substantial young women and dogs who desired thrown stones more than the bones of elephants. Recalcitrant uncles huddled, over luke ale, in the tiger-striped marquees. Mothers in black, like wobbling mountains, gasped under the discarded dresses of daughters who shrilly braved the gobbling waves. And fathers, in the once-a-year sun, took fifty winks. Oh, think of all the fifty winks along the paper-bagged sand.

Liquorice allsorts, and Welsh hearts, were melting. And the sticks of rock, that we all sucked, were like barbers' poles made of rhubarb.

In the distance, surrounded by disappointed theoreticians and an ironmonger with a drum, a cross man on an orange-box shouted that holidays were wrong. And the waves rolled in, with rubber ducks and clerks upon them.

I remember the patient, laborious and enamouring hobby, or profession, of burying relatives in sand.

I remember the princely pastime of pouring sand, from cupped hands or bucket, down collars of tops of dresses; the shriek, the shake, the slap.

I can remember the boy by himself, the beachcombing lone-wolf, hungrily waiting at the edge of family cricket; the friendless fielder, the boy uninvited to bat or to tea.

I remember the smell of sea and seaweed, wet flesh, wet hair, wet bathing-dresses, the warm smell as of a rabbity field after rain, the smell of pop and splashed sunshades and toffee, the stable-and-straw smell of hot, tossed, tumbled, dug and trodden sand, the swill-and-gaslamp smell of Saturday night, though the sun shone strong, from the bellying beer-tents, the smell of the vinegar on shelled cockles, winkle-smell, shrimp-smell, the dripping-oily backstreet winter-smell of chips in newspapers, the smell of ships from the sundazed docks round the corner of the sandhills, the smell of the known and paddled-in sea moving, full of the drowned and herrings, out and away and beyond and further still towards the antipodes that hung their koala-bears and Maoris, kangaroos and boomerangs, upside down over the backs of the stars.

And the noise of pummelling Punch and Judy falling, and a clock tolling or telling no time in the tenantless town; now and again a bell from a lost tower or a train on the lines behind us clearing its throat, and always the hopeless, ravenous swearing and pleading of the gulls, donkey-bray and hawker-cry, harmonicas and toy trumpets, shouting and laughing and singing, hooting of tugs and tramps, the clip of the chair-attendant's puncher, the motor-boat coughing in the bay, and the same hymn and washing of the sea that was heard in the Bible.

'If it could only just, if it could only just,' your lips said again and again as you scooped, in the hob-hot sand, dungeons, garages, torture-chambers, train tunnels, arsenals, hangars for zeppelins, witches' kitchens, vampires' parlours, smugglers' cellars, trolls' grog-shops, sewers, under the ponderous and cracking castle, 'If it could only just be like this for ever and ever amen.' August Monday all over the earth, from Mumbles where the aunties grew like ladies on a seaside tree to brown, bear-hugging Henty-land and the turtled Ballantyne Islands.

'Could donkeys go on the ice?'

'Only if they got snowshoes.'

We snowshoed a meek, complaining donkey and galloped him off in the wake of the ten-foot-tall and Atlas-muscled Mounties, rifled and pemmicanned, who always, in the white Gold Rush wastes, got their black-oathed-and-bearded Man.

'Are there donkeys on desert islands?'

'Only sort-of-donkeys.'

'What d'you mean, sort-of-donkeys?'

'Native donkeys. They hunt things on them!'

'Sort-of walruses and seals and things?'

'Donkeys can't swim!'

'These donkeys can. They swim like whales, they swim like anything, they swim like——'

'Liar.'

'Liar yourself.'

And two small boys fought fiercely and silently in the sand, rolling together in a ball of legs and bottoms. Then they went and saw the pierrots, or bought vanilla ices.

Lolling or larriking that unsoiled, boiling beauty of a common day, great gods with their braces over their vests sang, spat pips, puffed smoke at wasps, gulped and ogled, forgot the rent, embraced, posed for the dicky-bird, were coarse, had rainbow-coloured armpits, winked, belched, blamed the radishes, looked at Ilfracombe, played hymns on paper and comb, peeled bananas, scratched, found seaweed in their panamas, blew up paper-bags and banged them, wished for nothing. But over all the beautiful beach I remember most the children playing, boys and girls tumbling, moving jewels, who might never be happy again. And 'happy as a sandboy' is true as the heat of the sun.

Dusk came down; or grew up out of the sands and the sea; or curled around us from the calling docks and the bloodily smoking sun. The day was done, the sands brushed and ruffled suddenly with a sea-broom of cold wind. And we gathered together all the spades and buckets and towels, empty hampers and bottles, umbrellas and fishfrails, bats and balls and knitting, and went—oh, listen, Dad!—to the Fair in the dusk on the bald seaside field.

Fairs were no good in the day; then they were shoddy and tired; the voices of hoopla girls were crimped as elocutionists; no cannonball could shake the roosting coconuts; the gondolas mechanically repeated their sober lurch; the Wall of Death was safe as a governess-cart; the wooden animals were waiting for the night.

But in the night, the hoopla girls, like operatic crows, croaked at the coming moon; whizz, whirl and ten for a tanner, the coconuts rained from their sawdust like grouse from the Highland sky; tipsy the griffon-prowed gondolas weaved on dizzy rails, and the Wall of Death was a spinning rim of ruin, and the neighing wooden horses took, to a haunting hunting tune, a thousand Beecher's Brooks as easily and breezily as hooved swallows.

Approaching, at dusk, the Fair-field from the beach, we scorched and gritty boys heard above the belabouring of the batherless sea the siren voices of the raucous, horsy barkers.

'Roll up, roll up!'

In her tent and her rolls of flesh the Fattest Woman in the World sat sewing her winter frock, another tent, and fixed her little eyes, blackcurrants in blancmange, on the skeletons who filed and sniggered by.

'Roll up, roll up, roll up to see the Largest Rat on the Earth, the Rover or Bonzo of vermin.'

Here scampered the smallest pony, like a Shetland shrew. And here the Most Intelligent Fleas, trained, reined, bridled and bitted, minutely cavorted in their glass corral.

Round galleries and shies and stalls, pennies were burning holes in a hundred pockets. Pale young men with larded hair and Valentino-black sidewhiskers, fags stuck to their lower lips, squinted along their swivel-sighted rifles and aimed at ping-pong balls dancing on fountains. In knife-creased, silver-grey, skirt-like Oxford bags, and a sleeveless, scarlet, zip-fastened shirt with yellow horizontal stripes, a collier at the strength-machine spat on his hands, raised the hammer, and brought it Thor-ing down. The bell rang for Blaina.

Outside his booth stood a bitten-eared and barn-door-chested pug with a nose like a twisted swede and hair that startled from his eyebrows and three teeth yellow as a camel's, inviting any sportsman to a sudden and sickening basting in the sandy ring or a quid if he lasted a round; and wiry, cocky, bow-legged, coal-scarred, boozed sportsmen by the dozen strutted in and reeled out; and still those three teeth remained, chipped and camel-yellow in the bored, teak face.

Draggled and stout-wanting mothers, with haphazard hats, hostile hatpins, buns awry, bursting bags, and children at their skirts like pop-filled and jam-smeared limpets, screamed, before distorting mirrors, at their suddenly tapering or tubular bodies and huge ballooning heads, and the children gaily bellowed at their own reflected bogies withering and bulging in the glass.

Old men, smelling of Milford Haven in the rain, shuffled, badgering and cadging, round the edges of the swaggering crowd, their only wares a handful of damp confetti. A daring dash of schoolboys, safely, shoulder to shoulder, with their fathers' trilbies cocked at a desperate angle over one eye, winked at and whistled after the procession past the swings of two girls arm-in-arm: always one pert and pretty, and always one with glasses. Girls in skulled and cross-boned tunnels shrieked, and were comforted. Young men, heroic after pints, stood up on the flying chairaplanes, tousled, crimson and against the rules. Jaunty girls gave sailors sauce.

All the Fun of the Fair in the hot, bubbling night. The Man in the sand-yellow Moon over the hurdy of gurdies. The swingboats swimming to and fro like slices of the moon. Dragons and hippogriffs at the prows of the gondolas breathing fire and Sousa. Midnight roundabout rides tantivying under the fairylights, huntsmen on billygoats and zebras hallooing under a circle of glow-worms.

And as we climbed home, up the gas-lit hill, to the still house over the mumbling bay, we heard the music die and the voices drift like sand. And we saw the lights of the Fair fade. And, at the far end of seaside field, they lit their lamps, one by one, in the caravans.

1946

A Story

If you can call it a story. There's no real beginning or end and there's very little in the middle. It is all about a day's outing, by charabanc, to Porthcawl, which, of course, the charabanc never reached, and it happened when I was so high and much nicer.

I was staying at the time with my uncle and his wife. Although she was my aunt, I never thought of her as anything but the wife of my uncle, partly because he was so big and trumpeting and red-hairy and used to fill every inch of the hot little house like an old buffalo squeezed into an airing cupboard, and partly because she was so small and silk and quick and made no noise at all as she whisked about on padded paws, dusting the china dogs, feeding the buffalo, setting the moustraps that never caught her; and once she sleaked out of the room, to squeak in a nook or nibble in the hayloft, you forgot she had ever been there.

But there he was, always, a steaming hulk of an uncle, his braces straining like hawsers, crammed behind the counter of the tiny shop at the front of the house, and breathing like a brass band; or guzzling and blustery in the kitchen over his gutsy supper, too big for everything except the great black boats of his boots. As he ate, the house grew smaller; he billowed out over the furniture, the loud check meadow of his waistcoat littered, as though after a picnic, with cigarette ends, peelings, cabbage stalks, birds' bones, gravy; and the forest fire of his hair crackled among the hooked hams from the ceiling. She was so small she could hit him only if she stood on a chair; and every Saturday night at half-past ten he would lift her up, under his arm, on to a chair in the kitchen so that she could hit him on the head with whatever was handy, which was always a china dog. On Sundays, and when pickled, he sang high tenor, and had won many cups.

The first I heard of the annual outing was when I was sitting one evening on a bag of rice behind the counter,

A Story

under one of my uncle's stomachs, reading an advertisement
for sheep-dip, which was all there was to read. The shop was
full of my uncle, and when Mr Benjamin Franklyn, Mr
Weazley, Noah Bowen and Will Sentry came in, I thought it
would burst. It was like all being together in a drawer that
smelled of cheese and turps, and twist tobacco and sweet
biscuits and snuff and waistcoat. Mr Benjamin Franklyn said
that he had collected enough money for the charabanc and
twenty cases of pale ale and a pound apiece over that he
would distribute among the members of the outing when
they first stopped for refreshment, and he was about sick and
tired, he said, of being followed by Will Sentry.

'All day long, wherever I go,' he said, 'he's after me like a
collie with one eye. I got a shadow of my own *and* a dog. I
don't need no Tom, Dick or Harry pursuing me with his
dirty muffler on.'

Will Sentry blushed, and said, 'It's only oily. I got a
bicycle.'

'A man has no privacy at all,' Mr Franklyn went on. 'I tell
you he sticks so close I'm afraid to go out the back in case I sit
in his lap. It's a wonder to me,' he said, 'he don't follow me
into bed at night.'

'Wife won't let,' Will Sentry said.

And that started Mr Franklyn off again, and they tried to
soothe him down by saying, 'Don't you mind Will Sentry.'
'No harm in old Will.' 'He's only keeping an eye on the
money, Benjie.'

'Aren't I honest?' asked Mr Franklyn in surprise. There
was no answer for some time; then Noah Bowen said, 'You
know what the committee is. Ever since Bob the Fiddle they
don't feel safe with a new treasurer.'

'Do you think *I'm* going to drink the outing funds, like
Bob the Fiddle did?' said Mr Franklyn.

'You *might*,' said my uncle, slowly.

'I resign,' said Mr Franklyn.

'Not with our money you won't,' Will Sentry said.

'Who put the dynamite in the salmon pool?' said Mr
Weazley, but nobody took any notice of him. And, after a
time, they all began to play cards in the thickening dusk of

237

the hot, cheesy shop, and my uncle blew and bugled whenever he won, and Mr Weazley grumbled like a dredger, and I fell to sleep on the gravy-scented mountain meadow of uncle's waistcoat.

On Sunday evening, after Bethesda, Mr Franklyn walked into the kitchen where my uncle and I were eating sardines from the tin with spoons because it was Sunday and his wife would not let us play draughts. She was somewhere in the kitchen, too. Perhaps she was inside the grandmother clock, hanging from the weights and breathing. Then, a second later, the door opened again and Will Sentry edged into the room, twiddling his hard, round hat. He and Mr Franklyn sat down on the settee, stiff and moth-balled and black in their chapel and funeral suits.

'I brought the list,' said Mr Franklyn. 'Every member fully paid. You ask Will Sentry.'

My uncle put on his spectacles, wiped his whiskery mouth with a handkerchief big as a Union Jack, laid down his spoon of sardines, took Mr Franklyn's list of names, removed the spectacles so that he could read, and then ticked the names off one by one.

'Enoch Davies. Aye. He's good with his fists. You never know. Little Gerwain. Very melodious bass. Mr Cadwalladwr. That's right. He can tell opening time better than my watch. Mr Weazley. Of course. He's been to Paris. Pity he suffers so much in the charabanc. Stopped us nine times last year between the Beehive and the Red Dragon. Noah Bowen. Ah, very peaceable. He's got a tongue like a turtledove. Never a argument with Noah Bowen. Jenkins Loughor. Keep him off economics. It cost us a plateglass window. And ten pints for the Sergeant. Mr Jervis. Very tidy.'

'He tried to put a pig in the charra,' Will Sentry said.

'Live and let live,' said my uncle.

Will Sentry blushed.

'Sinbad the Sailor's Arms. Got to keep in with him. Old O. Jones.'

'Why old O. Jones?' said Will Sentry.

'Old O. Jones always goes,' said my uncle.

I looked down at the kitchen table. The tin of sardines was gone. By Gee, I said to myself, Uncle's wife is quick as a flash.

'Cuthbert Johnny Fortnight. Now there's a card,' said my uncle.

'He whistles after women,' Will Sentry said.

'So do you,' said Mr Benjamin Franklyn, 'in your mind.'

My uncle at last approved the whole list, pausing only to say, when he came across one name, 'If we weren't a Christian community, we'd chuck that Bob the Fiddle in the sea.'

'We can do that in Porthcawl,' said Mr Franklyn, and soon after that he went, Will Sentry no more than an inch behind him, their Sunday-bright boots squeaking on the kitchen cobbles.

And then, suddenly, there was my uncle's wife standing in front of the dresser, with a china dog in one hand. By Gee, I said to myself again, did you ever see such a woman, if that's what she is. The lamps were not lit yet in the kitchen and she stood in a wood of shadows, with the plates on the dresser behind her shining—like pink-and-white eyes.

'If you go on that outing on Saturday, Mr Thomas,' she said to my uncle in her small, silk voice, 'I'm going home to my mother's.'

Holy Mo, I thought, she's got a mother. Now that's one old bald mouse of a hundred and five I won't be wanting to meet in a dark lane.

'It's me or the outing, Mr Thomas.'

I would have made my choice at once, but it was almost half a minute before my uncle said, 'Well, then, Sarah, it's the outing, my love.' He lifted her up, under his arm, on to a chair in the kitchen, and she hit him on the head with the china dog. Then he lifted her down again, and then I said good night.

For the rest of the week my uncle's wife whisked quiet and quick round the house with her darting duster, my uncle blew and bugled and swole, and I kept myself busy all the time being up to no good. And then at breakfast time on Saturday morning, the morning of the outing, I found a note on the kitchen table. It said, 'There's some eggs in the pantry. Take your boots off before you go to bed.' My uncle's wife had gone, as quick as a flash.

When my uncle saw the note, he tugged out the flag of his handkerchief and blew such a hubbub of trumpets that the plates on the dresser shook. 'It's the same every year,' he said. And then he looked at me. 'But this year it's different. *You'll* have to come on the outing, too, and what the members will say I dare not think.'

The charabanc drew up outside, and when the members of the outing saw my uncle and me squeeze out of the shop together, both of us cat-licked and brushed in our Sunday best, they snarled like a zoo.

'Are you bringing a *boy?*' asked Mr Benjamin Franklyn as we climbed into the charabanc. He looked at me with horror.

'Boys is nasty,' said Mr Weazley.

'He hasn't paid his contributions,' Will Sentry said.

'No room for boys. Boys get sick in charabancs.'

'So do you, Enoch Davies,' said my uncle.

'Might as well bring *women.*'

The way they said it, women were worse than boys.

'Better than bringing grandfathers.'

'Grandfathers is nasty too,' said Mr Weazley.

'What can we do with him when we stop for refreshments?'

'I'm a grandfather,' said Mr Weazley.

'Twenty-six minutes to opening time,' shouted an old man in a panama hat, not looking at a watch. They forgot me at once.

'Good old Mr Cadwalladwr,' they cried, and the charabanc started off down the village street.

A few cold women stood at their doorways, grimly watching us go. A very small boy waved good-bye, and his mother boxed his ears. It was a beautiful August morning.

We were out of the village, and over the bridge and up the hill towards Steeplehat Wood when Mr Franklyn, with his list of names in his hand, called out loud, 'Where's Old O. Jones?'

'Where's old O.?'

'We've left old O. behind.'

'Can't go without old O.'

And though Mr Weazley hissed all the way, we turned and drove back to the village, where, outside the Prince of Wales, old O. Jones was waiting patiently and alone with a canvas bag.

'I didn't want to come at all,' old O. Jones said as they

hoisted him into the charabanc and clapped him on the back and pushed him on a seat and stuck a bottle in his hand, 'but I always go.' And over the bridge and up the hill and under the deep green wood and along the dusty road we wove, slow cows and ducks flying by, until 'Stop the bus!' Mr Weazley cried, 'I left my teeth on the mantelpiece.'

'Never you mind,' they said, 'you're not going to bite nobody,' and they gave him a bottle with a straw.

'I might want to smile,' he said.

'Not you,' they said.

'What's the time, Mr Cadwalladwr?'

'Twelve minutes to go,' shouted back the old man in the panama, and they all began to curse him.

The charabanc pulled up outside the Mountain Sheep, a small, unhappy public house with a thatched roof like a wig with ringworm. From a flagpole by the Gents fluttered the flag of Siam. I knew it was the flag of Siam because of cigarette cards. The landlord stood at the door to welcome us, simpering like a wolf. He was a long, lean, black-fanged man with a greased love-curl and pouncing eyes. 'What a beautiful August day!' he said, and touched his love-curl with a claw. That was the way he must have welcomed the Mountain Sheep before he ate it, I said to myself. The members rushed out, bleating, and into the bar.

'You keep an eye on the charra,' my uncle said, 'see nobody steals it now.'

'There's nobody to steal it,' I said, 'except some cows,' but my uncle was gustily blowing his bugle in the bar. I looked at the cows opposite, and they looked at me. There was nothing else for us to do. Forty-five minutes passed, like a very slow cloud. The sun shone down on the lonely road, the lost, unwanted boy, and the lake-eyed cows. In the dark bar they were so happy they were breaking glasses. A Shoni-Onion Breton man, with a beret and a necklace of onions, bicycled down the road and stopped at the door.

'*Quelle un grand matin, monsieur,*' I said.

'There's French, boy bach!' he said.

I followed him down the passage, and peered into the bar. I could hardly recognize the members of the outing. They had all changed colour. Beetroot, rhubarb and puce, they hollered and rollicked in that dark, damp hole like enormous ancient bad boys, and my uncle surged in the middle, all red whiskers and bellies. On the floor was broken glass and Mr Weazley.

'Drinks all round,' cried Bob the Fiddle, a small, absconding man with bright blue eyes and a plump smile.

'Who's been robbing the orphans?'

'Who sold his little babby to the gyppoes?'

'Trust old Bob, he'll let you down.'

'You will have your little joke,' said Bob the Fiddle, smiling like a razor, 'but I forgive you, boys.'

Out of the fug and babel I heard: 'Where's old O. Jones?' 'Where are you old O.?' 'He's in the kitchen cooking his dinner.' 'He never forgets his dinner time.' 'Good old O. Jones.' 'Come out and fight.' 'No, not now, later.' 'No, now when I'm in a temper.' 'Look at Will Sentry, he's proper snobbled.' 'Look at his wilful feet.' 'Look at Mr Weazley lording it on the floor.'

Mr Weazley got up, hissing like a gander. 'That boy pushed me down deliberate,' he said, pointing to me at the door, and I slunk away down the passage and out to the mild, good cows.

Time clouded over, the cows wondered, I threw a stone at them and they wandered, wondering, away. Then out blew my Uncle, ballooning, and one by one the members lumbered after him in a grizzle. They had drunk the Mountain Sheep dry. Mr Weazley had won a string of onions that the Shoni-Onion man had raffled in the bar.

'What's the good of onions if you left your teeth on the mantelpiece?' he said. And when I looked through the back window of the thundering charabanc, I saw the pub grow smaller in the distance. And the flag of Siam, from the flagpole by the Gents, fluttered now at half mast.

The Blue Bull, the Dragon, the Star of Wales, the Twll in the Wall, the Sour Grapes, the Shepherd's Arms, the Bells of Aberdovey: I had nothing to do in the whole wild August world but remember the names where the outing stopped and keep an eye on the charabanc. And whenever it passed a public house, Mr Weazley would cough like a billy goat and cry, 'Stop the bus, I'm dying of breath.' And back we would all have to go.

Closing time meant nothing to the members of that outing. Behind locked doors, they hymned and rumpused all the beautiful afternoon. And, when a policeman entered the Druid's Tap by the back door, and found them all choral with beer, 'Sssh!' said Noah Bowen, 'the pub is shut.'

'Where do you come from?' he said in his buttoned, blue voice.

They told him.

'I got a auntie there,' the policeman said. And very soon he was singing 'Asleep in the Deep.'

Off we drove again at last, the charabanc bouncing with tenors and flagons, and came to a river that rushed along among willows.

'Water!' they shouted.

'Porthcawl!' sang my uncle.

'Where's the donkeys?' said Mr Weazley.

And out they lurched, to paddle and whoop in the cool, white, winding water. Mr Franklyn, trying to polka on the slippery stones, fell in twice. 'Nothing is simple,' he said with dignity as he oozed up the bank.

'It's cold!' they cried.

'It's lovely!'

'It's smooth as a moth's nose!'

'It's *better* than Porthcawl!'

And dusk came down warm and gentle on thirty wild, wet, pickled, splashing men without a care in the world at the end of the world in the west of Wales. And, 'Who goes there?' called Will Sentry to a wild duck flying.

They stopped at the Hermit's Nest for a rum to keep out the cold. 'I played for Aberavon in 1898,' said a stranger to Enoch Davies.

'Liar,' said Enoch Davies.

'I can show you photos,' said the stranger.

'Forged,' said Enoch Davies.

'And I'll show you my cap at home.'

'Stolen.'

'I got friends to prove it,' the stranger said in a fury.

'Bribed,' said Enoch Davies.

On the way home, through the simmering moon-splashed dark, old O. Jones began to cook his supper on a primus stove in the middle of the charabanc. Mr Weazley coughed himself blue in the smoke. 'Stop the bus!' he cried, 'I'm dying of breath.' We all climbed down into the moonlight. There was not a public house in sight. So they carried out the remaining cases, and the primus stove, and old O. Jones himself, and took them into a field, and sat down in a circle in the field and drank and sang while old O. Jones cooked sausage and mash and the moon flew above us. And there I drifted to sleep against my uncle's mountainous waistcoat, and, as I slept, 'Who goes there?' called out Will Sentry to the flying moon.

1953

V. S. PRITCHETT

'Awful things happen to one every day.'

London W1, 1960

The Skeleton

Awful things happen to one every day: they come without warning and—this is the trouble, for who knows?—the next one may be the Great Awful Thing. Whatever that is.

At half-past seven, just as the new day came aching into the London sky, the waiter-valet went up in the old-fashioned lift of the service flats with a tray of tea to Mr Clark's flat at the top floor. He let himself in and walked down the long, tiled hallway, through part of Mr Clark's picture collection, into the large sitting-room and putting the tray down on the desk, drew back the curtains and looked down on the roofs. Arrows of fine snow had shot along the slate, a short sight of the Thames between the buildings was as black as iron, the trees stuck out their branches like sticks of charcoal and a cutting wind was rumbling and occasionally squealing against the large windows. The man wiped his nose and then went off to switch on one bar of the electric fire—he was forbidden to put on two—and moved the tray to a table by the fire. He had often been scolded for putting the tray upon Clark's valuable Chippendale desk, and he looked around to see if anything else was out of place in this gentlemanly room where every flash of polish or glass was as unnerving to him as the flash of old George Clark's glasses.

With its fine mahogany, its glazed bookcases which contained a crack regiment of books on art in dress uniform, its Persian rugs, its bronzes, figurines and silken-seated chairs and deep sofa that appeared never to have been sat on, and on the walls some twenty-five oil-paintings, the room had the air of a private museum. The valet respected the glass. He had often sat for a while at Mr Clark's desk gossiping with one of the maids while he saw to it that she did not touch the bronze and the Chinese figures—'He won't allow anyone to touch them. They're worth hundreds—thousands,' and making guesses at what the lot would fetch when the old man died. He made these guesses about the property of all the rich old people who lived in the flats.

The girls, an ignorant lot, Irish mainly these days, gaped at the pictures.

'He's left them all to the nation,' the valet would say importantly. He could not disguise his feeling that the poor old nation had a lot to put up with from the rich. He could always get in a sexy word to the maids when they looked at the cylindrical nude with a guitar lying across her canister-like knees. But the other pictures of vegetation—huge fruits, enormous flowers that looked tropical with gross veins and pores on stalk and leaves—looked humanly physical and made him feel sick. The flowers had large evil sucking mouths; there were veined intestinal marrows; there was a cauliflower like a gigantic brain that seemed to swell as you looked at it. Nature, to this painter, was a collection of clinical bodies and looked, as Seymour said, 'Nood.' The only living creature represented—apart from the cylindrical lady —was a fish, but it, too, was over-sized and gorged. Its scales, minutely enumerated, gave Seymour 'the pip'. It was hung over the central bookcase.

'It doesn't go with the furniture,' Seymour had often said. The comforting thing to him was that, at any rate, the collection could not move and get at him. Like the books, the pictures, too, were cased behind glass.

'All by the same man. Come into the bedroom. Come on. And don't touch anything there because he'll notice. He sees everything,' he'd say.

In the bedroom he would show the girls the small oil-painting of the head of a young man with almost white hair standing on end, and large blue eyes.

'That's the bloke,' the valet would say. 'He did it himself. Self-portrait. John Flitestone—see, the name's at the bottom—cut his throat. You watch—his eyes follow you,' he would say, steering the girl. 'He used to come here with the old man.'

'Oh,' the girls were apt to gasp.

'Stop it, Mr Seymour,' they added, taken off their guard.

'Years ago,' Seymour said, looking pious after the pinch he'd given them.

The valet left the room and went down the passage to George Clark's bedroom. Carpet stopped at the door of the room. Inside the room the curtains were blowing, the two sparse rugs lifting in the draught on the polished floor and snow spitting on the table beside the bed. He caught the curtains and drew them back and tried to shut the heavy window. The room contained a cheap yellow wardrobe and chest of drawers which old George Clark had had since he was a boy. The sitting-room was luxurious but his bedroom was as bleak as a Victorian servant's. On a very narrow iron bedstead he lay stiff as a frozen monk and still as a corpse, so paper thin as to look bodiless, his wiry black hair, his wiry black moustache and his greenish face and cold red nose showing like a pug's over the sheet. It sneered in sleep.

'Seven-thirty, sir. Terrible morning,' he said. There was no answer. 'By God,' the valet said after a pause, 'the old man's dead.' In death—if that was what it was—the face on the pillow looked as if it could bite. Then the old man gave a snuffle.

The old man opened a wicked eye.

'The old bastard,' murmured the valet. Often the old boy had terrified and tricked him with his corpse-like look. It was Clark's opening victory in a day, indeed a life, devoted to victory. Then he woke up fully, frightened, reaching for his glasses, to see Seymour's blood-coloured face looking down at him.

'What?' George Clark said. And then the valet heard him groan. These groans were awful.

'Oh my God!' George Clark groaned, but spoke the words in a whisper.

'It's a terrible morning. Shall I put on the fire?'

'No.' The old man sat up.

The valet sighed. He went and fetched a cup of tea.

'You'll need this,' he put on his bullying voice. 'Better drink it hot in here. You'd better have your lunch here today. Don't you go to the club. It's snowing, the wind's terrible.'

George Clark got out of bed in his flannel pyjamas. He stepped barefooted to the window, studying the driving grey sky, the slant of snow and the drift of chimney smoke.

'Who closed the window?' he said.

'Oh dear,' said the valet to himself, 'now he's going to begin.'

'The snow was coming in, Mr Clark. You'll get pneumonia. Please, sir.'

Clark was upright and tall. His small head jerked when he talked, on a long, wrinkled neck. His voice was naturally drawling but shortness of breath was in conflict with the drawl and the sounds that came out were jerky, military and cockerel-like. At eighty-two he looked about sixty, there was hardly any grey in his moustache, the bridge of his gold-framed glasses cut into his red nose. Seymour who was fifty was humped and lame and looked seventy. In a fight old George would win and he gave a sniff that showed he knew it. In fact, he got up every day to win; Seymour knew that and accepted it.

What reduced him to misery was that the old man would *explain* his victories. He was off on one now.

'No, I won't get pneumonia,' old George snapped. 'You see, Seymour, it's a north wind. The north wind doesn't touch me. There's no fat on me, I'm all bones. I'm a skeleton, there's nothing for it to bite on.'

'No, sir,' said Seymour wretchedly. Ten to one George Clark would now mention his family. He did.

'My father was thin, so was my grandfather, we're a thin family. My youngest sister—she's seventy-eight—she's all bones like me.'

Oh God (Seymour used to moan to himself), I forgot—he's got a sister! Two of them! He moved to get out of the room, but the old man followed him closely, talking fast.

'One day last week I thought we were going to catch it, oh yes. Now we're going to get it, I said! Awful thing! That clean white light in the sky, stars every night, everything clear, everything sparkling. I saw it and said, Oh no! No, no. I don't like this, oh no.'

He had now got Seymour in the doorway.

'You see—I know what *that* means.'

'Yes, sir.'

'East wind,' said George victoriously.

'That's it, sir.'

'Ah, then you've got to look out, Seymour. Oh yes, Awful business. That's what finishes old people. Awful thing.' He drove forward into the sitting-room and went to this window, studying the sky and sniffed two or three times at it.

'We're all right, Seymour. You see, I was right. It's in the north. I shall have lunch at the club. Bring my cup in here. Why did you take it to the bedroom?'

It was a cold flat. George Clark took a cold bath, as he had done ever since his schooldays. Then he ate a piece of toast and drank a second cup of tea and looked eagerly to see what was annoying in the papers—some new annoyance to add to a lifetime's accumulation of annoyances. It was one of the calamities of old age that one's memory went and one forgot a quite considerable number of exasperations and awful things in which, contrary to general expectation, one had been startlingly right. This forgetting was bad—as if one were the Duke of Wellington and sometimes forgot one had won the Battle of Waterloo.

In fact, George sat in comfort in a flat packed with past rows, annoyances and awful things, half-forgotten. It was an enormous satisfaction that many of his pictures annoyed the few people who came to see him nowadays. The Flitestones annoyed violently. They had indeed annoyed the nation to such an extent that, in the person of a 'nasty little man' called Gaiterswell, the nation had refused them. (Seymour was wrong there.) George was very proud of this: his denunciation of Gaiterswell was one of the major victories of his life. George had been the first to buy Flitestones and even Flitestone himself had warned the vain and swollen-headed young man against Gaiterswell, years and years ago.

'Modish, Jack, he's merely modish. He'll drop you when it suits him.'

At twelve o'clock George walked across the Park to one of his Clubs. He belonged to three. The Park was empty. He blew across it like a solitary, late leaf. The light snow was turning Whitehall black, and spat on his gold glasses; he arrived, a little breathless, but ready to deal with that bugbear of old men: protective sympathy.

'George! You ought not to be out on a day like this!' several said. One put his arm round his shoulder. They were a sneezing and coughing lot with slack affectionate faces, and friendly overburdened bellies, talking of snowed-up roads, late trains and scrambles for taxis.

'You *walked* through this! Why didn't you make your chauffeur bring you?'

'No car.'

'Or a cab?'

'Fares have gone up. I'm too mean.'

'Or a bus?'

'Oh no, no, you see,' said George glittering at them, 'I don't know if I told you'—he had told them innumerable times—'when you're brought up by a rich brute of a father, as I was—oh yes, he was very rich—you get stingy. I'm very stingy. I must have told you about my father. Oh well, now, there's a story,' he began eagerly. But the bar was crowded; slow to move, George Clark found his listener had been pushed away and had vanished. He stood suddenly isolated in his autobiography.

'Oh God,' he groaned loudly, but in a manner so sepulchral and private, that people moved respectfully away. It was a groan that seemed to come up from the earth, up from his feet, a groan of loneliness that was raging and frightening to the men around him. He had one of those moments which, he had to admit, were much commoner than they used to be, when he felt dizzy; when he felt he was lost among unrecognizable faces, without names, alone, in the wrong club, at the wrong address even, with the tottering story of his life, a story which he was offering or, rather, throwing out as a lifeline, for help. His hand shook as he finished his glass of sherry. The moment passed and, recovering and trembling, he aged as he left the bar and crossed the hall to the dining-room, saying aloud to himself, in his fighting drawl: 'Now, now, now, we must be careful.'

The side tables were already taken but there were gaps at the two long tables. George stood blinking at the battlefield. He had in the last years resigned from several clubs. Sometimes it was because of bridge, central heating, ventilation, smoking, about house committees, food and servants, usually over someone who, unknowingly, had become for a period uncommonly like the Arch Enemy, but who turned out to be no more than an understudy for the part. After a year or so George would rejoin the club. For him the dining-room was one more aspect of the general battlefield. Where should he place his guns? Next to Doyle? No, he was 'a Roman'. George hated 'Romans'. He hated 'Protestants' too. He was an atheist who never found anyone sufficiently atheistical. George was tired of telling Doyle how he had happened to be in Rome in '05 staying with one of the great families ('she was a cousin of the Queen's') and had, for a year, an unparalleled inside view of what was going on in the Vatican. 'Oh yes, you see, a Jesuit, one of their relations, became a great friend and exposed the whole hocus-pocus to me. You see, I have often been in a position to know more of what is going on than most people. I was close to Haig in the war.' There was Gregg, the painter; but it was intolerable to listen to Academicians; there was Foster who had been opposed to Munich and George could not stand that. There was Macdonald— but Scots climb. Look at Lang! There was Jefferies, such a bore about divorce reform; the bishops want it but daren't say so. 'I told the Archbishop in this club that the moment you drag in God you lose your reason. My mother ought to have got a divorce. You should have seen his face. Oh no, he didn't like it. Not a bit.'

George looked at the tops of heads and the table-loads of discarded enemies, casualties of his battles, with a grin. At last, glancing around him, he chose a seat beside a successful, smirking pink man of fifty whose name he had forgotten, 'Pretty harmless,' muttered George. 'He thinks Goya a great painter when we all know he is just a good painter of the second rank. Ah, he's eating oysters.' This stirred a memory. The man was talking to a deaf editor but on the other side there were empty chairs. It was against George's military sense to leave an exposed flank but the chance of attacking the club oysters was too good to miss.

'I see you've risked the oysters. I never eat oyster in this club,' said George, sitting down. 'Poisonous. Oh yes, yes—

didn't I tell you? Oh you see, it was an awful thing, last year...'

'Now George,' said the man. 'You told me that story before.'

'Did I? Nothing in that,' sniffed George. 'I always repeat myself, you see I make a point of telling my stories several times. I woke up in the night...'

'Please George,' said the man more sternly, 'I want to enjoy my lunch.'

'Oh ah, ah, ah,' said George sniffing away. 'I'll watch your plate. I'll warn you if I see a bad one.'

'Oh, really George!' said the young man.

'You're interrupting our conversation, George,' the editor called across. 'I was telling Trevor something very interesting about my trip to Russia.'

'I doubt if it is interesting,' said George in a loudish whisper to the other man. 'Interesting! I never found a Whig interesting.'

'Dear George is old. He talks too much,' said the deaf editor speaking louder than he knew.

'Not a lot of rot,' said George in a loud mutter.

'What's he say?' said the deaf editor.

'You see,' George continued to interrupt. 'I talk a lot because I live alone. I probably talk more than anyone in this club and I am more interesting than most people. You see, I've often been in a position to know more than most people here. I was in Rome in '05...'

But George looked restlessly at the vacant chair beside him. 'I hope,' he said, suddenly nervous, 'some awful bore is not going to sit here. You never know who, who—oh no, oh no, no...'

It happened as simply as that, when one was clean off one's guard. Not a single awful thing; but the Great Awful Thing. He saw a pair of small, polished, sunburned hands with soft black hair on them pull the chair and then a monkeyish man of seventy with wretched eyes and an academic heaving up of the right shoulder, sat beside him.

'Good morning, George,' uttering the name George as if it contained a lifetime's innuendo.

The Skeleton

'Oh God,' George said.

The man was the Arch Enemy and in a form he had never expected. Out of the future he should have come, a shape at a slowly opening door, pausing there, blocking it, so that one could not get out. Who he would be, what he would be, was unknown: he was hidden in next week, next year, as yet unborn.

But this man was known. He had sneaked in not from the future, but from the past. It was Gaiterswell.

'Just the man I want to speak to,' said Gaiterswell, picking up the menu in hands that George could only think of as thieving.

'I didn't know you were a member,' George choked out in words like lead shot.

'Just elected.'

George gave a loud sniff.

'Monstrous,' said George, but, holding on to manners, said it under his breath. He grasped his table napkin, ready to fly off and at once, resign. It was unbelievable that the Committee, knowing his feelings as they must do, had allowed this man in. Gaiterswell who had stolen Flitestone from him: who had turned down Flitestone; who had said in *The Times*—in a letter above all—that George's eccentric tastes had necessarily taught him nothing about the chemical composition of oil-paint; Gaiterswell of the scandalous official appointment!

George had forgotten these Waterloos; but now the roar of them woke up in his brain. The fusillades he had let off in committees were heard again. The letters to *The Times* were shot off once more. Gaiterswell had said there were too many 'gentlemen' in the art world. It was a pity (he was known to have said), it was a pity that the Empire had gone and there were no more natives for them to pester. George had replied, around the clubs, that the 'nasty little man' suffered glaringly from merit and the path of the meritorious was strewn with the bodies they had kicked down the ladder as they climbed.

After he had said things like this, George considered that Gaiterswell was dead. The body could no doubt be found still lying after twenty-five years, in that awful office of his with the fake Manet—of course it was a fake—on the wall.

253

'Just the man I want to speak to,' Gaiterswell said to the menu. (You noticed he never looked you in the face.)

'Wants to speak to me. For no good reason,' George murmured loudly to the man sitting on the other side of him.

'I bet you won't guess who came to see me the other day,' Gaiterswell said. 'Gloria Archer, Stokes that was. She's married to a Frenchman called Duprey. You remember her? What are you eating? The pie! Is it any good? She's got a lot of poor Jack Flitestone's letters. She's short of money. You wrote the *Memoir*, didn't you, George? Charming little book, charming. I told her to drop in on you. I said you'd be delighted to see her.'

George was about to put a piece of pie into his mouth. He put his fork down. He was shaking. He was choking.

'Drop in!' he said, astounded. 'Drop in?'

'Look here,' he called out, pushing his chair from the table. 'Oh, this is monstrous.' And he called to one of the waiters who rushed past and ignored him. 'Look here, I say, why do we have to have meat like this in this club ... It's uneatable ... I shall find the Secretary...'

And getting up, with his table napkin waving from his hand, he hurried to the end of the room, the light tossing in his glasses, and then after wild indecision, left the room.

'Where has George Clark gone?' said an old gentleman who had been sitting opposite. 'He never finishes a meal.'

'It's his teeth,' the deaf editor said.

George had made for the morning-room of the Club where he circled like a dog.

'What manners!' he said to the portraits of dead members on the wall. Happier than he, they were together, he was alone. He was older than most of them had been and, with a flick of ironic pride which never quite left him in any distress, he could not but notice that he was rather better connected and had more inside knowledge than most of them had had. He addressed them again:

'Drop in! What manners! I shall resign.'

The Arch Enemy had appeared in a fashion unpredictable: from the past—and now he saw—not as a male but as a female. Gloria Archer—as he had always said: 'What a

254

name!' It recalled (as he firmly pronounced it), the 'Kinema', striking a blow for classical scholarship. Her portrait, if one could call it that, was in his sitting-room, cylindrical and naked. It had been there for over twenty-five years, with the other Flitestones and he had long ago stopped remembering her or even Flitestone himself as human beings he had known. They were not life; they were art—not even art now, but furniture of his self-esteem. He had long ago closed his mind to them as persons. They had become fossilizations of mere anecdote. Now that damn little shot-up official, Gaiterswell who had been polished off long ago, had brought first Gloria back to life, and the name of Gloria had brought Flitestone back. The seals of anecdote were broken; one of the deepest wounds of George's existence was open and raw again. A woman's work; it was Gloria who had shown how dangerous Flitestone was to him: it was Gloria who had shown him the chaos of his heart.

He left the morning-room, got his hat and coat, buttoned himself up to the neck and walked out into the street where the snow was coming in larger shots. At once he felt something like a film of ice form between his shirt and his bony chest and he stepped back afraid.

'No, no,' he said very loudly and passers-by raised their ducked heads thinking he was talking to them. But he was speaking to the wind: it had gone round to the east.

Seymour met him in the lift at the flat. He smelled of beer.

'You shouldn't have gone out, sir,' said Seymour.

Seymour looked murderous with self-righteousness.

George sat down on his sofa, frightened and exhausted. He was assaulted by real memories and was too weak to fend them off: he had felt frightened to death—he now admitted—in that so enjoyable 1914 war. Flitestone's pictures took on life. Flitestone, too. The cliché vanished—'Not a bad minor painter, like a good many others ruined by the school of Paris'—the dangerous Flitestone appeared. He saw again the poor boy from a Scottish mill town, with gaunt cheeks, light blue eyes and almost white hair that stood up like a dandelion clock—('took hours brushing it, always going to expensive hairdressers'). A pedant, too, with morbid and fanatical patience: it took him longer to paint a picture than anyone George Clark had ever known; the young man was rather deaf which made him seem to be an unworldly, deeply innocent listener, but there was—as George Clark saw—nothing innocent about him, there was a mean calculating streak—('After all he realized I was a rich man,' George swaggered) and he was soon taken up by wealthy people. He was clever and made them laugh. He was in trouble all the time with women, chasing them like a maniac and painting them with little heads and large bottoms, like pairs of enormous pink poppies.

('Now, there's a bloody fine bottom, George.')

Very annoying he was, too, especially when he got into Society. That was one thing George Clark knew all about and to be told about Lord This or That or a lot of duchesses, by a crude young genius from the slums, was infuriating.

'He's got five bloody great castles...'

'Only one. Forstairs and Aldbaron belong to his half-brother who married Glasnevin's sister. Jack, I wish you wouldn't pick your teeth at meals. I can't bear it. It's such frightful manners.'

'Lord Falconer does. He's got a gold toothpick.'

But these squabbles were merely annoying. Flitestone was the only human being George ever loved. Jealously loved. He was his prize and his possession. And the boy liked him. Here was the danger. George had dreaded to be liked. You lose something when people like you. You are in danger of being stripped naked and of losing a skin. With Flitestone he felt—ah there was the danger: he did not know what he felt except that it was passion. He could listen to him for hours. For eleven years, George had the sensation that he had married late in life someone who, fortunately, did not exist, and that Flitestone was their fantastic, blindly-invented son. Like a son he clawed at George's bowels.

His love affairs? Well, one had to avert the eye. They were nevertheless, an insurance against George's instant jealous fear: that Flitestone would marry. The thought of that made George shrink. 'Marriage will ruin you'—he nagged at it. And that was where Gloria came in.

When Gaiterswell spoke of Gloria, a shot of jealous terror and satisfaction had gone through George. She bored him, of course. Yet in the last years of their friendship, Flitestone's insane love for this girl who would have nothing to do with him, was the real guarantee. George even admired the young girl for the cruelty of her behaviour, for being so complete an example of everything that made women impossible. He was so absorbed in this insurance that he forgot the obvious: that Gloria might marry. She did. In a month on the rebound, Flitestone had married some milky, student girl whose first act was to push her husband into the influence of Gaiterswell. For Gaiterswell was the nation. A breach with George was inevitable.

He went to his desk and started writing to Gaiterswell.

I shall be obliged if you will inform Miss Stokes, Mrs Archer or whatever her name is, that I have no desire to meet her or enter into correspondence ... His hand shook. He could not continue.

'Awful business' was all he could say. The Arch Enemy had deprived him even of the power to talk to himself.

The east wind. Impossible to go out to any of his clubs that night. After dinner, he poured himself a very large whisky and left the bottle, uncorked, on his desk—a sinister breach of habit, for he always locked up his drink.

'I always reckon to be rather drunk every evening,' George used to say. It was a gesture to the dignity of gentlemanly befuddlement. But now, he felt his legs go; he was rapidly very drunk. He tottered to his bedroom, dropped his clothes on the floor and got into bed with his shirt, collar and tie on and was asleep at once. Often at night he had enjoyable dreams of social life at Staff H.Q. in the 1914 war. Haig, Ronnie Blackwater and others would turn up. A bit of gunfire added an interest: but this night he had a frightful dream. He dreamed that at the club, before all the members, he had kissed the teeth of George the Fifth.

This woke him up and he saw that it was daylight. His heart was racing. He could not find his glasses. He got out of bed. The room was getting light; he wondered if he were dead and he pulled back the curtain and what he saw convinced him that he was. The snow has stopped, the sky was hard and clear, and the sun was coming up in a gap between two high buildings. It was still low and this made it an enormous raw yellow football that someone had kicked there, without heat or radiance yet. It looked like a joke or some aimless idea; one more day (George realized as he became more conscious) had begun its unsolicited course over the blind slates of the city. 'Old men are lonely,' he often said but now he saw a greater loneliness than his own.

'I want those letters.' The desire came out before he could stop it. 'I must see Gloria. I must get Gaiterswell's dirty little hands off them.' He was longing for the past. Then he saw he was wearing his day shirt, his collar and tie.

'Oh God,' he said. And he got into his pyjamas and back into bed before Seymour should catch him.

At half-past seven Seymour let himself into the flat. His demeanour was of one whose expectations were at last being fulfilled. He had warned several of the old people in the flats about the weather; he had seen Mr Clark come back yesterday exhausted when, against all advice, he had gone to the club. Reaching the sitting-room Seymour saw a decanter of whisky standing on the table. This was a sight that he had thirsted for for years and he gazed at it entranced, unbelieving and with suspicion. He listened. There was no sound. Seymour made a grab at the decanter and took a long swig, letting a drop rest on his chin while he replaced what he had drunk with water from the hot-water pot on the tea-tray. He stood still trying to lick the drip off his chin but, failing, he wiped it off with his sleeve and after looking at the letters on Mr Clark's desk, walked confidently to Mr Clark's bedroom.

'Good morning, Seymour. Half-past seven,' said George. He was sitting up in bed. Seymour heard this reversal of their usual greeting with alarm. He stood well away and slopped the tea in its saucer. He was even more alarmed to see Mr Clark had switched on his own fire and that his clothes were dropped in a muddle on the floor. George caught his glance and got out of bed to show that he was properly dressed and stood with one foot on his rumpled jacket. Panic and the whisky brought guilt into Seymour's face: he suddenly remembered he had made a disastrous mistake. He had forgotten to give Mr Clark a message.

'A lady rang last night, sir, when you were at dinner.'

'A lady—why didn't you tell me?'

'The head waiter took the call. He said you were out. She didn't leave a name.'

To distract an angry question, Seymour looked at the clothes on the floor.

'Dear, dear, dear, what a way to leave a suit.' He pulled the trouser leg from under George's foot and held the trousers up. 'Look at it.'

'What lady?' said George.

'She didn't leave a name. She said she'd drop in.'

'Drop in!' The horrible phrase.

'That's what she said, she'd drop in.'

'Who was it?'

'I don't know, sir. I never took the message. I told you—it was the new head waiter.'

'Don't stand there waving my trousers about like a fool, Seymour. It's your business to know.'

'They're all foreigners downstairs.'

George had his glasses on now and Seymour stepped away. In his panic he took a gamble.

'Might have been Miss Stokes,' he said. He had read the name on George's unfinished letter. The gamble was a mistake.

'Archer!' cried George. 'Where is the head waiter?' And hurrying to the sitting-room, he started banging the telephone. There was no answer.

'What time do the servants come on?' he called to Seymour. Seymour came in and listened to George banging away. He was very scared now. He dreaded that the head waiter would answer.

'They come when it suits them, now. They suit themselves,' said Seymour putting on a miserable manner. And then he got in his blow, the sentence he often used to the old people in the flats when they got difficult. It always silenced them.

'Might just as well sell the place,' he said.

'Sell!' George was silenced, too. He stared at Seymour who straightened himself and said, accusingly:

'Where's the jacket of this? Dear, dear, I suppose that's on the floor too.' And walked out, leaving George shivering where he stood.

'Sell?' said George.

On a long ledge of the stained building opposite, thirty or forty dirty pigeons were huddled, motionless, with puffed out feathers, too cold to fly.

'Out on the street! Homeless.' Like Stebbing-Walker crippled and deaf who had married Kepton's half-sister—she was a Doplestone—and now lay in his nursing home, or Ronnie Blackwater who sat paralysed in the army infirmary. Sell—it was the awful word anxiously whispered in the lift by the old ladies, as they went up and down to their meals. Was the place being sold? Were the rents going up? Were they going to pull the whole place down? For months there would be silence; everyone breathed again; then once more, mostly from Seymour, the rumours began. Fear made them sly and they believed Seymour rather than the management. He moved among them like a torment.

George Clark went down early to luncheon, to get in before the restaurant vanished; rushed upstairs afterwards to barricade himself, so to speak, in his flat. There were few pigeons on the ledge now. What? Had tenancy gone out of Nature too? At seven o'clock he went to dinner. Instead of the two or three tables of old doll-like couples in the middle of the room, there was a large table at which ten large young men, loud and commercial, were laughing together. One or two had briefcases with them. Obviously this was the group who were going to pull down the flats. George raced through the meal, feeling that, possibly, even before the apples and custard, he might be sitting out alone on a vacant site. George's fighting spirit revived over his wine. 'Ha,' he sneered at them as he left the table and went to the lift, 'I'll be dead before you can turn me out.'

The lift wheezed and wobbled upwards, making the sound of all the elderly throats in the building. He was startled to see the door of his flat open and, for a moment, thought the men had broken in already; but Seymour was standing in the cold hall. His heavy face looked criminal. In an insinuating, lugubrious voice he said:

'The lady's waiting to see you, sir.'

'Seymour, I've told you, never...' George hurried to his sitting-room. Gloria was standing by his desk reading the letter he had begun so often.

Dear Gaiterswell, I would have thought that common decency...

'Oh, oh, no, no, I say,' said George greeting her, but was stopped.

A fur coat and a close fitting black hat like a faded turban with brass colour hair sticking out of it, rushed at him, a hot powdery face kissed him with a force that made him crack in his joints like a stick.

'Oh George, darling, I dropped in.' Gloria shouted at him through large stained teeth and laughed.

All he could see was these teeth and lipstick and blue eyes and she was laughing and laughing as she wiped the lipstick off his face.

'Oh well,' he said, 'they're selling the place...' Then she stood back in a pair of cracking shoes.

'George,' she said in a Cockney voice. 'It's marvellous. You haven't changed at all. You're not a day older.'

And she let her fur coat fall open and slip back on her shoulders and he saw the cigarette ash and one or two marks on the bosom of her black dress. She was a big woman.

'Oh,' George recovered and gave a victorious sniff. 'I'm eighty-two.'

'You're a boy,' she cried.

'Oh no, don't think I'm deceived by that sort of talk—er, well, you see I mean...' George nearly smiled. By his reckoning she was in her fifties and he could see what she wanted, what all women wanted, compliments. He was not, at his age, going to fall for that old game. She sat down on the sofa so as to show off her fine legs.

'Did you recognize me?' she asked.

'Oh well, you know...'

'Oh come on, George.'

'I dare say I—er—might have done. You see, I forget names and faces, it's an awful business ... old people ... they're selling this place...'

'Oh you crusty old thing. What do you mean—selling?' she said. 'You always were crusty. I knew you'd be at dinner, so I got that man to bring me up. What is his name? Is he all right? I didn't feel very comfortable with him in the lift.'

She moved her body and pouted.

'When your lady friends call you ought to tell them to keep an eye—well, George, how are you? How many years is it? It must be twenty-five. You weren't living here then.'

'It was the beginning of the war,' said George, but he could not remember. He had discarded memory as useless a long time back. He had seen her a lot, yet one of his few clear recollections was of sitting with Flitestone in the old Café Royal waiting for her to come in and arguing with him that she was not a woman who would stick to any man: he remembered her really as an absence.

'You've put on weight,' he said. But she hadn't changed much.

'Yes,' she said. 'I like it, don't you?'

The Cockney voice came warm and harsh out of the wide mouth. Her skin was rougher and was now looser on her bones but still had a wide-pored texture and the colourlessness which Flitestone used to say was like linen. One spot of colour in her cheeks and Flitestone would probably never have fallen for her. 'She's like a canvas. I'd like to paint *on* her,' Flitestone used to say to George. He did remember. The bare maleness of face on a girlish body was still there on the body of the full woman.

George stood, shaking at the sight of her.

'You're still an old bachelor, George?' she said. 'You didn't marry?'

'No,' said George with a grin of victory. 'You see, in my day, one never met any girls, everyone was chaperoned, you couldn't speak and we had no one to the house, oh no, my father wouldn't allow anyone and then the war, and all that. I told you about my father, oh, now, there's a story...'

'Oh, I've been. Three times,' she cut in, parading herself.

'Oh three! Well, that's interesting. Or I suppose it is. It doesn't surprise me. Please sit down. Let me get you a drink. Now let me see, keys. I have to keep it locked, well with the servants it isn't fair to leave drink about. Ah, in this pocket. I keep them here.'

He fussed at the cupboard and brought out a bottle of whisky and a bottle of sherry.

'Oh gin please,' she said. 'Can I help?'

'No, no, it's here. I keep it at the back. I'll put this bottle down here, yes, that's the way...' he chattered to himself.

Gloria walked across the room to look at the pictures, but stopped instead to look at her reflection in the glass of the bookcases and to rearrange the frilled neck of her dress. Then she looked up at the large picture of the fish.

'George! You've got my fish.'

'Ah yes, the fish. He painted four fish pictures. One is in the Tate, one is ... now where is it?'

'*My* fish, I mean,' she said. 'Don't you remember, it's the one I made you carry to Jack's place and the paper came off...'

'No, no,' said George.

'Yes, you must remember. You're not still cross, are you? You looked so funny.'

She took a deep breath in front of the picture, inhaling it.

'I don't know why we didn't eat it.'

'Ah yes. Awful business. Café Royal,' said George, a memory coming back.

She turned to the cylindrical woman in a shift, with enormous column-like legs, who was playing a guitar, and looked with flirtatious annoyance at it, paying off an old score.

'That's me,' she said.

'Oh, no,' said George sarcastically. He was beginning to enjoy himself. 'It was done in Paris.'

'It's me,' said Gloria. 'But they're Violet's legs.' Gloria turned abruptly away, insulted, and taking her drink from George went back to the sofa. Once more she gave a large sigh and gazed with admiring calculation at the room. She leaned her head to one side and smiled at George.

'You are a dear, George. How cosy you are! It's wonderful to see old friends,' said Gloria sweetly. 'It brings it all back.'

She got up and put more gin in her drink and then leaned over his chair as she passed him and kissed the top of his head.

'Dear George,' she said and sat down. 'And you live here,

all alone! Well, George, I've brought the letters, all Jack's letters to me. I didn't know I had them. It's a funny thing: François found them, my husband, he's French. We live in France and he has an antique business. He said "They ought to fetch a bit," you know what the French are about money, so I remembered Monkey...'

'Monkey?'

'Monkey Gaiterswell, I always used to call him Monkey. We used,' said Gloria very archly, 'to be friends and he said "Sell them to America." Do you think he's right—I mean Monkey said you'd written a book about Jack and you'd know? He said I'd get five hundred pounds for them. I mean they're all about painting, famous people, the whole circle...'

Ah, it was a plot!

'Five hundred,' said George. 'You won't get five hundred pounds. No one has ever heard of Flitestone in America. None of his pictures went there.'

'But the letters are very *personal*, George. Naturally you're in them.'

'I doubt it.'

'Oh you are. I remember. I know you are. You were his best friend. And you wrote so beautifully about him. Monkey says so.'

'Obviously there was a plot between Monkey and Gloria.'

'I've no doubt they are full of slanders. I should tear them up,' said George shortly.

'George,' she appealed. 'I need the money. François has gone off with some woman and I'm broke. Look.'

She opened her black shopping bag and took out a parcel of crumpled brown paper and put it on George's desk.

'Open it. I'll leave them with you to look at. You'll see.'

'Oh no. I can't do that,' said George. 'I don't care to be responsible. It leads to all sorts of awful business.'

'Read them. Open it. Here.'

She put down her empty glass and untied the string. A pile of letters of all sizes in Flitestone's large hand, each word formed carefully like the words of a medieval manuscript, slid on to George's desk.

George was sitting there and he withdrew his hand so as

not to touch the letters. They brought Jack Flitestone into the room. George wanted them. He knew now what was meant when she said *he* was in them. It was not what *she* meant. The letters contained the, to him, affronting fact that he had not after all succeeded in owning his own life and closing it to others; that he existed in other people's minds and that all people dissolved in this way, becoming fragments of one another, and nothing in themselves. He had known that once, when Jack Flitestone had brought him to life. He knew, too, that he had once lived or nearly lived. Flitestone, in his dangerous way, had lived for him. One letter had fallen to the floor and Gloria read aloud:

... Archie's car broke down outside Medley and we didn't get to Gorse until the middle of dinner. La Tarantula was furious and I offered to eat in the kitchen and the Prime Minister who was already squiffy...

'There you are, George. The Prime Minister,' cried Gloria. George took the letter in the tips of his fingers and Gloria helped herself to another drink.

'Jack was an awful snob,' said George, but admiringly, putting the letter back. 'No manners, writing about people when he was a guest.'

'Oh come off it, George,' said Gloria, picking out one or two more. 'You know, I haven't read them for years. Actually Jack frightened me. So morbid. Here's one. Oh, this is good. It's about the time you and Jack went to Chartres. The tie drawer, George!'

The new blow from the past struck him. He remembered it: the extraordinary thing about small French hotels: they never gave you a drawer for your ties. He took the letter and read:

... George surpassed himself this morning...

He had walked down the corridor to Flitestone's room and knocked.

'Here. I say, Jack. I want to speak to you.'

'What is it?' Flitestone called. Ordinary manners, one

would have thought, would at least have led Flitestone to open the door, Jack was so *thoughtless*.

'Jack, Jack, I've got no tie drawer in my room.'

Flitestone came to the door naked and pushed a drawer from his wardrobe into George's hand.

'Take mine.'

'Jack, here I say, dear fellow. Chambermaid.'

'Umph,' said George to Gloria. 'Inaccurate.'

He reached out for the next letter she offered to him. He looked at it distantly, read a few lines and stopped.

'Here, I say, I can't read this. It is to you,' he sneered a little.

'They're all to me.'

'Yes, but this is—er—private, personal.'

George looked quizzically and sternly at her; it was 'not done' to look into another's moral privacy. It was also shameless and woman-like to show letters like these to him. But the phrases he had run into head-on had frightened him, they brought back to him the danger he had once lived in: his heart had been invaded, he had been exposed once to a situation in which the question of a victory or a defeat vanished.

'You see,' he said turning his head away nervously from her as he handed back the letter to her.

Gloria took it. She put on her glasses and read. Immediately she smiled. The smile became wider and she gave pleased giggles. She was blushing.

'Jack ought to have been a writer,' she said. 'I hated his paintings. It's quite true what he says, George. I was very attractive. I had marvellous legs.'

She turned to look at her reflection in the glass of the bookcase and took her fur coat off and posed. Gradually she lifted her skirt above her knees and pleased by what she saw, she lifted her skirt higher, putting one leg forward, then the other.

'Look, George,' she said. 'Look. They're still good. There aren't many women of my age with legs like these. They're damn fine, George. You've never seen a pair like that.' She turned sideways and pranced with pleasure.

'Gloria, please,' said George sharply.

But she marched over to the picture of the woman with cylindrical legs and said:

'I could have killed him for that. What's the matter with painters? Didn't he have enough to eat when he was a boy? He was always carrying on about his hard times.'

She lowered her dress and sat down to go on reading the letter.

'The pink peony, did you get to that?' she said. 'Really, Jack's ideas! Not very nice, is it? I mean, not in a letter. He wasn't very...' she stopped and was sad. 'No,' she checked herself. 'I'll tell you something, George: we only went to bed together once...'

'Gloria,' said George in agitation. 'Give me the letter. I'll put it with the others...'

She was making Flitestone far too alive.

'It was your fault, George. It was the dinner you gave us that night, the night I bought the fish. You say you don't remember? At the Café Royal. I made you go off to the Café Royal kitchen and get the largest fish they had. I don't know why. I wanted to get rid of you and I thought it would annoy you. I was getting plastered. Don't you remember? I said: "Tell them we want it for our cat. Our cat is enormous. It eats a salmon a day." And Jack kept on saying—we were both drunk—"I want to paint a large salmon. You're bloody stingy, George, you won't buy me a salmon."'

'Awful business,' snapped George. 'Jack never understood money.'

'You remember! Isn't that wonderful?' cried Gloria pulling off her hat and looking into her empty glass.

'You followed us out of the restaurant, all up Shaftesbury Avenue and he was going to show me his new pictures. You had no tact, George. He was carrying the fish and he suddenly gave it to you and made you carry it and the paper blew off. George,' she said, 'do you mind if I have just a teeny-weeny one? There's a letter about it.'

And she pushed him aside and got at the parcel on his desk.

'I think you've had enough, Gloria.'

'For old times' sake,' said Gloria, filling her glass. She unfolded the parcel again and scattered the letters. George looked at the clock.

'I can't find it,' she said. 'It's here somewhere.'

'Gloria, I don't want drink spilled on my desk. I've forbidden Seymour ...'

Gloria stopped and, now red in the face, smiled amorously. 'That man?' she said. 'Is he here?'

'Gloria,' said George. 'I'll have to—er—I'll have to—It's eleven o'clock, I ...'

Gloria replied with dignity.

'Jack had no sense of behaviour. I could see it was spoiling your suit. I begged him, begged him,' she said grandly, 'to carry it himself. I was furious with him. He could see you had an umbrella as well, you always carried one and wore a bowler hat. He said "Stick it on the umbrella." I was terribly upset when he slammed the door in your face when we got to the studio. We had a terrible row and I made him swear to go around to your flat and apologize. It was awful. George. What did you do?'

'I took a cab, of course,' said George.

'Well, I mean, you couldn't leave a salmon in the street,' said Gloria. 'It was a suit like the one you are wearing now, dark grey. That isn't the one, is it? It can't be.'

'Gloria, I am sorry, but ...'

Gloria frowned.

'I am sure it's there,' she said and went to the letters on the desk again. 'No, not that. Not that,' she began throwing the letters on the floor. 'Ah, here.'

She waved the letter and looked through it in silence until she read aloud:

'... I apologized to George and he said he had left the fish with the hall porter, so I went down there. We had a bit of a row about my low class manners. I said I thought half the salmon in England had been to Eton. He told me to ask Seymour, the hall porter for it ...'

'Inaccurate,' interrupted George. 'Seymour was never hall porter.'

'... I said I have called for the specimen I loaned to Sir George Clark, the marine biologist, who is doing research on spawn ...

'You see, George,' she said. She went back to the sofa. 'Come and sit here, George, don't be so stuffy. We can talk, can't we, after all these years? We are friends. That is what we all need, George, friends. I'm serious, George.' She had tears in her eyes.

'It was wicked of Jack to call you stingy. You gave him money. You bought his pictures.'

'But I *am* stingy,' said George. 'You see, rich people never give their children a penny. We never had anyone to the house at Maddings...'

'It was his jealousy,' said Gloria darkly. 'He was jealous of you.'

'Oh well, class envy...' George began.

'No, of you and me,' she said. 'Oh yes, George, he really was. That's why he tried to shake you off, that night, that's why we had such terrible scenes... You were rich...'

'Don't be ludicrous, Gloria.'

'Letters by every post, pursuing, bombarding me, I couldn't stand it.'

'Nonsense.'

'It isn't nonsense. You were very blind, George. And so you live in this place, alone. Jealous men are so *boring*, George. I've had four. I said "Oh to hell" and I went off to France. Vive de Gaulle! You know?' she said, raising her glass.

'To *les feuilles mortes d'automne*,' she said. 'That's what my husband says.'

He bent to take her glass to prevent her drinking more and she stroked his spiky hair. He put the glass away out of reach.

'That is why Jack married that stupid student girl,' she said in a suddenly sharp calculating voice. 'That broke up you and Jack, didn't it?'

'I don't wish to talk about it,' said George. 'It ruined him. Marriage is the ruin of painters.'

'George, come clean. After all, we all know it. You were in love with him, weren't you?'

There was silence.

'Weren't you?' she persisted.

He recovered and achieved his worldly drawl.

'Oh I know there's a lot of that sort of thing about, was in my time, too. I paid no attention to it... Women don't understand talent. I understood Jack's talent. Women ruined it.'

'Jack said you'd never been to bed with a woman in your life,' she said.

'It wasn't possible, it wasn't possible,' said George angrily. 'Not in my day. Not for a gentleman.' And he turned on her. 'I won't be questioned. I should burn those letters. You treated him badly. You killed his imagination. It's obvious in his work.'

He looked at the clock.

'George,' she said. 'You don't mean that. You don't know what you are saying. You were always so sweet to me.'

'I do mean what I said. Read your letters,' said George. And briskly he collected them off the floor and packed them up and tied the parcel. He was going to turn her out now.

She was staring stupidly.

'You don't want them?' she said. 'Monkey said you'd jump at them.'

'You've got one in your hands,' he said. 'No, I won't give a penny for them. I won't be blackmailed.'

Gloria got up to give the letter to him. She could not walk and put her hand on the table beside the sofa. It fell over, carrying her glass with it.

'What's that man Seymour doing in here? Tell him to get out. Out with Seymour,' she suddenly shouted. 'Out. Out. What d'you mean? Stop playing the innocent. You've never lived. That's you, George, that fish?' And she tried to point at the picture.

'Gloria, I won't have this,' shouted George. 'You're drunk.'

'You won't have it? You've never had it. My coat, who's taken that?'

But when she turned she fell heavily on to the sofa, twisted her body, and her skirt above her knees and one majestic leg trailing on the floor.

'Gloria. How dare you! In my house!'

'Darling,' she smiled and fell asleep instantly.

'Women,' George always said, glittering dryly, 'they contribute nothing.' She was contributing a stentorian snore.

He had couples up after dinner sometimes, elderly friends and you could see how it was: they either couldn't let their husbands speak—poor Caldicott, for instance—or they sat as stupid as puddings. The men aged as they sat: rather them than me. Eighty-two and not a day's illness.

Gloria was contributing more than a snore. She was contributing an enormous haunch, an indecent white thigh— 'Really.' He would have to cover it. Couldn't she pull her skirt down. Couldn't she be drunk like a—like a lady! She contributed brutality, an awful animality to the room.

He went over and tried to pull her skirt down.

'Gloria,' he shouted.

He couldn't move the skirt. He gave her a shake. It stirred an enormous snore and a voluptuous groan and it seemed that she was going to roll off the sofa on to the floor. He couldn't have women lying on the floor in his flat. He could never get her up. He moved a chair against the sofa.

He sat down and waited. Gaiterswell was responsible for this. In the promiscuous Bohemian set he had lived in, the dirty little man would be used to it.

George could not ring for Seymour. Think of the scandal. She had trapped him. He hated her for what she had done to Jack, driving him out of his mind with jealousy of other men, encouraging him, evading him, never letting go. She, more than his expensive wife, was responsible for Jack's suicide. Gloria had paralysed him. You could see it in his paintings, after they had broken up: the paintings had become automatic, academic, dead, without air, without life. There were ten drawings of that fish. He had become obsessed with it.

It was a death of the heart; of George's heart as well. This body lying in the room, was like the brutal body of his father. The old brute with his rages and his passions, his disgraceful affairs with governesses and maids in the very next room to where he slept as a boy—awful business—he would never forget that—the manners!—the shouts, his terrible behaviour to his wife: it had paralysed the whole family. They all hated him so violently, with a violence that so magnetized them all, that none of them had heart for others. He had killed their hearts; not one of them had been able to love. For a moment, George left these exact memories and went off into anecdotes about how he fought back against his father, sniffing triumphantly, as he did at the club. But the sight of

Gloria there smashed the anecdotal in him. He recognized that he had *not* fought back and had not been victorious. He had risked nothing. He had been whipped into the life of a timid, self-absorbed scholar.

He poured himself a large whisky. It was gone midnight. Perhaps by the time he checked up on the windows in the flat and saw all the doors were closed, she would wake up. He carried his glass to his bedroom and put it by the bedside; and there exhaustion drove him to his habits. He took off his watch and put it on the table. He forgot why he had come into the room. It was not what he intended to do but he was tired, murmuring to himself 'Coat, hanger, shirt, trousers, shoes, socks,' he undressed and shivering he got into bed. He finished his whisky, turned out the light and—Gloria forgotten he was at once asleep. And at once dreaming he was back in the sitting-room, parcelling the letters, watching her. He dreamed that he called Seymour who got a taxi and they hauled her into it. But as fast as they got her into the cab she was back upstairs on the sofa and his father and Jack were there too, but ignoring him, standing a yard or two away, though he shouted at them to help. And then the awful thing happened. He picked her up himself. He was at a railway station: he could go no farther: he dropped her. With an appalling noise, the enormous body fell just as a train came, steaming, blasting, wheels grinding, a massive black engine, advancing upon him. He gave a shout. It had hit him and crushed him. He was dying. He had had a heart attack. He screamed and he woke up shouting, sitting up in bed.

In the bedroom Gloria was standing in her stockinged feet and her petticoat, holding her skirt in her hand, her hair in disorder.

'What's the matter, George?' she said thickly. George could not speak.

'What is it? I woke up. I heard you shout.' Her breathing was heavy, it was the sound of the engine he had heard. George gaped at her.

'Are you ill?' she said. 'I passed out.'

'I—I—I...,' he could say nothing more. He got out of bed. George was shuddering. 'What's the time?'

'Get into bed. You're freezing. You're ill.' She came over

and took him by the arm and he allowed himself to be put back to bed.

'What an ice-box,' she said. She shut the window, switched on the fire.

'I'd better get a doctor,' she said.

'No,' said George. 'I'm all right.' He was panting. She felt his head.

'Where's my watch?'

'It's half-past three nearly. George, for God's sake don't do that again. Have you got any aspirins? What happens when you're alone and there is no one here?'

'Ah, you see, I have an arrangement with the...'

'What? The doctor?'

'The telephone,' said George.

'The telephone? What the hell's the good of that? You might die, George. Where are those aspirins, be a dear and tell me. I'm sorry, George. You screamed. God, I hadn't time to put a skirt on,' she said archly.

'Oh well, so I see,' said George sarcastically.

'Ah, thank God,' said Gloria sighing. 'Now you sound more like yourself. You gave me a turn. I would have fallen on the floor if you hadn't put the chair there. I'll make you a cup of tea. Can you make tea in this awful museum?'

'No,' said George victoriously. 'You can't. I never keep tea here. Tea, I never drink it. Seymour brings it.'

'Well, my God, how you live, George, in this expensive barn,' she said, sitting on the bed.

'Awful business. Awful dream,' said George, coming round. 'I had an awful dream the other night, oh yes...'

'You look green, George. I'll get you a drink.'

She brought it to him and watched him drink it.

'I've been round your flat. There are no beds. If you don't mind I'll go back to the sofa. Now, stop talking.'

For George was off on some tale of a night in the war.

'This is the only bed,' he said. 'I used to keep a spare bed but I stopped that. People exploit you. Want to stay the night. It upsets the servants here.'

'There's not room for two in it, George,' she said. George stopped his drink.

'Gloria,' he stammered in terror of her large eyes. She

273

came closer and sat on the bed. She took his free hand.

'You're cold,' she said.

'No,' he said. 'I'm not. All bone, you see, skeleton. My sister...'

She stood up and then bent over him and kissed him.

'I'll find a blanket,' she said. 'I'll go back to the sofa. I'm terribly sorry, George. George, I really am.'

'Well,' said George.

'George, forgive me,' she said and suddenly kneeled at the bed and put her arms round him. 'Let me warm you.'

At the Club George was sitting at luncheon.

'You're looking well, George,' said the academician who had just passed him the decanter.

'I never drink until the evening. I always reckon to drink a bottle of wine at dinner, a couple of glasses of port. I usually have a whisky here and one more back at the flat when I get home. I walk home, taxis are expensive and oh, oh, oh, I don't like the underground. Oh no, I don't like that.'

'You're looking fine.'

'I have been very ill. I had pneumonia. I was taken very ill a month ago, in the night. Lucky my sister has been looking after me. That is the trouble with old people who live alone, no one knows. They can't reach the bell. I told you about that awful night when I ate the oysters...'

'George, not now, please. I didn't know you had a sister?'

'Oh yes, oh yes. Two,' said George sharply. 'One is very thin, all bones like me, the other very fat.'

'But you're better? You look fine. I hear, by the way, that Sanders is getting married.'

'Oh, I knew about that. I advised him to, at his age. I warned him about the loneliness of bachelors in old age. I'm used to it. Keep occupied. See people. That's the secret. Oh yes, I worked it out. My father lived till he was ninety. You see, when I was young one never met any women. Just girls at deb parties, but speak to them, oh dear no. Not done. That's a big change. The bishops don't like sex, though Canterbury is beginning to come round. The Pope will have to make a move, he's been the stumbling block. A scandal. Oh yes, I happened to be in Rome in '05, staying with a Papal Count and, well, I was able to tell him the whole inside story at the

Vatican, you see I knew a very able Jesuit who was very frank about it privately...'

'What happened about Gloria?' said a voice. It was the Arch Enemy, sitting opposite.

'Hah,' said George. 'I recommended her not to sell. She offered to give me the letters, but I didn't care to take them. They were very intimate, personal.'

'I thought her husband had left her and she was short of money?'

'Oh no, no. No. Awful business,' said George.

She went away. George heard her opening cupboards, looking for blankets. He listened to every movement. He thought, Seymour will find her in the morning. Where could he hide her? Could he make her go to the bathroom and stay there till Seymour left? No, Seymour always ran his bath. He was trapped. He heard her go to the sitting-room. It was six before he fell asleep again.

At half-past seven she came to his room with Seymour.

'My brother was taken very ill in the night,' she was saying to Seymour. 'I cannot find out who his doctor is? He oughtn't to be alone like this. At his age.'

'No ma'am,' said Seymour, looking guilty.

'Bring me his tea. Where does he keep his thermometer? Get me one.'

'I told him not to go out, ma'am,' said Seymour.

'Thank Heaven I came in.'

When Seymour left she said to George:

'Don't talk. It's tiring. A little scandal would have done you good, George, but not at your age.'

'Umph,' said George. 'That man knows my sister. She's as thin as a pole. She's meaner than me,' he cackled. 'She never tips anyone.'

'I told him I was the fat one,' she said. 'You stay there. I'm calling a doctor.'

Waiting for him to come was a nuisance. 'Awful business' having a woman in the house. They spend half their lives in the bathroom. You can't get into it. When George did get to it he was so weak he had to call for her. She was sitting in a chair reading Flitestone's letters and smiling. She had—

George had to admit—made herself presentable.

'You're right, George,' she said. 'I'm going to keep them. He was so full of news. They're too,' she said demurely '... personal.'

And then the doctor came.

'That's not the worst thing to be short of,' sniffed George.

'The trouble with Gloria was that she was also so sentimental,' said the Arch Enemy. 'The moment she sees a man her mind simply goes. Still does, and she must be sixty if she's a day,' he said, looking at George.

By God, George thought, the Arch Enemy is a fool.

WILLIAM TREVOR

'One takes liberties, I suppose, in describing people.'

Barnes Common, 1972

Access to the Children

Malcolmson, a fair, tallish man in a green tweed suit that required pressing, banged the driver's door of his ten-year-old Volvo and walked quickly away from the car, jangling the keys. He entered a block of flats that was titled—gold engraved letters on a granite slab—The Quadrant.

It was a Sunday afternoon in late October. Yellow-brown leaves patterned grass that was not for walking on. Some scurried on the steps that led to the building's glass entrance doors. Rain was about, Malcolmson considered.

At three o'clock precisely he rang the bell of his ex-wife's flat on the third floor. In response he heard at once the voices of his children and the sound of their running in the hall. 'Hullo,' he said when one of them, Deirdre, opened the door. 'Ready?'

They went with him, two little girls, Deirdre seven and Susie five. In the lift they told him that a foreign person, the day before, had been trapped in the lift from eleven o'clock in the morning until teatime. Food and cups of tea had been poked through a grating to this person, a Japanese businessman who occupied a flat at the top of the block. 'He didn't get the hang of an English lift,' said Deirdre. 'He could have died there,' said Susie.

In the Volvo he asked them if they'd like to go to the Zoo and they shook their heads firmly. On the last two Sundays he'd taken them to the Zoo, Susie reminded him in her specially polite, very quiet voice: you got tired of the Zoo, walking round and round, looking at all the same animals. She smiled at him to show she wasn't being ungrateful. She suggested that in a little while, after a month or so, they could go to the Zoo again, because there might be some new animals. Deirdre said that there wouldn't be, not after a month or so: why should there be? 'Some old animals might have died,' said Susie.

Malcolmson drove down the Edgware Road, with Hyde Park in mind.

'What have you done?' he asked.

'Only school,' said Susie.

'And the news cinema,' said Deirdre. 'Mummy took us to a news cinema. We saw a film about how they make wire.'

'A man kept talking to Mummy. He said she had nice hair.'

'The usherette told him to be quiet. He bought us ice-creams, but Mummy said we couldn't accept them.'

'He wanted to take Mummy to a dance.'

'We had to move to other seats.'

'What else have you done?'

'Only school,' said Susie. 'A boy was sick on Miss Bawden's desk.'

'After school stew.'

'It's raining,' said Susie.

He turned the windscreen-wipers on. He wondered if he should simply bring the girls to his flat and spend the afternoon watching television. He tried to remember what the Sunday film was. There often was something suitable for children on Sunday afternoons, old films with Deanna Durbin or Nelson Eddy and Jeanette MacDonald.

'Where're we going?' Susie asked.

'Where d'you want to go?'

'*A Hundred and One Dalmatians.*'

'Oh, please,' said Susie.

'But we've seen it. We've seen it five times.'

'Please, Daddy.'

He stopped the Volvo and bought a *What's On*. While he leafed through it they sat quietly, willing him to discover a cinema, anywhere in London, that was showing the film. He shook his head and started the Volvo again.

'Nothing else?' Deirdre asked.

'Nothing suitable.'

At Speakers' Corner they listened to a Jehovah's Witness and then to a woman talking about vivisection. 'How horrid,' said Deirdre. 'Is that true, Daddy?' He made a face. 'I suppose so,' he said.

In the drizzle they played a game among the trees, hiding and chasing one another. Once when they'd been playing this game a woman had brought a policeman up to him. She'd seen him approaching the girls, she said; the girls had been playing alone and he'd joined in. 'He's our daddy,' Susie had said, but the woman had still argued, claiming that he'd given them sweets so that they'd say that. 'Look at him,' the woman had insultingly said. 'He needs a shave.' Then she'd gone away, and the policeman had apologized.

'The boy who was sick was Nicholas Barnet,' Susie said. 'I think he could have died.'

A year and a half ago Malcolmson's wife, Elizabeth, had said he must choose between her and Diana. For weeks they had talked about it; she knowing that he was in love with Diana and was having some kind of an affair with her, he caught between the two of them, attempting the impossible in his effort not to hurt anyone. She had given him a chance to get over Diana, as she put it, but she couldn't go on for ever giving him a chance, no woman could. In the end, after the shock and the tears and the period of reasonableness, she became bitter. He didn't blame her: they'd been in the middle of a happy marriage, nothing was wrong, nothing was lacking.

He'd met Diana on a train; he'd sat with her, talking for a long time, and after that his marriage didn't seem the same. In her bitterness Elizabeth said he was stupidly infatuated: he was behaving like a murderer: there was neither dignity nor humanity left in him. Diana she described as a flat chested American nymphomaniac and predator, the worst type of woman in the world. She was beautiful herself, more beautiful than Diana, more gracious, warmer and funnier: there was a sting of truth in what she said; he couldn't understand himself. In the very end, after they'd been morosely drinking gin and lime-juice, she'd suddenly shouted at him that he'd better pack his bags. He sat unhappily, gazing at the green bottle of Gordon's gin on the carpet between his chair and hers. She screamed; tears poured in a torrent from her eyes. 'For God's sake go away,' she cried, on her feet, turning away from him. She shook her head in a wild gesture, causing her long fair hair to move like a horse's mane. Her hands, clenched into fists, beat at his cheeks, making bruises that Diana afterwards tended.

For months after that he saw neither Elizabeth nor his children. He tried not to think about them. He and Diana took a flat in Barnes, near the river, and in time he became used to the absence of the children's noise in the mornings, and to Diana's cooking and her quick efficiency in little things, and the way she always remembered to pass on telephone messages, which was something that Elizabeth had always forgotten to do.

Then one day, a week or so before the divorce was due, Diana said she didn't think there was anything left between them. It hadn't worked, she said; nothing was quite right. Amazed and bewildered, he argued with her. He frowned at her, his eyes screwed up as though he couldn't properly see her. She was very poised, in a black dress, with a necklace at her throat, her hair pulled smooth and neatly tied. She'd met a man called Abbotforth, she said, and she went on talking about that, still standing.

'We could go to the Natural History Museum,' Deirdre said.

'Would you like to, Susie?'

'Certainly not,' said Susie.

They were sitting on a bench, watching a bird that Susie said was a yellow-hammer. Deirdre disagreed: at this time of year, she said, there were no yellow-hammers in England, she'd read it in a book. 'It's a little baby yellow-hammer,' said Susie. 'Miss Bawden said you see lots of them.'

The bird flew away. A man in a raincoat was approaching them, singing quietly. They began to giggle. 'Sure, maybe some day I'll go back to Ireland,' sang the man, 'if it's only at the closing of my day.' He stopped, noticing that they were watching him.

'Were you ever in Ireland?' he asked. The girls, still giggling, shook their heads. 'It's a great place,' said the man. He took a bottle of VP wine from his raincoat pocket and drank from it.

'Would you care for a swig, sir?' He said to Malcolmson, and Malcolmson thanked him and said he wouldn't. 'It would do the little misses no harm,' suggested the man. 'It's good, pure stuff.' Malcolmson shook his head. 'I was born in County Clare,' said the man, 'in 1928, the year of the Big Strike.' The girls, red in the face from containing their laughter, poked at one another with their elbows. 'Aren't they the great little misses?' said the man. 'Aren't they the fine credit to you, sir?'

In the Volvo on the way to Barnes they kept repeating that he was the funniest man they'd ever met. He was nicer than the man in the news cinema, Susie said. He was quite like him, though, Deirdre maintained: he was looking for company in just the same way, you could see it in his eyes. 'He was staggering,' Susie said. 'I thought he was going to die.'

Before the divorce he had telephoned Elizabeth, telling her that Diana had gone. She hadn't said anything, and she'd put the receiver down before he could say anything else. Then the divorce came through and the arrangement was that the children should remain with Elizabeth and that he should have reasonable access to them. It was an extraordinary expression, he considered: reasonable access.

The Sunday afternoons had begun then, the ringing of a doorbell that had once been his own doorbell, the children in the hall, the lift, the Volvo, tea in the flat where he and Diana had lived and where now he lived on his own. Sometimes, when he was collecting them, Elizabeth spoke to him, saying in a matter-of-fact way that Susie had a cold and should not be outside too much, or that Deirdre was being bad about practising her clarinet and would he please speak to her. He loved Elizabeth again; he said to himself that he had never not loved her; he wanted to say to her that she'd been right about Diana. But he didn't say anything, knowing that wounds had to heal.

Every week he longed more for Sunday to arrive. Occasionally he invented reasons for talking to her at the door of the flat, after the children had gone in. He asked questions about their progress at school, he wondered if there were ways in which he could help. It seemed unfair, he said, that she should have to bring them up single-handed like this; he made her promise to telephone him if a difficulty arose; and if ever she wanted to go out in the evenings and couldn't find a baby-sitter, he'd willingly drive over. He always hoped that if he talked for long enough the girls would become so noisy in their room that she'd be forced to ask him in so that she could quieten them, but the ploy never worked.

In the lift on the way down every Sunday evening he thought she was more beautiful than any woman he'd ever seen, and he thought it was amazing that once she should have been his wife and should have borne him children, that once they had lain together and loved, and that he had let her go. Three weeks ago she had smiled at him in a way that was like the old way. He'd been sure of it, positive, in the lift on the way down.

He drove over Hammersmith Bridge, along Castelnau and into Barnes High Street. No one was about on the pavements; buses crept sluggishly through the damp afternoon.

'Miss Bawden's got a black boy-friend,' Susie said, 'called Eric Mantilla.'

'You should see Miss Bawden,' murmured Deirdre. 'She hasn't any breasts.'

'She has lovely breasts,' shouted Susie, 'and lovely jumpers and lovely skirts. She has a pair of earrings that once belonged to an Egyptian empress.'

'As flat as a pancake,' said Deirdre.

After Diana had gone he'd found it hard to concentrate. The managing director of the firm where he worked, a man with a stout red face called Sir Gerald Travers, had been sympathetic. He'd told him not to worry. Personal troubles, Sir Gerald had said, must naturally affect professional life; no one would be human if that didn't happen. But six months later, to Malcolmson's surprise, Sir Gerald had suddenly suggested to him that perhaps it would be better if he made a move. 'It's often so,' Sir Gerald had said, a soft smile gleaming between chubby cheeks. 'Professional life can be affected by the private side of things. You understand me, Malcolmson?' They valued him immensely, Sir Gerald said, and they'd be generous when the moment of departure came. A change was a tonic; Sir Gerald advised a little jaunt somewhere.

In reply to all that Malcolmson said that the upset in his

private life was now over; nor did he feel, he added, in need of recuperation. 'You'll easily find another berth,' Sir Gerald Travers replied, with a wide, confident smile. 'I think it would be better.'

Malcolmson had sought about for another job, but had not been immediately successful: there was a recession, people said. Soon it would be better, they added, and because of Sir Gerald's promised generosity Malcolmson found himself in a position to wait until things seemed brighter. It was always better, in any case, not to seem in a hurry.

He spent the mornings in the Red Lion, in Barnes, playing dominoes with an old-age pensioner, and when the pensioner didn't turn up owing to bronchial trouble Malcolmson would borrow a newspaper from the landlord. He slept in the afternoons and returned to the Red Lion later. Occasionally when he'd had a few drinks he'd find himself thinking about his children and their mother. He always found it pleasant then, thinking of them with a couple of drinks inside him.

'It's *The Last of the Mohicans*,' said Deirdre in the flat, and he guessed that she must have looked at the *Radio Times* earlier in the day. She'd known they'd end up like that, watching television. Were they bored on Sundays? he often wondered.

'Can't we have *The Golden Shot*?' demanded Susie, and Deirdre pointed out that it wasn't on yet. He left them watching Randolph Scott and Binnie Barnes, and went to prepare their tea in the kitchen.

On Saturdays he bought meringues and brandy-snaps in Frith's Patisserie. The elderly assistant smiled at him in a way that made him wonder if she knew what he wanted them for; it occurred to him once that she felt sorry for him. On Sunday mornings, listening to the omnibus edition of *The Archers*, he made Marmite sandwiches with brown bread and tomato sandwiches with white. They loved sandwiches, which was something he remembered from the past. He remembered parties, Deirdre's friends sitting around a table, small and silent, eating crisps and cheese puffs and leaving all the cake.

When *The Last of the Mohicans* came to an end they watched *Going for a Song* for five minutes before changing the channel for *The Golden Shot*. Then Deirdre turned the television off and they went to the kitchen to have tea. 'Wash your hands,' said Susie, and he heard her add that if a germ got into your food you could easily die. 'She kept referring to death,' he would say to Elizabeth when he left them back. 'D'you think she's worried about anything?' He imagined Elizabeth giving the smile she had given three weeks ago and then saying he'd better come in to discuss the matter.

'Goody,' said Susie, sitting down.

'I'd like to marry a man like that man in the park,' said Deirdre. 'It'd be much more interesting, married to a bloke like that.'

'He'd be always drunk.'

'He wasn't drunk, Susie. That's not being drunk.'

'He was drinking out of a bottle——'

'He was putting on a bit of flash, drinking out of a bottle and singing his little song. No harm in that, Susie.'

'I'd like to be married to Daddy.'

'You couldn't be married to Daddy.'

'Well, Richard then.'

'Ribena, Daddy. Please.'

He poured drops of Ribena into two mugs and filled them up with warm water. He had a definite feeling that today she'd ask him in, both of them pretending a worry over Susie's obsession with death. They'd sit together while the children splashed about in the bathroom; she'd offer him gin and lime-juice, their favourite drink, a drink known as a Gimlet, as once he'd told her. They'd drink it out of green glasses that they'd bought, years ago, in Italy, The girls would dry themselves and come and say good night. They'd go to bed. He might tell them a story, or she would. 'Stay to supper,' she would say, and while she made risotto he would go to her and kiss her hair.

'I like his eyes,' said Susie. 'One's higher than another.'

'It couldn't be.'

'It is.'

'He couldn't see, Susie, if his eyes were like that. Every-one's eyes are——'

'He isn't always drunk like the man in the park.'

'Who?' he asked.

'Richard,' they said together, and Susie added: 'Irishmen are always drunk.'

'Daddy's an Irishman and Daddy's not always——'

'Who's Richard?'

'He's Susie's boy-friend.'

'I don't mind,' said Susie. 'I like him.'

'If he's there tonight, Susie, you're not to climb all over him.'

He left the kitchen and in the sitting-room he poured himself some whisky. He sat with the glass cold between his hands, staring at the grey television screen. 'Sure, maybe some day I'll go back to Ireland,' Deirdre sang in the kitchen, and Susie laughed shrilly.

He imagined a dark-haired man, a cheerful man, intelligent and subtle, a man who came often to the flat, whom his children knew well and were already fond of. He imagined him as he had imagined himself ten minutes before, sitting with Elizabeth, drinking Gimlets from the green Italian glasses. 'Say good night to Richard,' Elizabeth would say, and the girls would go to him and kiss him good night.

'Who's Richard?' he asked, standing in the kitchen doorway.

'A friend,' said Deirdre, 'of Mummy's.'

'A nice friend?'

'Oh, yes.'

'I love him,' said Susie.

He returned to the sitting-room and quickly poured himself more whisky. Both of his hands were shaking. He drank quickly, and then poured and drank some more. On the pale carpet, close to the television set, there was a stain where Diana had spilt a cup of coffee. He hated now this memory of her, he hated her voice when it came back to him, and the memory of her body and her mind. And yet once he had been rendered lunatic with the passion of his love for her. He had loved her more than Elizabeth, and in his madness he had spoilt everything.

'Wash your hands,' said Susie, close to him. He hadn't heard them come into the room. He asked them, mechanically, if they'd had enough to eat. 'She hasn't washed her hands,' Susie said. 'I washed mine in the sink.'

He turned the television on. It was the girl ventriloquist Shari Lewis, with Lamb Chop and Charley Horse.

Well, he thought under the influence of the whisky, he had had his fling. He had played the pins with a flat-chested American nymphomaniac and predator, and he had lost all there was to lose. Now it was Elizabeth's turn: why shouldn't she have, for a time, the dark-haired Richard who took another man's children on to his knee and kissed them good night? Wasn't it better that the score should be even before they all came together again?

He sat on the floor with his daughters on either side of him, his arms about them. In front of him was his glass of whisky. They laughed at Lamb Chop and Charley Horse, and when the programme came to an end and the news came on he didn't want to let his daughters go. An electric fire glowed cosily. Wind blew the rain against the windows, the autumn evening was dark already.

He turned the television off. He finished the whisky in his glass and poured some more. 'Shall I tell you,' he said, 'about when Mummy and I were married?'

They listened while he did so. He told them about meeting Elizabeth in the first place, at somebody else's wedding, and of the days they had spent walking about together, and about the wet, cold afternoon on which they'd been married.

'February the twenty-fourth,' Deirdre said.

'Yes.'

'I'm going to be married in summer-time,' Susie said, 'when the cow-parsley's out.'

His birthday and Elizabeth's were on the same day, April 21st. He reminded the girls of that; he told them of the time he and Elizabeth had discovered they shared the date, a date shared also with Hitler and the Queen. They listened quite politely, but somehow didn't seem much interested.

They watched *What's in a Game?* He drank more. He wouldn't be able to drive them back. He'd pretend he couldn't start the Volvo and then he'd telephone for a taxi. It had happened once before that in a depression he'd begun to drink when they were with him on a Sunday afternoon. They'd been to Madame Tussaud's and the Planetarium, which Susie had said frightened her. In the flat, just as this time, while they were eating their sandwiches, he'd been overcome with the longing that they should all be together again. He'd begun to drink and in the end, while they watched television, he'd drunk quite a lot. When the time came to go he'd said that he couldn't find the keys of the Volvo and that they'd have to have a taxi. He'd spent five minutes brushing his teeth so that Elizabeth wouldn't smell the alcohol when she opened the door. He'd smiled at her with his well-brushed teeth but she, not then being over her bitterness, hadn't smiled back.

The girls put their coats on. Deirdre drank some Ribena; he had another small tot of whisky. And then, as they were leaving the flat, he suddenly felt he couldn't go through the farce of walking to the Volvo, putting the girls into it and then pretending he couldn't start it. 'I'm tired,' he said instead. 'Let's have a taxi.'

They watched the Penrhyn Male Voice Choir in *Songs of Praise* while they waited for it to arrive. He poured himself another drink, drank it slowly and then went to the bathroom to brush his teeth. He remembered the time Deirdre had been born, in a maternity home in the country because they'd lived in the country then. Elizabeth had been concerned because she'd thought one of Deirdre's fingers was bent and had kept showing it to nurses who said they couldn't see anything the matter. He hadn't been able to see anything the matter either, nor had the doctor. 'She'll never be as beautiful as you,' he'd said and quite soon after that she'd stopped talking about the finger and had said he was nice to her. Susie had been born at home, very quickly, very easily.

The taxi arrived. 'Soon be Christmas,' said the taximan. 'You chaps looking forward to Santa Claus?' They giggled because he had called them chaps. 'Fifty-six more days,' said Susie.

He imagined them on Christmas Day, with the dark-haired Richard explaining the rules of a game he'd bought them. He imagined all four of them sitting down at Christmas dinner, and Richard asking the girls which they liked, the white or the brown of the turkey, and then cutting them small slices. He'd have brought, perhaps, champagne, because he was that kind of person. Deirdre would sip from his glass, not liking the taste. Susie would love it.

He counted in his mind: if Richard had been visiting the flat for, say, six weeks already and assuming that his love affair with Elizabeth had begun two weeks before his first visit, that left another four months to go, allowing the affair ran an average course of six months. It would therefore come to an end at the beginning of March. His own affair with Diana had lasted from April until September. 'Oh darling,' said Diana, suddenly in his mind, and his own voice replied to her, caressing her with words. He remembered the first time they had made love and the guilt that had hammered at him and the passion there had been between them. He imagined Elizabeth naked in Richard's naked arms, her eyes open, looking at him, her fingers touching the side of his face, her lips slightly smiling. He reached forward and pulled down the glass shutter. 'I need cigarettes,' he said. 'There's a pub in Shepherd's Bush Road, the Laurie Arms.'

He drank two large measures of whisky. He bought cigarettes and lit one, rolling the smoke around in his mouth to disguise the smell of the alcohol. As he returned to the taxi, he slipped on the wet pavement and almost lost his balance. He felt very drunk all of a sudden. Deirdre and Susie were telling the taximan about the man in Hyde Park.

He was aware that he walked unsteadily when they left the taxi and moved across the forecourt of the block of flats. In the hall, before they got into the lift, he lit another cigarette, rolling the smoke about his mouth. 'That poor Japanese man,' said Deirdre.

He rang the bell, and when Elizabeth opened the door the girls turned to him and thanked him. He took the cigarette from his mouth and kissed them. Elizabeth was smiling: if only she'd ask him in and give him a drink he wouldn't have to worry about the alcohol on his breath. He swore to himself that she was smiling as she'd smiled three weeks ago. 'Can I come in?' he asked, unable to keep the words back.

'In?' The smile was still there. She was looking at him quite closely. He released the smoke from his mouth. He tried to remember what it was he'd planned to say, and then it came to him.

'I'm worried about Susie,' he said in a quiet voice. 'She talked about death all the time.'

'Death?'

'Yes.'

'There's someone here actually,' she said, stepping back into the hall. 'But come in, certainly.'

In the sitting-room she introduced him to Richard who was, as he'd imagined, a dark-haired man. The sitting-room was much the same as it always had been. 'Have a drink,' Richard offered.

'D'you mind if we talk about Susie?' Elizabeth asked Richard. He said he'd put them to bed if she liked. She nodded. Richard went away.

'Well?'

He stood with the familiar green glass in his hand, gazing at her. He said:

'I haven't had gin and lime-juice since——'

'Yes. Look, I shouldn't worry about Susie. Children of that age often say odd things, you know——'

'I don't mind about Richard, Elizabeth, I think it's your due. I worked it out in the taxi. It's the end of October now——'

'My due?'

'Assuming your affair has been going on already for six weeks——'

'You're drunk.'

He closed one eye, focusing. He felt his body swaying and he said to himself that he must not fall now, that no matter what his body did his feet must remain firm on the carpet. He sipped from the green glass. She wasn't, he noticed, smiling any more.

'I'm actually not drunk,' he said. 'I'm actually sober. By the time our birthday comes round, Elizabeth, it'll all be over. On April the twenty-first we could have family tea.'

'What the hell are you talking about?'

'The future, Elizabeth. Of you and me and our children.'

'How much have you had to drink?'

'We tried to go to *A Hundred and One Dalmatians*, but it wasn't on anywhere.'

'So you drank instead. While the children——'

'We came here in a taxi-cab. They've had their usual tea, they've watched a bit of *The Last of the Mohicans* and a bit of *Going for a Song* and all of *The Golden Shot* and *The Shari Lewis Show* and——'

'You see them for a few hours and you have to go and get drunk——'

'I am not drunk, Elizabeth.'

He crossed the room as steadily as he could. He looked aggressively at her. He poured gin and lime-juice. He said:

'You have a right to your affair with Richard, I recognize that.'

'A *right*?'

'I love you, Elizabeth.'

'You loved Diana.'

'I have never not loved you. Diana was nothing—nothing, nothing at all.'

'She broke our marriage up.'

'No.'

'We're divorced.'

'I love you, Elizabeth.'

'Now listen to me——'

'I live from Sunday to Sunday. We're a family, Elizabeth; you and me and them. It's ridiculous, all this. It's ridiculous making Marmite sandwiches with brown bread and tomato sandwiches with white. It's ridiculous buying meringues and going five times to *A Hundred and One Dalmatians* and going up the Post Office Tower until we're sick of the sight of it, and watching drunks in Hyde Park and poking about at the Zoo——'

'You have reasonable access——'

'Reasonable access, my God!' His voice rose. He felt sweat on his forehead. Reasonable access, he shouted, was utterly no good to him; reasonable access was meaningless and stupid; a day would come when they wouldn't want to go with him on Sunday afternoons, when there was nowhere left in London that wasn't an unholy bore. What about reasonable access then?

'Please be quiet.'

He sat down in the armchair that he had always sat in. She said:

'You might marry again. And have other children.'

'I don't want other children. I have children already. I want us all to live together as we used to——'

'Please listen to me——'

'I get a pain in my stomach in the middle of the night. Then I wake up and can't go back to sleep. The children will grow up and I'll grow old. I couldn't begin a whole new thing all over again: I haven't the courage. Not after Diana. A mistake like that alters everything.'

'I'm going to marry Richard.'

'Three weeks ago,' he said, as though he hadn't heard her, 'you smiled at me.'

'Smiled?'

'Like you used to, Elizabeth. Before——'

'You made a mistake,' she said, softly. 'I'm sorry.'

'I'm not saying don't go on with your affair with this man. I'm not saying that, because I think in the circumstances it'd be a cheek. D'you understand me, Elizabeth?'

'Yes, I do. And I think you and I can be perfectly good friends. I don't feel sour about it any more: perhaps that's what you saw in my smile.'

'Have a six-month affair——'

'I'm in love with Richard.'

'That'll all pass into the atmosphere. It'll be nothing at all in a year's time——'

'No.'

'I love you, Elizabeth.'

They stood facing one another, not close. His body was still swaying. The liquid in his glass moved gently, slurping to the rim and then settling again. Her eyes were on his face: it was thinner, she was thinking. Her fingers played with the edge of a cushion on the back of the sofa.

'On Saturdays,' he said, 'I buy the meringues and the brandy-snaps in Frith's Patisserie. On Sunday morning I make the sandwiches. Then I cook sausages and potatoes for my lunch, and after that I come over here.'

'Yes, yes——'

'I look forward all week to Sunday.'

'The children enjoy their outings, too.'

'Will you think about it?'

'About what?'

'About all being together again.'

'Oh, for heaven's sake.' She turned away from him. 'I wish you'd go now,' she said.

'Will you come out with me on our birthday?'

'I've told you.' Her voice was loud and angry, her cheeks were flushed. 'Can't you understand? I'm going to marry Richard. We'll be married within a month, when the girls have had time to get to know him a little better. By Christmas we'll be married.'

He shook his head in a way that annoyed her, seeming in his drunkenness to deny the truth of what she was saying. He tried to light a cigarette; matches dropped to the floor at his feet. He left them there.

It enraged her that he was sitting in an armchair in her flat with his eyelids drooping through drink and an unlighted cigarette in his hand and his matches spilt all over the floor. They were his children, but she wasn't his wife: he'd destroyed her as a wife, he'd insulted her, he'd left her to bleed and she had called him a murderer.

'Our birthday,' he said, smiling at her as though already she had agreed to join him on that day. 'And Hitler's and the Queen's.'

'On our birthday if I go out with anyone it'll be Richard.'

'Our birthday is beyond the time——'

'For God's sake, there is no beyond the time. I'm in love with another man——'

'No.'

'On our birthday,' she shouted at him, 'on the night of our birthday Richard will make love to me in the bed you slept in for nine years. You have access to the children. You can demand no more.'

He bent down and picked up a match. He struck it on the side of the empty box. The cigarette was bent. He lit it with a wobbling flame and dropped the used match on to the carpet. The dark-haired man, he saw, was in the room again. He'd come in, hearing her shouting like that. He was asking her if she was all right. She told him to go away. Her face was hard; bitterness was there again. She said, not looking at him:

'Everything was so happy. We had a happy marriage. For

nine years we had a perfectly happy marriage.'

'We could——'

'Not ever.'

Again he shook his head in disagreement. Cigarette ash fell on to the green tweed of his suit. His eyes were narrowed, watching her, seemingly suspicious.

'We had a happy marriage,' she repeated, whispering the words, speaking to herself, still not looking at him. 'You met a woman on a train and that was that: you murdered our marriage. You left me to plead, as I am leaving you now. You have your Sunday access. There is that legality between us. Nothing more.'

'Please, Elizabeth——'

'Oh for God's sake, stop.' Her rage was all in her face now. Her lips quivered as though in the effort to hold back words that would not be denied. They came from her, more quietly but with greater bitterness. Her eyes roved over the green tweed suit of the man who once had been her husband, over his thin face and his hair that seemed, that day, not to have been brushed.

'You've gone to seed,' she said, hating herself for saying that, unable to prevent herself. 'You've gone to seed because you've lost your self-respect. I've watched you, week by week. The woman you met on a train took her toll of you and now in your seediness you want to creep back. Don't you know you're not the man I married?'

'Elizabeth——'

'You didn't have cigarette burns all over your clothes. You didn't smell of toothpaste when you should have smelt of drink. You stand there, pathetically, Sunday after Sunday, trying to keep a conversation going. D'you know what I feel?'

'I love——'

'I feel sorry for you.'

He shook his head. There was no need to feel sorry for him, he said, remembering suddenly the elderly assistant in Frith's Patisserie and remembering also, for some reason, the woman in Hyde Park who peculiarly had said that he wasn't shaved. He looked down at his clothes and saw the burn marks she had mentioned. 'We think it would be better,' said the voice of Sir Gerald Travers unexpectedly in his mind.

'I'll make some coffee,' said Elizabeth.

She left him. He had been cruel, and then Diana had been cruel, and now Elizabeth was cruel because it was her right and her instinct to be so. He recalled with vividness Diana's face in those first moments on the train, her eyes looking at him, her voice. 'You have lost all dignity,' Elizabeth had whispered, in the darkness, at night. 'I despise you for that.' He tried to stand up but found the effort beyond him. He raised the green glass to his lips. His eyes closed and when he opened them again he thought for a drunken moment that he was back in the past, in the middle of his happy marriage. He wiped at his face with a handkerchief.

He saw across the room the bottle of Gordon's gin so nicely matching the green glasses, and the lime-juice, a lighter shade of green. He made the journey, his legs striking the arms of chairs. There wasn't much gin in the bottle. He poured it all out; he added lime-juice, and drank it.

In the hall he could hear voices, his children's voices in the bathroom, Elizabeth and the man speaking quietly in the kitchen. 'Poor wretch,' Elizabeth was saying. He left the flat and descended to the ground floor.

The rain was falling heavily. He walked through it, thinking that it was better to go, quietly and without fuss. It would all work out; he knew it; he felt it definitely in his bones. He'd arrive on Sunday, a month or so before their birthday, and something in Elizabeth's face would tell him that the dark-haired man had gone for ever, as Diana had gone. By then he'd be established again, with better prospects than the red-faced Sir Gerald Travers had ever offered him. On their birthday they'd both apologize to one another, wiping the slate clean: they'd start again. As he crossed the Edgware Road to the public house in which he always spent an hour or so on Sunday nights, he heard his own voice murmuring that it was understandable that she should have taken it out on him, that she should have tried to hurt him by saying he'd gone to seed. Naturally, she'd say a thing like that; who could blame her after all she'd been through? At night in the flat in Barnes he watched television until the programmes closed down. He usually had a few drinks, and as often as not he dropped off to sleep with a cigarette between his fingers: that was how the burns occurred on his clothes.

He nodded to himself as he entered the saloon bar, thinking he'd been wise not to mention any of that to Elizabeth. It would only have annoyed her, having to listen to a lot of stuff about late-night television and cigarettes. Monday, Tuesday, Wednesday, he thought, Thursday, Friday. On Saturday he'd buy the meringues and brandy-snaps, and then it would be Sunday. He'd make the sandwiches listening to *The Archers*, and at three o'clock he'd ring the bell of the flat. He smiled in the saloon bar, thinking of that, seeing in his mind the faces of his children and the beautiful face of their mother. He'd planted an idea in Elizabeth's mind and even though she'd been a bit shirty she'd see when she thought about it that it was what she wanted, too.

He went on drinking gin and lime-juice, quietly laughing over being so upset when the children had first mentioned the dark-haired man who took them on to his knee. Gin and lime-juice was a Gimlet, he told the barmaid. She smiled at him. He was celebrating, he said, a day that was to come. It was ridiculous, he told her, that a woman casually met on a train should have created havoc, that now, at the end of it all, he should week by week butter bread for Marmite and tomato sandwiches. 'D'you understand me?' he drunkenly asked the barmaid. 'It's *too* ridiculous to be true—that man will go because none of it makes sense the way it is.' The barmaid smiled again and nodded. He bought her a glass of beer, which was something he did every Sunday night. He wept as he paid for it, and touched his cheeks with the tips of his fingers to wipe away the tears. Every Sunday he wept, at the end of the day, after he'd had his access. The barmaid raised her glass, as always she did. They drank to the day that was to come, when the error he had made would be wiped away, when the happy marriage could continue. 'Ridiculous,' he said. 'Of course it is.'

SAUL BELLOW

'I overheard my Russian mother calling me "Krasa-
vitz ..." But my vanity could no longer give me much
mileage and to tell you the truth I'm not even greatly
impressed by my own tortured heart.'

Mexico, 1968

Mosby's Memoirs

The birds chirped away. Fweet, Fweet, Bootchee-Fweet.
Doing all the things naturalists say they do. Expressing
abysmal depths of aggression, which only Man—Stupid Man—
heard as innocence. We feel everything is so innocent—because our wickedness is so fearful. Oh, very fearful!

Mr Willis Mosby, after his siesta, gazing down-mountain at
the town of Oaxaca, where all were snoozing still—mouths,
rumps, long black Indian hair, the antique beauty photo-
graphically celebrated by Eisenstein in *Thunder over Mexico*. Mr Mosby—Dr Mosby really; erudite, maybe even profound; thought much, accomplished much—had made some
of the most interesting mistakes a man could make in the
twentieth century. He was in Oaxaca now to write his
memoirs. He had a grant for the purpose, from the Guggenheim Foundation. And why not?

Bougainvillaea poured down the hillside, and the hum-
mingbirds were spinning. Mosby felt ill with all this whirl-
ing, these colours, fragrances, ready to topple on him. Liveli-
ness, beauty, seemed very dangerous. Mortal danger. Maybe
he had drunk too much mescal at lunch (beer, also). Behind
the green and red of Nature, dull black seemed to be thickly
laid like mirror backing.

Mosby did not feel quite well; his teeth, gripped tight,
made the muscles stand out in his handsome, elderly tanned
jaws. He had fine blue eyes, light-pained, direct, intelligent,
disbelieving; hair still thick, parted in the middle; and strong

vertical grooves between the brows, beneath the nostrils, and at the back of the neck.

The time had come to put some humour into the memoirs. So far it had been: Fundamentalist family in Missouri—Father the successful builder—Early schooling—The State University—Rhodes Scholarship—Intellectual friendships—What I learned from Professor Collingwood—Empire and the mental vigour of Britain—My unorthodox interpretation of John Locke—I work for William Randolph Hearst in Spain—The personality of General Franco—Radical friendships in New York—Wartime service with the OSS—The limited vision of Franklin D. Roosevelt—Comte, Proudhon and Marx revisited—De Tocqueville once again.

Nothing very funny here. And yet thousands of students and others would tell you, 'Mosby had a great sense of humour.' Would tell their children, 'This Mosby in the OSS,' or 'Willis Mosby, who was in Toledo with me when the Alcázar fell, made me die laughing.' 'I shall never forget Mosby's observations on Harold Laski.' 'On packing the Supreme Court.' 'On the Russian purge trials.' 'On Hitler.'

So it was certainly high time to do something. He had given it some consideration. He would say, when they sent down his ice from the hotel bar (he was in a cottage below the main building, flowers heaped upon it; envying a little the unencumbered mountains of the Sierra Madre) and when he had chilled his mescal—warm, it tasted rotten—he would write that in 1947, when he was living in Paris, he knew any number of singular people. He knew the Comte de la Mine-Crevée, who sheltered Gary Davis the World Citizen after the World Citizen had burnt his passport publicly. He knew Mr Julian Huxley at UNESCO. He discussed social theory with Mr Lévi-Straus but was not invited to dinner—they ate at the Musée de l'Homme. Sartre refused to meet with him; he thought all Americans, Negroes excepted, were secret agents. Mosby for his part suspected all Russians abroad of working for the GPU. Mosby knew French well; extremely fluent in Spanish; quite good in German. But the French cannot identify originality in foreigners. That is the curse of an old civilization. It is a heavier planet. Its best minds must double their horsepower to overcome the gravitational field of tradition. Only a few will ever fly. To fly away from Descartes. To fly away from the political anachronisms of left, centre and right persisting since 1789. Mosby found these French exceedingly banal. These French found him lean and tight. In well-tailored clothes, elegant and dry, his good Western skin, pale eyes, strong nose, handsome mouth and virile creases. *Un type sec.*

Both sides—Mosby and the French, that is—with highly developed attitudes. Both, he was lately beginning to concede, quite wrong. Possibly equidistant from the truth, but lying in different sectors of error. The French were worse off because their errors were collective. Mine, Mosby believed, were at least peculiar. The French were furious over the collapse in 1940 of *La France Pourrie,* their lack of military will, the extensive collaboration, the massive deportations unopposed (the Danes, even the *Bulgarians* resisted Jewish deportations), and, finally, over the humiliation of liberation by the Allies. Mosby, in the OSS, had information to support such views. Within the State Department, too, he had university colleagues—former students and old acquaintances. He had expected a high post-war appointment, for which, as director of counterespionage in Latin America, he was ideally qualified. But Dean Acheson personally disliked him. Nor did Dulles approve. Mosby, a fanatic about *ideas*, displeased the institutional gentry. He had said that the Foreign Service was staffed by rejects of the power structure. Young gentlemen from good Eastern colleges who couldn't make it as Wall Street lawyers were allowed to interpret the alleged interests of their class in the State Department bureaucracy. In foreign consulates they could be rude to DPs and indulge their country-club anti-Semitism, which was dying out even in the country clubs. Besides, Mosby had sympathized with the Burnham position on managerialism, declaring, during the war, that the Nazis were winning because they had made their managerial revolution first. No Allied combination could conquer, with its obsolete industrialism, a nation which had reached a new state of history and tapped the power of the inevitable, etc. And then Mosby, holding forth in Washington, among the elite Scotch drinkers, stated absolutely that however deplorable the concentration camps had been, they showed at least the rationality of German political ideas. The Americans had no such ideas. They didn't know what they were doing. No design existed. The British were not much better. The Hamburg fire-bombing, he argued in his clipped style, in full declarative phrases, betrayed the idiotic emptiness and planlessness of Western leadership. Finally, he said that when Acheson blew his nose, there were maggots in his handkerchief.

Among the defeated French, Mosby admitted that he had a galled spirit. (His jokes were not too bad.) And of course he drank a lot. He worked on Marx and Tocqueville, and he drank. He would not cease from mental strife. The Comte de la Mine-Crevée (Mosby's own improvisation on a noble and ancient name) kept him in PX booze and exchanged his money on the black market for him. He described his swindles and was very entertaining.

Mosby now wished to say, in the vein of Sir Harold Nicolson or Santayana or Bertrand Russell, writers for whose memoirs he had the greatest admiration, that Paris in 1947, like half a Noah's Ark, was waiting for the second of each kind to arrive. There was one of everything. Something of this sort. Especially among Americans. The city was very bitter, grim; the Seine looked and smelled like medicine. At an American party, a former student of French from Minnesota, now running a shady enterprise, an agency which specialized in bribery, private undercover investigations and procuring broads for VIPs, said something highly emotional about the City of Man, about the meaning of Europe for Americans, the American failure to preserve human scale. Not omitting to work in Man the Measure. And every other tag he could bring back from Randall's *Making of the Modern Mind* or *Readings in the Intellectual History of Euope*. 'I was tempted,' Mosby meant to say (the ice arrived in a glass jar with tongs; the natives no longer wore the dirty white drawers of the past). 'Tempted...' He rubbed his forehead, which projected like the back of an observation car. 'To tell this sententious little drunkard and gyp artist, formerly a pacifist and vegetarian, follower of Gandhi at the University of Minnesota, now driving a very handsome Bentley to the Tour d'Argent to eat duck *à l'orange*. Tempted to say, "Yes, but we come here across the Atlantic to relax a bit in the past. To recall what Ezra Pound had once said. That we would make another Venice, just for the hell of it, in the Jersey marshes any time we liked. Toying. To divert ourselves in the time of colossal mastery to come. Reproducing anything, for fun. Baboons trained to row will bring us in gondolas to discussions of astrophysics. Where folks burn garbage now, and fatten pigs and junk their old machines, we will debark to hear a concert." '

Mosby the thinker, like other busy men, never had time for music. Poetry was not his cup of tea. Members of Congress, Cabinet officers, Organization Men, Pentagon planners, Party leaders, Presidents had no such interest. They could not be what they were and read Eliot, hear Vivaldi, Cimarosa. But they planned that others might enjoy these things and benefit by their power. Mosby perhaps had more in common with political leaders and Joint Chiefs and Presidents. At least, they were in his thoughts more often than Cimarosa and Eliot. With hate, he pondered their mistakes, their shallowness. Lectured on Locke to show them up. Except by the will of the majority, unambiguously expressed, there was no legitimate power. The only absolute democrat in America (perhaps in the world—although who can know what there is in the world, among so many billions of minds and souls) was Willis Mosby. Notwithstanding his terse, dry, intolerant style of conversation (more precisely, examination), his lank dignity of person, his aristocratic bones. Dark long nostrils hinting at the afflictions that needed the strength you could see in his jaws. And, finally, the light-pained eyes.

A most peculiar, ingenious, hungry, aspiring and heartbroken animal, who, by calling himself Man, thinks he can escape being what he really is. Not a matter of his definition, in the last analysis, but of his being. Let him say what he likes.

> *Kingdoms are clay: our dungy earth alike*
> *Feeds beast as man; the nobleness of life*
> *Is to do thus.*

Thus being love. Or any other sublime option. (Mosby

knew his Shakespeare anyway. *There* was a difference from the President. And of the Vice-President he said, 'I wouldn't trust him to make me a pill. A has-been druggist!')

With sober lips he sipped the mescal, the servant in the coarse orange shirt enriched by metal buttons reminding him that the car was coming at four o'clock to take him to Mitla, to visit the ruins.

'*Yo mismo soy una ruina,*' Mosby joked.

The stout Indian, giving only so much of a smile—no more—withdrew with quiet courtesy. Perhaps I was fishing, Mosby considered. Wanted him to say I was *not* a ruin. But how could he? Seeing that for him I *am* one.

Perhaps Mosby did not have a light touch. Still, he thought he did have an eye for certain kinds of comedy. And he *must* find a way to relieve the rigor of this account of his mental wars. Besides, he could really remember that in Paris at that time people, one after another, revealed themselves in a comic light. He was then seeing things that way. Rue Jacob, Rue Bonaparte, Rue du Bac, Rue de Verneuil, Hôtel de l'Université—filled with funny people.

He began by setting down a name: Lustgarten. Yes, there was the man he wanted. Hymen Lustgarten, a Marxist, or former Marxist, from New Jersey. From Newark, I think. He had been a shoe salesman, and belonged to any number of heretical, fanatical, bolshevistic groups. He had been a Leninist, a Trotskyist, then a follower of Hugo Oehler, then of Thomas Stamm, and finally of an Italian named Salemme who gave up politics to become a painter, an abstractionist. Lustgarten also gave up politics. He wanted now to be successful in business—rich. Believing that the nights he had spent poring over *Das Kapital* and Lenin's *State and Revolution* would give him an edge in business dealings. We were staying in the same hotel. I couldn't at first make out what he and his wife were doing. Presently I understood. The black market. This was not then reprehensible. Postwar Europe was like that. Refugees, adventurers, G.Is. Even the Comte de la M.-C. Europe still shuddering from the blows it had received. Governments new, uncertain, infirm. No reason to respect their authority. American soldiers led the way. Flamboyant business schemes. Machines, whole factories,

stolen, treasures shipped home. An American colonel in the
lumber business started to saw up the Black Forest and send it
to Wisconsin. And, of course, Nazis concealing their concen-
tration-camp loot. Jewels sunk in Austrian lakes. Art works
hidden. Gold extracted from teeth in extermination camps,
melted into ingots and mortared like bricks into the walls
of houses. Incredibly huge fortunes to be made, and Lustgarten intended to make one of them. Unfortunately, he was
incompetent.

You could see at once that there was no harm in him. Despite the bold revolutionary associations and fierceness of
doctrine. Theoretical willingness to slay class enemies. But
Lustgarten could not even hold his own with pushy people in a
pissoir. Strangely meek, stout, swarthy, kindly, grinning with
mulberry lips, a froggy, curving mouth which produced
wrinkles like gills between the ears and the grin. And perhaps, Mosby thought, he comes to mind in Mexico because of
his Toltec, Mixtec, Zapotec look, squat and black-haired, the
tip of his nose turned downward and the black nostrils shyly
widening when his friendly smile was accepted. And a bit sick
with the wickedness, the awfulness of life but, respectfully
persistent, bound to get his share. Efficiency was his style—
action, determination, but a traitorous incompetence trembled within. Wrong calling. Wrong choice. A bad mistake.
But he was persistent.

His conversation amused me, in the dining-room. He was
proud of his revolutionary activities, which had consisted
mainly of cranking the mimeograph machine. Internal Bul-
letins. Thousands of pages of recondite examination of fine
points of doctrine for the membership. Whether the American
working class should give *material* aid to the Loyalist Government of Spain, controlled as that was by Stalinists and
other class enemies and traitors. You had to fight Franco, and
you had to fight Stalin as well. There was, of course, no
material aid to give. But *had* there been any, *should* it have
been given? This purely theoretical problem caused splits
and expulsions. I always kept myself informed of these
curious agonies of sectarianism, Mosby wrote. The single
effort made by Spanish Republicans to purchase arms in the
United States was thwarted by that friend of liberty Franklin

Delano Roosevelt, who allowed one ship, the *Mar Cantá-
brico*, to be loaded but set the Coast Guard after it to turn it
back to port. It was, I believe, that *genius* of diplomacy, Mr
Cordell Hull, who was responsible, but the decision, of
course, was referred to F.D.R., whom Huey Long amusingly
called Franklin de la *No*! But perhaps the most refined of
these internal discussions left of left, the documents for which
were turned out on the machine by that Jimmy Higgins, the
tubby devoted party-worker Mr Lustgarten, had to do with
the Finnish War. Here the painful point of doctrine to be re-
solved was whether a Workers' State like the Soviet Union,
even if it was a *degenerate* Workers' State, a product of the
Thermidorian Reaction following the glorious Proletarian
Revolution of 1917, could wage an Imperialistic War. For
only the *bourgeoisie* could be Imperialistic. Technically,
Stalinism could not be Imperialism. By definition. What then
should a Revolutionary Party say to the Finns? Should they
resist Russia or not? The Russians were monsters, but they
would expropriate the Mannerheim White-Guardist land-
owners and move, painful though it might be, in the correct historical direction. This, as a sect-watcher, I greatly
relished. But it was too foreign a subtlety for many of the
sectarians. Who were, after all, Americans. Pragmatists at
heart. It was *too* far out for Lustgarten. He decided, after the
war, to become (it shouldn't be hard) a rich man. Took his
savings and, I believe his wife said, his mother's savings, and
went abroad to build a fortune.

Within a year he had lost it all. He was cheated. By a German partner, in particular. But also he was caught smuggling
by Belgian authorities.

When Mosby met him (Mosby speaking of himself in the
third person as Henry Adams had done in *The Education
of Henry Adams*)—when Mosby met him, Lustgarten was
working for the American Army, employed by Graves Registration. Something to do with the procurement of crosses. Or
with the supervision of the lawns. Official employment gave
Lustgarten PX privileges. He was rebuilding his financial
foundations by the illegal sale of cigarettes. He dealt also in
gas-ration coupons which the French Government, anxious to
obtain dollars, would give you if you exchanged your money

at the legal rate. The gas coupons were sold on the black market. The Lustgartens, husband and wife, persuaded Mosby to do this once. For them, he cashed his dollars at the bank, not with la Mine-Crevée. The occasion seemed important. Mosby gathered that Lustgarten had to drive at once to Munich. He had gone into the dental-supply business there with a German dentist who now denied that they had ever been partners.

Many consultations between Lustgarten (in his international intriguer's trenchcoat, ill-fitting; head, neck and shoulders sloping backward in a froggy curve) and his wife, a young woman in an eyelet-lace blouse and black velveteen skirt, a velveteen ribbon tied on her round, healthy neck. Lustgarten, on the circular floor of the bank, explaining as they stood apart. And sweating blood; being reasonable with Trudy, detail by tortuous detail. It grated away poor Lustgarten's patience. Hands feebly remonstrating. For she asked female questions or raised objections which gave him agonies of patient rationality. Only there was nothing rational to begin with. That is, he had had no legal right to go into business with the German. All such arrangements had to be licensed by Military Government. It was a black-market partnership and when it began to show a profit, the German threw Lustgarten out. With what they call impunity. Germany as a whole having discerned the limits of all civilized systems of punishment as compared with the unbounded possibilities of crime. The bank in Paris, where these explanations between Lustgarten and Trudy were taking place, had an interior of some sort of red porphyry. Like raw meat. A colour which bourgeois France seemed to have vested with ideas of potency, mettle and grandeur. In the Invalides also, Napoleon's sarcophagus was of polished red stone, a great, swooping, polished cradle containing the little green corpse. (We have the testimony of M. Rideau, the Bonapartist historian, as to the colour.) As for the living Bonaparte, Mosby felt, with Auguste Comte, that he had been an anachronism. The Revolution was historically necessary. It was socially justified. Politically, economically, it was a move towards industrial democracy. But the Napoleonic drama itself belonged to an archaic category of personal ambitions, feudal ideas of war.

Older than feudalism. Older than Rome. The commander at the head of armies—nothing rational to recommend it. Society, increasingly rational in its organization, did not need it. But humankind evidently desired it. War is a luxurious pleasure. Grant the first premise of hedonism and you must accept the rest also. Rational foundations of modernity are cunningly accepted by man as the launching platform of ever wilder irrationalities.

Mosby, noting these reflections in a blue-green colour of ink which might have been extracted from the landscape. As his liquor had been extracted from the green spikes of the mescal, the curious sharp, dark-green fleshy limbs of the plant covering the fields.

The dollars, the francs, the gas rations, the bank like the beefsteak mine in which W. C. Fields invested, and shrinking but persistent dark Lustgarten getting into his little car on the sodden Parisian street. There were few cars then in Paris. Plenty of parking space. And the streets were so yellow, grey, wrinkled, dismal. But the French were even then ferociously telling the world that they had the *savoir-vivre*, the *gai savoir*. Especially Americans, haunted by their Protestant Ethic, had to hear this. My God—sit down, sip wine, taste cheese, break bread, hear music, know love, stop running and learn ancient life-wisdom from Europe. At any rate, Lustgarten buckled up his trenchcoat, pulled down his big hoodlum's fedora. He was bunched up in the seat. Small brown hands holding the steering wheel of the Simca Huit, and the grinning despair with which he waved.

'*Bon voyage*, Lustgarten.'

His Zapotec nose, his teeth like white pomegranate seeds. With a sob of the gears he took off for devastated Germany.

Reconstruction is big business. You demolish a society, you decrease the population and off you go again. New fortunes. Lustgarten may have felt, *qua* Jew, that he had a right to grow rich in the German boom. That all Jews had natural claims beyond the Rhine. On land enriched by Jewish ashes. And you never could be sure, seated on a sofa, that it was not stuffed or upholstered with Jewish hair. And he would not use German soap. He washed his hands, Trudy told Mosby, with Lifebuoy from the PX.

Trudy, a graduate of Montclair Teachers' College in New Jersey, knew French, studied composition, had hoped to work with someone like Nadia Boulanger, but was obliged to settle for less. From the bank, as Lustgarten drove away in a kind of doomed, latently tearful daring in the rain-drenched street, Trudy invited Mosby to the Salle Pleyel, to hear a Czech pianist performing Schönberg. This man, with muscular baldness, worked very hard upon the keys. The difficulty of his enterprise alone came through—the labour of culture, the trouble it took to preserve art in tragic Europe, the devoted drill. Trudy had a nice face for concerts. Her odour was agreeable. She shone. In the left half of her countenance, one eye kept wandering. Stone-hearted Mosby, making fun of flesh and blood, of these little humanities with their short inventories of bad and good. The poor Czech in his blazer with chased buttons and the muscles of his forehead rising in protest against *tabula rasa*—the bare skull.

Mosby could abstract himself on such occasions. Shut out the piano. Continue thinking about Comte. Begone, old priests and feudal soldiers! Go, with Theology and Metaphysics! And in the Positive Epoch Enlightened Woman would begin to play her part, vigilant, preventing the managers of the new society from abusing their powers. Over Labour, the supreme good.

Embroidering the trees, the birds of Mexico, looking at Mosby, and the hummingbird, so neat in its lust, vibrating tinily, and the lizard on the soil drinking heat with its belly. To bless small creatures is supposed to be real good.

Yes, this Lustgarten was a funny man. Cheated in Germany, licked by the partner, and impatient with his slow progress in Graves Registration, he decided to import a Cadillac. Among the new postwar millionaires of Europe there was a big demand for Cadillacs. The French Government, moving slowly, had not yet taken measures against such imports for rapid resale. In 1947, no tax prevented such transactions. Lustgarten got his family in Newark to ship a new Cadillac. Something like four thousand dollars was raised by his brother, his mother, his mother's brother for the purpose. The car was sent. The customer was waiting. A down payment had already been given. A double profit was expected. Only, on the day the car was unloaded at Le Havre new regulations went into effect. The Cadillac could not be sold. Lustgarten was stuck with it. He couldn't even afford to buy gas. The Lustgartens were seen one day moving out of the hotel, into the car. Mrs Lustgarten went to live with musical friends. Mosby offered Lustgarten the use of his sink for washing and shaving. Weary Lustgarten, defeated, depressed, frightened at last by his own plunging, scraped at his bristles, mornings, with a modest cricket noise, while sighing. All that money—mother's savings, brother's pension. No wonder his eyelids turned blue. And his smile, like a spinster's sachet, the last fragrance ebbed out long ago in the trousseau never used. But the long batrachian lips continued smiling.

Mosby realized that compassion should be felt. But passing in the night the locked, gleaming car, and seeing huddled Lustgarten, sleeping, covered with two coats, on the majestic seat, like Jonah inside Leviathan, Mosby could not say in candour that what he experienced was sympathy. Rather he reflected that this shoe salesman, in America attached to foreign doctrines, who could not reliquish Europe in the New World, was now, in Paris, sleeping in the Cadillac, encased in this gorgeous Fisher Body from Detroit. At home exotic, in Europe a Yankee. His timing was off. He recognized this himself. But believed, in general, that he was too early. A pioneer. For instance, he said, in a voice that creaked with shy assertiveness, the French were only now beginning to be Marxians. He had gone through it all years ago. What did these people know! Ask them about the Shakhty Engineers! About Lenin's Democratic Centralism! About the Moscow Trials! About 'Social Fascism'! They were ignorant. The Revolution having been totally betrayed, these Europeans suddenly discovered Marx and Lenin. 'Eureka!' he said in a high voice. And it was the Cold War, beneath it all. For should America lose, the French intellectuals were preparing to collaborate with Russia. And should America win, they could still be free, defiant radicals under American protection.

'You sound like a patriot,' said Mosby.

'Well, in a way I am,' said Lustgarten. 'But I am getting to be objective. Sometimes I say to myself, "If you were outside the world, if you, Lustgarten, didn't exist as a man, what would your opinion be of this or that?"'

'Disembodied truth.'

'I guess that's what it is.'

'And what are you going to do about the Cadillac?' said Mosby.

'I'm sending it to Spain. We can sell it in Barcelona.'

'But you have to get it there.'

'Through Andorra. It's all arranged. Klonsky is driving it.'

Klonsky was a Polish Belgian in the hotel. One of Lustgarten's associates, congenitally dishonest, Mosby thought. Kinky hair, wrinkled eyes like Greek olives and a cat nose and cat lips. He wore Russian boots.

But no sooner had Klonsky departed for Andorra, than Lustgarten received a marvellous offer for the car. A capitalist in Utrecht wanted it at once and would take care of all excise problems. He had all the necessary *tuyaux*, unlimited drag. Lustgarten wired Klonsky in Andorra to stop. He raced down on the night train, recovered the Cadillac and started driving back at once. There was no time to lose. But after sitting up all night on the *rapide*, Lustgarten was drowsy in the warmth of the Pyrenees and fell asleep at the wheel. He was lucky, he later said, for the car went down a mountainside and might have missed the stone wall that stopped it. He was only a foot or two from death when he was awakened by the crash. The car was destroyed. It was not insured.

Still faintly smiling, Lustgarten, with his sling and cane, came to Mosby's café table on the Boulevard Saint-Germain. Sat down. Removed his hat from dazzling black hair. Asked permission to rest his injured foot on a chair. 'Is this a private conversation?' he said.

Mosby had been chatting with Alfred Ruskin, an American poet. Ruskin, though some of his front teeth were missing, spoke very clearly and swiftly. A perfectly charming man. Inveterate theoretical. He had been saying, for instance, that France had shot its collaborationist poets. America, which had no poets to spare, put Ezra Pound in Saint Elizabeth's. He then went on to say, barely acknowledging Lustgarten, that America had had no history, was not a historical society. His proof was from Hegel. According to Hegel, history was the history of wars and revolutions. The United States had had only one revolution and very few wars. Therefore it was historically empty. Practically a vacuum.

Ruskin also used Mosby's conveniences at the hotel, being too fastidious for his own latrine in the Algerian backstreets of the Left Bank. And when he emerged from the bathroom, he invariably had a topic sentence.

'I have discovered the main defect of Kierkegaard.'

Or, 'Pascal was terrified by universal emptiness, but Valery says the difference between empty space and space in a bottle is only quantitative, and there is nothing intrinsically terrifying about quantity. What is your view?'

We do not live in bottles—Mosby's reply.

Lustgarten said when Ruskin left us, 'Who is that fellow? He mooched you for the coffee.'

'Ruskin,' said Mosby.

'*That* is Ruskin?'

'Yes, why?'

'I hear my wife was going out with Ruskin while I was in the hospital.'

'Oh, I wouldn't believe such rumours,' said Mosby. 'A cup of coffee, an apéritif together, maybe.'

'When a man is down on his luck,' said Lustgarten, 'it's the rare woman who won't give him hell in addition.'

'Sorry to hear it,' Mosby replied.

And then, as Mosby in Oaxaca recalled, shifting his seat from the sun—for he was already far too red, and his face, bones, eyes, seemed curiously thirsty—Lustgarten had said, 'It's been a terrible experience.'

'Undoubtedly so, Lustgarten. It must have been frightening.'

'What crashed was my last stake. It involved family. Too bad in a way that I wasn't killed. My insurance would at least have covered my kid brother's loss. And my mother and uncle.'

Mosby had no wish to see a man in tears. He did not care to sit through these moments of suffering. Such unmastered emotion was abhorrent. Though perhaps the violence of this abomination might have told Mobsy something about his own moral constitution. Perhaps Lustgarten did not want his face to be working. Or tried to subdue his agitation, seeing from Mosby's austere, though not unkind, silence that this was not his way. Mosby was by taste a Senecan. At least he admired Spanish masculinity—the *varonil* of Lorca. The *clavel varonil*, the manly red carnation, the clear classic hardness of honourable control.

'You sold the wreck for junk, I assume?'

'Klonsky took care of it. Now look, Mosby. I'm through with that. I was reading, thinking in the hospital. I came over to make a pile. Like the gold rush. I really don't know what got into me. Trudy and I were just sitting around during the war. I was too old for the draft. And we both wanted action. She in music. Or life. Excitement. You know, dreaming at Montclair Teachers' College of the Big Time. I wanted to make it possible for her. Keep up with the world, or something. But really—in my hospital bed I realized—I was right the first time. I am a Socialist. A natural idealist. Reading about Attlee, I felt at home again. It became clear that I am still a political animal.'

Mosby wished to say, 'No, Lustgarten. You're a dandler of swarthy little babies. You're a piggyback man—a giddyap horsie. You're a sweet old Jewish Daddy.' But he said nothing.

'And I also read,' said Lustgarten, 'about Tito. Maybe the Tito alternative is the real one. Perhaps there is hope for Socialism somewhere between the Labour Party and the Yugoslav type of leadership. I feel it my duty,' Lustgarten told Mosby, 'to investigate. I'm thinking of going to Belgrade.'

'As what?'

'As a matter of fact, that's where you could come in,' said Lustgarten. 'If you would be so kind. You're not *just* a scholar. You wrote a book on Plato, I've been told.'

'On the *Laws*.'

'And other books. But in addition you know the Movement. Lots of people. More connections than a switchboard ...'

The slang of the forties.

'You know people at the *New Leader*?'

'Not my type of paper,' said Mosby. 'I'm actually a political conservative. Not what you would call a Rotten Liberal but an out-and-out conservative. I shook Franco's hand, you know.'

'Did you?'

'This very hand shook the hand of the Caudillo. Would you like to touch it for yourself?'

'Why should I?'

'Go on,' said Mosby. 'It may mean something. Shake the hand that shook the hand.'

Very strangely, then, Lustgarten extended padded, swarthy fingers. He looked partly subtle, partly ill. Grinning, he said, 'Now I've made contact with real politics at last. But I'm serious about the *New Leader*. You probably know Bohn. I need credentials for Yugoslavia.'

'Have you ever written for the papers?'

'For the *Militant*.'

'What did you write?'

Guilty Lustgarten did not lie well. It was heartless of Mosby to amuse himself in this way.

'I have a scrapbook somewhere,' said Lustgarten.

But it was not necessary to write to the *New Leader*. Lustgarten, encountered two days later on the Boulevard, near the pork butcher, had taken off the sling and scarcely needed the cane. He said, 'I'm going to Yugoslavia. I've been invited.'

'By whom?'

'Tito. The Government. They're asking interested people to come as guests to tour the country and see how they're building Socialism. Oh, I know,' he quickly said, anticipating standard doctrinal objection, 'you don't build Socialism in one country, but it's no longer the same situation. And I really believe Tito may redeem Marxism by actually transforming the dictatorship of the proletariat. This brings me back to my first love—the radical movement. I was never meant to be an entrepreneur.'

'Probably not.'

'I feel some hope,' Lustgarten shyly said. 'And then also, it's getting to be spring.' He was wearing his heavy moose-coloured bristling hat, and bore many other signs of interminable winter. A candidate for resurrection. An opportunity for the grace of life to reveal itself. But perhaps, Mosby thought, a man like Lustgarten would never, except with supernatural aid, exist in a suitable form.

'Also,' said Lustgarten touchingly, 'this will give Trudy time to reconsider.'

'Is that the way things are with you two? I'm sorry.'

'I wish I could take her with me, but I can't swing that with the Yugoslavs. It's sort of a VIP deal. I guess they want to affect the foreign radicals. There'll be seminars in dialectics, and so on. I love it. But it's not Trudy's dish.'

Steady-handed, Mosby on his patio took ice with tongs, and poured more mescal flavoured with *gusano de maguey*—a worm or slug of delicate flavour. These notes on Lustgarten pleased him. It was essential, at this point in his memoirs, to disclose new depths. The preceding chapters had been heavy. Many unconventional things were said about the state of political theory. The weakness of conservative doctrine, the lack, in America, of conservative alternatives, of resistance to the prevailing liberalism. As one who had personally tried to create a more rigorous environment for slovenly intellectuals, to force them to do their homework, to harden the categories of political thought, he was aware that on the Right as on the Left the results were barren. Absurdly, the college-bred dunces of America had longed for a true Left Wing movement on the European model. They still dreamed of it. No less absurd were the Right Wing idiots. You cannot grow a rose in a coal mine. Mosby's own Right Wing graduate students had disappointed him. Just a lot of television actors. Bad guys for the Susskind interview programmes. They had transformed the master's manner of acid elegance, logical tightness, factual punctiliousness and merciless laceration in debate into a sort of shallow Noël Coward style. The real, the original Mosby approach brought Mosby hatred, got Mosby fired. Princeton University had offered Mosby a lump sum to retire seven years early. One hundred and forty thousand dollars. Because his mode of discourse was so upsetting to the academic community. Mosby was invited to no television programmes. He was like the Guerrilla Mosby of the Civil War. When he galloped in, all were slaughtered.

Most carefully, Mosby had studied the memoirs of Santa-yana, Malraux, Sartre, Lord Russell and others. Unfortunately, no one was reliably or consistently great. Men whose lives had been devoted to thought, who had tried mightily to govern the disorder of public life, to put it under some sort of intellectual authority, to get ideas to save mankind or to offer it mental aid in saving itself, would suddenly turn into gruesome idiots. Wanting to kill everyone. For instance, Sartre calling for the Russians to drop A-bombs on American bases in the Pacific because America was now presumably monstrous. And exhorting the Blacks to butcher the Whites. This moral philosopher! Or Russell, the Pacifist of World War I, urging the West to annihilate Russia after World War II. And sometimes, in his memoirs—perhaps he was gaga— strangely illogical. When, over London, a Zeppelin was shot down, the bodies of Germans were seen to fall, and the brutal men in the street horribly cheered, Russell wept and had there not been a beautiful woman to console him in bed that night, this heartlessness of mankind would have broken him utterly. What was omitted was the fact that these same Germans who fell from the Zeppelin had come to bomb the city. They were going to blow up the brutes in the street, explode the lovers. This Mosby saw.

It was earnestly to be hoped—this was the mescal attempting to invade his language—that Mosby would avoid the common fate of intellectuals. The Lustgarten digression should help. The correction of pride by laughter.

There were twenty minutes yet before the chauffeur came to take the party to Mitla, to the ruins. Mosby had time to continue. To say that in September the Lustgarten who reappeared looked frightful. He had lost no less than fifty pounds. Sun-blackened, creased, in a filthy stained suit, his eyes infected. He said he had had diarrhoea all summer.

'What did they feed their foreign VIPs?'

And Lustgarten shyly bitter—the lean face and inflamed eyes materializing from a spiritual region very different from any heretofore associated with Lustgarten by Mosby—said, 'It was just a chain gang. It was hard labour. I didn't understand the deal. I thought we were invited, as I told you. But we turned out to be foreign volunteers of construction. A labour brigade. And up in the mountains. Never saw the Dalmatian coast. Hardly even shelter for the night. We slept on the ground and ate shit fried in rancid oil.'

'Why didn't you run away?' asked Mosby.

'How? Where?'

'Back to Belgrade. To the American Embassy at least?'

'How could I? I was a guest. Came at their expense. They held the return ticket.'

'And no money?'

'Are you kidding? Dead broke. In Macedonia. Near Skoplje. Bug-stung, starved and running to the latrine all night. Labouring on the roads all day, with pus in my eyes, too.'

'No first aid?'

'They may have had the first, but they didn't have the second.'

Mosby thought it best to say nothing of Trudy. She had divorced him.

Commiseration, of course.

Mosby shaking his head.

Lustgarten with a certain skinny dignity walking away. He himself seemed amused by his enounters with Capitalism and Socialism.

The end? Not quite. There was a coda: The thing had quite good form.

Lustgarten and Mosby met again. Five years later. Mosby enters an elevator in New York. Express to the forty-seventh floor, the executive dining-room of the Rangeley Foundation. There is one other passenger, and it is Lustgarten. Grinning. He is himself again, filled out once more.

'Lustgarten!'

'Willis Mosby!'

'How are you, Lustgarten?'

'I'm great. Things are completely different. I'm happy. Successful. Married. Children.'

'In New York?'

'Wouldn't live in the US again. It's godawful. Inhuman. I'm visiting.'

Without a blink in its brilliancy, without a hitch in its smooth, regulated power, the elevator containing only the two of us was going up. The same Lustgarten. Strong words, vocal insufficiency, the Zapotec nose and under it the frog smile, the kindly gills.

'Where are you going now?'

'Up to *Fortune*,' said Lustgarten. 'I want to sell them a story.'

He was on the wrong elevator. This one was not going to *Fortune*. I told him so. Perhaps I had not changed either. A voice which for many years had informed people of their errors said, 'You'll have to go down again. The other bank of elevators.'

At the forty-seventh floor we emerged together.

'Where are you settled now?'

'In Algiers,' said Lustgarten. 'We have a Laundromat there.'

'We?'

'Klonsky and I. You remember Klonsky?'

They had gone legitimate. They were washing burnooses. He was married to Klonsky's sister. I saw her picture. The image of Klonsky, a cat-faced woman, head ferociously encased in kinky hair, Picasso eyes at different levels, sharp teeth. If fish, dozing in the reefs, had nightmares, they would be of such teeth. The children also were young Klonskys. Lustgarten had the snapshots in his wallet of North African leather. As he beamed, Mosby recognized that pride in his success was Lustgarten's opiate, his artificial paradise.

'I thought,' said Lustgarten, 'that *Fortune* might like a piece on how we made it in North Africa.'

We then shook hands again. Mine the hand that had shaken Franco's hand—his that had slept on the wheel of the Cadillac. The lighted case opened for him. He entered in. It shut.

Thereafter, of course, the Algerians threw out the French, expelled the Jews. And Jewish-Daddy-Lustgarten must have moved on. Passionate fatherhood. He loved those children. For Plato this childbreeding is the lowest level of creativity.

Still, Mosby thought, under the influence of mescal, my parents begot me like a committee of two.

From a feeling of remotion, though he realized that the car from Mitla had arrived, a shining conveyance waited, he noted the following as he gazed at the afternoon mountains:

Until he was some years old
People took care of him
Cooled his soup, sang, chirked,
Drew on his long stockings,
Carried him upstairs sleeping.
He recalls at the green lakeside
His father's solemn navel,
Nipples like dog's eyes in the hair
Mother's thigh with wisteria of blue veins.

After they retired to death,
He conducted his own business
Not too modestly, not too well
But here he is, smoking in Mexico
Considering the brown mountains
Whose fat laps are rolling
On the skulls of whole families.

Two Welsh women were his companions. One was very ancient, lank. The Wellington of lady travellers. Or like C. Aubrey Smith, the actor, who used to command Gurkha regiments in movies about India. A great nose, a gaunt jaw, a pleated lip, a considerable mustache. The other was younger. She had a small dewlap, but her cheeks were round and dark eyes witty. A very satisfactory pair. Decent was the word. English traits. Like many Americans, Mosby desired such traits for himself. Yes, he was pleased with the Welsh ladies. Though the guide was unsuitable. Overweening. His fat cheeks a red pottery colour. And he drove too fast.

The first stop was at Tule. They got out to inspect the celebrated Tule tree in the churchyard. This monument of vegetation, intricately and densely convolved, a green cypress, more than two thousand years old, roots in a vanished lake bottom, older than the religion of this little heap of white and gloom, this charming peasant church. In the comfortable dust a dog slept. Disrespectful. But unconscious. The old lady, quietly dauntless, tied on a scarf and entered the church. Her stiff genuflection had real quality. She must be Christian. Mosby looked into the depths of the Tule. A world in itself! It could contain communities. In fact, if he recalled his Gerald Heard, there was supposed to be a primal tree occupied by early ancestors, the human horde housed in such appealing, dappled, commodious, altogether beautiful organisms. The facts seemed not to support this golden myth of an encompassing paradise. Earliest man probably ran about on the ground, horribly violent, killing everything. Still, this dream of gentleness, this aspiration for arboreal peace was no small achievement for the descendants of so many killers. For his religion, this tree would do, thought Mosby. No church for him.

He was sorry to go. *He* could have lived up there. On top, of course. The excrements would drop on you below. But the Welsh ladies were already in the car, and the bossy guide began to toot the horn. Waiting was hot.

The road to Mitla was empty. The heat made the landscape beautifully crooked. The driver knew geology, archaeology. He was quite ugly with his information. The Water Table, the Caverns, the Triassic Period. Inform me no further! Vex not my soul with more detail. I cannot use what I have! And now Mitla appeared. The right fork continued to Tehuantepec. The left brought you to the Town of Souls. Old Mrs Parsons (Elsie Clews Parsons, as Mosby's mental retrieval system told him) had done ethnography here, studied the Indians in the baked streets of adobe and fruit garbage. In the shade, a dark urinous tang. A long-legged pig struggling on a tether. A sow. From behind, observant Mosby identified its pink small female opening. The dungy earth feeding beast as man.

But here were fascinating temples, almost intact. This place the Spanish priests had not destroyed. All others they had razed, building churches on the same sites, using the same stones.

A tourist market. Coarse cotton dresses, Indian embroidery, hung under flour-white tarpaulins, the dust settling on the pottery of the region, black saxophones, black trays of glazed clay.

Following the British travellers and the guide, Mosby was going once more through an odd and complex fantasy. It was that he was dead. He had died. He continued, however, to live. His doom was to live life to the end as Mosby. In the fantasy, he considered this his purgatory. And when had death occurred? In a collision years ago. He had thought it a near thing then. The cars were demolished. The actual Mosby was killed. But another Mosby was pulled from the car. A trooper asked, 'You okay?'

Yes, he was okay. Walked away from the wreck. But he still had the whole thing to do, step by step, moment by moment. And now he heard a parrot blabbing, and children panhandled him and women made their pitch, and he was getting his shoes covered with dust. He had been working at his memoirs and had provided a diverting recollection of a funny man—Lustgarten. In the manner of Sir Harold Nicolson. Much less polished, admittedly, but in accordance with a certain protocol, the language of diplomacy, of mandarin irony. However certain facts had been omitted. Mosby had arranged, for instance, that Trudy should be seen with Alfred Ruskin. For when Lustgarten was crossing the Rhine, Mosby was embracing Trudy in bed. Unlike Lord Russell's beautiful friend, she did not comfort Mosby for the disasters he had (by intellectual commitment) to confront. But Mosby had not advised her about leaving Lustgarten. He did not mean to interfere. However, his vision of Lustgarten as a funny man was transmitted to Trudy. She could not be the wife of such a funny man. But he *was*, he *was* a funny man! He was, like Napoleon in the eyes of Comte, an anachronism. Inept, he wished to be a colossus, something of a Napoleon himself, make millions, conquer Europe, retrieve from Hitler's fall a colossal fortune. Poorly imagined, unoriginal, the rerun of old ideas, and so inefficient. Lustgarten didn't have to happen. And so he *was* funny. Trudy too was funny, however. What a large belly she had. Since individuals are sometimes born from a twin impregnation, the organism carrying the undeveloped brother or sister in vestigial form—at times no more than an extra organ, a rudimentary eye buried in the leg, or a kidney or the beginnings of an ear somewhere in the back—Mosby often thought that Trudy had a little sister inside her. And to him she was a clown. This need not mean contempt. No, he liked her. The eye seemed to wander in one hemisphere. She did not know how to use perfume. Her atonal compositions were foolish.

At this time, Mosby had been making fun of people.

'Why?'

'Because he had needed to.'

'Why?'

'Because!'

The guide explained that the buildings were raised without mortar. The mathematical calculations of the priests had been perfect. The precision of the cut stone was absolute. After centuries you could not find a chink, you could not insert a razor blade anywhere. These geometrical masses were balanced by their own weight. Here the priests lived. The walls had been dyed. The cochineal or cactus louse provided the dye. Here were the altars. Spectators sat where you are standing. The priests used obsidian knives. The beautiful youths played on flutes. Then the flutes were broken. The bloody knife was wiped on the head of the executioner. Hair must have been clotted. And here, the tombs of the nobles. Stairs leading down. The Zapotecs, late in the day, had practiced this form of sacrifice, under Aztec influence.

How game this Welsh crone was. She was beautiful. Getting in and out of these pits, she required no assistance.

Of course you cannot make yourself an agreeable, desirable person. You can't will yourself into it without regard to the things to be done. Imperative tasks. Imperative comprehensions, monstrous compulsions of duty which deform. Men will grow ugly under such necessities. This one a director of espionage. That one a killer.

Mosby had evoked, to lighten the dense texture of his memoirs, a Lustgarten whose doom was this gaping comedy. A Lustgarten who didn't have to happen. But himself, Mosby, also a separate creation, a finished product, standing under the sun on large blocks of stone, on the stairs descending into this pit, he was complete. He had completed himself in this cogitating, unlaughing, stone, iron, nonsensical form.

Having disposed of all things human, he should have encountered God.

Would this occur?

But having so disposed, what God was there to encounter?

But they had now been led below, into the tomb. There was a heavy grille, the gate. The stones were huge. The vault was close. He was oppressed. He was afraid. It was very damp. On the elaborately zigzag-carved walls were thin, thin pipings of fluorescent light. Flat boxes of ground lime were here to absorb moisture. His heart was paralysed. His lungs would not draw. Jesus! I cannot catch my breath! To be shut in here! To be dead here! Suppose one were! Not as in accidents which ended, but did not quite end, existence. *Dead*-dead. Stooping, he looked for daylight. Yes, it was there. The light was there. The grace of life still there. Or, if not grace, air. Go while you can.

'I must get out,' he told the guide. 'Ladies, I find it very hard to breathe.'

JOHN HAWKES

'The eyes of certain people are never without a redness
inside the lids.'

Germany, 1950s

The Traveller

Early one morning in a town famous for the growing of some
grape, I arose from my bed in the inn and stepped outside
alone to the automobile. I smelled the odour of flowers thirst-
ing early for the sun; deep green fields stretched to either side
of the road, wet and silent; it was the cold dawn of the traveller and I wished suddenly for a platter of home-cooked
sausage. The car was covered with the same white dew as the
grass, and when I opened the door I smelled the damp
leather, the still cold oil and the gasoline that had been standing the night long. Soon the hot day would be upon us; the
dust of driving would whirl us into villages, every hour or
two whirl chickens and small children across the road like
weeds.

Down the road came a young bent-backed girl. On her
shoulders she carried a yoke from either end of which hung a
milk can, and over her shoulders she wore a shawl. Her legs
were bare and scratched by the thistle. Slowly she came into
the inn yard and approached me, each step loudly sloshing
the milk.

'Your name, Fräulein?'

'Just Milkmaid,' she said.

'Well, Milkmaid, how many cows have you milked this
morning?'

'Five, Mein Herr,' she said. Her arms were pimpled with a
curious raw colour as if they had been sunburned the day
before but now were cold. The girl tugged at her shawl, trying to hide the hump of her spine below the yoke. She
seemed to know that I, Justus Kümmerlich, would miss nothing. She took the lid from one of her buckets—a steam rose

323

from the white milk lying flat now inside—and offered me a ladleful small and thick.

'But it is still warm,' I exclaimed.

'Yes,' she laughed, 'I have only now stripped it from them.' And she made a milking motion with her hands and peered up at me.

I put the wood to my lips and quickly drank down the milk still raw with the warmth of the cows that gave suck to this community. I paid her and she walked again to the road, herself sloshing like a cow. Long and carefully I wiped my mouth.

Then, having drunk of the rich countryside, I climbed behind the wheel of my car and started the engine. I leaned from the door: 'Auf Wiedersehen, Milkmaid!' I put my foot on the accelerator, once, twice, and the engine rocked full throttle in several explosions of cylinders and exhaust. Smoke filled the yard. I raced the engine again and took hold of the hand brake; the pressure of the automobile filled the dashboard; vibrations possessed the automobile in all its libertine mechanization, noise and saliency.

'Wait!' At first I hardly heard the cry, 'Wait, wait!' But from the inn ran my wife, calling loudly the word shaped in vapour, twisting her ankles with every step, and one could see she felt the possibility of being left behind, left all alone, so driven was she to run like a wasp across this strange and empty yard. I imagined how she must have been wakened from her country sleep and how she must have started, frightened at the roar of the racing engine.

'What, Sesemi,' allowing the engine to cool down and idle, 'no hat?' But she did not smile and did not stop her trembling until I had silenced the machine.

So we journeyed, bearing always south, bearing down upon the spike-helmeted policemen of small villages, coming abreast of flocks of geese by the road, driving towards some church spire in the distance, racing down our rich continent all that summer and settling ourselves to sleep each night in the spring-weakened hollows of familiar beds which, no matter how old we grow, tell us always of mother and father and sick child as we roll from side to side through the years.

'Justus, do you know what day this is?'

'No,' I replied and kept my eyes to the road so flat now against the contour of the sea.

'They sent little Mauschel out of the house...'

'No riddles, Sesemi. No riddles.'

The sun was hot on the roof of the automobile and I sat with my chin lifted. Always I drove with my head raised slightly and looked clearly and relentlessly at the space ahead and now and then swabbed my neck, leaving the handkerchief to soak, so to speak, around my collar. That day the countryside was sunswept and a pale blue as if at any moment the earth itself might turn to water.

'Don't you recall it, Justus? Don't you recall the wreath?' Sesemi peered out of the window into the blue stratum of air spread over the sand. She was remembering, of course, and seemed to be washing her little eyes in that blue air, cleansing her sight if only to enjoy the scratching progress of the impurity across the conjunctiva. What memories she retained: only the unpleasant ones, the specks of gloom, the grains in the eye which, months later, she would tell me about. But the eyes of certain people are never without a redness inside the lids.

'I do not remember. Perhaps this is not a special day after all, Sesemi.'

'It was evening, Justus.'

'Then perhaps it was not a special evening, Sesemi.'

'Oh, yes. How lonely your brother would be now, except for Metze and Mauschel. And you and me, Justus.'

'Don't taunt me, Sesemi. Please.'

Late that afternoon we approached a small city and I steered the automobile quickly as I could through the outskirts to the centre of this traveller's resting place until I found the bank and parked in front of it. A group of children collected immediately around my automobile and began to touch the hood, the fenders, the spokes in the wheels.

There are banks all over the world and I am always at home in a bank. Nothing else is needed when one brushes off his coat and makes his appearance before the faceless tellers of these institutions. The clerk did not ask to see my credentials, sensing at once that his bank with its gold clock was my hostel, that some of my assets, a stranger's assets, were vaulted there waiting only upon my demand and my signature—Justus Kümmerlich. I noted that the pen trembled when he thrust it, his fingers pinching the wet point, through the grille.

'Thank you,' I said shortly and raised my eyes.

There was a hair on the pen point. I handed it back to the clerk, indicating the dirt, and lit a cigar. I could not hurry bank business. I looked around the room—the same, all the same, this very bastion in Zurich, Paris, Milan, even small Tiergarten, retaining faithfully all one's fortunes, the scruples of one's piety and reserve.

'A traveller must be cautious, I imagine,' came the sudden whisper.

'I beg pardon?'

'Cautious with money, Mein Herr. I imagine one does well to carry little.' He dropped the pen, then reappeared, attempting to wipe dry that face and quiet those round eyes. 'Travelling, sir, I should think one would take only the barest amount ... thieves, chambermaids, accidents. Nicht wahr?'

I began to write. The round worried face hovered there behind the mesh.

'If one is ordained to have it, one's money is not stolen, my friend. If there is money in your pocket, it will stay. If money is your domesticity, you will have only to be a good house-keeper. When travelling, my friend, it is simple: one has merely to know how to pin one's pocketbook inside the pillow.' I laughed and pushed the pen and the cheque into those reaching fingers.

He murmured something and then, smiling, sucking his breath, began to count with a terrible aimless dexterity, an inhuman possessiveness, confident but suffering while my money passed through his hands.

'Mein Herr,' he whispered, 'don't leave these bills in your hotel room.'

I took the packet and counted it quickly myself. The grill-work closed without a sound.

I reached the automobile and wrenched open the door. 'Mein Herr, Mein Herr,' begged the children, 'take us with

326

you!' Against the hot leather seat I lay back my head and smiled, though my eyes were shut. 'Well, Sesemi. The Riviera?'

I paid the hotel manager in advance. I stared into his small French eyes carefully and signed my name on his register. I guessed immediately that there was no sand in his shoes and that he drank a good deal of wine.

'But the linen,' staring at him again, 'what of the linen?'

'Herr Kümmerlich, smooth and white, of course! Perfectly white!'

The room was small. It contained a white bed and a few white mats placed on the empty table and on the arms of the chair, a room facing the ocean and filled with that tomb odour of habitations built by the sea. Each time I entered there was the sensation of a mild loneliness, a realization that it was not one's own.

In the beginning I thought that if we tired of going to the beach, we might sun ourselves on the porch completely encircling our floor of the hotel. But those who walked the porch at night spoiled it for the day. It was not long before I moved my chair so that it blocked our own screened doors, which opened upon the rotting and down-sloping porch. The first night the sea was loud; we could hear it green and barbarous, having emptied itself of humans there below. The sun sank like a woman into a hot bath; it became dark and the night was suddenly singing with mosquitoes and violins.

Sesemi was at last done with her kneeling at the bedside and climbed in beside me. We lay in the dark. Someone, perhaps a child, had fastened two large starfish to the screens of our porch door and now I saw them, silhouetted in dead sea fashion, between the blue night outside and the blackness within, all around us. From the next room came a little voice:

'Mamma, a drink of water, bitte.'

We lay still. The starfish rustled against the screen in a slight wind. The sea was beginning now to turn to foam, the hopeless separation of day and night, against all shores.

'Mamma. A drink of water, bitte.'

'Sesemi,' I said in the dark, 'if the child will not be quiet and go to sleep, you must fetch some water.'

'Ja, Justus.'

My eyes would not close. Even an older man—I was pleased to count myself among them—watches the stars when he lies down in a strange place, watches them in their cold heaven as he wonders what he may find on the beach when next the sun rises and the sea grows calm. I reached out and reassured myself of the light switch, relaxed my arms straight by my sides, thought of the meal I should order at dawn, and subsided into that state of alertness which for those who have found the middle of life is called sleep.

But I woke and the violins, not the insects, were still. Some equatorial disturbance was reflected now in the sea, which mounted steadily upon the scales of the shore, that sea which drowned the midnight suicides. I lifted my head quickly. There were two in embrace. Together they leaned heedlessly into our screened doors as if they thought the room empty, the two become a single creature that rolled its back and haunches into the mesh, scraped its four feet now and then on the porch wood. Their single body moved, scratched the wire, intent upon the revealing introspection of the embrace, immobile, swept by the black sea breezes.

'Pfui! Pfui!' I cried, clutching at the top of my pyjamas. And they were gone, drifting down the porch.

I got out of bed and trembled in the cold. Deftly, overcome with conscience, I pulled the billfold from my linen coat and opened my valise.

'Justus. What are you doing?'

'The pins,' I hissed over my shoulder, 'the pins!'

I did not eat heavily the next morning. But with the ringing of the gong and the screeching of a pack of gulls that early took flight from the roof of the hotel, Sesemi and I appeared among the first breakfasters and met, as we met morning and morning again, those old ladies who sat one to a table drinking their black coffee. It was said in the hotel that we Germans would not miss a meal, and that we even sat in the midst of the deaf ladies that we might eat the sooner. The old ladies were all grandmothers who had survived their young. All of them wore violet shawls over the quick irregular protrusions that were their backs and shoulder blades. They stayed in the dining-room a precise time, each of them; and then, before the sun was fully risen, they retreated up to their drawn rooms to wait through the long day for sundown. They preferred the cool, they sought the shade like snails and feared what they called the stroke.

Whenever we entered the dining-room Sesemi helped one of them to sit whenever we left the dining-room Sesemi helped one of them to exit. Every morning the hotel manager came among the tables and spoke to each old woman and finally to myself, urging his guests to enjoy some special luxury, but knowing all too well the fruitlessness of his invitation. The dining-room was a quiet place; the old women hardly tinkled spoon to cup until, in French, one of them would say, 'Ladies, ladies, here comes the sun!' And, putting down their napkins, they would faintly stir, then flee.

And a moment later the beach would be turned to fire, scattered over with the burning bathers and their umbrellas, bathers who were as eager to lie in the violet rays as the ladies were to escape them. The young ate no breakfast but went directly from their beds to the beach as if their youthful bodies and anonymous lively figures needed no food, except the particles of sunshine, to exist upon. The Germans were good at volley ball. The others, the French, rarely played the game, but paired off, man and woman, woman and man, to lie on their bright blankets and hold hands, inert about the beach like couples of black and slender seals.

The sun was always upon its dial, sending down to the beach intangible rays of heat and fomenting over this area its dangerous diffusion of light. The world came to us behind shut eyes. A silent bombardment descended upon the women with dark glasses while old gentlemen stuck out their legs as for treatment, expecting the sun to excite those shrunken tendons. Feet ran close to our heads on the sand. The catchers of star-fish came dangerously near and a small boy stepped on my arm at midmorning. The immensity of the sun was challenging, all the biology of myself, Justus, my lungs and liver, my blood-pumping system, cried out to meet the sun, to withstand the rising temperature, to survive the effects, the dehydration, of such a sun. We saw the child who had called for water in the darkness; well might it thirst.

When I went down to the water, Sesemi, sitting upon a towel, waved good-bye and admonished me to return if the seas were too cold or if I felt cramps. Women have no place in the water. What is the sea if not for the washing of dead relatives and for the swimming of fish and men? On this trip, only a few steps, I left behind my wife, my housecoat, the muffler, the partially smoked cigar that marked me for this world, and then, feeling the sands go wet, braced myself for that plunge into the anonymous black.

When I began walking upon that nearer undersurface which can never breathe the air and upon which the less heroic sea creatures move, I saw the thirsty child standing knee-deep and not far off, watching me. The child did not wave or smile but merely watched as if its parents had perhaps told it something about Herr Kümmerlich. But no, as I splashed forward, I realized that the child was speculating, trying to calculate the moment when I should leave my feet and thrust myself to ride upon the waves. I shut my eyes and heard it calling suddenly for its papa to come and see.

I was an excellent floater. I could drift farther from shore than anyone, buoyed and perfectly calm, flat on my back, so unsinkable was my body, classic and yet round with age as my father's. Floating is a better test of character than swimming—creatures that float are indestructible and children beware of them. Their parents have only admiration for him who moves effortlessly, purposefully, out to sea.

'That is Herr Kümmerlich out there.'

'What? That far?'

'Ja. Herr Kümmerlich. And, see, not a splash.'

Now I was floating, perfectly proportioned, helmeted in my old bathing cap and rocking steadily. What a swim it was, what sport! The water carried me fathoms high and I lay on the surface, the plane, from which the winds started and across which grew the salt in its nautical gardens. I was the master and the ship. Now and then my breast went under, I rolled for a long while in the hollow of a swell. My feet cut the water like a killer shark's fins, I breathed deep—Justus Kümmerlich—in the world of less-than-blood temperature.

The knees float, the head floats, the scrotum is awash; here is a man upon the sea, a rationalist thriving upon the great green spermary of the earth!

I might never have returned. The sea is made of male elements and I was vigorously contented there on the crest of it all. But at that instant there came suddenly the cutting of two sharp arms and the beating of a swimmer's legs. He made straight for me and at the last moment lifted his mouth to exclaim: 'Mein Herr, Frau Kümmerlich is worried. She would be pleased if you returned to shore,' and he shot by, racing, his head buried again in the foam of his blind channel. He was carrying on his back his little thin thirsty son, the boy sitting upright as on a dolphin and unconcerned with the violence of his father's strokes.

Sesemi was waiting on the dry sand with the towel. It was a noon sun, straight above us and near to the earth. I exposed myself to it and the thousand molecules of salt crystallized on my freshened skin. My hair was suddenly dry as straw. I heard her saying, 'Justus, Justus,' but I never moved and heard nothing but the swishing of the sun's tails. After all the peace of the ocean, now there was none; there was only the immoderate heat and a sudden blackness that fell upon me in the form of a great dead gull filled with fish. And so I stayed in the sun too long, and so I burned.

For three days I lay in our room occupying the bed alone, and blistered. A thick warm water swelled under the skin of my red body, my temperature would drop suddenly, chilled, and nausea would come in a storm. I knew the twilight of the sunburn, the sheet stuck to me like a crab. In the dead of night I would hear the speechless methodical striking of my compatriots' fists into the gasping sides of the volley ball. All memory, the entire line of my family, was destroyed in the roaring of the sea and the roaring of the sun. What horror when the bed turned and rocked gently out on the thick swells.

At last I woke. Like a gangrenous general waking from a stupor in his hot, fly-filled field tent, I peered through the sticky substance of eyeball and eyelid and saw the grey of the late afternoon, the grey of the dying window blinds tightly drawn. The room was dishevelled and torn as if their attendance upon me had been a violent thing. But now they too were serene.

Sesemi and the child were huddled together in the corner in the half-turned chair. They were watching me and smiling. Wearily and happily they were hugging each other—little Frau Kümmerlich, her hair undone, was hugging the child about the waist. They came to the bed together; Sesemi held his hand.

'Justus,' she said, and looked into the diffused parts of my eyes. 'Justus,' she whispered, 'it has been a long while.'

Then I was able to think of them and my lips slid open long enough for me to say, 'Yes, Sesemi. Yes, it has.'

'O die Fröhlichkeit!' she whispered, dropping her head to the tepid, sun-smelling sheet. The boy picked up the pan and went out the door, as habit had taught him, to empty it.

When I was able to travel, when I was able once more to hum the *Lorelei*, and we quit the town, I stopped the automobile before a butcher's shop and ordered the throat cut and the lamb packed whole with ice and rock salt in a wooden box.

'The whole lamb,' I explained to Sesemi, 'is for my brother. For Lebrecht! You see, Sesemi, I am the father after all.'

We started home.

ISAAC BASHEVIS SINGER

'I said, "You are a ball of fire.'
'Yes, fire from Gehenna"'

Israel, 1955. New York, 1965

The Mentor

1

When I arrived in Israel in 1955, I met two kinds of acquaintances: those I hadn't seen since 1935, when I left Warsaw for
the United States, and those I hadn't seen since 1922, when I
left Jadow for Warsaw. Those from Warsaw had known me as
a young author, a member of the writers' association and of
the Yiddish section of the PEN club; those from Jadow remembered me as an adolescent who tutored Hebrew, sent
poems to magazines that were immediately rejected, believed
himself deeply in love with a sixteen-year-old girl and in-
dulged in all sorts of Bohemian activities. The Warsaw people
called me by my literary pen name; the Jadower called me
Itche, or Itche the rabbi's, because I was the rabbi's grandson.

In Tel Aviv, the Yiddish writers held a reception for me
and made speeches. They swore that I had changed little.
The Jadower all asked the same question—'What happened
to your red hair?' They gathered in the house of a *landsman*
who had become rich from his business in leather. There I
had a strange experience: former servant girls and coachmen
spoke to me in fluent Hebrew. Some of those who spoke Yiddish spoke with a Russian or Lithuanian accent because they
had fled from Poland during the Second World War and spent
years in Vilna, Bialystok, Jambul or Tashkent. Girls I had
kissed on the sly and who used to call me *Moreh*—teacher—
told me about their married children and even of their grandchildren. Faces and figures had changed beyond recognition.

Slowly I began to orient myself. Several of the Jadow
women confided that they had never forgotten me. My boyhood companions reminded me of the wild pranks I played,
the fantastic stories I told and even of my jokes about the old

townspeople. Many of the Jadower were missing. They had perished in the ghettoes and concentration camps or had died in Russia of hunger, typhoid fever and scurvy. Some of the Jadower had lost children in the war against the Arabs in 1948. My *landsleit* both laughed and sighed. They prepared a banquet for me, and a memorial evening for those who had not survived.

Since they called me Itche and spoke familiarly, I felt young in this crowd. I began to babble again, telling all kinds of jokes about Berl, the village idiot, and Reb Mordecai Meyer, the Jadower preacher of morality. I spoke to these middle-aged men and women as if they were still boys and girls. I even tried to renew my old romances. Good-naturedly, the Jadower made fun of me and said, 'Really, Itche, you are still the same!'

Among the Jadower who came to meet me was Freidl, a former pupil of mine who was now a doctor. She was about ten years younger than I. When I was seventeen, she was eight. Her father, Avigdor Rosenbach, was one of the enlightened, a rich lumber dealer. In Israel, Freidl had Hebraized her name and was called Ditza. Before I left Jadow, Freidl was already known for her sharp mind. She spoke Yiddish and Polish, studied French with one teacher and piano with another. She quickly mastered the Hebrew I taught her. She was a pretty little girl, with black hair, a white skin and green eyes. She plagued me with all sorts of questions that I could not answer. In her childish way she flirted with me, and after every lesson I had to kiss her. She promised to marry me when she grew up. Later, in Warsaw, I learned that Freidl had finished *Gymnasium* with honours and studied medicine at the Sorbonne. Somebody told me that she knew eight languages. One day, I heard the strange news that she had married a Jadower boy, Tobias Stein. Tobias was a youth of my age; his ideal was to be a chalutz in Palestine. Although his father was a wealthy merchant, he learned carpentry in order to become a builder in the settlements. He was dark, with laughing black eyes and a head of curly black hair. He wore a blouse with a sash, and a white-and-blue cap embroidered with the Star of David to express his Zionistic fervour. Besides carpentry, he learned to shoot a rifle so he could become a guard in Palestine and protect the colonies from Arab attack. He knew the geography of Palestine better than any of us, sang all the Zionist songs, and declaimed Bialik's poems. Some time after I left Warsaw, Tobias received a certificate to enter Palestine, but it seems that he returned to Europe long enough to marry Freidl. I didn't know the details; neither did I care to know them.

Years after the Second World War, I learned that Freidl had a daughter with Tobias and that the two had separated. Freidl had made a career in Israel; she was a neurologist and had written a book, which was translated into other languages. She was said to have had all kinds of affairs—among others, with a high officer of the English Army. Tobias lived in a remote kibbutz. He was still in love with Freidl. Their daughter had remained with him.

Freidl's entrance that evening into the home of the rich leather dealer created a sensation among the Jadower. She had avoided all their gatherings, and they considered her a snob. The woman who came into the room would have been over forty but looked much younger: a little taller than medium height, slender, with closely cropped black hair, her skin still white, her eyes green. I recognized the Freidl of long ago—only her nose had become that of a grown-up, serious person. Although she did not wear glasses, there were marks on the skin, as if she had just removed her pince-nez. She wore a suit of English tweed, with a woman's tie; her purse resembled an attaché case. On her finger sat a large emerald ring. Worldliness, energy and resolution emanated from her. She looked at me in perplexity. Then she called out, '*Moreh!*' and we kissed. I imagined that the smell of all the men with whom she had had affairs still clung to her. After the first sentences, she spoke to me in Yiddish instead of Hebrew. I was embarrassed—I, who had taught her the Hebrew alphabet, could not keep up with her Hebrew, which she spoke rapidly, in a strong voice, and with the modern Sephardic accent. She told me that she was connected with the university in Jerusalem. She also had contacts with universities abroad—even in the United States. The Jadower became silent. They listened to our talk with awe.

I asked, 'May I still call you Friedl?'

And she answered, 'For you, I will always be Freidl.'

2

After the reception, a number of the Jadower wanted to accompany me to the hotel, but Freidl announced that she had her car and would drive me, and no one dared to contradict her. In the car, Freidl said to me, 'Are you in a hurry? It's a beautiful night. Let's go for a ride.'

'Yes, with pleasure.'

We drove through the city. How strange it was to be in a Jewish country, to read shop signs in the latest created Hebrew to pass streets with the names of rabbis, Zionist leaders, writers. The day had been a hot one—actually, a chamsin, though not the worst kind. I saw women covering their faces with kerchiefs to keep from breathing in the fine desert sand that the wind carried. The sun had set—large, red, not round as usual but pointed towards the bottom, like a fruit with a stem. Usually in Tel Aviv it cools off after dark, but on this night the hot breeze continued. Gasoline fumes mixed with the smell of softening asphalt and with the freshness that drifted in from the fields, the hills, the valleys. From the sea came the stench of dead fish and the city's refuse. The moon stood low, dark red, half erased, and I had a feeling that it might be falling to earth in a cosmic catastrophe. The stars shook like little lamps suspended from unseen wires. We took the road towards Jaffa. On my right the sea sparkled silvery. Green shadows passed across its surface. Freidl said, 'On nights like this I cannot sleep anyhow. I walk around and smoke cigarettes.'

I wanted to ask her why she had left Tobias, but I knew that the question should be put in other terms: Why had she married him? However, I waited till she would begin to talk. We passed Arabic houses with many cupolas, like the breasts of mythical beasts. Some of the houses had beaded curtains instead of doors. Freidl pointed out a mosque and a minaret from which the muezzins call the faithful five times a day. After a while, she began.

'It was crazy, the whole business. I remembered him from

the time I was still a child, and I was left with a romantic illusion. I belong to the type of woman who is attracted to older men—you know how they call it in Freudian jargon. The truth is I also had a crush on you, but I heard that you were married. I realized early that we Jews had no future in the Diaspora. Not only Hitler—the whole world was ready to tear us to pieces. You were right when you wrote that modern Jews are suicidal. The modern Jew can't live without anti-Semitism. If it's not there, he's driven to create it. He has to bleed for humanity—battle the reactionaries, worry about the Chinese, the Manchurians, the Russians, the untouchables in India, the Negroes in America. He preaches revolution and at the same time he wants all the privileges of capitalism for himself. He tries to destroy nationalism in others but prides himself on belonging to the Chosen People. How can a tribe like this exist among strangers? I wanted to settle here, with my so-called brothers and sisters, and there was Tobias—an idealist, a pioneer. I had visited here, and I imagined that I loved him. Even as I stood with him under the canopy, I knew I'd made a mistake. I'd convinced myself that he was a hero, but I soon saw that he was a schlemiel, softheaded, as sentimental as an old maid. In the beginning, his Hebrew dazzled me, but when I listened closely I realized that banalities poured from his mouth. He parroted all the brochures, all the editorials in the newspapers. He sang cheap songs with gusto. He fell in love with me in a sick way, and that love completely crushed me. There isn't a greater pain than to be loved by a fool. He makes you frigid and ashamed of your sex. Near him I became cruel and bitchy. I immediately wanted to end it, but then our Rina came. A child is a child. She took after our family, not his. But he keeps her as a pawn. He has set her against me until she has become my adversary in every way. I am disappointed in the kibbutz, too. It has the faults of Communism along with those of capitalism. What kind of person can she become there? A half-educated peasant. Do you smoke?'

'No.'

'I hear you don't eat meat, either.'

'No.'

'What's the sense of it? Nature knows no compassion. As far

as nature is concerned, we are like worms. You taught me the Bible, and my father stuffed me with the miracles that God performed for the Jews. But after what happened to them one must be absolutely stupid and insensitive to believe in God and all that drivel. What's more, to believe in a compassionate God is the worst betrayal of the victims. A rabbi from America visited here, and he preached that all the six million Jews sit in Paradise, gorge themselves on the meat of the Leviathan and study the Torah with angels. You don't need to be a psychologist to figure out what that kind of belief compensates for. In Jerusalem there's a group that dabbles in psychic research. I became involved a little—I even attended their séances. It's all fake. If they don't swindle others, they deceive themselves. Without a functioning brain, there is no thought. If a hereafter really existed, it would be the greatest cruelty. Why should a soul remember all the pettiness of its existence? What would be so wonderful if my father's soul continued to live and recall how his partner stole from him, how his house burned down, how my sister Mirele died in childbirth and then the ghettoes, the camps and the Nazi ovens. If there is one iota of justice in nature, it is the obliteration of the spirit when the body decays. I don't understand how one can think differently.'

'If one thinks that way, there is no reason one should not be a Nazi.'

'It's not a question of should or should not. Nazis are enemies of the human race, and people must be allowed to exterminate them like bedbugs.'

'How about the weak ones? What rights do they have?'

'They have the right to unite and become strong.'

'Why not enjoy all the privileges and injustices meanwhile?' I asked.

'We do enjoy them. The fact that at this moment we find ourselves riding in a car, instead of pulling somebody in a rickshaw or standing in a rice field up to our knees in water and working for six piastres a day is already a privilege and even an injustice. Let's end this talk. It leads nowhere. You yourself believe in nothing.'

'Someone takes charge of this world.'

'Who? Nonsense. Sheer nonsense!'

'What about the stars?'

Freidl lifted her head for a second. 'The stars are stars.'

We became silent. The road ran through fields and orchards—or perhaps they were orange groves; it was too dark to see. From time to time a light flickered in the distance. I did not ask where we were going. I had already crossed the land in its length and breadth and my curiosity was quenched. We had travelled for half an hour without encountering a single car. A midnight silence hovered over the earth. The wind had stopped. The noise of the motor was overlaid by the chirping of crickets, the croaking of frogs and the rustle of myriads of insects that lived in this Holy Land, searched for food, protection, mates.

Freidl said, 'If you are sleepy, I will turn back. For me, there is no greater pleasure than such a trip in the night.'

I wanted to ask Freidl about her affairs, but I restrained myself. I knew that most people like to confess but can't stand having someone force the truth from them with open curiosity. I don't remember how it came about, but Freidl began to talk again.

'What was there to stop me?' she said. 'I didn't love him, and even if I did I would have wanted to taste others. I had men before him, with him and after him. I had somebody on our what you call honeymoon. There are monogamous women and even men, but I don't belong to them. I feel like de Maupassant: two lovers are better than one, and three are better than two. Naturally, I had to turn away some, but never out of moral motives. I share Mme Kollontai's opinion that my body is my private property. Exactly what love is I don't know and probably never will know. Everyone understands it in his own way. I've heard countless stories from my patients. But there isn't any explanation for human behaviour—there are only patterns. Lately, I became a disciple of Gestalt psychology because it doesn't try to find motivations. A cat catches mice. A bee makes honey. Stalin craved power. Modern Jews also crave power—not directly but only through working behind the scenes. In that sense they are like women. The Jew is a born critic. He has to tear things down. Here he cannot belittle everything, and this makes him mad. I am, as you see, a complete hedonist. But there are inhibitions that don't allow one to enjoy things. You won't believe it, but my daughter is the main disturbance in my life. A hundred times a day I tell myself that a child is nothing more than an accidentally fertilized egg and that all the love and loyalty one feels towards it are only blind instinct—or call it what you will. But it bothers me just the same. Her hatred, her complaints make me miserable. It grows worse from day to day. I literally hear how she talks back to me, scolds me and tries to revenge the wrongs I am supposed to have done her father. I wanted to send her abroad to study, but she refuses to take anything from me. She doesn't answer my letters. When I telephone her—and in a kibbutz it's not an easy thing to get a connection—she hangs up on me. There would be one remedy—to go back to live with Tobias—but the very thought of it makes me vomit. How he managed to implant such hatred is a riddle to me. This has actually become the essence of his life. He appears to be saccharin sweet, but inside he is bitter and malicious. The things he says are baffling in their stupidity, and yet they frighten me, too. There is some mysterious strength in fools. They are deeply rooted in the primeval chaos. You are the only man in the world I have confided this to. I have lost my brothers, and to me you are like an older brother. Thirty-three years is a long time, but somehow I remembered you. Many times I wanted to write to you. However, for me writing a letter is an impossible task. Aren't you sleepy?'

'No.'

'Why not? It's late.'

'The history in this land doesn't let me sleep.'

'Who? Father Abraham?'

'The prophets.'

'The first time I was afraid I wouldn't be able to go to the toilet in Jerusalem, it was so holy, but you get accustomed to it. Are you ready to ride with me the whole night?'

'Yes, but where?'

'Don't laugh at me. I want to take you to my daughter's kibbutz. I stopped visiting her. I've taken an oath—a secular oath; by what can we swear?—that I will never visit her. Every time I go there, she shows her hostility. She is simply possessed by her hatred for me. She refuses to sit with me in the dining hall. She has spit in my face. The reason I want to take you is this. Tobias will be happy to see you. You and he were supposed to be bosom friends. He reads you faithfully. Rina also knows of you. She boasts that you are her father's friend. Here a writer still commands some respect. In that sense, Israel is like Jadow. I can't rest in bed anyhow, and I don't take tranquillizers any more. I'd like to go and have a look at her. Then we will drive back and you will be in the hotel by ten o'clock. I have to be at the clinic, but since you have no work here, you can close the shutters and sleep as long as you wish.'

'All right, I agree.'

'I am exploiting you, eh? I know I am being weak, but there is some weakness even in the strong. We will be in the kibbutz at daybreak. They have a high school there, and Rina is in the senior class. She works there, too. She has chosen the stable, just to spite me. She milks the cows and cleans away the dung. There is one sphere in which everyone is a genius, and that is in being spiteful.'

'What kind of a kibbutz is it?'

Freidl mentioned a name.

'Isn't that a leftist kibbutz?'

'Yes, they are leftists. He, as well as his daughter. Their god is Borokhov. They went there to spread the Torah of revolution directly from Zion. The others have cooled off somewhat, but for the two of them Lenin is still Moses. It's all personal. Just because I make fun of it. She is good-looking, an absolute beauty—clever also. In America, Hollywood would have snapped her up, but here she became a stablemaid.'

'Does she go out with boys?'

'Yes, but not seriously. She'll marry some boor, and that will be it.'

'She will give you grandchildren.'

'For this I have no feeling at all.'

'Who is your present lover?'

Freidl was silent for a while. 'Oh, there is one. A lawyer, an *orech-din*. He has a wife and children. When I want him he's here, and when I don't want him he's off. Tobias wouldn't divorce me anyhow. I am past forty, and the great desire is over. Once, I had a passion for my work; now even this isn't what it used to be. I would like to write a novel, but no one is waiting for my fiction. Besides, I am actually left without a language. Hebrew is not my mother tongue. To write in Yiddish here makes no sense. I know French fluently, but I haven't used it in years. My English is quite good, but not good enough for writing. Anyhow, I'm not going to become your competitor. Lean back and try to sleep.'

'I assure you, I'm not sleepy.'

'If you had come a few years sooner, I might have started something with you, but for some time now I've had the feeling that it's late for everything. Perhaps this is the beginning of my menopause, or a presage of death. This daughter has robbed me of all my joy.'

'Really, you should be psychoanalysed.'

'What? I don't believe in it. It wouldn't help. All my life I've had one main neurosis and a lot of little ones I called the "candidates". When one stepped out, another rose to take its place. They kept on changing, like a clique of politicians. One became the leader for a few years, and then he handed over power to the next. In a few cases, something like a court revolution occurred. This with my daughter is relatively new, but not so new. It grew like a cancer, and I felt it growing.'

'What is it that you want of her?'

'That she should love me.'

'And what will this bring you?'

'I'm asking you.'

I leaned back and began to doze.

3

I was neither awake nor asleep. I dreamed, and in the middle of my dreams I opened one eye and saw that the moon had vanished. The black night lay heavily over the earth, and it reminded me of the darkness in the beginning of creation before God said, 'Let there be light!' The insects had become silent. Freidl drove quickly, and I had the uncanny feeling that we were sliding downhill into an abyss. The glowing tip of her cigarette shook upwards, downwards, sidewise. She seemed to be signalling to someone in a fiery code. You never know who is going to be your angel of death, I thought. It's

Freidl from Jadow. I slept again and saw craggy mountains and shadowy giants. They tried to lay a bridge from summit to summit. They spoke an ancient tongue in booming voices and reached out long arms to the edge of the horizon. Below, waters were raging, foaming, throwing up boulders. 'Can this be the river Sambation?' I asked myself. 'In that case, it's not just a legend...' I opened my eyes, and from behind a hill the sun emerged, bathed and Biblical, casting a light that was neither night nor day. In my half sleep, this scene was somehow connected with the priests' blessing of the Jews, which one is not permitted to look upon lest one become blind. I dozed again.

Freidl woke me. We had arrived at the kibbutz. In the twilight of dawn I saw cactus trees gleaming with dew, beds of flowers, and huts with open doors from which half-dressed men and women came out. They were all sunburned, almost black. Some carried towels, cakes of soap, toothbrushes. Freidl said to me, 'You slept like a god.'

She took my arm and led me on a narrow path overgrown with wet grass. She knocked at a door, and when no one responded she knocked louder. I heard a hoarse voice, and Freidl answered. The door opened and out came a man with dishevelled black hair streaked with white, barefoot, in an unbuttoned shirt that exposed a hairy chest. One side of his face was more wrinkled than the other—raw and red as from a rash. He held up his pants with one hand. 'Can this be Tobias?' I asked myself. He had broad shoulders, a thick nose and a heavily veined neck.

Freidl said to him, 'Forgive me for waking you. I brought you a guest.'

I was beginning to find some resemblance between this elderly person and Tobias from Jadow. But he blinked sleepily and did not recognize me.

Freidl smiled. 'It's Itche the rabbi's, from Jadow.'

'Itche,' Tobias repeated and stood there bewildered, with his hand on his unbuttoned pants. After a while, he embraced me with his free hand. We kissed, and his beard pricked me like nails.

Freidl said, 'I want to see Rina. I will just take a look at her. We have to go straight back.'

'Rina isn't home,' Tobias answered hesitantly, in a flat voice.

Freidl became tense. 'Where is she?'

'Not home.'

'Where?'

'With a girl friend.'

'Who? You're lying.'

Husband and wife began to bicker in Hebrew. I heard Tobias say, 'She is with her mentor.'

'With her mentor? In the middle of the night?'

'With her mentor,' Tobias repeated.

'Are you crazy, or do you think that I am?'

'She sleeps there.' Tobias spoke as if to himself.

Although the sun threw purple flecks on Freidl's face, I saw that she paled. Her lips trembled. Her expression became angry, aggrieved. She said, 'A girl of sixteen goes to sleep at a boy's? You shame me before Itche.'

'She learned it from her mother.' Tobias's eyes beneath his bushy brows were piercing and cold. I saw in them an expression of mockery. I stepped back. Tobias made a sign with his hand that I should wait. He smiled, and for the first time I really recognized the Tobias from Jadow. He went inside.

Freidl called a name after him. She turned to me. 'He's mad. A mad degenerate.'

We stood still, apart from one another. Tobias was not in a hurry to come out. Freidl's face seemed set and older. 'It's all malice. To spite me, he's making a whore of his daughter. Well, I have no more daughter.'

'Perhaps it isn't true.'

'Come, let's see.'

Freidl walked in front of me, and I followed. My pants and socks became wet with dew. We passed a truck into which men with bare chests were loading crates of live chickens. They clucked in their sleep. We approached a building that looked half-way between a hayloft and a watchtower. There was a weathercock on its roof. This was where the mentor lived. A ladder led up to the entrance. Freidl called, 'Rina!' Her voice sounded shrill, with a tremor of crying. She called many times, but no one looked out from the open window. Freidl gave me a sidewise glance, as if to ask, 'Should I climb up?'

I felt cold; my knees were shaky. It all seemed without substance—one of those nightmares that vanish as soon as one wakens. I wanted to tell Freidl there was no purpose in standing here, it would be best to go back, but at that moment the face of a girl appeared. It passed like a shadow. Freidl must have seen it also. She stood openmouthed. This was no longer the doctor who had spoken those clever words this night but a shocked Jewish mother. It seemed that she wanted to cry out, but she was silent. It was now full day, and a mist drifted from somewhere. I said, 'Come, Freidl, it makes no sense.'

'Yes, you are right.'

I was apprehensive that Freidl would take me back to Tobias's house and begin a quarrel with him, but she led me in another direction. She walked so quickly I could barely follow her. We passed the empty dining hall. Naked bulbs lighted the room. A girl was spreading paper on narrow tables. A boy washed the stone floor with a rag mop. The air was pungent with disinfectant. Soon we reached Freidl's car.

She drove fast. I leaned back and stared ahead. It was cold and I shivered. I turned up the collar of my jacket. Thank God I have no daughters, I thought. In the east, a cloud spread out like a huge bed of fiery coals. A long row of birds flew by screeching. We passed a flock of sheep that seemed to be feeding on the sandy soil of a barren field. Although I had doubts about God, His mercy, and Providence, passages from the Bible came to my mind—Isaiah's admonitions of doom: 'A sinful nation, a people laden with iniquity, a seed of evil-doers... They have forsaken the Lord. They have provoked the Holy One of Israel...' I had an urge to prove to Freidl that she was using a double standard—one for herself and a different one for others—but I knew that her contradictions were also my contradictions. The powers that rule history had brought us back to the land of our ancestors, but we had already defiled it with abominations. The sun became hot and sulphurous yellow. Sparks and little flames fell from it, as from a torch. It threw a light shadowy and gloomy, as at a time of eclipse. A dry wind blew from the desert, sweeping in fine sand. Freidl's face became ashen grey and sunken. At this moment I saw in her a resemblance to her mother, Deborah Ita.

We pulled up at a gas station with a sign in Hebrew, and Freidl said to me, 'Where shall we go from here? If this is a mentor, everything is lost. I am cured, cured for ever!'

Translated by the author and Evelyn Torton Beck

The Cafeteria

1

Even though I have reached the point where a great part of
my earnings is given away in taxes, I still have the habit of
eating in cafeterias when I am by myself. I like to take a tray
with a tin knife, fork, spoon and paper napkin and to choose
at the counter the food I enjoy. Besides, I meet there the
landsleit from Poland, as well as all kinds of literary begin-
ners and readers who know Yiddish. The moment I sit down
at a table, they come over. 'Hello, Aaron!' they greet me, and
we talk about Yiddish literature, the Holocaust, the state of
Israel and often about acquaintances who were eating rice
pudding or stewed prunes the last time I was here and are
already in their graves. Since I seldom read a paper, I learn
this news only later. Each time, I am startled, but at my age
one has to be ready for such tidings. The food sticks in the
throat; we look at one another in confusion, and our eyes ask
mutely, Whose turn is next? Soon we begin to chew again. I
am often reminded of a scene in a film about Africa. A lion
attacks a herd of zebras and kills one. The frightened zebras
run for a while and then they stop and start to graze again.
Do they have a choice?

I cannot spend too long with these Yiddishists, because I
am always busy. I am writing a novel, a story, an article. I
have to lecture today or tomorrow; my datebook is crowded
with all kinds of appointments for weeks and months in
advance. It can happen that an hour after I leave the cafeteria
I am on a train to Chicago or flying to California. But meanwhile we converse in the mother language and I hear of
intrigues and pettiness about which, from a moral point of
view, it would be better not to be informed. Everyone tries in
his own way with all his means to grab as many honours and
as much money and prestige as he can. None of us learns from

347

all these deaths. Old age does not cleanse us. We don't repent at the gate of hell.

I have been moving around in this neighbourhood for over thirty years—as long as I lived in Poland. I know each block, each house. There has been little building here on uptown Broadway in the last decades, and I have the illusion of having put down roots here. I have spoken in most of the synagogues. They know me in some of the stores and in the vegetarian restaurants. Women with whom I have had affairs live on the side streets. Even the pigeons know me; the moment I come out with a bag of feed, they begin to fly towards me from blocks away. It is an area that stretches from Ninety-sixth Street to Seventy-second Street and from Central Park to Riverside Drive. Almost every day on my walk after lunch, I pass the funeral parlour that waits for us and all our ambitions and illusions. Sometimes I imagine that the funeral parlour is also a kind of cafeteria where one gets a quick eulogy or Kaddish on the way to eternity.

The cafeteria people I meet are mostly men: old bachelors like myself, would-be writers, retired teachers, some with dubious doctorate titles, a rabbi without a congregation, a painter of Jewish themes, a few translators—all immigrants from Poland or Russia. I seldom know their names. One of them disappears and I think he is already in the next world; suddenly he reappears and he tells me that he has tried to settle in Tel Aviv or Los Angeles. Again he eats his rice pudding, sweetens his coffee with saccharin. He has a few more wrinkles, but he tells the same stories and makes the same gestures. It may happen that he takes a paper from his pocket and reads me a poem he has written.

It was in the fifties that a woman appeared in the group who looked younger than the rest of us. She must have been in her early thirties; she was short, slim, with a girlish face, brown hair that she wore in a bun, a short nose and dimples in her cheeks. Her eyes were hazel—actually, of an indefinite colour. She dressed in a modest European way. She spoke Polish, Russian and an idiomatic Yiddish. She always carried Yiddish newspapers and magazines. She had been in a prison camp in Russia and had spent some time in the camps in Germany before she obtained a visa for the United States. The men all hovered around her. They didn't let her pay the check. They gallantly brought her coffee and cheese cake. They listened to her talk and jokes. She had returned from the devastation still gay. She was introduced to me. Her name was Esther. I didn't know if she was unmarried, a widow, a divorcée. She told me she was working in a factory, where she sorted buttons. This fresh young woman did not fit into the group of elderly has-beens. It was also hard to understand why she couldn't find a better job than sorting buttons in New Jersey. But I didn't ask too many questions. She told me that she had read my writing while still in Poland, and later in the camps in Germany after the war. She said to me, 'You are my writer.'

The moment she uttered those words I imagined I was in love with her. We were sitting alone (the other man at our table had gone to make a telephone call), and I said, 'For such words I must kiss you.'

'Well, what are you waiting for?'

She gave me both a kiss and a bite.

I said, 'You are a ball of fire.'

'Yes, fire from Gehenna.'

A few days later, she invited me to her home. She lived on a street between Broadway and Riverside Drive with her father, who had no legs and sat in a wheelchair. His legs had been frozen in Siberia. He had tried to run away from one of Stalin's slave camps in the winter of 1944. He looked like a strong man, had a head of thick white hair, a ruddy face and eyes full of energy. He spoke in a swaggering fashion, with boyish boastfulness and a cheerful laugh. In an hour, he told me his story. He was born in White Russia but he had lived long years in Warsaw, Lodz and Vilna. In the beginning of the thirties, he became a Communist and soon afterwards a functionary in the Party. In 1939 he escaped to Russia with his daughter. His wife and the other children remained in Nazi-occupied Warsaw. In Russia, somebody denounced him as a Trotskyite and he was sent to mine gold in the north. The G.P.U. sent people there to die. Even the strongest could not survive the cold and hunger for more than a year. They were exiled without a sentence. They died together: Zionists,

349

Bundists, members of the Polish Socialist Party, Ukrainian
Nationalists and just refugees, all caught because of the
labour shortage. They often died of scurvy or beriberi. Boris
Merkin, Esther's father, spoke about this as if it were a big
joke. He called the Stalinists outcasts, bandits, sycophants. He
assured me that had it not been for the United States Hitler
would have overrun all of Russia. He told how prisoners
tricked the guards to get an extra piece of bread or a double
portion of watery soup, and what methods were used in picking lice.

Esther called out, 'Father, enough!'

'What's the matter—am I lying?'

'One can have enough even of *kreplach.*'

'Daughter, you did it yourself.'

When Esther went into the kitchen to make tea, I learned
from her father that she had had a husband in Russia—a
Polish Jew who had volunteered in the Red Army and
perished in the war. Here in New York she was courted by a
refugee, a former smuggler in Germany who had opened a
bookbinding factory and become rich. 'Persuade her to marry
him,' Boris Merkin said to me. 'It would be good for me, too.'

'Maybe she doesn't love him.'

'There is no such thing as love. Give me a cigarette. In the
camp, people climbed on one another like worms.'

2

I had invited Esther to supper, but she called to say she had
the grippe and must remain in bed. Then in a few days time
a situation arose that made me leave for Israel. On the way
back, I stopped over in London and Paris. I wanted to write
to Esther, but I had lost her address. When I returned to New
York, I tried to call her, but there was no telephone listing
for Boris Merkin or Esther Merkin—father and daughter
must have been boarders in somebody else's apartment. Weeks
passed and she did not show up in the cafeteria. I asked the
group about her; nobody knew where she was. 'She has most
probably married that bookbinder,' I said to myself. One
evening, I went to the cafeteria with the premonition that I
would find Esther there. I saw a black wall and boarded

windows—the cafeteria had burned. The old bachelors were no doubt meeting in another cafeteria, or an Automat. But where? To search is not in my nature. I had plenty of complications without Esther.

The summer passed; it was winter. Late one day, I walked by the cafeteria and again saw lights, a counter, guests. The owners had rebuilt. I entered, took a check and saw Esther sitting alone at a table reading a Yiddish newspaper. She did not notice me, and I observed her for a while. She wore a man's fur fez and a jacket trimmed with a faded fur collar. She looked pale, as though recuperating from a sickness. Could that grippe have been the start of a serious illness? I went over to her table and asked, 'What's new in buttons?'

She started and smiled. Then she called out, 'Miracles do happen!'

'Where have you been?'

'Where did you disappear to?' she replied. 'I thought you were still abroad.'

'Where are our *cafeterianiks*?'

'They now go to the cafeteria on Fifty-seventh Street and Eighth Avenue. They only reopened this place yesterday.'

'May I bring you a cup of coffee?'

'I drink too much coffee. All right.'

I went to get her coffee and a large egg cookie. While I stood at the counter, I turned my head and looked at her. Esther had taken off her mannish fur hat and smoothed her hair. She folded the newspaper, which meant that she was ready to talk. She got up and tilted the other chair against the table as a sign that the seat was taken. When I sat down, Esther said, 'You left without saying good-bye, and there I was about to knock at the pearly gates of heaven.'

'What happened?'

'Oh, the grippe became pneumonia. They gave me penicillin, and I am one of those who cannot take it. I got a rash all over my body. My father, too, is not well.'

'What's the matter with your father?'

'High blood pressure. He had a kind of stroke and his mouth became all crooked.'

'Oh, I'm sorry. Do you still work with buttons?'

'Yes, with buttons. At least I don't have to use my head,

only my hands. I can think my own thoughts.'

'What do you think about?'

'What not. The other workers are all Puerto Ricans. They rattle away in Spanish from morning to night.'

'Who takes care of your father?'

'Who? Nobody. I come home in the evening to make supper. He has one desire—to marry me off for my own good and, perhaps, for his comfort, but I can't marry a man I don't love.'

'What is love?'

'You ask me! You write novels about it. But you're a man—I assume you really don't know what it is. A woman is a piece of merchandise to you. To me a man who talks nonsense or smiles like an idiot is repulsive. I would rather die than live with him. And a man who goes from one woman to another is not for me. I don't want to share with anybody.'

'I'm afraid a time is coming when everybody will.'

'That is not for me.'

'What kind of person was your husband?'

'How did you know I had a husband? My father, I suppose. The minute I leave the room, he prattles. My husband believed in things and was ready to die for them. He was not exactly my type but I respected him and loved him, too. He wanted to die and he died like a hero. What else can I say?'

'And the others?'

'There were no others. Men were after me. The way people behaved in the war—you will never know. They lost all shame. On the bunks near me one time, a mother lay with one man and her daughter with another. People were like beasts—worse than beasts. In the middle of it all, I dreamed about love. Now I have even stopped dreaming. The men who come here are terrible bores. Most of them are half mad, too. One of them tried to read me a forty-page poem. I almost fainted.'

'I wouldn't read you anything I'd written.'

'I've been told how you behave—no!'

'No is no. Drink your coffee.'

'You don't even try to persuade me. Most men around here plague you and you can't get rid of them. In Russia people suffered, but I have never met as many maniacs there as in

New York City. The building where I live is a madhouse. My neighbours are lunatics. They accuse each other of all kinds of things. They sing, cry, break dishes. One of them jumped out of the window and killed herself. She was having an affair with a boy twenty years younger. In Russia the problem was to escape the lice; here you're surrounded by insanity.'

We drank coffee and shared the egg cookie. Esther put down her cup. 'I can't believe that I'm sitting with you at this table. I read all your articles under all your pen names. You tell so much about yourself I have the feeling I've known you for years. Still, you are a riddle to me.'

'Men and women can never understand one another.'

'No—I cannot understand my own father. Sometimes he is a complete stranger to me. He won't live long.'

'Is he so sick?'

'It's everything together. He's lost the will to live. Why live without legs, without friends, without a family? They have all perished. He sits and reads the newspapers all day long. He acts as though he were interested in what's going on in the world. His ideals are gone, but he still hopes for a just revolution. How can a revolution help him? I myself never put my hopes in any movement or party. How can we hope when everything ends in death?'

'Hope in itself is a proof that there is no death.'

'Yes, I know you often write about this. For me, death is the only comfort. What do the dead do? They continue to drink coffee and eat egg cookies? They still read newspapers? A life after death would be nothing but a joke.'

3

Some of the *cafeterianiks* came back to the rebuilt cafeteria. New people appeared—all of them Europeans. They launched into long discussions in Yiddish, Polish, Russian, even Hebrew. Some of those who came from Hungary mixed German, Hungarian, Yiddish-German then all of a sudden they began to speak plain Galician Yiddish. They asked to have their coffee in glasses, and held lumps of sugar between their teeth when they drank. Many of them were my readers. They introduced themselves and reproached me for all kinds of literary errors: I contradicted myself, went too far in descriptions of sex, described Jews in such a way that anti-Semites could use it for propaganda. They told me their experiences in the ghettoes, in the Nazi concentration camps, in Russia. They pointed out one another. 'Do you see that fellow—in Russia he immediately became a Stalinist. He denounced his own friends. Here in America he has switched to anti-Bolshevism.' The one who was spoken about seemed to sense that he was being maligned, because the moment my informant left he took his cup of coffee and his rice pudding, sat down at my table and said, 'Don't believe a word of what you are told. They invent all kinds of lies. What could you do in a country where the rope was always around your neck? You had to adjust yourself if you wanted to live and not die somewhere in Kazakhstan. To get a bowl of soup or a place to stay you had to sell your soul.'

There was a table with a group of refugees who ignored me. They were not interested in literature and journalism but strictly in business. In Germany they had been smugglers. They seemed to be doing shady business here, too; they whispered to one another and winked, counted their money, wrote long lists of numbers. Somebody pointed out one of them. 'He had a store in Auschwitz.'

'What do you mean, a store?'

'God help us. He kept his merchandise in the straw where he slept—a rotten potato, sometimes a piece of soap, a tin spoon, a little fat. Still, he did business. Later, in Germany, he became such a big smuggler they once took forty thousand dollars away from him.'

Sometimes months passed between my visits to the cafeteria. A year or two had gone by (perhaps three or four; I lost count), and Esther did not show up. I asked about her a few times. Someone said that she was going to the cafeteria on Forty-second Street; another had heard that she was married. I learned that some of the *cafeterianiks* had died. They were beginning to settle down in the United States, had remarried, opened businesses, workshops, even had children again. Then came cancer or a heart attack. The result of the Hitler and Stalin years, it was said.

One day, I entered the cafeteria and saw Esther. She was

sitting alone at a table. It was the same Esther. She was even wearing the same fur hat, but a strand of grey hair fell over her forehead. How strange—the fur hat, too, seemed to have greyed. The other *cafeterianiks* did not appear to be interested in her any more, or they did not know her. Her face told of the time that had passed. There were shadows under her eyes. Her gaze was no longer so clear. Around her mouth was an expression that could be called bitterness, disenchantment. I greeted her. She smiled, but her smile immediately faded away. I asked, 'What happened to you?'

'Oh, I'm still alive.'

'May I sit down?'

'Please—certainly.'

'May I bring you a cup of coffee?'

'No. Well, if you insist.'

I noticed that she was smoking, and also that she was reading not the newspaper to which I contribute but a competition paper. She had gone over to the enemy. I brought her coffee and for myself stewed prunes—a remedy for constipation. I sat down. 'Where were you all this time? I have asked for you.'

'Really? Thank you.'

'What happened?'

'Nothing good.' she looked at me. I knew that she saw in me what I saw in her: the slow wilting of the flesh. She said, 'You have no hair but you are white.'

For a while we were silent. Then I said, 'Your father—' and as I said it I knew that her father was not alive.

Esther said, 'He has been dead for almost a year.'

'Do you still sort buttons?'

'No, I became an operator in a dress shop.'

'What happened to you personally, may I ask?'

'Oh nothing—absolutely nothing. You will not believe it, but I was sitting here thinking about you. I have fallen into some kind of trap. I don't know what to call it. I thought perhaps you could advise me. Do you still have the patience to listen to the troubles of little people like me? No, I didn't mean to insult you. I even doubted you would remember me. To make it short, I work but work is growing more difficult for me. I suffer from arthritis. I feel as if my bones would

355

crack. I wake up in the morning and can't sit up. One doctor tells me it's a disc in my back, others try to cure my nerves. One took X-rays and says that I have a tumour. He wanted me to go to the hospital for a few weeks, but I'm in no hurry for an operation. Suddenly a little lawyer showed up. He is a refugee himself and is connected with the German government. You know they're now giving reparation money. It's true that I escaped to Russia, but I'm a victim of the Nazis just the same. Besides, they don't know my biography so exactly. I could get a pension plus a few thousand dollars, but my dislocated disc is no good for the purpose because I got it later—after the camps. This lawyer says my only chance is to convince them that I am ruined psychically. It's the bitter truth, but how can you prove it? The German doctors, the neurologists, the psychiatrists require proof. Everything has to be according to the textbooks—just so and no different. The lawyer wants me to play insane. Naturally, he gets twenty per cent of the reparation money—maybe more. Why he needs so much money I don't understand. He's already in his seventies, an old bachelor. He tried to make love to me and whatnot. He's half *meshugga* himself. But how can I play insane when actually I *am* insane? The whole thing revolts me and I'm afraid it will really drive me crazy. I hate swindle. But this shyster pursues me. I don't sleep. When the alarm rings in the morning, I wake up as shattered as I used to be in Russia when I had to walk to the forest and saw logs at four in the morning. Naturally, I take sleeping pills—if I didn't, I couldn't sleep at all. That is more or less the situation.'

'Why don't you get married? You are still a good-looking woman.'

'Well, the old question—there is nobody. It's too late. If you knew how I felt, you wouldn't ask such a question.'

4

A few weeks passed. Snow had been falling. After the snow came rain, then frost. I stood at my window and looked out at Broadway. The passers-by half walked, half slipped. Cars moved slowly. The sky above the roofs shone violet, without a moon, without stars, and even though it was eight o'clock in the evening the light and the emptiness reminded me of dawn. The stores were deserted. For a moment, I had the feeling I was in Warsaw. The telephone rang and I rushed to answer it as I did ten, twenty, thirty years ago—still expecting the good tidings that a telephone call was about to bring me. I said hello, but there was no answer and I was seized by the fear that some evil power was trying to keep back the good news at the last minute. Then I heard a stammering. A woman's voice muttered my name.

'Yes, it is I.'

'Excuse me for disturbing you. My name is Esther. We met a few weeks ago in the cafeteria—'

'Esther!' I exclaimed.

'I don't know how I got the courage to phone you. I need to talk to you about something. Naturally, if you have the time and—please forgive my presumption.'

'No presumption. Would you like to come to my apartment?'

'If I will not be interrupting. It's difficult to talk in the cafeteria. It's noisy and there are eavesdroppers. What I want to tell you is a secret I wouldn't trust to anyone else.'

'Please come up.'

I gave Esther directions. Then I tried to make order in my apartment, but I soon realized this was impossible. Letters, manuscripts lay around on tables and chairs. In the corners books and magazines were piled high. I opened the closets and threw inside whatever was under my hand: jackets, pants, shirts, shoes, slippers. I picked up an envelope and to my amazement saw that it had never been opened. I tore it open and found a cheque. 'What's the matter with me—have I lost my mind?' I said out loud. I tried to read the letter that came with the cheque, but I had misplaced my glasses; my fountain pen was gone, too. Well—and where were my keys? I heard a bell ring and I didn't know whether it was the door or the telephone. I opened the door and saw Esther. It must have been snowing again, because her hat and the shoulders of her coat were trimmed with white. I asked her in, and my neighbour, the divorcée, who spied on me openly with no shame—and, God knows, with no sense of purpose—opened her door and stared at my guest.

Esther removed her boots and I took her coat and put it on the case of the *Encyclopaedia Britannica*. I shoved a few manuscripts off the sofa so she could sit down. I said, 'In my house there is sheer chaos.'

'It doesn't matter.'

I sat in an armchair strewn with socks and handkerchiefs. For a while we spoke about the weather, about the danger of being out in New York at night—even early in the evening. Then Esther said, 'Do you remember the time I spoke to you about my lawyer—that I had to go to a psychiatrist because of the reparation money?'

'Yes, I remember.'

'I didn't tell you everything. It was too wild. It still seems unbelievable, even to me. Don't interrupt me, I implore you. I'm not completely healthy—I may even say that I'm sick— but I know the difference between fact and illusion. I haven't slept for nights, and I kept wondering whether I should call you or not. I decided not to—but this evening it occurred to me that if I couldn't trust you with a thing like this, then there is no one I could talk to. I read you and I know that you have a sense of the great mysteries—' Esther said all this stammering and with pauses. For a moment her eyes smiled, and then they became sad and wavering.

I said, 'You can tell me everything.'

'I am afraid that you'll think me insane.'

'I swear I will not.'

Esther bit her lower lip. 'I want you to know that I saw Hitler,' she said.

Even though I was prepared for something unusual, my throat constricted. 'When—where?'

'You see, you are frightened already. It happened three years ago—almost four. I saw him here on Broadway.'

'On the street?'

'In the cafeteria.'

I tried to swallow the lump in my throat. 'Most probably someone resembling him,' I said finally.

'I knew you would say that. But remember, you've promised to listen. You recall the fire in the cafeteria?'

'Yes, certainly.'

'The fire has to do with it. Since you don't believe me anyhow, why draw it out? It happened this way. That night I
didn't sleep. Usually when I can't sleep, I get up and make
tea, or I try to read a book, but this time some power commanded me to get dressed and go out. I can't explain to you
how I dared walk on Broadway at that late hour. It must have
been two or three o'clock. I reached the cafeteria, thinking
perhaps it stays open all night. I tried to look in, but the large
window was covered by a curtain. There was a pale glow
inside. I tried the revolving door and it turned. I went in and
saw a scene I will not forget to the last day of my life. The
tables were shoved together and around them sat men in
white robes, like doctors or orderlies, all with swastikas on
their sleeves. At the head sat Hitler. I beg you to hear me
out—even a deranged person sometimes deserves to be listened to. They all spoke German. They didn't see me. They
were busy with the Führer. It grew quiet and he started to
talk. That abominable voice—I heard it many times on the
radio. I didn't make out exactly what he said. I was too terrified to take it in. Suddenly one of his henchmen looked
back at me and jumped up from his chair. How I came out
alive I will never know. I ran with all my strength, and I was
trembling all over. When I got home, I said to myself, "Esther,
you are not right in the head." I still don't know how I lived
through that night. The next morning, I didn't go straight to
work but walked to the cafeteria to see if it was really there.
Such an experience makes a person doubt his own senses.
When I arrived, I found the place had burned down. When I
saw this, I knew it had to do with what I had seen. Those who
were there wanted all traces erased. These are the plain facts. I
have no reason to fabricate such queer things.'

We were both silent. Then I said, 'You had a vision.'

'What do you mean, a vision?'

'The past is not lost. An image from years ago remained
present somewhere in the fourth dimension and it reached
you just at that moment.'

'As far as I know, Hitler never wore a long white robe.'

'Perhaps he did.'

'Why did the cafeteria burn down just that night?' Esther
asked.

'It could be that the fire evoked the vision.'

'There was no fire then. Somehow I foresaw that you would give me this kind of explanation. If this was a vision, my sitting here with you is also a vision.'

'It couldn't have been anything else. Even if Hitler is living and is hiding out in the United States, he is not likely to meet his cronies at a cafeteria on Broadway. Besides, the cafeteria belongs to a Jew.'

'I saw him as I am seeing you now.'

'You had a glimpse back in time.'

'Well, let it be so. But since then I have had no rest. I keep thinking about it. If I am destined to lose my mind, this will drive me to it.'

The telephone rang and I jumped up with a start. It was a wrong number. I sat down again. 'What about the psychiatrist your lawyer sent you to? Tell it to him and you'll get full compensation.'

Esther looked at me sidewise and unfriendly. 'I know what you mean. I haven't fallen that low yet.'

5

I was afraid that Esther would continue to call me. I even planned to change my telephone number. But weeks and months passed and I never heard from her or saw her. I didn't go to the cafeteria. But I often thought about her. How can the brain produce such nightmares? What goes on in that little marrow behind the skull? And what guarantee do I have that the same sort of thing will not happen to me? And how do we know that the human species will not end like this? I have played with the idea that all of humanity suffers from schizophrenia. Along with the atom, the personality of *Homo sapiens* has been splitting. When it comes to technology, the brain still functions, but in everything else degeneration has begun. They are all insane: the Communists, the Fascists, the preachers of democracy, the writers, the painters, the clergy, the atheists. Soon technology, too, will disintegrate. Buildings will collapse, power plants will stop generating electricity. Generals will drop atomic bombs on their own populations. Mad revolutionaries will run in the streets, crying fantastic slogans. I have often thought that it would begin in New York. This metropolis has all the symptoms of a mind gone berserk.

But since insanity has not yet taken over altogether, one had to act as though there were still order—according to Vaihinger's principle of 'as if'. I continued with my scribbling. I delivered manuscripts to the publisher. I lectured. Four times a year, I sent cheques to the federal government, the state. What was left after my expenses I put in the savings bank. A teller entered some numbers in my bank book and this meant that I was provided for. Somebody printed a few lines in a magazine or newspaper, and this signified that my value as a writer had gone up. I saw with amazement that all my efforts turned into paper. My apartment was one big wastepaper basket. From day to day, all this paper was getting drier and more parched. I woke up at night fearful that it would ignite. There was not an hour when I did not hear the sirens of fire engines.

A year after I had last seen Esther, I was going to Toronto to read a paper about Yiddish in the second half of the nineteenth century. I put a few shirts in my valise as well as papers of all kinds, among them one that made me a citizen of the United States. I had enough paper money in my pocket to pay for a taxi to Grand Central. But the taxis seemed to be taken. Those that were not refused to stop. Didn't the drivers see me? Had I suddenly become one of those who see and are not seen? I decided to take the subway. On my way, I saw Esther. She was not alone but with someone I had known years ago, soon after I arrived in the United States. He was a frequenter of a cafeteria on East Broadway. He used to sit at a table, express opinions, criticize, grumble. He was a small man, with sunken cheeks the colour of brick, and bulging eyes. He was angry at the new writers. He belittled the old ones. He rolled his own cigarettes and dropped ashes into the plates from which we ate. Almost two decades had passed since I had last seen him. Suddenly he appears with Esther. He was even holding her arm. I had never seen Esther look so well. She was wearing a new coat, a new hat. She smiled at me and nodded. I wanted to stop her, but my watch showed that it was late. I barely managed to catch the train. In my bedroom, the bed was already made. I undressed and went to sleep.

In the middle of the night, I awoke. My car was being switched, and I almost fell out of bed. I could not sleep any more and I tried to remember the name of the little man I had seen with Esther. But I was unable to. The thing I did remember was that even thirty years ago he had been far from young. He had come to the United States in 1905 after the revolution in Russia. In Europe, he had a reputation as a speaker and public figure. How old must he be now? According to my calculations, he had to be in the late eighties— perhaps even ninety. Is it possible that Esther could be intimate with such an old man? But this evening he had not looked old. The longer I brooded about it in the darkness, the stranger the encounter seemed to me. I even imagined that somewhere in a newspaper I had read that he had died. Do corpses walk around on Broadway? This would mean that Esther, too, was not living. I raised the window shade and sat up and looked out into the night—black, impenetrable, without a moon. A few stars ran along with the train for a while and then they disappeared. A lighted factory emerged; I saw machines but no operators. Then it was swallowed in the darkness and another group of stars began to follow the train. I was turning with the earth on its axis. I was circling with it around the sun and moving in the direction of a constellation whose name I had forgotten. Is there no death? Or is there no life?

I thought about what Esther had told me of seeing Hitler in the cafeteria. It had seemed utter nonsense, but now I began to reappraise the idea. If time and space are nothing more than forms of perception, as Kant argues, and quality, quantity, causality are only categories of thinking, why shouldn't Hitler confer with his Nazis in a cafeteria on Broadway? Esther didn't sound insane. She had seen a piece of reality that the heavenly censorship prohibits as a rule. She had caught a glimpse behind the curtain of the phenomena. I regretted that I had not asked for more details.

In Toronto, I had little time to ponder these matters, but when I returned to New York I went to the cafeteria for some private investigation. I met only one man I knew: a rabbi who had become an agnostic and given up his job. I asked him about Esther. He said, 'The pretty little woman who used to come here?'

'Yes.'

'I heard that she committed suicide.'

'When—how?'

'I don't know. Perhaps we are not speaking about the same person.'

No matter how many questions I asked and how much I described Esther, everything remained vague. Some young woman who used to come here had turned on the gas and made an end of herself—that was all the ex-rabbi could tell me.

I decided not to rest until I knew for certain what had happened to Esther and also to that half writer, half politician I remembered from East Broadway. But I grew busier from day to day. The cafeteria closed. The neighbourhood changed. Years have passed and I have never seen Esther again. Yes, corpses do walk on Broadway. But why did Esther choose that particular corpse? She could have got a better bargain even in this world.

Translated by the author and Dorothea Straus

RICHARD BRAUTIGAN

'America, often only a place in the mind.'

San Francisco, 1960s

My Name

I guess you are kind of curious as to who I am, but I am one of those who do not have a regular name. My name depends on you. Just call me whatever is in your mind.

If you are thinking about something that happened a long time ago: somebody asked you a question and you did not know the answer.

That is my name.

Perhaps it was raining very hard.

That is my name.

Or somebody wanted you to do something. You did it. Then they told you what you did was wrong—'Sorry for the mistake'—and you had to do something else.

That is my name.

Perhaps it was a game that you played when you were a child or something that came idly into your mind when you were old and sitting in a chair near the window.

That is my name.

Or you walked some place. There were flowers all around.

That is my name.

Perhaps you stared into a river. There was somebody near you who loved you. They were about to touch you. You could feel this before it happened. Then it happened.

That is my name.

Or you heard someone calling from a great distance. Their voice was almost an echo.

That is my name.

Perhaps you were lying in bed, almost ready to go to sleep, and you laughed at something, a joke unto yourself, a good way to end the day.

That is my name.

Or you were eating something good and for a second forgot what you were eating, but still went on, knowing it was good.

That is my name.

Perhaps it was around midnight and the fire tolled like a bell inside the stove.

That is my name.

Or you felt bad when she said that thing to you. She could have told it to someone else: somebody who was more familiar with her problems.

That is my name.

Perhaps the trout swam in the pool but the river was only eight inches wide and the moon shone on DEATH and the watermelon fields glowed out of proportion, dark and the moon seemed to rise from every plant.

That is my name.

And I wish Margaret would leave me alone.

The Cleveland Wrecking Yard

Until recently my knowledge about the Cleveland Wrecking
Yard had come from a couple of friends who's bought things
there. One of them bought a huge window: the frame, glass
and everything for just a few dollars. It was a fine-looking
window.

Then he chopped a hole in the side of his house up on
Potrero Hill and put the window in. Now he has a panoramic
view of the San Francisco County Hospital.

He can practically look right down into the wards and see
old magazines eroded like the Grand Canyon from endless
readings. He can practically hear the patients thinking about
breakfast: *I hate milk*, and thinking about dinner: *I hate
peas*, and then he can watch the hospital slowly drown at
night, hopelessly entangled in huge bunches of brick seaweed.

He bought that window at the Cleveland Wrecking Yard.

My other friend bought an iron roof at the Cleveland
Wrecking Yard and took the roof down to Big Sur in an old station wagon and then he carried the iron roof on his back up
the side of a mountain. He carried up half the roof on his back.
It was no picnic. Then he bought a mule, George, from Pleasanton. George carried up the other half of the roof.

The mule didn't like what was happening at all. He lost a
lot of weight because of the ticks, and the smell of the wildcats up on the plateau made him too nervous to graze there.
My friend said jokingly that George had lost around two
hundred pounds. The good wine country around Pleasanton
in the Livermore Valley probably had looked a lot better to
George than the wild side of the Santa Lucia Mountains.

My friend's place was a shack right beside a huge fireplace
where there had once been a great mansion during the 1920s,
built by a famous movie actor. The mansion was built before
there was even a road down at Big Sur. The mansion had
been brought over the mountains on the backs of mules,

strung out like ants, bringing visions of the good life to the poison oak, the ticks and the salmon.

The mansion was on a promontory, high over the Pacific. Money could see farther in the 1920s, and one could look out and see whales and the Hawaiian Islands and the Kuomintang in China.

The mansion burned down years ago.

The actor died.

His mules were made into soap.

His mistresses became bird nests of wrinkles.

Now only the fireplace remains as a sort of Carthaginian homage to Hollywood.

I was down there a few weeks ago to see my friend's roof. I wouldn't have passed up the chance for a million dollars, as they say. The roof looked like a colander to me. If that roof and the rain were running against each other at Bay Meadows, I'd bet on the rain and plan to spend my winnings at the World's Fair in Seattle.

My own experience with the Cleveland Wrecking Yard began two days ago when I heard about a used trout stream they had on sale out at the Yard. So I caught the Number 15 bus on Columbus Avenue and went out there for the first time.

There were two Negro boys sitting behind me on the bus. They were talking about Chubby Checker and the Twist. They thought that Chubby Checker was only fifteen years old because he didn't have a moustache. Then they talked about some other guy who did the twist forty-four hours in a row until he saw George Washington crossing the Delaware.

'Man, that's what I call twisting,' one of the kids said.

'I don't think I could twist no forty-four hours in a row,' the other kid said. 'That's a lot of twisting.'

I got off the bus right next to an abandoned Time Gasoline filling station and an abandoned fifty-cent self-service car wash. There was a long field on one side of the filling station. The field had once been covered with a housing project during the war, put there for the shipyard workers.

On the other side of the Time filling station was the Cleveland Wrecking Yard. I walked down there to have a look at the used trout stream. The Cleveland Wrecking Yard has a very long front window filled with signs and merchandise.

There was a sign in the window advertising a laundry marking machine for $65.00. The original cost of the machine was $175.00. Quite a saving.

There was another sign advertising new and used two and three ton hoists. I wondered how many hoists it would take to move a trout stream.

There was another sign that said:

THE FAMILY GIFT CENTRE,
GIFT SUGGESTIONS FOR THE ENTIRE FAMILY

The window was filled with hundreds of items for the entire family. *Daddy, do you know what I want for Christmas? What, son? A bathroom. Mommy, do you know what I want for Christmas? What, Patricia? Some roofing material.*

There were jungle hammocks in the window for distant relatives and dollar-ten-cent gallons of earth-brown enamel paint for other loved ones.

There was also a big sign that said:

USED TROUT STREAM FOR SALE.
MUST BE SEEN TO BE APPRECIATED.

I went inside and looked at some ship's lanterns that were for sale next to the door. Then a salesman came up to me and said in a pleasant voice, 'Can I help you?'

'Yes,' I said. 'I'm curious about the trout stream you have for sale. Can you tell me something about it? How are you selling it?'

'We're selling it by the foot length. You can buy as little as you want or you can buy all we've got left. A man came in here this morning and bought 563 feet. He's going to give it to his niece for a birthday present,' the salesman said.

'We're selling the waterfalls separately of course, and the trees and birds, flowers, grass and ferns we're also selling extra. The insects we're giving away free with a minimum purchase of ten feet of stream.'

'How much are you selling the stream for?' I asked.

'Six dollars and fifty-cents a foot,' he said. 'That's for the first hundred feet. After that it's five dollars a foot.'

'How much are the birds?' I asked.

'Thirty-five cents apiece,' he said. 'But of course they're used. We can't guarantee anything.'

'How wide is the stream?' I asked. 'You said you were selling it by the length, didn't you?'

'Yes,' he said. 'We're selling it by the length. Its width runs between five and eleven feet. You don't have to pay anything extra for width. It's not a big stream, but it's very pleasant.'

'What kinds of animals do you have?' I asked.

'We only have three deer left,' he said.

'Oh ... What about flowers?'

'By the dozen,' he said.

'Is the stream clear?' I asked.

'Sir,' the salesman said. 'I wouldn't want you to think that we would ever sell a murky trout stream here. We always make sure they're running crystal clear before we even think about moving them.'

'Where did the stream come from?' I asked.

'Colorado,' he said. 'We moved it with loving care. We've never damaged a trout stream yet. We treat them all as if they were china.'

'You're probably asked this all the time, but how's fishing in the stream?' I asked.

'Very good,' he said. 'Mostly German browns, but there are a few rainbows.'

'What do the trout cost?' I asked.

'They come with the stream,' he said. 'Of course it's all luck. You never know how many you're going to get or how big they are. But the fishing's very good, you might say it's excellent. Both bait and dry fly,' he said smiling.

'Where's the stream at?' I asked. 'I'd like to take a look at it.'

'It's around in back,' he said. 'You go straight through that door and then turn right until you're outside. It's stacked in lengths. You can't miss it. The waterfalls are upstairs in the used plumbing department.'

'What about the animals?'

'Well, what's left of the animals are straight back from the stream. You'll see a bunch of our trucks parked on a road by the railroad tracks. Turn right on the road and follow it down past the piles of lumber. The animal shed's right at the end of the lot.'

'Thanks,' I said. 'I think I'll look at the waterfalls first. You don't have to come with me. Just tell me how to get there and I'll find my own way.'

'All right,' he said. 'Go up those stairs. You'll see a bunch of doors and windows, turn left and you'll find the used plumbing department. Here's my card if you need any help.'

'Okay,' I said. 'You've been a great help already. Thanks a lot. I'll take a look around.'

'Good luck,' he said.

I went upstairs and there were thousands of doors there. I'd never seen so many doors before in my life. You could have built an entire city out of those doors. Doorstown. And there were enough windows up there to build a little suburb entirely out of windows. Windowville.

I turned left and went back and saw the faint glow of pearl-coloured light. The light got stronger and stronger as I went farther back, and then I was in the used plumbing department, surrounded by hundreds of toilets.

The toilets were stacked on shelves. They were stacked five toilets high. There was a skylight above the toilets that made them glow like the Great Taboo Pearl of the South Sea movies.

Stacked over against the wall were the waterfalls. There were about a dozen of them, ranging from a drop of a few feet to a drop of ten or fifteen feet.

There was one waterfall that was over sixty feet long. There were tags on the pieces of the big falls describing the correct order for putting the falls back together again.

The waterfalls all had price tags on them. They were more expensive than the stream. The waterfalls were selling for $19.00 a foot.

I went into another room where there were piles of sweet-smelling lumber, glowing a soft yellow from a different colour skylight above the lumber. In the shadows at the edge of the room under the sloping roof of the building were many sinks and urinals covered with dust, and there was also another waterfall about seventeen feet long, lying there in two lengths and already beginning to gather dust.

I had seen all I wanted of the waterfalls, and now I was very curious about the trout stream, so I followed the salesman's directions and ended up outside the building.

O I had never in my life seen anything like that trout stream. It was stacked in piles of various lengths: ten, fifteen, twenty feet, etc. There was one pile of hundred-foot lengths. There was also a box of scraps. The scraps were in odd sizes ranging from six inches to a couple of feet.

There was a loudspeaker on the side of the building and soft music was coming out. It was a cloudy day and seagulls were circling high overhead.

Behind the stream were big bundles of trees and bushes. They were covered with sheets of patched canvas. You could see the tops and roots sticking out the ends of the bundles.

I went up close and looked at the lengths of stream. I could see some trout in them. I saw one good fish. I saw some crawdads crawling around the rocks at the bottom.

It looked like a fine stream. I put my hand in the water. It was cold and felt good.

I decided to go around to the side and look at the animals. I saw where the trucks were parked beside the railroad tracks. I followed the road down past the piles of lumber, back to the shed where the animals were.

The salesman had been right. They were practically out of animals. About the only thing they had left in any abundance were mice. There were hundreds of mice.

Beside the shed was a huge wire birdcage, maybe fifty feet high, filled with many kinds of birds. The top of the cage had a piece of canvas over it, so the birds wouldn't get wet when it rained. There were woodpeckers and wild canaries and sparrows.

On my way back to where the trout stream was piled, I found the insects. They were inside a prefabricated steel building that was selling for eighty-cents a square foot. There was a sign over the roof. It said

INSECTS

Footnote Chapter to 'Red Lid'

Living in the California bush we had no garbage service. Our garbage was never greeted in the early morning by a man with a big smile on his face and a kind word or two. We couldn't burn any of the garbage because it was the dry season and everything was ready to catch on fire anyway, including ourselves. The garbage was a problem for a little while and then we discovered a way to get rid of it.

We took the garbage down to where there were three abandoned houses in a row. We carried sacks full of tin cans, papers, peelings, bottles and Popeyes.

We stopped at the last abandoned house where there were thousands of old receipts to the San Francisco *Chronicle* thrown all over the bed and the children's toothbrushes were still in the bathroom medicine cabinet.

Behind the place was an old outhouse and to get down to it, you had to follow the path down past some apple trees and a patch of strange plants that we thought were either a good spice that would certainly enhance our cooking or the plants were deadly nightshade that would cause our cooking to be less.

We carried the garbage down to the outhouse and always opened the door slowly because that was the only way you could open it, and on the wall there was a roll of toilet paper, so old it looked like a relative, perhaps a cousin, to the Magna Carta.

We lifted up the lid of the toilet and dropped the garbage down into the darkness. This went on for weeks and weeks until it became very funny to lift the lid of the toilet and instead of seeing darkness below or maybe the murky abstract outline of garbage, we saw bright, definite and lusty garbage heaped up almost to the top.

If you were a stranger and went down there to take an

innocent crap, you would've had quite a surprise when you lifted up the lid.

We left the California bush just before it became necessary to stand on the toilet seat and step into that hole, crushing the garbage down like an accordion into the abyss.

Cameron (44:40)

When I knew Cameron he was a very old man and wore carpet slippers all the time and didn't talk any more. He smoked cigars and occasionally listened to Burl Ives' records. He lived with one of his sons who was now a middle-aged man himself and starting to complain about growing old.

'God-damn it, there's no getting around the fact that I'm not as young as I used to be.'

Cameron had his own easy chair in the front room. It was covered with a wool blanket. Nobody else ever sat in that chair, but it was always as if he were sitting there, anyway. His spirit had taken command of that chair. Old people have a way of doing that with the furniture they end their lives sitting in.

He didn't go outside any more during the winter, but he would sit out on the front porch sometimes in the summer and stare past the rose bushes in the front yard to the street beyond where life calendared its days without him as if he had never existed out there at all.

That wasn't true, though. He used to be a great dancer and would dance all night long in the 1890s. He was famous for his dancing. He sent many a fiddler to an early grave and when the girls danced with him, they always danced better and they loved him for it and just the mention of his name in that county made the girls feel good and would get them blushing and giggling. Even the 'serious' girls would get excited by his name or the sight of him.

There were a lot of broken hearts when he married the youngest of the Singleton girls in 1900.

'She's not that pretty,' refrained the sore losers and they all cried at the wedding.

He was also a hell of a good poker player in a county where people played very serious poker for high stakes. Once a man sitting next to him was caught cheating during a game.

There was a lot of money on the table and a piece of paper

that represented twelve head of cattle, two horses and a wagon. That was part of a bet.

The man's cheating was made public by one of the other men at the table reaching swiftly across without saying a word and cutting the man's throat.

Cameron automatically reached over and put his thumb on the man's jugular vein to keep the blood from getting all over the table and held him upright, though he was dying until the hand was finished and the ownership of the twelve head of cattle, two horses and a wagon was settled.

Though Cameron didn't talk any more, you could see events like that in his eyes. His hands had been made vegetable-like by rheumatism but there was an enormous dignity to their repose. The way he lit a cigar was like an act of history.

Once he had spent a winter as a sheepherder in 1889. He was a young man, not yet out of his teens. It was a long lonely winter job in God-forsaken country, but he needed the money to pay off a debt that he owed his father. It was one of those complicated family debts that its best not to go into detail about.

There was very little exciting to do that winter except look at sheep but Cameron found something to keep his spirits up.

Ducks and geese flew up and down the river all winter and the man who owned the sheep had given him and the other sheepherders a lot, an almost surrealistic amount, of 44:40 Winchester ammunition to keep the wolves away, though there weren't any wolves in that country.

The owner of the sheep had a tremendous fear of wolves getting to his flock. It bordered on the ridiculous if you were to go by all the 44:40 ammunition he supplied his sheepherders.

Cameron heavily favoured this ammunition with his rifle that winter by shooting at the ducks and geese from a hillside about two hundred yards from the river. A 44:40 isn't exactly the greatest bird gun in the world. It lets go with a huge slow-moving bullet like a fat man opening a door. Cameron wanted those kind of odds.

The long months of that family-debted exile winter passed

slowly day after day, shot after shot until it was finally spring and he had maybe fired a few thousand shots at those ducks and geese without hitting a single one of them.

Cameron loved to tell that story and thought it was very funny and always laughed during the telling. Cameron told that story about as many times as he had fired at those birds years in front of and across the bridge of 1900 and up the decades of this century until he stopped talking.

A Note on the Camping Craze that is Currently Sweeping America

As much as anything else, the Coleman lantern is the symbol of the camping craze that is currently sweeping America, with its unholy white light burning in the forests of America.

Last summer, a Mr Norris was drinking at a bar in San Francisco. It was Sunday night and he'd had six or seven. Turning to the guy on the next stool, he said, 'What are you up to?'

'Just having a few,' the guy said.

'That's what I'm doing,' Mr Norris said. 'I like it.'

'I know what you mean,' the guy said. 'I had to lay off for a couple of years. I'm just starting up again.'

'What was wrong?' Mr Norris said.

'I had a hole in my liver,' the guy said.

'In your liver?'

'Yeah, the doctor said it was big enough to wave a flag in. It's better now. I can have a couple once in a while. I'm not supposed to, but it won't kill me.'

'Well, I'm thirty-two years old,' Mr Norris said. 'I've had three wives and I can't remember the names of my children.'

The guy on the next stool, like a bird on the next island, took a sip from his Scotch and soda. The guy liked the sound of the alcohol in his drink. He put the glass back on the bar.

'That's no problem,' he said to Mr Norris. 'The best thing I know for remembering the names of children from previous marriages, is to go out camping, try a little trout fishing. Trout fishing is one of the best things in the world for remembering children's names.'

'Is that right?' Mr Norris said.

'Yeah,' the guy said.

'That sounds like an idea,' Mr Norris said. 'I've got to do something. Sometimes I think one of them is named Carl, but that's impossible. My third-ex hated the name Carl.'

'You try some camping and that trout fishing,' the guy on

378

the next stool said. 'And you'll remember the names of your unborn children.'

'Carl! Carl! Your mother wants you!' Mr Norris yelled as a kind of joke, then he realized that it wasn't very funny. He was getting there.

He'd have a couple more and then his head would always fall forward and hit the bar like a gunshot. He'd always miss his glass, so he wouldn't cut his face. His head would always jump up and look startled around the bar, people staring at it. He'd get up then, and take it home.

The next morning Mr Norris went down to a sporting goods store and charged his equipment. He charged a 9 x 9 foot dry finish tent with an aluminium centre pole. Then he charged an Arctic sleeping bag filled with eiderdown and an air mattress and an air pillow to go with the sleeping bag. He also charged an air alarm clock to go along with the idea of night and waking in the morning.

He charged a two-burner Coleman stove and a Coleman lantern and a folding aluminium table and a big set of inter-locking aluminium cookware and a portable ice box.

The last things he charged were his fishing tackle and a bottle of insect repellent.

He left the next day for the mountains.

Hours later, when he arrived in the mountains, the first sixteen campgrounds he stopped at were filled with people. He was a little surprised. He had no idea the mountains would be so crowded.

At the seventeenth campground, a man had just died of a heart attack and the ambulance attendants were taking down his tent. They lowered the centre pole and then pulled up the corner stakes. They folded the tent neatly and put it in the back of the ambulance, right beside the man's body.

They drove off down the road, leaving behind them in the air, a cloud of brilliant white dust. The dust looked like the light from a Coleman lantern.

Mr Norris pitched his tent right there and set up all his equipment and soon had it all going at once. After he finished eating a dehydrated beef Stroganoff dinner, he turned off all his equipment with the master air switch and went to sleep, for it was now dark.

It was about midnight when they brought the body and placed it beside the tent, less than a foot away from where Mr Norris was sleeping in his Arctic sleeping bag.

He was awakened when they brought the body. They weren't exactly the quietest body bringers in the world. Mr Norris could see the bulge of the body against the side of the tent. The only thing that separated him from the dead body was a thin layer of 6 oz. water resistant and mildew resistant DRY FINISH green AMERIFLEX poplin.

Mr Norris unzipped his sleeping bag and went outside with a gigantic hound-like flashlight. He saw the body bringers walking down the path towards the creek.

'Hey, you guys!' Mr Norris shouted. 'Come back here. You forgot something.'

'What do you mean?' one of them said. They both looked very sheepish, caught in the teeth of the flashlight.

'You know what I mean,' Mr Norris said. 'Right now!'

The body bringers shrugged their shoulders, looked at each other and then reluctantly went back, dragging their feet like children all the way. They picked up the body. It was heavy and one of them had trouble getting hold of the feet.

That one said, kind of hopelessly to Mr Norris, 'You won't change your mind?'

'Good night and good-bye,' Mr Norris said.

They went off down the path towards the creek, carrying the body between them. Mr Norris turned his flashlight off and he could hear them, stumbling over the rocks along the bank of the creek. He could hear them swearing at each other. He heard one of them say, 'Hold your end up.' Then he couldn't hear anything.

About ten minutes later he saw all sorts of lights go on at another campsite down along the creek. He heard a distant voice shouting. 'The answer is no! You already woke up the kids. They have to have their rest. We're going on a four-mile hike tomorrow up to Fish Konk Lake. Try some place else.'

Partners

I like to sit in the cheap theatres of America where people live and die with Elizabethan manners while watching the movies. There is a theatre down on Market Street where I can see four movies for a dollar. I really don't care how good they are either. I'm not a critic. I just like to watch movies. Their presence on the screen is enough for me.

The theatre is filled with black people, hippies, senior citizens, soldiers, sailors and the innocent people who talk to the movies because the movies are just as real as anything else that has ever happened to them.

'No! No! Get back in the car, Clyde. Oh, God, they're killing Bonnie!'

I am the poet-in-residence at these theatres but I don't plan on getting a Guggenheim for it.

Once I went into the theatre at six o'clock in the evening. At seven I crossed my legs and they stayed that way until ten and I never did stand up.

In other words, I am not an art film fan. I do not care to be aesthetically tickled in a fancy theatre surrounded by an audience drenched in the confident perfume of culture. I can't afford it.

I was sitting in a two-pictures-for-seventy-five-cents theatre called the Times in North Beach last month and there was a cartoon about a chicken and a dog.

The dog was trying to get some sleep and the chicken was keeping him awake and what followed was a series of adventures that always ended up in cartoon mayhem.

There was a man sitting next to me.

He was WHITEWHITEWHITE; fat, about fifty years old, balding sort of and his face was completely minus any human sensitivity.

His baggy no-style clothes covered him like the banner of a defeated country and he looked as if the only mail he had ever got in his life were bills.

381

Just then the dog in the cartoon let go with a huge yawn because the chicken was still keeping him awake and before the dog had finished yawning, the man next to me started yawning, so that the dog in the cartoon and the man, this living human being, were yawning together, partners in America.

Room 208, Hotel
Trout Fishing in America

Half a block from Broadway and Columbus is Hotel Trout Fishing in America, a cheap hotel. It is very old and run by some Chinese. They are young and ambitious Chinese and the lobby is filled with the smell of Lysol.

The Lysol sits like another guest on the stuffed furniture, reading a copy of the *Chronicle*, the Sports Section. It is the only furniture I have ever seen in my life that looks like baby food.

And the Lysol sits asleep next to an old Italian pensioner who listens to the heavy ticking of the clock and dreams of eternity's golden pasta, sweet basil and Jesus Christ.

The Chinese are always doing something to the hotel. One week they paint a lower banister and the next week they put some new wallpaper on part of the third floor.

No matter how many times you pass that part of the third floor, you cannot remember the colour of the wallpaper or what the design is. All you know is that part of the wallpaper is new. It is different from the old wallpaper. But you cannot remember what that looks like either.

One day the Chinese take a bed out of a room and lean it up against the wall. It stays there for a month. You get used to seeing it and then you go by one day and it is gone. You wonder where it went.

I remember the first time I went inside Hotel Trout Fishing in America. It was with a friend to meet some people.

'I'll tell you what's happening,' he said. 'She's an ex-hustler who works for the telephone company. He went to medical school for a while during the Great Depression and then he went into show business. After that, he was an errand boy for an abortion mill in Los Angeles. He took a fall and did some time in San Quentin.

'I think you'll like them. They're good people.

'He met her a couple of years ago in North Beach. She was hustling for a spade pimp. It's kind of weird. Most women have the temperament to be a whore, but she's one of these rare women who just don't have it—the whore temperament. She's Negro, too.

'She was a teenage girl living on a farm in Oklahoma. The pimp drove by one afternoon and saw her playing in the front yard. He stopped his car and got out and talked to her father for a while.

'I guess he gave her father some money. He came up with something good because her father told her to go and get her things. So she went with the pimp. Simple as that.

'He took her to San Francisco and turned her out and she hated it. He kept her in line by terrorizing her all the time. He was a real sweetheart.

'She had some brains, so he got her a job with the telephone company during the day, and he had her hustling at night.

'When Art took her away from him, he got pretty mad. A good thing and all that. He used to break into Art's hotel room in the middle of the night and put a switchblade to Art's throat and rant and rave. Art kept putting bigger and bigger locks on the door, but the pimp just kept breaking in—a huge fellow.

'So Art went out and got a .32 pistol, and the next time the pimp broke in, Art pulled the gun out from underneath the covers and jammed it into the pimp's mouth and said, "You'll be out of luck the next time you come through that door, Jack." This broke the pimp up. He never went back. The pimp certainly lost a good thing.

'He ran up a couple thousand dollars worth of bills in her name, charge accounts and the like. They're still paying them off.

'The pistol's right there beside the bed, just in case the pimp has an attack of amnesia and wants to have his shoes shined in a funeral parlour.

'When we go up there, he'll drink the wine. She won't. She'll have a little bottle of brandy. She won't offer us any of it. She drinks about four of them a day. Never buys a fifth. She always keeps going out and getting another half-pint.

'That's the way she handles it. She doesn't talk very much, and she doesn't make any bad scenes. A good-looking woman.'

My friend knocked on the door and we could hear somebody get up off the bed and come to the door.

'Who's there?' said a man on the other side.

'Me,' my friend said, in a voice deep and recognizable as any name.

'I'll open the door.' A simple declarative sentence. He undid about a hundred locks, bolts and chains and anchors and steel spikes and canes filled with acid, and then the door opened like a classroom of a great university and everything was in its proper place: the gun beside the bed and a small bottle of brandy beside an attractive Negro woman.

There were many flowers and plants growing in the room, some of them were on the dresser, surrounded by old photographs. All of the photographs were of white people, including Art when he was young and handsome and looked just like the 1930s.

There were pictures of animals cut out of magazines and tacked to the wall, with crayola frames drawn around them and crayola picture wires drawn holding them to the wall. They were pictures of kittens and puppies. They looked just fine.

There was a bowl of goldfish next to the bed, next to the gun. How religious and intimate the goldfish and the gun looked together.

They had a cat named 208. They covered the bathroom floor with newspaper and the cat crapped on the newspaper. My friend said that 208 thought he was the only cat left in the world, not having seen another cat since he was a tiny kitten. They never let him out of the room. He was a red cat and very aggressive. When you played with that cat, he really bit you. Stroke 208's fur and he'd try to disembowel your hand as if it were a belly stuffed full of extra-soft intestines.

We sat there and drank and talked about books. Art had owned a lot of books in Los Angeles, but they were all gone now. He told us that he used to spend his spare time in secondhand bookstores buying old and unusual books when he was in show business, travelling from city to city across America. Some of them were very rare autographed books, he told us, but he had bought them for very little and was forced to sell them for very little.

'They'd be worth a lot of money now,' he said.

The Negro woman sat there very quietly studying her brandy. A couple of times she said yes, in a sort of nice way. She used the word yes to its best advantage, when surrounded by no meaning and left alone from other words.

They did their own cooking in the room and had a single hot plate sitting on the floor, next to half a dozen plants, including a peach tree growing in a coffee can. Their closet was stuffed with food. Along with shirts, suits and dresses, were canned goods, eggs and cooking oil.

My friend told me that she was a very fine cook. That she could really cook up a good meal, fancy dishes, too, on that single hot plate, next to the peach tree.

They had a good world going for them. He had such a soft voice and manner that he worked as a private nurse for rich mental patients. He made good money when he worked, but sometimes he was sick himself. He was kind of run down. She was still working for the telephone company, but she wasn't doing that night work any more.

They were still paying off the bills that pimp had run up. I mean, years had passed and they were still paying them off: a Cadillac and a hi-fi set and expensive clothes and all those things that Negro pimps do love to have.

I went back there half a dozen times after that first meeting. An interesting thing happened. I pretended that the cat, 208, was named after their room number, though I knew that their number was in the three hundreds. The room was on the third floor. It was that simple.

I always went to their room following the geography of Hotel Trout Fishing in America, rather than its numerical layout. I never knew what the exact number of their room was. I knew secretly it was in the three hundreds and that was all.

Anyway, it was easier for me to establish order in my mind by pretending that the cat was named after their room number. It seemed like a good idea and the logical reason for a cat to have the name 208. It, of course, was not true. It was a fib. The cat's name was 208 and the room number was in the three hundreds.

Where did the name 208 come from? What did it mean?

I thought about it for a while, hiding it from the rest of my mind. But I didn't ruin my birthday by secretly thinking about it too hard.

A year later I found out the true significance of 208's name, purely by accident. My telephone rang one Saturday morning when the sun was shining on the hills. It was a close friend of mine and he said, 'I'm in the slammer. Come and get me out. They're burning black candles around the drunk tank.'

I went down to the Hall of Justice to bail my friend out, and discovered that 208 is the room number of the bail office. It was very simple. I paid ten dollars for my friend's life and found the original meaning of 208, how it runs like melting snow all the way down the mountainside to a small cat living and playing in Hotel Trout Fishing in America, believing itself to be the last cat in the world, not having seen another cat in such a long time, totally unafraid, newspaper spread out all over the bathroom floor and something good cooking on the hot plate.

Perfect California Day

I was walking down the railroad tracks outside of Monterey on Labour Day in 1965, watching the Sierra shoreline of the Pacific Ocean. It has always been a constant marvel to me how much the ocean along there is like a high Sierra river with a granite shore and fiercely-clear water and turns of green and blue with chandelier foam shining in and out of the rocks like the currents of a river high in the mountains.

It's hard to believe that it's the ocean along there if you don't look up. Sometimes I like to think of that shore as a small river and carefully forget that it's 11,000 miles to the other bank.

I went around a bend in the river and there were a dozen or so frog people having a picnic on a sandy little beach surrounded by granite rocks. They were all in black rubber suits. They were standing in a circle eating big slices of watermelon. Two of them were pretty girls who wore soft felt hats on top of their suits.

The frog people were of course all talking frog people talk. Often they were child-like and a summer of tadpole dialogue went by in the wind. Some of them had weird blue markings on the shoulders and down the arms of their suits like a brand-new blood system.

There were two German police dogs playing around the frog people. The dogs were not wearing black rubber suits and I did not see any suits lying on the beach for them. Perhaps their suits were behind a rock.

A frog man was floating on his back in the surf, eating a slice of watermelon. He swirled and eddied with the tide.

A lot of their equipment was leaning against a large theatre-like rock that would have given Prometheus a run for his money. There were some yellow oxygen tanks lying next to the rock. They looked like flowers.

The frog people changed into a half-circle and then two of them ran into the sea and turned back to throw pieces of

388

watermelon at the others and two of them started wrestling on the shore in the sand and the dogs were barking around them.

The girls were very pretty in their poured-on black rubber suits and gentle clowning hats. Eating watermelon, they sparkled like jewels in the crown of California.

A Walden Pond For Winos

The autumn carried along with it, like the roller coaster of a flesh-eating plant, port wine and the people who drank that dark sweet wine, people long since gone, except for me.

Always wary of the police, we drank in the safest place we could find, the park across from the church.

There were three poplar trees in the middle of the park and there was a statue of Benjamin Franklin in front of the trees. We sat there and drank port.

At home my wife was pregnant.

I would call on the telephone after I finished work and say, 'I won't be home for a little while. I'm going to have a drink with some friends.'

The three of us huddled in the park, talking. They were both broken-down artists from New Orleans where they had drawn pictures of tourists in Pirate's Alley.

Now in San Francisco, with the cold autumn wind upon them, they had decided that the future held only two directions: They were either going to open up a flea circus or commit themselves to an insane asylum.

So they talked about it while they drank wine.

They talked about how to make little clothes for fleas by pasting pieces of coloured paper on their backs.

They said the way that you trained fleas was to make them dependent upon you for their food. This was done by letting them feed off you at an appointed hour.

They talked about making little flea wheelbarrows and pool tables and bicycles.

They would charge fifty-cents admission for their flea circus. The business was certain to have a future to it. Perhaps they would even get on the Ed Sullivan Show.

They of course did not have their fleas yet, but they could easily be obtained from a white cat.

Then they decided that the fleas that lived on Siamese cats would probably be more intelligent than the fleas that lived on just ordinary alley cats. It only made sense that drinking intelligent blood would make intelligent fleas.

And so it went on until it was exhausted and we went and bought another fifth of port wine and returned to the trees and Benjamin Franklin.

Now it was close to sunset and the earth was beginning to cool off in the correct manner of eternity and office girls were returning like penguins from Montgomery Street. They looked at us hurriedly and mentally registered: winos.

Then the two artists talked about committing themselves to an insane asylum for the winter. They talked about how warm it would be in the insane asylum, with television, clean sheets on soft beds, hamburger gravy over mashed potatoes, a dance once a week with the lady kooks, clean clothes, a locked razor and lovely young student nurses.

Ah, yes, there was a future in the insane asylum. No winter spent there could be a total loss.

The Last Year the Trout came up
Hayman Creek

Gone now the old fart. Hayman Creek was named for Charles Hayman, a sort of half-assed pioneer in a country that not many wanted to live in because it was poor and ugly and horrible. He built a shack, this was in 1876, on a little creek that drained a worthless hill. After a while the creek was called Hayman Creek.

Mr Hayman did not know how to read or write and considered himself better for it. Mr Hayman did odd jobs for years and years and years and years.

Your mule's broke?

Get Mr Hayman to fix it.

Your fences are on fire?

Get Mr Hayman to put them out.

Mr Hayman lived on a diet of stone-ground wheat and kale. He bought the wheat by the hundred-pound sack and ground it himself with a mortar and pestle. He grew the kale in front of his shack and tended the kale as if it were prize-winning orchids.

During all the time that was his life, Mr Hayman never had a cup of coffee, a smoke, a drink or a woman and thought he'd be a fool if he did.

In the winter a few trout would go up Hayman Creek, but by early summer the creek was almost dry and there were no fish in it.

Mr Hayman used to catch a trout or two and eat raw trout with his stone-ground wheat and his kale, and then one day he was so old that he did not feel like working any more, and he looked so old that the children thought he must be evil to live by himself, and they were afraid to go up the creek near his shack.

It didn't bother Mr Hayman. The last think in the world he had any use for were children. Reading and writing and children were all the same, Mr Hayman thought, and ground his wheat and tended his kale and caught a trout or two when they were in the creek.

He looked ninety years old for thirty years and then he got the notion that he would die, and did so. The year he died the trout didn't come up Hayman Creek, and never went up the creek again. With the old man dead, the trout figured it was better to stay where they were.

The mortar and pestle fell off the shelf and broke.

The shack rotted away.

And the weeds grew into the kale.

Twenty years after Mr Hayman's death, some fish and game people were planting trout in the streams around there.

'Might as well put some here,' one of the men said.

'Sure,' the other one said.

They dumped a can full of trout in the creek and no sooner had the trout touched the water, than they turned their white bellies up and floated dead down the creek.

SAMUEL BECKETT

'But not so fast, all cities are not eternal ...'

Dublin Bay, 1945

The End

They clothed me and gave me money. I knew what the money was for, it was to get me started. When it was gone I would have to get more, if I wanted to go on. The same for the shoes, when they were worn out I would have to get them mended, or get myself another pair, or go on barefoot, if I wanted to go on. The same for the coat and trousers, needless to say, with this difference, that I could go on in my shirt-sleeves, if I wanted. The clothes—shoes, socks, trousers, shirt, coat, hat—were not new, but the deceased must have been about my size. That is to say, he must have been a little shorter, a little thinner, for the clothes did not fit me so well in the beginning as they did at the end, the shirt especially, and it was many a long day before I could button it at the neck, or profit by the collar that went with it, or pin the tails together between my legs in the way my mother had taught me. He must have put on his Sunday best to go to the consultation, perhaps for the first time, unable to bear it any longer. Be that as it may the hat was a bowler, in good shape. I said, Keep your hat on and give me back mine. I added, Give me back my greatcoat. They replied that they had burnt them, together with my other clothes. I understood then that the end was near, at least fairly near. Later on I tried to exchange this hat for a cap, or a slouch which could be pulled down over my face, but without much success. And yet I could not go about bare-headed, with my skull in the state it was. At first this hat was too small, then it got used to me. They gave me a tie, after long discussion. It seemed a pretty tie to me, but I didn't like it. When it came at last I was too tired to send it back. But in the end it came in useful. It was blue, with kinds of little stars. I didn't feel well, but they told me I was well enough. They didn't say so in so many words that I was as well as I would ever be, but that was the implication. I lay inert on the bed and it took three women to put on my trousers. They didn't seem to take much interest in my private parts which to tell the truth were nothing to write home about, I didn't take much interest in them myself. But they might have passed some remark. When they had finished I got up and finished dressing unaided. They told me to sit on the bed and wait. All the bedding had disappeared. It made me angry that they had not let me wait in the familiar bed, instead of leaving me standing in the cold, in these clothes that smelt of sulphur. I said, You might have left me in the bed till the last moment. Men all in white came in with mallets in their hands. They dismantled the bed and took away the pieces. One of the women followed them out and came back with a chair which she set before me. I had done well to pretend I was angry. But to make it quite clear to them how angry I was that they had not left me in my bed I gave the chair a kick that sent it flying. A man came in and made a sign to me to follow him. In the hall he gave me a paper to sign. What's this, I said, a safe-conduct? It's a receipt, he said, for the clothes and money you have received. What money? I said. It was then I received the money. To think I had almost departed without a penny in my pocket. The sum was not large, compared to other sums, but to me it seemed large. I saw the familiar objects, companions of so many bearable hours. The stool, for example, dearest of all. The long afternoons together, waiting for it to be time for bed. At times I felt its wooden life invade me, till I myself became a piece of old wood. There was even a hole for my cyst. Then the window pane with the patch of frosting gone, where I used to press my eye in the hour of need, and rarely in vain. I am greatly obliged to you, I said, is there a law which prevents you from throwing me out naked and penniless? That would damage our reputation in the long run, he replied. Could they not possibly keep me a little longer, I said, I could make myself useful. Useful, he said, joking apart you would be willing to make yourself useful? A moment later he went on, If they believed you were really willing to make yourself useful they would keep you, I am sure. The number of times I had said I was going to make myself useful, I wasn't going to start that again. How weak I felt! Perhaps I said, they would consent to take back the money and keep me a little longer. This is a charitable institution, he said, and the money is a gift you receive when you leave. When it is gone you will have to get more, if you want to go on. Never come back here whatever you do, you would not be let in. Don't go to any of our branches either, they would turn you away. Exelmans! I cried. Come come, he said, and anyway no one understands a tenth of what you say. I'm so old, I said. You are not so old as all that, he said. May I stay here just a little longer, I said, till the rain is over? You may wait in the cloister, he said, the rain will go on all day. You may wait in the cloister till six o'clock, you will hear the bell. If anyone challenges you, you need only say you have permission to shelter in the cloister. Whose name will I give? I said. Weir, he said.

I had not been long in the cloister when the rain stopped and the sun came out. It was low and I reckoned it must be getting on for six, considering the season. I stayed there looking through the archway at the sun as it went down behind the cloister. A man appeared and asked me what I was doing. What do you want? were the words he used. Very friendly. I replied that I had Mr Weir's permission to stay in the cloister till six o'clock. He went away, but came back immediately. He must have spoken to Mr Weir in the interim, for he said, You must not loiter in the cloister now the rain is over.

Now I was making my way through the garden. There was that strange light which follows a day of persistent rain, when the sun comes out and the sky clears too late to be of any use. The earth makes a sound as of sighs and the last drops fall from the emptied cloudless sky. A small boy, stretching out his hands and looking up at the blue sky, asked his mother how such a thing was possible. Fuck off, she said. I suddenly remembered I had not thought of asking Mr Weir for a piece of bread. He would surely have given it to me. I had as a matter of fact thought of it during our conversation in the hall, I had said to myself, Let us first finish our conversation, then I'll ask. I knew well they would not keep me. I would gladly have turned back, but I was afraid one of the guards would stop me and tell me I would never see Mr Weir again. That might have added to my sorrow. And anyway I never turned back on such occasions.

In the street I was lost. I had not set foot in this part of the city for a long time and it seemed greatly changed. Whole buildings had disappeared, the palings had changed position and on all sides I saw, in great letters, the names of tradesmen I had never seen before and would have been at a loss to pronounce. There were streets where I remembered none, some I did remember had vanished and others had completely changed their names. The general impression was the same as before. It is true I did not know the city very well. Perhaps it was quite a different one. I did not know where I was supposed to be going. I had the great good fortune, more than once, not to be run over. My appearance still made people laugh, with that hearty jovial laugh so good for the health. By keeping the red part of the sky as much as possible on my right hand I came at last to the river. Here all seemed at first sight more or less as I had left it. But if I had looked more closely I would doubtless have discovered many changes. And indeed I subsequently did so. But the general appearance of the river, flowing between its quays and under its bridges, had not changed. Yes, the river still gave the impression it was flowing in the wrong direction. That's all a pack of lies I feel. My bench was still there. It was shaped to fit the curves of the seated body. It stood beside a watering trough, gift of a Mrs Maxwell to the city horses, according to the inscription. During the short time I rested there several horses took advantage of this monument. The iron shoes approached and the jingle of the harness. Then silence. That was the horse looking at me. Then the noise of pebbles and mud that horses make when drinking. Then the silence again. That was the horse looking at me again. Then the pebbles again. Then the silence again. Till the horse had finished drinking or the driver deemed it had drunk its fill. The horses were uneasy. Once, when the noise stopped, I turned and saw the horse looking at me. The driver too was looking at me. Mrs Maxwell would have been pleased if she could have seen her trough rendering such services to the city horses. When it was night, after a tedious twilight, I took off my hat which was paining me. I longed to be under cover again, in an empty place, close and warm, with artificial light, an oil lamp for choice, with a pink shade for preference. From time to time someone would come to make sure I was all right and needed nothing. It was long since I had longed for anything and the effect on me was horrible.

In the days that followed I visited several lodgings, without much success. They usually slammed the door in my face, even when I showed my money and offered to pay a week in advance, or even two. It was in vain I put on my best manners, smiled and spoke distinctly, they slammed the door in my face before I could even finish my little speech. It was at this time I perfected a method of doffing my hat at once courteous and discreet, neither servile nor insolent. I slipped it smartly forward, held it a second poised in such a way that the person addressed could not see my skull, then slipped it back. To do that naturally, without creating an unfavourable impression, is no easy matter. When I deemed that to tip my hat would suffice, I naturally did no more than tip it. But to tip one's hat is no easy matter either. I subsequently solved this problem, always fundamental in time of adversity, by wearing a kepi and saluting in military fashion, no, that must be wrong, I don't know, I had my hat at the end. I never made the mistake of wearing medals. Some landladies were in such need of money that they let me in immediately and showed me the room. But I couldn't come to an agreement with any of them. Finally I found a basement. With this woman I came to an agreement at once. My oddities, that's the expression she used, did not alarm her. She nevertheless insisted on making the bed and cleaning the room once a week, instead of once a month as I requested. She told me that while she was cleaning, which would not take long, I could wait in the area. She added, with a great deal of feeling, that she would never put me out in bad weather. This woman was Greek, I think, or Turkish. She never spoke about herself. I somehow got the idea she was a widow or at least that her husband had left her. She had a strange accent. But so had I with my way of assimilating the vowels and omitting the consonants.

Now I didn't know where I was. I had a vague vision, not a real vision, I didn't see anything, of a big house five or six stories high, one of a block perhaps. It was dusk when I got there and I did not pay the same heed to my surroundings as I might have done if I had suspected they were to close about me. And by then I must have lost all hope. It is true that when I left this house it was a glorious day, but I never look back when leaving. I must have read somewhere, when I was small and still read, that it is better not to look back when leaving. And yet I sometimes did. But even without looking back it seems to me I should have seen something when leaving. But there it is. All I remember is my feet emerging from my shadow, one after the other. My shoes had stiffened and the sun brought out the cracks in the leather.

I was comfortable enough in this house, I must say. Apart from a few rats I was alone in the basement. The woman did her best to respect our agreement. About noon she brought me a big tray of food and took away the tray of the previous day. At the same time she brought me a clean chamber-pot. The chamber-pot had a large handle which she slipped over her arm so that both her hands were free to carry the tray. The rest of the day I saw no more of her except sometimes when she peeped in to make sure nothing had happened to me. Fortunately I did not need affection. From my bed I saw the feet coming and going on the sidewalk. Certain evenings, when the weather was fine and I felt equal to it, I fetched my chair into the area and sat looking up into the skirts of the women passing by. Once I sent for a crocus bulb and planted it in the dark area, in an old pot. It must have been coming up to spring, it was probably not the right time for it. I left the pot outside, attached to a string I passed through the window. In the evening, when the weather was fine, a little light crept up the wall. Then I sat down beside the window and pulled on the string to keep the pot in the light and warmth. That can't have been easy, I don't see how I managed it. It was probably not the right thing for it. I manured it as best I could and pissed on it when the weather was dry. It may not have been the right thing for it. It sprouted, but never any flowers, just a wilting stem and a few chlorotic leaves. I would have liked to have a yellow crocus, or a hyacinth, but there, it was not to be. She wanted to take it away, but I told her to leave it. She wanted to buy me another, but I told her I didn't want another. What lacerated me most was the din of the newspaper boys. They went pounding by every day at the same hours, their heels thudding on the sidewalk, crying the names of their papers and even the headlines. The house noises disturbed me less. A little girl, unless it was a little boy, sang every evening at the same hour, somewhere above me. For a long time I could not catch the words. But hearing them day after day I finally managed to catch a few. Strange words for a little girl, or a little boy. Was it a song in my head or did it merely come from without? It was a sort of lullaby, I believe. It often sent me to sleep, even me. Sometimes it was a little girl who came. She had long red hair hanging down in two braids. I didn't know who she was. She lingered awhile in the room, then went away without a word. One day I had a visit from a policeman. He said I had to be watched, without explaining why. Suspicious, that was it, he told me I was suspicious. I let him talk. He didn't dare arrest me. Or perhaps he had a kind heart. A priest too, one day I had a visit from a priest. I informed him I belonged to a branch of the reformed church. He asked me what kind of clergyman I would like to see. Yes, there's that about the reformed church, you're lost, it's unavoidable. Perhaps he had a kind heart. He told me to let him know if I ever needed a helping hand. A helping hand! He gave me his name and explained where I could reach him. I should have made a note of it.

One day the woman made me an offer. She said she was in urgent need of cash and that if I could pay her six months in advance she would reduce my rent by one fourth during that period, something of that kind. This had the advantage of saving six weeks' (?) rent and the disadvantage of almost exhausting my small capital. But could you call that a disadvantage? Wouldn't I stay on in any case till my last penny was gone, and even longer, till she put me out? I gave her the money and she gave me a receipt.

One morning, not long after this transaction, I was awakened by a man shaking my shoulder. It could not have been much past eleven. He requested me to get up and leave his house immediately. He was most correct, I must say. His surprise, he said, was no less than mine. It was his house. His property. The Turkish woman had left the day before. But I saw her last night, I said. You must be mistaken, he said, for she brought the keys to my office no later than yesterday afternoon. But I just paid her six months' rent in advance, I said. Get a refund, he said. But I don't even know her name, I said, let alone her address. You don't know her name? he said. He must have thought I was lying. I'm sick, I said, I can't leave like this, without any notice. You're not so sick as all that, he said. He offered to send for a taxi, even an ambulance if I preferred. He said he needed the room immediately for his pig which even as he spoke was catching cold in a cart before the door and no one to look after him but a stray urchin whom he had never set eyes on before and who was probably busy tormenting him. I asked if he couldn't let me have another place, any old corner where I could lie down long enough to recover from the shock and decide what to do. He said he could not. Don't think I'm being unkind, he added. I could live here with the pig, I said, I'd look after him. The long months of peace, wiped out in an instant! Come now, come now, he said, get a grip on yourself, be a man, get up, that's enough. After all it was no concern of his. He had really been most patient. He must have visited the basement while I was sleeping.

I felt weak. Perhaps I was. I stumbled in the blinding light. A bus took me into the country. I sat down in a field in the sun. But it seems to me that was much later. I stuck leaves under my hat, all the way round, to make a shade. The night was cold. I wandered for hours in the fields. At last I found a heap of dung. The next day I started back to the city. They made me get off three buses. I sat down by the roadside and dried my clothes in the sun. I enjoyed doing that. I said to myself. There's nothing more to be done now, not a thing, till they are dry. When they were dry I brushed them with a brush, I think a kind of curry-comb, that I found in a stable. Stables have always been my salvation. Then I went to the house and begged a glass of milk and a slice of bread and butter. They gave me everything except the butter. May I rest in the stable? I said. No, they said. I still stank, but with a stink that pleased me. I much preferred it to my own which moreover it prevented me from smelling, except a waft now and then. In the days that followed I took the necessary steps to recover my money. I don't know exactly what happened, whether I couldn't find the address, or whether there was no such address, or whether the Greek woman was unknown there. I ransacked my pockets for the receipt, to try and decipher the name. It wasn't there. Perhaps she had taken it back while I was sleeping. I don't know how long I wandered thus, resting now in one place, now in another, in the city and in the country. The city had suffered many changes. Nor was the country as I remembered it. The general effect was the same. One day I caught sight of my son. He was striding along with a briefcase under his arm. He took off his hat and bowed and I saw he was as bald as a coot. I was almost certain it was he. I turned round to gaze after him. He went bustling along on his duck feet, bowing and scraping and flourishing his hat left and right. The insufferable son of a bitch.

One day I met a man I had known in former times. He lived in a cave by the sea. He had an ass that grazed winter and summer, over the cliffs, or along the little tracks leading down to the sea. When the weather was very bad this ass came down to the cave of his own accord and sheltered there till the storm was past. So they had spent many a night huddled together, while the wind howled and the sea pounded on the shore. With the help of this ass he could deliver sand, sea-wrack and shells to the townsfolk, for their gardens. He couldn't carry much at a time, for the ass was old and small and the town was far. But in this way he earned a little money, enough to keep him in tobacco and matches and to buy a piece of bread from time to time. It was during one of these excursions that he met me, in the suburbs. He was delighted to see me, poor man. He begged me to go home with him and spend the night. Stay as long as you like, he said. What's wrong with your ass? I said. Don't mind him, he said, he doesn't know you. I reminded him that I wasn't in the habit of staying more than two or three minutes with anyone and that the sea did not agree with me. He seemed

deeply grieved to hear it. So you won't come, he said. But
to my amazement I got up on the ass and off we went, in the
shade of the red chestnuts springing from the sidewalk. I
held the ass by the mane, one hand in front of the other. The
little boys jeered and threw stones, but their aim was poor,
for they only hit me once, on the hat. A policeman stopped
us and accused us of disturbing the peace. My friend replied
that we were as nature had made us, the boys too were
as nature had made them. It was inevitable, under these
conditions, that the peace should be disturbed from time
to time. Let us continue on our way, he said, and order will
soon be restored throughout your beat. We followed the quiet,
dustwhite inland roads with their hedges of hawthorn and
fuchsia and their footpaths fringed with wild grass and
daisies. Night fell. The ass carried me right to the mouth of
the cave, for in the dark I could not have found my way down
the path winding steeply to the sea. Then he climbed back
to his pasture.

I don't know how long I stayed there. The cave was nicely
arranged, I must say. I treated my crablice with salt water
and seaweed, but a lot of nits must have survived. I put
compresses of seaweed on my skull, which gave me great
relief, but not for long. I lay in the cave and sometimes
looked out at the horizon. I saw above me a vast trembling
expanse without islands or promontories. At night a light
shone into the cave at regular intervals. It was here I found
the phial in my pocket. It was not broken, for the glass was
not real glass. I thought Mr Weir had confiscated all my
belongings. My host was out most of the time. He fed me on
fish. It is easy for a man, a proper man, to live in a cave, far
from everybody. He invited me to stay as long as I liked. If I
preferred to be alone he would gladly prepare another cave
for me further on. He would bring me food every day and
drop in from time to time to make sure I was all right and
needed nothing. He was kind. Unfortunately I did not need
kindness. You wouldn't know of a lake dwelling? I said. I
couldn't bear the sea, its splashing and heaving, its tides and
general convulsiveness. The wind at least sometimes stops.
My hands and feet felt as though they were full of ants. This
kept me awake for hours on end. If I stayed here something

awful would happen to me, I said, and a lot of good that would do me. You'd get drowned, he said. Yes, I said, or jump off the cliff. And to think I couldn't live anywhere else, he said, in my cabin in the mountains I was wretched. Your cabin in the mountains? I said. He repeated the story of his cabin in the mountains, I had forgotten it, it was as though I were hearing it for the first time. I asked him if he still had it. He replied he had not seen it since the day he fled from it, but that he believed it was still there, a little decayed no doubt. But when he urged me to take the key I refused, saying I had other plans. You will always find me here, he said, if you ever need me. Ah people. He gave me his knife.

What he called his cabin in the mountains was a sort of wooden shed. The door had been removed, for firewood, or for some other purpose. The glass had disappeared from the window. The roof had fallen in at several places. The interior was divided, by the remains of a partition, into two unequal parts. If there had been any furniture it was gone. The vilest acts had been committed on the ground and against the walls. The floor was strewn with excrements, both human and animal, with condoms and vomit. In a cowpad a heart had been traced, pierced by an arrow. And yet there was nothing to attract tourists. I noticed the remains of abandoned nose-gays. They had been greedily gathered, carried for miles, then thrown away, because they were cumbersome or already withered. This was the dwelling to which I had been offered the key.

The scene was the familiar one of grandeur and desolation. Nevertheless it was a roof over my head. I rested on a bed of ferns, gathered at great labour with my own hands. One day I couldn't get up. The cow saved me. Goaded by the icy mist she came in search of shelter. It was probably not the first time. She can't have seen me. I tried to suck her, without much success. Her udder was covered with dung. I took off my hat and, summoning all my energy, began to milk her into it. The milk fell to the ground and was lost, but I said to myself, No matter, it's free. She dragged me across the floor, stopping from time to time only to kick me. I didn't know our cows too could be so inhuman. She must have recently been milked. Clutching the dug with one hand I kept my hat under it with the other. But in the end she prevailed. For she dragged me across the threshold and out into the giant streaming ferns, where I was forced to let go.

As I drank the milk I reproached myself with what I had done. I could no longer count on this cow and she would warn the others. More master of myself I might have made a friend of her. She would have come every day, perhaps accompanied by other cows. I might have learnt to make butter, even cheese. But I said to myself, No, all is for the best.

Once on the road it was all downhill. Soon there were carts, but they all refused to take me up. In other clothes, with another face, they might have taken me up. I must have changed since my expulsion from the basement. The face notably seemed to have attained its climacteric. The humble, ingenuous smile would no longer come, nor the expression of candid misery, showing the stars and the distaff. I summoned them, but they would not come. A mask of dirty old hairy leather, with two holes and a slit, it was too far gone for the old trick of please your honour and God reward you and pity upon me. It was disastrous. What would I crawl with in future? I lay down on the side of the road and began to writhe each time I heard a cart approaching. That was so they would not think I was sleeping or resting. I tried to groan, Help! Help! But the tone that came out was that of polite conversation. My hour was not yet come and I could no longer groan. The last time I had cause to groan I had groaned as well as ever, and no heart within miles of me to melt. What was to become of me? I said to myself, I'll learn again. I lay down across the road at a narrow place, so that the carts could not pass without passing over my body, with one wheel at least, or two if there were four. But the day came when, looking round me, I was in the suburbs, and from there to the old haunts it was not far, beyond the stupid hope of rest or less pain.

So I covered the lower part of my face with a black rag and went and begged at a sunny corner. For it seemed to me my eyes were not completely spent, thanks perhaps to the dark glasses my tutor had given me. He had given me the *Ethics* of Geulincz. They were a man's glasses, I was a child. They found him dead, crumpled up in the water closet, his clothes in awful disorder, struck down by an infarctus. Ah what peace. The *Ethics* had his name (Ward) on the fly-leaf, the glasses had belonged to him. The bridge, at the time I am speaking of, was of brass wire, of the kind used to hang pictures and big mirrors, and two long black ribbons served as wings. I wound them round my ears and then down under my chin where I tied them together. The lenses had suffered, from rubbing in my pocket against each other and against the other objects there. I thought Mr Weir had confiscated all my belongings. But I had no further need of these glasses and used them merely to soften the glare of the sun. I should never have mentioned them. The rag gave me a lot of trouble. I got it in the end from the lining of my greatcoat, no, I had no greatcoat now, of my coat then. The result was a grey rag rather than a black, perhaps even chequered, but I had to make do with it. Till afternoon I held my face raised towards the southern sky, then towards the western till night. The bowl gave me a lot of trouble. I couldn't use my hat because of my skull. As for holding out my hand, that was quite out of the question. So I got a tin and hung it from a button of my greatcoat, what's the matter with me, of my coat, at pubis level. It did not hang plumb, it leaned respectfully towards the passer-by, he had only to drop his mite. But that obliged him to come up close to me, he was in danger of touching me. In the end I got a bigger tin, a kind of big tin box, and I placed it on the sidewalk at my feet. But people who give alms don't much care to toss them, there's something contemptuous about this gesture which is repugnant to sensitive natures. To say nothing of their having to aim. They are prepared to give, but not for their gift to go rolling under the passing feet or under the passing wheels, to be picked up perhaps by some undeserving person. So they don't give. There are those, to be sure, who stoop, but generally speaking people who give alms don't much care to stoop. What they like above all is to sight the wretch from afar, get ready their penny, drop it in their stride and hear the God bless you dying away in the distance. Personally I never said that, nor anything like it, I wasn't much of a believer, but I did make a noise with my mouth. In the end I got a kind of board or tray and tied it to my neck and waist. It jutted out just at the right height, pocket height, and its edge was far enough from my person for the coin to be bestowed without danger. Some days I strewed it with flowers, petals, buds and that herb which men call fleabane, I believe, in a word whatever I could find. I didn't go out of my way to look for them, but all the pretty things of this description that came my way were for the board. They must have thought I loved nature. Most of the time I looked up at the sky, but without focusing it, for why focus it? Most of the time it was a mixture of white, blue and grey, and then at evening all the evening colours. I felt it weighing softly on my face, I rubbed my face against it, one cheek after the other, turning my head from side to side. Now and then to rest my neck I dropped my head on my chest. Then I could see the board in the distance, a haze of many colours. I leaned against the wall, but without nonchalance, I shifted my weight from one foot to the other and my hands clutched the lapels of my coat. To beg with your hands in your pockets makes a bad impression, it irritates the workers, especially in winter. You should never wear gloves either. There were guttersnipes who swept away all I had earned, under cover of giving me a coin. It was to buy sweets. I unbuttoned my trousers discreetly to scratch myself. I scratched myself in an upward direction, with four nails. I pulled on the hairs, to get relief. It passed the time, time flew when I scratched myself. Real scratching is superior to masturbation, in my opinion. One can masturbate up to the age of seventy, and even beyond, but in the end it becomes a mere habit. Whereas to scratch myself properly I would have needed a dozen hands. I itched all over, on the privates, in the bush up to the navel, under the arms, in the arse and then patches of eczema and psoriasis that I could set raging merely by thinking of them. It was in the arse I had the most pleasure, I stuck in my forefinger up to the knuckle. Later, if I had to shit, the pain was atrocious. But I hardly shat any more. Now and then a flying machine flew by, sluggishly it seemed to me. Often at the end of the day I discovered the legs of my trousers all wet. That must have been the dogs. I personally pissed very little. If by chance the need came on me a little squirt in my fly was enough to relieve it. Once at my post I did not leave it till nightfall. I had no appetite, God tempered the wind to me. After work I bought a bottle of milk and drank it in the evening in the shed. Better still, I got a little boy to buy it for me, always the same, they wouldn't serve me, I don't know why. I gave him a penny for his pains. One day I witnessed a strange scene. Normally I didn't see a great deal. I didn't hear a great deal either. I didn't pay attention. Strictly speaking I wasn't there. Strictly speaking I believe I've never been anywhere. But that day I must have come back. For some time past a sound had been scarifying me. I did not investigate the cause, for I said to myself, It's going to stop. But as it did not stop I had no choice but to find out the cause. It was a man perched on the roof of a car and haranguing the passers-by. That at least was my interpretation. He was bellowing so loud that snatches of his discourse reached my ears. Union ... brothers ... Marx ... capital ... bread and butter ... love. It was all Greek to me. The car was drawn up against the kerb, just in front of me, I saw the orator from behind. All of a sudden he turned and pointed at me, as at an exhibit. Look at this down and out, he vociferated, this leftover. If he doesn't go down on all fours, it's for fear of being impounded. Old, lousy, rotten, ripe for the muckheap. And there are a thousand like him, worse than him, ten thousand, twenty thousand. A voice, Thirty thousand. Every day you pass them by, resumed the orator, and when you have backed a winner you fling them a farthing. Do you ever think? The voice, God forbid. A penny, resumed the orator, tuppence. The voice, thruppence. It never enters your head, resumed the orator, that your charity is a crime, an incentive to slavery, stultification and organized murder. Take a good look at this living corpse. You may say it's his own fault. Ask him if it's his own fault. The voice, Ask him yourself. Then he bent forward and took me to task. I had perfected my board. It now consisted of two boards hinged together, which enabled me, when my work was done, to fold it and carry it under my arm. I liked doing little odd jobs. So I took off the rag, pocketed the few coins I had earned, untied the board, folded it and put it under my arm. Do you hear me, you crucified bastard! cried the orator. Then I went away, although it was still light. But generally speaking it was a quiet corner, busy but not overcrowded, thriving and well-frequented. He must have been a religious fanatic, I could find no other explanation. Perhaps he was an escaped lunatic. He had a nice face, a little on the red side.

I did not work every day. I had practically no expenses. I even managed to put a little aside, for my very last days. The days I did not work I spent lying in the shed. The shed was on a private estate, or what had once been a private estate, on the riverside. This estate, the main entrance to which opened on a narrow, dark and silent street, was enclosed with a wall, except of course on the river front, which marked its northern boundary for a distance of about thirty yards. From the last quays beyond the water the eyes rose to a confusion of low houses, wasteland, hoardings, chimneys, steeples and towers. A kind of parade ground was also to be seen, where soldiers played football all the year round. Only the ground-floor windows—no, I can't. The estate seemed abandoned. The gates were locked and the paths overgrown with grass. Only the ground-floor windows had shutters. The others were sometimes lit at night, faintly, now one, now another. At least that was my impression. Perhaps it was reflected light. In this shed, the day I adopted it, I found a boat, upside down. I righted it, chocked it up with stones and pieces of wood, took out the thwarts and made my bed inside. The rats had difficulty in getting at me, because of the bulge of the hull. And yet they longed to. Just think of it, living flesh, for in spite of everything I was still living flesh. I had lived too long among rats, in my chance dwellings, to share the dread they inspire in the vulgar. I even had a soft spot in my heart for them. They came with such confidence towards me, it seemed without the least repugnance. They made their toilet with catlike gestures. Toads at evening, motionless for hours, lap flies from the air. They like to squat where cover ends and open air begins, they favour thresholds. But I had to contend now with water rats, exceptionally lean and ferocious. So I made a kind of lid with stray boards. It's incredible the number of boards I've come across in my lifetime, I never needed a board but there it was, I had only to stoop and pick it up. I liked doing little odd jobs, no, not particularly, I didn't mind. It completely covered the boat, I'm referring

again to the lid. I pushed it a little towards the stern, climbed
into the boat by the bow, crawled to the stern, raised my feet
and pushed the lid back towards the bow till it covered me
completely. But what did my feet push against? They pushed
against a cross-bar I nailed to the lid for that purpose, I liked
these little odd jobs. But it was better to climb into the boat
by the stern and pull back the lid with my hands till it
completely covered me, then push it forward in the same way
when I wanted to get out. As holds for my hands I planted
two spikes just where I needed them. These little odds and
ends of carpentry, if I may so describe it, carried out with
whatever tools and material I chanced to find, gave me a
certain pleasure. I knew it would soon be the end, so I played
the part, you know, the part of—how shall I say, I don't
know. I was comfortable enough in this boat, I must say. The
lid fitted so well I had to pierce a hole. It's no good closing
your eyes, you must leave them open in the dark, that is my
opinion. I am not speaking of sleep, I am speaking of what I
believe is called waking. In any case, I slept very little at this
period, I wasn't sleepy, or I was too sleepy, I don't know, or I
was afraid, I don't know. Flat then on my back I saw nothing
except, dimly, just above my head, through the tiny chinks,
the grey light of the shed. To see nothing at all, no, that's too
much. I heard faintly the cries of the gulls ravening about the
mouth of the sewer near by. In a spew of yellow foam, if my
memory serves me right, the filth gushed into the river and
the slush of birds above screaming with hunger and fury. I
heard the lapping of water against the slip and against the
bank and the other sound, so different, of open wave, I heard
it too. I too, when I moved, felt less boat than wave, or so it
seemed to me, and my stillness was the stillness of eddies.
That may seem impossible. The rain too, I often heard it, for
it often rained. Sometimes a drop, falling through the roof of
the shed, exploded on me. All that composed a rather liquid
world. And then of course there was the voice of the wind or
rather those, so various, of its playthings. But what does it
amount to? Howling, soughing, moaning, sighing. What I
would have liked was hammer strokes, bang bang bang,
clanging in the desert. I let farts to be sure, but hardly ever a
real crack, they oozed out with a sucking noise, melted in the

mighty never. I don't know how long I stayed there. I was very snug in my box, I must say. It seemed to me I had grown more independent of recent years. That no one came any more, that no one could come any more to ask me if I was all right and needed nothing, distressed me then but little. I was all right, yes, quite so, and the fear of getting worse was less with me. As for my needs, they had dwindled as it were to my dimensions and become, if I may say so, of so exquisite a quality as to exclude all thought of succour. To know I had a being, however faint and false, outside of me, had once had the power to stir my heart. You become unsociable, it's inevitable. It's enough to make you wonder sometimes if you are on the right planet. Even the words desert you, it's as bad as that. Perhaps it's the moment when the vessels stop communicating, you know, the vessels. There you are still between the two murmurs, it must be the same old song as ever, but Christ you wouldn't think so. There were times when I wanted to push away the lid and get out of the boat and couldn't, I was so indolent and weak, so content deep down where I was. I felt them hard upon me, the icy, tumultuous streets, the terrifying faces, the noises that slash, pierce, claw, bruise. So I waited till the desire to shit, or even to piss, lent me wings. I did not want to dirty my nest! And yet it sometimes happened, and even more and more often. Arched and rigid I edged down my trousers and turned a little on my side, just enough to free the hole. To contrive a little kingdom, in the midst of the universal muck, then shit on it, ah that was me all over. The excrements were me too, I know, I know, but all the same. Enough, enough, the next thing I was having visions, I who never did, except sometimes in my sleep, who never had, real visions, I'd remember, except perhaps as a child, my myth will have it so. I knew they were visions because it was night and I was alone in my boat. What else could they have been? So I was in my boat and gliding on the waters. I didn't have to row, the ebb was carrying me out. Anyway I saw no oars, they must have taken them away. I had a board, the remains of a thwart perhaps, which I used when I came too close to the bank, or when a pier came bearing down on me or a barge at its moorings. There were stars in the sky, quite a few. I didn't know what the weather was doing, I was neither cold nor warm and all seemed calm. The banks receded more and more, it was inevitable, soon I saw them no more. The lights grew fainter and fewer as the river widened. There on the land men were sleeping, bodies were gathering strength for the toil and joys of the morrow. The boat was not gliding now, it was tossing, buffeted by the choppy waters of the bay. All seemed calm and yet foam was washing aboard. Now the sea air was all about me, I had no other shelter than the land, and what does it amount to, the shelter of the land, at such a time. I saw the beacons, four in all, including a lightship. I knew them well, even as a child I had known them well. It was evening, I was with my father on a height, he held my hand. I would have liked him to draw me close with a gesture of protective love, but his mind was on other things. He also taught me the names of the mountains. But to have done with these visions I also saw the lights of the buoys, the sea seemed full of them, red and green and to my surprise even yellow. And on the slopes of the mountain, now rearing its unbroken bulk behind the town, the fires turned from gold to red, from red to gold. I knew what it was, it was the gorse burning. How often I had set a match to it myself, as a child. And hours later, back in my home, before I climbed into bed, I watched from my high window the fires I had lit. That night then, all aglow with distant fires, on sea, on land and in the sky, I drifted with the currents and the tides. I noticed that my hat was tied, with a string I suppose, to my buttonhole. I got up from my seat in the stern and a great clanking was heard. That was the chain. One end was fastened to the bow and the other round my waist. I must have pierced a hole beforehand in the floorboards, for there I was down on my knees prying out the plug with my knife. The hole was small and the water rose slowly. It would take a good half hour, everything included, barring accidents. Back now in the stern-sheets, my legs stretched out, my back well propped against the sack stuffed with grass I used as a cushion, I swallowed my calmative. The sea, the sky, the mountains and the islands closed in and crushed me in a mighty systole, then scattered to the uttermost confines of space. The memory came faint and cold of the story I might have told, a story in the likeness of my life, I mean without the courage to end or the strength to go on.

*Translated by Richard Seaver
in collaboration with the author.*